Praise for "Though War Shall Rise Against Me

"I loved it :) Historically correct with glimpses into the lives of 4 women and they're small town as the civil war breaks out. Ms. LaPres, what an outstanding debut! You must read it, I promise you won't be disappointed."

"I totally enjoyed the writing of this first time author. It was clear, concise and factually accurate to the era. I would not hesitate to read another of her works!!"

"I love historical fiction and I felt that this book was well written and factual. I can't wait for the sequels to come out. Nice job for a first time author."

"I had trouble putting the book down. Couldn't wait to find out what was going to happen next. I look forward to reading more about the other characters."

"Well written and factual. Couldn't put it down. Looking forward to the next book."

"This is an awesome book to read. It got me so involved it was hard to put down. I can't wait to read the next one. I highly recommend this book."

"I just finished the book and thoroughly enjoyed it. You included so many elements in your book that are often overlooked with the "strategy" of war. Through the relationship of 4 amazing women (and one antagonist), you were able to discuss the personal relationships of friends, husbands, and families. You presented the struggles of these women and the prejudiced that existed besides that of color. And you added the struggle of faith as well."

"Read your book today. It was AWESOME! And I really mean it. Interesting characters, great plot, even had tears in my eyes a couple of times!"

Though War Shall Rise Against Me

Book #1 in the Turner Daughters Series

Marie LaPres

Cover photograph taken at the Gettysburg National Battlefield Park by Susan Marie Emelander

Dedicated to Sue, my mother and great friend, for all her support and assistance and always believing in me!

Red Flannel Days - Cedar Springs 2016

Rita,

Thanks so much for reading!

Erica "Martha Pres" Emelander

Gettysburg-The Town

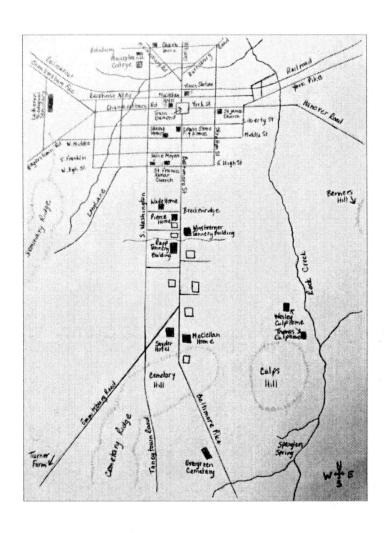

Gettysburg-Surrounding Areas

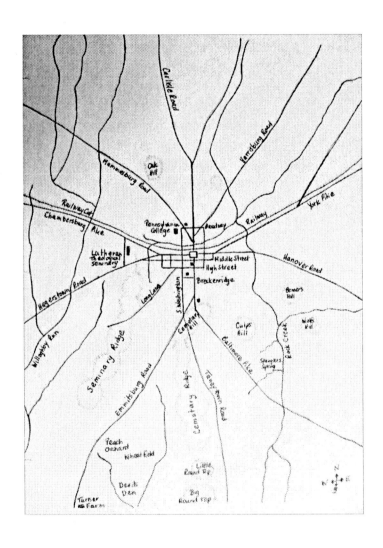

The LORD is my light and my salvation;
whom should I fear?
The LORD is my life's refuge;
of whom should I be afraid?
When evildoers come at me
to devour my flesh,
these my enemies and foes
themselves stumble and fall.
Though an army encamp against me,
my heart does not fear;
Though war shall rise against me,
even then do I trust.

Psalm 27:1-3

To the reader…

This is a fiction novel based in Gettysburg, Pennsylvania during the Civil War. It follows four young women and details their wartime experiences. Throughout the novel, the main characters have flashback memories to recall things that have happened in the past. When this happens, the text will appear in italics. There are also letters written to and from the home front to the soldiers. When this happens, the text is in bold.

This is a historical fiction novel. Some characters are fiction, while other characters are based on actual historic figures that lived in Gettysburg or were in Gettysburg during the war. Be sure to read the Authors Note at the end of the book to learn more about the characters.

Family Trees

Turner Family

Hiram ——— Caroline (Deceased)

Charlotte

Wade Family

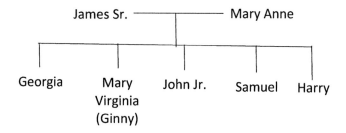

James Sr. ——— Mary Anne

Georgia | Mary Virginia (Ginny) | John Jr. | Samuel | Harry

Clark Family

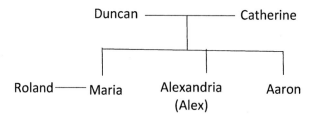

Duncan ——— Catherine

Roland ——— Maria | Alexandria (Alex) | Aaron

Lewis/Byron Family

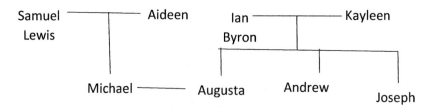

Samuel Lewis ——— Aideen   Ian Byron ——— Kayleen

Michael ——— Augusta   Andrew   Joseph

8

Part One:

1861

Charlotte Turner quickly made her way through the streets of Gettysburg. She glanced both ways before crossing Baltimore Street, heading toward Breckenridge Road and the home of her best friend, Mary Virginia Wade, also known as Ginny. The small borough was abuzz with war news and war fever. The night before, Southern forces had fired upon the Federal Fort Sumter in Charleston, South Carolina. It was believed that this act would finally throw the country into a war between the states. Men and boys were preparing to leave to fight the rebels, gathering supplies, having wives and mothers prepare uniforms, and practicing with firearms.

Charlotte glanced up the street and stopped when she noticed Alexandria Clark heading her way. Alex, who was a good friend of Charlotte, gave a gentle smile and wave. Charlotte waved back.

"Have you heard the news?" Alex asked, her blue eyes brighter than usual reflecting off of the blue and white checked day dress she was wearing. "I cannot believe it's actually happening." She pushed an errant dark brown lock of curly hair from her face and adjusted her straw bonnet. Charlotte couldn't help but compare herself to her friend. Alex was one year older than Charlotte at 20. While Charlotte had plain blue eyes and dark blonde hair, Alex's features were striking. She had the type of figure that all women envied and all men appreciated, while Charlotte had an average figure. Alex had many of the men in Gettysburg vying for her attention, but had only recently found one who caught her interest. She had been born and raised in Philadelphia, and was elegant, refined, quick to smile and never hesitated to laugh or share her opinion, whether it was favorable or not. In contrast, Charlotte only opened up to people who she was close to and found it difficult to make small talk. Alex was friendly, outgoing and well-liked. She also had a strong faith that Charlotte envied. Alex was kind and saw people for who they really were. It didn't matter that

Ginny Wade was poor and unpopular with the townspeople and Charlotte was considered a "country farm girl". Alex preferred their company to any of the other girls in town.

"I can hardly believe the news myself." Charlotte said, taking her friend's arm and continuing towards the Wade home. "Have you spoken to Will?" Will Sadler was Alexandria's beau. Even though they had not been courting long, most people in town knew they would get married. Will was a student at Pennsylvania College in Gettysburg and they had met through her father, a professor at the school.

"No, I haven't." Alex answered as she looked longingly toward the railway station. "He left the day before yesterday to go see his family." She sighed. "I'm not quite sure when he will be back." She paused, then asked. "Are you heading to Ginny's?"

"Yes, I am. I finished all my chores and wanted to catch up with her. Would you like to join me?"

"I would."

The two arrived at the Wade house, knocked twice on the door, opened it and then walked in. The girls were so close that some formalities had been forgone long ago.

"Hello!" Charlotte called out, and immediately spotted her best friend at the stove, boiling water for laundry. Ginny brushed damp locks of brown hair from her sweating forehead. Her hair which had surely been neatly tied back and braided this morning, had completely fallen out of its pins throughout the course of the day. 18-year-old Ginny was tall, with brown eyes and an average figure. She was quiet, except around those who knew her well. Even though Ginny was a hard worker, many of the people in town looked down on her, as well as the whole Wade family, because of their lack of money.

"Alex! Charlie!" Ginny poured a steaming pail of water into the wash bucket and turned back around. "It is so good to see you! What brings you over here? I'm sure it's not just to help with the laundry."

"We don't need an excuse to visit you." Alex said, arranging her skirts as she sat down, her hands folded neatly in her lap, her posture perfect.

"I suppose not." Ginny replied with a smile. Charlotte grabbed the basket of mending and sat at the drop-leaf table. The chores never seemed to end at the Wade home. With Ginny, her mother, her older sister, Georgia, and three boys living in the house, there was always work to do. They were continually taking in mending and other odd jobs just to survive.

Georgia Wade walked in the room and smiled at the two visitors. She pushed a strand of her dark hair from her face. "Charlotte, Alex, how are you?"

"Very well." Charlotte smiled back. "And how is Mr. McClellan?"

"John is doing well." Georgia said. "Although now that war is going to break out, he will most likely drop out of school and join the army." John McClellan was the young man who was courting Georgia.

"I'm sure a lot of the students will do the same." Alex said, thinking of Will.

"Ginny, has Jack stopped by to say anything about this Fort Sumter business?" Charlotte asked.

"No," Ginny said. "He has not..." A knock at the door cut her sentence off and Jack Skelly walked into the house. Tall and of average build, 20-year-old Jack was a handsome man. He had brown hair and eyes, and had recently began growing a moustache. His father was a tailor, and Jack knew that trade, but his chosen career was a stonemason and granite cutter. Ginny and Jack had gotten to know one another when Ginny's father worked for Jack's father. The Wade and Skelley families had worked closely together for years. Jack was a very close friend of Alex, Charlotte and Ginny, but in the past few years, the friendship between Ginny and Jack had been developing into something more, much to the dismay of Jack's mother, who disapproved of Jack's relationship with Ginny.

"Hello, ladies," Jack said in his quiet voice.

"Hi, Jack!" Charlotte smiled, waving at him.

"Have you heard the news?" He crossed the room and stood next to Ginny.

"We heard some of the news. What's the official word?" Ginny looked at him, concern in her face.

"Forces from the newly declared Confederate States fired on a fort in Charleston Harbor, South Carolina to take it away from Union forces. The Union army was refusing to leave just because the South declared themselves a separate country."

"Was anyone killed?" Alex asked.

"I don't think so." Jack rubbed at the new hair on his upper lip.

"What does this mean, Jack?" Ginny turned and faced him. He didn't meet her eyes.

"It means that our country is going to war and that you and I need to talk." He placed a hand on Ginny's elbow, gently and quietly, not to attract too much attention. He looked into her eyes, wordlessly communicating that he had something important to tell her.

"If you'll excuse us." Ginny said to Alex and Charlotte, then allowed Jack to lead her out the door, his hand on the small of her back. As the door closed behind them, Charlotte and Alex exchanged a glance.

"War?" Alex asked, still a bit in shock from that terrible revelation. She knew it was unavoidable, but now it was upon them.

"It was only a matter of time." Charlotte said, jamming her needle through the shirt she had been working on.

"I know that, it's just…so soon." *Way too soon.* She thought. *Just as Will and I were getting closer, he is going to leave.* She knew he would enlist. He hated school and would jump at the chance to go off and fight. There was no way he would stay behind. "And to hear the word "war" spoken aloud, so definite."

"Yes, I agree."

Alex nodded toward the door that Ginny and Jack had walked out. "What do you think that's all about?"

"Well, if Jack's smart, he'll finally propose. He's been delaying long enough. Knowing him though, he probably just wants to say goodbye. He's cautious."

"So there *is* something going on between the two of them." Alex confirmed.

"You are just now figuring that out?" Charlotte asked with a smile.

"Well, Ginny is always so quiet about her relationship with Jack and everything else for that matter. I guessed they were more than friends but I really just wasn't sure. I didn't want to say something and stick my foot in my mouth."

"No, because you never speak before thinking." Charlotte tried not to laugh.

Alex did laugh. "My father always says that I am so unpredictable that even *I* do not know what I am going to do next."

******

Jack led Ginny down Baltimore Street, away from the town towards a huge rock hill known locally as Devil's Den. He remained silent and Ginny didn't push him to communicate. She knew that he would talk when he was ready. They continued walking until they got to the hill of boulders. He helped her up to lean against a boulder and then turned away, still collecting his thoughts. She looked at him, drinking in the sight of the man she had come to love. It made her think of how lucky she was. They had always been such good friends, and had only recently made the transition from just friends to something more. As he continued to think, her mind turned back to the day when she had finally realized that she cared for Jack as more than a friend. It was back when their friend Wesley Culp was still around, and before Alex had come to town. Back when they could all afford to be a little more carefree…

April 1855
Culp's Hill, Outside of Gettysburg, Pennsylvania

Ginny sat in the soft spring grass, leaning against a large budding maple tree, working on some stitching she had brought. Through the leaves of the tree, she felt the sunlight wash upon her face. April was her favorite month. After the long months of winter, there was nothing better than a blue sky with fluffy white clouds and warm gentle breezes. Ginny's mother seldom let her work outside the home. The thirteen-year-old was usually stuck in the dark, crowded house. With her husband in the asylum, Mary Anne Wade needed a lot of help running the household. Even when Ginny was attending school, she had to work after school hours to help earn money by sewing for Mr. Skelly, Jack's father, who ran the tailor shop. Ginny's father had once been an apprentice to Mr. Skelly and the Skelly men still did their best to help the Wade family out whenever possible.

Charlotte lay next to her, eyes closed, her copy of Jane Austen's Pride and Prejudice *next to her, soaking in the spring sunlight. It was the first warm Saturday of the year. She had taken off her shoes and stockings, and had pulled her blue cotton work dress to her mid-shin. Rock Creek trickled by, almost lulling Charlotte to sleep. She spread out her fingers and threaded them through the sun-warmed grass. She had almost drifted off to sleep when a loud yell broke the tranquility.*

"Whoooo-ahhh!" The cry was followed by a loud splash. Before Charlotte could react, strong arms went under her and she was lifted into the air. Her eyes flew open.

"Wesley Culp!" Charlotte yelled, her eyes locked on the smiling face of the boy who held her. He headed towards the river, where Jack was emerging from the crisp water. Jack shook his head and cold water flew from his shaggy hair spattering both Wesley and Charlotte.

"Wesley, put me down!" Charlotte screeched. He smiled and shook his own shaggy brown head.

"Nope!"

Charlotte struggled to free herself from his arms; as warm as the day was, she did not want to get wet.

"Jonathan Wesley Culp, you put me down right now!" She demanded.

Ginny observed the scene from her spot on the grass. She had laid her sewing down and crossed her legs at the ankles, doing her best to smother her laughter behind her hands. Wesley reached the water and began wading in.

"Wesley!" Charlotte yelled.

"You want me to put you down?" He asked, loosening his grip.

"No!" She threw her arms around his neck. "Not now. Don't you dare think about it!" He tightened his arms and looked down at her, smiling a crooked smile that showed a dimple in his left cheek.

"What will you give me for not dropping you?" He asked.

"I won't pummel you." Charlotte exclaimed, tightening her grip around his neck.

He sighed. "Like that would even hurt." He looked at her expression and chuckled. "Ahh, it's a good thing that I'm so nice." He stepped back onto the bank and set her down.

"Thank you." She said, brushing at the wrinkles on her dress. Wesley bowed and smiled.

"Wes, get in here!" Jack splashed some water in the direction of his friends. More icy water hit Charlotte and she scrambled out of the water's reach and up towards Ginny.

"Cold enough for you?" Ginny asked, a grin on her face.

"Those boys..." Charlotte said, but she was smiling, it was hard to be mad at Wes and Jack for long. Wesley stripped his shirt off and flung it in the direction of the girls before he leapt into the water, tackling Jack.

"Do you know how scandalized people would be if they realized what we were watching right now?" Charlotte asked. Ginny continued to stare in the direction of Jack and Wesley's water wrestling match. Wesley had the advantage. He was stocky, but had lost the fat he had as a child and was now more muscular. His father had recently told Wesley that, at fifteen, he was old enough to go to work and get a job, and start earning his own way. He had started working part-time for a carriage maker in town.

"I'm sure they would be." Ginny said, not taking her eyes off the boys. "But we've been going off and playing with them for so long that I don't think folks even realize it."

"True." Charlotte nodded. "Don't' you think Wesley looks good now that he's grown into his weight?"

"Yes. Jack's grown up quite a bit as well." Ginny smiled. With the exception of Charlotte, Jack was the one friend who had always been there for her. No matter what happened, with her family scandals

15

and financial problems, he stood by her. He had been a friend for so long, but now, they were getting older. They were not children anymore. She was starting to notice the little things, like his smile, and the way he smelled and the stubble that formed on his chin when he didn't shave. She was noticing him as a man. She prayed to God every day that He would help Jack to notice her as a young woman for she was growing up too. When she thought she might be seeing him, when she went out to do errands or on her way to work she would do her hair just a little nicer. She would make sure her dress was just right, even though it may not be in style, and she would pinch her cheeks to give them color.

It wasn't too long before the boys, tired of their game, scrambled out of the water and up the bank to join the girls, pulling their shirts back on. The cool air didn't seem to bother them in the least.

"I can't believe this is all gonna be over soon." Wesley commented.

"What do you mean?" Charlotte asked. "What's going to be over?"

"Carefree life like this, as we know it."

"What are you talking about?" Charlotte was beginning to get irritated. "You are being way too enigmatic, Wesley Culp."

"He means that our days of carefree fun are over." Jack said, shaking his wet head again. "Won't be too long before we all have to concentrate on being adults."

"Yeah." Wesley began pulling at the grass absentmindedly. "Time to grow up and start working. No more time for fun"

Ginny was pulled back to reality as Jack cleared his throat and turned towards her. She realized that whatever he said to her here and now would change their relationship. Finally, he spoke.

"I'm going to join the Union army." He still didn't look at her, afraid to see her reaction.

"I gathered that." She nodded and clasped her hands in front of her.

"I just need you to know that I am not joining up because I want glory and adventure. I mean, I want that too, kind of. I just…it's not the only reason, and I want you to know that." He finally looked into her eyes, "I also signed up because it's the right thing to do. I feel it is my duty; what God is asking me to do. And…" He paused and stood closer, there was still an arm's length between them. "I need to get

16

away from Gettysburg. Not from you, not at all from you." He took a deep breath. "I need to get away from my parents. You know my father can be overbearing, even though I have chosen a different profession, he just can be too...you know. And mother, well, she..."

"Doesn't like me." Ginny finished his statement.

"It's not that, Gin. It's just that she doesn't like us together. I'm her son and she..."

"She thinks that you can do better than a poor girl whose father was arrested and then sent to the Almshouse because he was mentally..."

"Ginny, no! No one holds you accountable for your father's mistakes." Jack placed a hand on her arm.

"You know that's not true, Jack. My whole family suffers for what he did."

"And I am sorry that some hold his actions against you. You know I am. Not everyone feels that way." He put his other hand on her shoulder and took a step closer. "But you're not usually this defensive about your father. What's really bothering you?"

Ginny clenched her fists. "You're leaving me. You're the one person who has always..." She whispered. "The reasons why you're enlisting don't really matter Jack, you're still leaving me to go and fight." Tears formed in the corners of her eyes. "I'm sure you realize that you could be killed."

"Of course I realize that, Gin."

"Well, then..." Ginny's mind flew in all different directions. She wanted to be alone to think things through, but she also wanted to spend as much time with Jack as possible, and yet another part of her wanted to go and share her thoughts with Alex and Charlotte. He still hadn't said what she wanted to hear. "Well... then.... was that all you wanted to say to me? To tell me that?"

"That is not all I wanted." Jack smiled and closed the space between them. He touched her cheek. "I love you, Ginny. I just wanted you to know that. I needed you to know that."

"I do know, Jack, and I love you too." He kissed her gently and Ginny gave him a long hug. "I just needed to hear the words from you."

"I love you, Gin." He pulled away then pressed his forehead against hers. "When I come back, if I come back...will you marry me?"

"Of course I will. You know how happy I would be to be your wife. I would marry you anytime." She moved her hands to his face and tears began welling up in her eyes again. Tears of happiness for the love he gave her, tears of fear for the dangers he would be facing, tears of sorrow from missing him already. "I have always prayed that someday we would be together."

"God willing, it will happen. I would marry you tomorrow if I could." He smiled sadly.

"Why can't we?" She whispered.

"Lots of reasons. You're still young, only 18, which isn't young, it's just...and anyways I will be back soon enough. Everyone says the war should be over in one big battle. I'll be home before you know it and we can start planning our lives together then. Besides, I don't want people thinking that the only reason we're getting married is because I'm going off to war."

Ginny reached up and kissed him. "I suppose if I must wait, I will." He hugged her tightly. "I also suppose I should be getting back. The laundry won't wash itself." She sighed. He took her hand and threaded their fingers together as they started walking back towards town. "Will you join us for dinner tonight?"

"I can't. Mother is having company for dinner and I must be there." He shook his head. "But will you meet me later tonight?"

"Tonight? Is there something special going on?" Ginny's heart fluttered in anticipation.

"No, nothing special. Just to talk, to just be together. I am not sure when my division will be getting organized to leave, but when we do, I will be going right away."

Ginny sighed again. She knew deep down that meeting Jack that night would mean making some tough decisions. She knew what most men would want in a situation like this. But she also knew that taking that step before being married would be a big mistake. She knew that being alone with him at night would make it hard to keep things the way God wanted. She was a girl who always tried to do what God wanted, and she knew Jack would never pressure her to do anything. However, with his leaving so quickly, she wasn't sure what would happen.

"Jack, I...I am not sure that's such a good idea. I want to, I just..." He looked at her, and as if reading her mind, gave her a small smile. "I'm not sure I can trust myself alone with you."

"What if I just come over to your house later and we can talk there? I would like to see your brothers anyway."

She smiled, thankful again for the man God had given her. "I would love that." She said.

April 15,

Washington DC

Michael Lewis, a native of Gettysburg, lay in bed with his wife, stroking her arm. He smiled and kissed her temple, still not quite sure how he had won such a wonderful girl. Augusta stirred and opened her sharp blue eyes, giving him a sleepy smile.

"Hey, there." She murmured, turning in his arms and kissing his cheek, her blonde hair falling over her shoulder. "What are you smiling about?" She was unable to keep from smiling herself. Her husband was an amazing man. Kind, honest, and endearingly shy, it had taken him quite a while to speak to her. When they met, he had been unusually tall and lanky, with dark brown hair and dark blue eyes. It had been his eyes that had first attracted her to him. She felt as though she could stare at them forever. Now, after years in the military, four at West Point, and then two more with the Corps of Engineers, he had filled out, still tall, but now having the muscular body to go with it. He was also more outwardly confident, but she knew he still had some shyness in him.

"Just thinking about you. The day we met. How lucky I am. Thanking the good Lord for all my blessings."

"Ah, the day we met. The day that you couldn't even speak to me because you were so nervous." She teased him.

"Don't give me a hard time. You were, and still are the most beautiful woman I have ever met." He leaned back and looked at her. Augusta truly was the most beautiful girl he knew, both inside and out. She was taller than most women, which was okay with him because he was taller than most men. When she was out in the sun even for a short time, a smattering of freckles would show up on her nose, which was not considered elegant, but he found endearing. He continued his thought. "All I knew about Southern women was that they were spoiled and persnickety. That they only liked the elegant, fancy men with money and property."

"Oh, you're using that excuse again." She laughed. "Well, I should thank you again for getting up the courage to talk to me."

19

She paused, and thought back to the path that had taken her from her plantation home in South Carolina, where she grew up, to being the wife of a Northern army officer. It hadn't been easy, and she still wondered if her father would ever really accept the marriage. Always able to read her expression, Michael commented about the worried look on her face.

"What are you thinking about?" Michael whispered against her ear. "Your family again?"

"Yes." She said. "I wish I could see them again. It's been almost a year since I have seen Matthew or my father. And with Joey leaving last week…with this war almost on our doorstep, I wonder if I'll ever see them again." Her voice turned to a whisper, her vulnerability apparent.

"I miss Joe too. He's my best friend and I'm not too happy about his decision to go south and fight for the Confederacy. I do understand, I suppose. It only makes sense that he would choose to fight for his land and family" He sighed. "This horrible conflict is finally here. I knew it was inevitable. It will be hard when I have to leave you."

"I hate the senselessness of it all. I can't stand it. I can't stand that men are too prideful to work out their differences peacefully." Augusta felt a tear roll down her cheek. She knew her next sentence would cause a disagreement. "I wonder how father will act towards me when I go home, because I will go home, to wait for you there…" The slight hesitant look in Michael's eyes made Augusta's stomach tighten.

"Augusta, you can't go south. I won't allow it." He averted his eyes.

"Yes, I can and I will!"

"It's way too dangerous. You cannot go back to Byron Hill."

"But I have to. And what do you mean it will be too dangerous? The war's not supposed to last long. I'll just go home to be sure everyone is alright and visit a spell, then come back home to you when your tour of duty is complete. I surely can't stay here. This being the capitol, well, that's what would be dangerous. Where else am I supposed to go?"

"Augusta, listen to me. This war is going to be longer than a lot of people realize. Neither side will give up easily. The North has more men and a lot more factories for supplies and munitions. The South may have fewer men but those men will be the more experienced

20

soldiers, plus they have that southern pride you're always talking about. Most of them have spent a good deal of their lives hunting and riding horses, you know that." He hesitated and continued, "I also believe that most of the war will be fought in the southern states. The Southerners will be fighting a defensive war; will be fighting on land they have grown up on. The Union army will have to be the aggressor. I can't have you in harm's way. Besides, even if you left tomorrow, the trip would be too dangerous and difficult. There is no easy route to get you there."

"Then what am I supposed to do, Michael? Stay here in Washington all by myself and be worried out of my mind about you and my family?" She pushed him over and sat up, then leaned back on an arm and looked down at him. She was angry, and frustrated at the whole situation. She had known this time would come and that he would be leaving her. They had avoided talking about it, both hating to even think about it. But the time to discuss it had come. They could no longer avoid it.

"As you said, that won't be such a good idea either. Washington could be too dangerous as well, it being the capital city. I'd like you to go to Gettysburg. Stay with my mother and father. Gettysburg is a small town. It'll be safe."

Augusta blinked, and then ran her hand through her blonde waves. "Gettysburg? But I've never been there and I've only met your parents twice. I won't know anybody there."

"But you'll adapt. You're outgoing and friendly. People love you. You'll make friends fast."

"When my family is fighting for the Confederacy? My southern accent will be frowned upon and you know it. What makes Gettysburg any different than Washington? I don't think I'll be making any friends at all."

"There are some good people in Gettysburg, Augusta and my parents love you. Trust me." He leaned over and kissed the tear off her cheek. "I know it will be tough." He spoke in a soft voice. "We knew this would be."

"I know." She reached up and wove her hands through his hair. "I'm not mad because you want me to go to Gettysburg. I would rather just go home. I miss my family. I understand why you don't want me to. It's more ...I just don't want to leave you. When you go...I just don't know how I'll say goodbye. What if...what if you

21

don't come back?" The last sentence was spoken so softly, he almost missed it.

"I'll have God with me. He'll watch over the both of us. I'll visit you if I ever get the chance and I'll write frequently. We will get through this. I can't promise that I'll come back alive; I won't make a promise like that, but one way or another, we'll see each other again."

She gently moved her hands around his face, as if trying to memorize the feel of it. She finally pulled his head down and kissed him.

"I love you, Michael."

April 15
Gettysburg, Pennsylvania

Alexandra was up to her elbows in a sticky, pasty mixture of biscuits. She didn't have to cook often, but she knew how, and the family's cook had left to take care of her sick mother in Philadelphia. Alex was flush with perspiration; the oven had been warm all day and it was hot in the kitchen. Her dark hair clung to her forehead and the back was coming out of the chignon she had tied it into earlier. She looked a mess but she couldn't escape baking today. With her mother feeling poorly, Alex was doing all the housework. As she kneaded the dough she sang her favorite folk song that she had learned as a child.

"There is a young maiden, she lives all alone. She lives all alone on the shore-oh. And there was nothing she could find that would comfort her mind than to roam all alone on the shore, shore shore. Then to roam all alone on the shore."

She took a deep breath to continue the next lines, but a deep baritone voice joined in.

"There is a young captain who sailed the salt sea. Let the wind blow high, blow low-oh." Alex turned and looked in shock and embarrassment at Will, who strode into the kitchen with a grin. *"I will die I will die, that young captain did cry..."* His voice was strong and she was surprised at how good it sounded. *"If I can't have that maid on the shore-oh shore. If I can't have that maid on the shore."* He came behind her and wrapped his arms around her. He kissed her neck and held her close. "I could call you my own maid from the shore." He spoke softly, "Would you, like the maiden, deceive me, your captain, if I took you and stowed you away in my cabins below?" He referred to the next verse of the song.

"I probably would." She grinned back and turned around, wrapping her own arms around him. "I can be quite stubborn sometimes, you know that. I may have escaped you just because I knew you wanted me."

"I do want you." He brushed a strand of hair away from her eyes. "Will you come for a walk with me?"

Alex threw her hands out to show Will her disheveled dress. "Look at me Will, I'm a mess. I've been baking and preparing dinner. I can't just leave. Besides," She gave him a puzzled look. "Why are you not in class?"

"I can answer that question if you come with me." He slid his hands down her arm to her hands and gave her a small tug. "Come on. Your parents will understand."

She gave very little resistance. "I don't know, Will. Have you ever been around my father when he's hungry?" But she knew she would go with him. She found it so hard to say no to this man. She sighed. "Just give me a moment to clean up."

When she was ready, the couple walked towards the new railroad cut. She kept her hand in his and walked closely next to him. As they walked, Alex thought back to the day he walked into her life…

October 13, 1860
Clark Home

 Alex, Ginny and Charlotte sat together in the Clark parlor on a Saturday afternoon. The skies were gray that day, and rain threatened. Ginny was enjoying some rare time off, and Alex was filling the two in on some news from town. Jack had the day off from work as well, and though the girls would have loved to have him come visit with them, his mother found many chores that only he could take care of. Alex found it more than a coincidence that Jack's mother had found all that work for him only after she had learned Ginny was free that day as well. She and Charlotte felt that Jack's mother didn't quite approve of his relationship with Ginny. They never discussed it with Ginny because they didn't want to hurt her feelings. Ginny was very self-conscious of the way the townspeople viewed her and her family.

 Rain began to fall heavily, the patter on the roof was calming in a way. The girls' discussion ranged from many different topics: the young men in the community to the town's upcoming Harvest Dance. It was easy to see that Alex loved social functions. It gave her the perfect opportunity to meet new people and talk. Ginny and Charlotte had quickly discovered that Alex had the type of personality that drew people in. Her wit, her smile, and her friendly manner was magnetic. She enjoyed flirting with the men, but in such a way that was socially acceptable.

 The talk turned to Abigail Williams, a rich, spoiled girl who liked nothing better than to make others around her feel inferior. Ginny, and by association Alex and Charlotte, had been favorite targets of hers. Abigail always wanted what others had, including Jack Skelley. Alex began her perfect impersonation of the socialite, pretending to flounce around and hang on every single male between the ages of 16 and 30.

 Alex was interrupted by a crisp knock on the door. Only the three girls were in the house, so Alex rose to answer it.

 A young man stood on the porch, soaking wet from the rain. He was about their age or perhaps a few years older. He was tall and well dressed in dark blue trousers and a white button-down shirt that clung to his wide shoulders and muscular chest. A dark maroon cravat was tied around his neck, looking out of place without a jacket. His midnight black hair lay flat on his head dripping water, and his bright blue expressive eyes scanned the room. Alex took in a sharp breath, she was speechless. He was the best-looking man she had ever seen.

"Excuse me, but is Professor Clark at home?" His voice was low and smooth.

"I am so sorry, but the professor, my father, is currently not at home. He is out with my mother." She invited him in out of the rain and closed the door behind him. Ginny went to the linen closet, pulled out a towel then handed it to Alex who offered it to the young man.

"Thank you." He said. "I am sorry for the intrusion. My name is William Sadler, and I'm a student of your father's. Actually, I am his student assistant. I just stopped by with a question on some papers I was reading for him."

"There is no need to apologize, Mr. Sadler." Alex smiled. "I'm Alexandria, and these are my good friends, Miss Charlotte Turner and Miss Virginia Wade."

"It is a pleasure to meet you both." As he ran the towel over his face and arms, drying off what he could, Will Sadler's eyes moved around the room. They touched on all three of the girls, but his gaze lingered on Alex the longest.

"Come over and sit by the stove, Mr. Sadler." Alex invited. "You can try to get warm and dry while you wait with us. My father should return soon and hopefully this rain will let up."

"Thank you very much, Miss Clark." He headed for the warmth of the stove. "I really shouldn't impose but I need to talk to your father."

"It's not an imposition at all, Mr. Sadler." Alex smiled. "We were just talking and relaxing, passing the time."

"Well don't let me interrupt you. Continue as if I am not even here." He flashed a charming smile.

"I suppose we could do that, but we would much rather have you join in the conversation."

"Of course, I would be delighted, thank you, Miss Clark." Will ran a hand through his wet hair, trying to fix his appearance.

The next hour passed by quickly. Will was a charming, outgoing, funny young man who was very easy to like. He shared many stories from his past, and at times dominated the conversation. The girls learned that he was not interested in college at all, but his father had insisted since he would one day be expected to take over the family's small textile factory in Northern Pennsylvania.

"Is that what you want to do with your life?" Alex asked. Will shook his head.

"No, running a factory that makes clothing doesn't really interest me at all. I've always wanted to do something else." He said. "If I had my way, I would be working out of doors, doing something more physical, not intellectual, something like farming, exploring, or something where I can work with my hands. But I am the only son in a family of five and have no real choice in the matter."

"That is unfortunate." Charlotte said.

"I've learned to accept it." Will shrugged. "Besides, if the problems between the north and south continue, there might be a war and I can always sign on with the army."

"Do you really believe that it is inevitable?" Ginny asked.

"Well, yes, everyone says so. Tensions are high and the Southern politicians, especially those in South Carolina, keep trying to break off from the Union. Parts of the south really want secession."

"They've tried that before and failed." Alex said.

"That's true. It's said that if they don't get their way in the election this November, they'll try again, and this time they might succeed." Will continued.

"And the Northern states would never sit back and let that happen." Alex replied.

"No, they won't." Will shook his head. He looked at Alex. "You are very well informed about current events, Miss Clark."

"Well, do remember who my father is; he never stops teaching even when he is at home." Alex smiled.

"Yes, I imagine that is very true." Will smiled back. He turned to Ginny and Charlotte. "So what do you ladies think?"

Before either girl could answer, the door opened and Alex's parents entered. Will stood and explained his presence.

"Dinner should be ready soon. Would you care to join us?" Mr. Clark asked. "You would be most welcome and after dinner we could discuss the papers in more detail. You ladies can stay as well." Charlotte glanced at the clock ticking on the mantle.

"Thank you for the invitation Mr. Clark, but I really should be leaving. I left a stew on the stove and Father will expect me home for dinner." Charlotte said.

"I can't stay either." Ginny said. "I promised my mother I'd be back before dinner but thank you for the invitation."

"Well, sir, I would be delighted. Thank you." Will said with a smile.

As the rain started to let up the two girls said their goodbyes and headed out the door. Alex went into the kitchen to help her mother finish the dinner preparations. That night had been the most enjoyable dinner Alex had ever had and it wasn't because of the food. Will was wonderful. He was funny, knowledgeable, and the perfect gentleman. He even seemed to appreciate the fact that Alex had a mind and liked discussing politics and current events. Most men didn't like that side of her. She was especially happy to learn that he shared her faith.

"So what is so important that I deserted my dinner chores?" Alex asked, taking a deep breath of the fresh spring air. "What is it you need to tell me?" It had been humid and rainy the past few days and the air was still slightly damp, but the grass and plants were green and lush. She looked out at the landscape, fields rolling gently until they emerged as mountains. The sun was just beginning to set, over them, a splash of pink and red forming over them.

"Well, as you know the war has started." Will began quickly. He wanted to get the most difficult part of the conversation over with.

"Yes." Alex immediately had a dreadful feeling. She knew exactly what Will was going to say next.

"Well, President Lincoln has made a call to arms. He's asking men to join the army, become soldiers and fight the states that are in rebellion." He paused, waiting for any comment she might have. She usually had something to say, but when she remained silent he continued.

"So I'm going to. Sign up that is. What do you think about that?" His voice was so anxious, and excited, Alex felt like she would crush his feelings if she said what was really on her mind. Despite this she had to be truthful and tell him. When she hesitated too long, he stopped walking and pulled her around to face him,

"Alexandra? I thought you would be excited for me. Please, say something."

"What should I say, Will?" Her voice was hoarse, as she was trying not to cry. "That I want you to go, that I want you to leave? That I want you to go off to fight and possibly be killed?"

"I won't be killed, Allie." His use of the personal nickname he gave her was in the hopes of calming her, making her see where he was coming from.

28

"If you think that you're either more arrogant than I thought or just plain stupid." she said angrily, giving him a small shove. "How can you even say something like that? People will die in this fight, Will."

"The rebellion isn't supposed to last that long. Everyone has been saying that the war will be over in one big battle anyways. I can get a different view of life before I am tied down to my father's factory."

"I'm sure the British thought the rebellion would be a quick one back in 1776. Besides, Will, men will still die in that one big battle. I don't want you to be one of them."

"Allie, I have to do this. You know me, you know I'm telling the truth. I have to get out and do something. I can't spend the rest of my life stuck behind a desk, buried in paperwork and you know I don't like school. I have to go out and do this one thing before I have to take over Father's business."

Alex took a deep breath. She knew arguing would do no good. Will's mind was made up. He would go and fight in this stupid war and risk possibly being killed. She had not known him for long, but over the past few months, she realized she was in love with him. She could not imagine what her life would be like if she lost him.

"Will, you know I would never keep you from doing anything that you really wanted. It isn't like I have any right to tell you what to do."

"That's not true, Allie. I value your opinion and I greatly value you. You must know that." He reached up to gently run his finger down her cheek.

"I love you, Alexandria." His voice was so soft it was almost a whisper. Her eyes flew up to his, surprised. She knew that he cared for her, but had no idea it was something as strong as love.

"Will…" she started to speak, but he interrupted her.

"I know, we haven't known each other that long. But I know what is in my heart. I love you and I want to spend the rest of my life with you. I think I have known I loved you from the moment I saw you."

"When you came to my home asking about a paper from Father?"

Will grinned. "Actually, I saw your image before that. A daguerreotype on your father's desk. It was from your sister's wedding. I saw that and knew I had to meet you. The need for asking your father about that paper was just an excuse to meet you."

"I never knew that." Alex said.

"It's true." Will paused, taking a quick breath. "I have spoken with your father. He approves, although I know you well enough to realize

that you wouldn't need his permission, if it was something that you truly wanted. I did want his blessing, though. At any rate, like I said, he approves of the marriage, just thought that it was a little soon..."
Will was talking fast now, rambling really, and his nervousness was showing. Alex smiled, then reached up to touch a strand of hair that had fallen onto his face. Will continued talking. "But your father said all I had to do was ask you and he would support whatever decision..."
Alex moved her hand to pull Will's face down to hers. Their lips met gently, briefly. It was their first real kiss. Will pulled back, stunned at her forwardness.

"Well, I had to get you to stop talking somehow." She explained with a smile. "I love you too, Will." She knew it now. Loved his smile, his carefree and easygoing nature, how he could always make her laugh. Everything about him made her smile.

He slid his hands down her arms, leaned close and whispered. "I want to be with you as much as possible while we have the time."

She put her own arms around him. "Well, then we'll just have to make wedding arrangements quickly."

The next day
Gettysburg, Pennsylvania

"Will and I are getting married!" Alex exclaimed, out of nowhere. The three friends were at the Wade's house, working on mending and other small projects from their respective homes. At Alex's news, Charlotte stuck herself with the needle she was using. She had expected the couple to get married but this seemed so sudden.

"Alex, you met him only a few months ago." Ginny said, the voice of reason.

"I know. But I love him. He loves me. When he asked me, I didn't hesitate at all. I want to be with him so much. Not only that, but he will be leaving for camp soon. He really dislikes being in school and will do anything to get away. He said the only positive thing about coming to school in Gettysburg was meeting me. It must have been Divine Providence." She blushed. "Sometimes, you just know who you are meant to be with. Father approves wholeheartedly. Mother's only issue is that it's so soon."

"Well, good for you. I'm really happy for you both." Charlotte told her. "This is exciting news! When will you have the ceremony? "

"Saturday. I know it doesn't give us a lot of time to prepare, but we want to spend some time together before he has to go."

"Where will you stay?" Charlotte asked.

"Well, my parents said we could stay with them, but...I just feel that would be strange. Since it will only be a week or so before Will is mustered in, we are going to stay at the McClellan Hotel. He wired his family to tell them the news and they said they would send some money as a gift to put us up there. We can still eat with my family, but we will be able to spend some time alone. It will be nice, especially since we are not going to be able to take a proper wedding trip."

"This just seems like it is happening so fast." Ginny commented.

"I know." Alex said. "I have a dress that I can wear, it will just need a few alterations."

"I can help with that." Ginny said.

"I hoped you would say that." Alex grinned. "I would be so grateful. And Will's cousin will be coming here in the next few days to be his best man, but that is it from his family. His friend and roommate from school, Daniel Gilchrist will also stand up with him. I wanted to ask you two..." She looked at both of them, a smile still on her face. "You have been two of the best friends I could have asked for. Even

31

in Philadelphia, I didn't have friends as close as you, I just had my sister. Most likely, she won't be able to make it in from the city. She's with child, due next month as you both know, so that will complicate traveling for her. I was wondering if you two would stand up with me."

"I would be honored." Charlotte said with a smile.

"Yes, of course." Ginny replied. Alex hugged first Charlotte, then Ginny.

"I am so happy." Alex said, sitting back down and picking up her sewing.

"You know, Ginny and I are really happy for you, but I do know someone who will be quite upset by this news." Charlotte said, picking up her sewing needle and the shirt she was mending.

"And who would that be?" Alex asked, defensively. She didn't like the idea of anyone interfering with her marriage.

"Well, the last few Sundays at church, Abigail has been making eyes at Will and talking to him."

"Well, Abigail Williams can just…"

"Woah, easy, Alex." Ginny said with a smile. "Charlotte was just teasing you." Since Abigail was always dressed in the finest, newest fashion and always had to have the best accessories, Charlotte suspected that was the main reason she liked Will, who was very handsome. The man would perfectly compliment her walking through town. When Alex had first come to town, Abigail had wanted to befriend the fashionable new girl from Philadelphia. Luckily, Charlotte and Ginny had been able to help prevent that …

February, 1859
Gettysburg, Pennsylvania

Pastor Reynolds started the church service by introducing a new family. Mr. Duncan Clark was a new professor at the Pennsylvania College. He was a stern looking man, with a dark, bushy mustache tinged with gray, with his hair the same coloring. His wife was a tiny woman, blonde, with a kind face and sharp, angular features. They had a daughter, a pretty girl who appeared the same age as Charlotte and Ginny. She was tall, with long, dark hair and a big, friendly smile. Their son, who looked to be about John Wade's age of 13, had the same dark features as his sister and a mischievous grin.

After the service, Ginny and Charlotte quickly found one another. Jack and some of the other boys were under a grouping of trees nearby. The new girl stood to the side of her parents, who were being welcomed by members of the church. Abigail Williams had already approached the new girl.

"Oh dear." Ginny said. "That poor Clark girl is going to get ambushed."

"I absolutely cannot tolerate Abigail." Charlotte muttered. "She is so pretentious and full of herself and..."

"Well, I can't stand to be around her either, but we just can't leave the new girl to Abigail's wonderful personality."

"That would be terribly cruel of us." Charlotte nodded and they headed over to where Abigail was talking to Alex. Abigail was dominating the conversation, as always. The new girl was trying to speak, but not having much of a chance to do so. The two girls wove through the crowd until they could speak to Abigail and the Clark girl.

"Abbie, how are you?" Charlotte said, using a nickname that everyone knew she hated.

"I'm doing well, Charlotte, thank you. I was just welcoming the town's newest member, Alexandria Clark, to Gettysburg." She smiled a fake smile. It was clear that Abigail was flustered at the interruption, especially since one of the culprits was Ginny Wade. Abigail was one of the townspeople who considered Ginny to be of a lower class; one who was way beneath her and seldom worth her notice. To make matters worse, Abigail had recently gotten it in her head that Jack Skelly would be the perfect beau for herself and she was jealous of the relationship between Jack and Ginny.

"Hello, Alexandria, my name is Charlotte Turner and this is my best friend, Ginny Wade." Charlotte gave a small curtsey. "Welcome to Gettysburg. Where are you from?"

"She is from..." Abigail started to answer, but a quick hand up from Alex stopped her.

"I am from Philadelphia, thank you for asking." Alex's green eyes flashed as she smiled at Abigail patronizingly. "I appreciate the gesture, Abigail, but you will soon realize that I am able to answer for myself. In fact, I usually prefer it." She gave Charlotte and Ginny a smile.

"My father and I live on a farm just outside of town." Charlotte said. "Ginny, her mother and sister are tailors. If you ever have a need of one, they do good work."

"I also have three brothers." Ginny said. "John Jr. is thirteen. How old is your brother?"

"Aaron just turned fourteen. I also have a sister, Maria, but she is recently married and stayed in Philadelphia with her husband."

Abigail looked from Alex to Charlotte, then gave Ginny what could only be called an annoyed look, and left the small group in a huff.

Alexandria rolled her eyes. "Is she always that irritating? I'm sorry to be judgmental, and I usually am not, but she was insufferable. I thank you for coming over." She looked over to where Abigail now was. "And she was kind of rude."

"That's Abigail. She thinks she is better than everyone else just because her father has money and her mother claims that her family has been in town since the 1760's and her great-great-whatever grandfather was a relative of James Gettys . He was one of the first settlers of the town."

"Well, then, I am especially glad you two came over. I would really rather not associate with girls like that."

And from that day on, Alex, Charlotte and Ginny became best of friends.

April 20
Gettysburg, Pennsylvania

Alex stood in front of her mother's looking glass, straightening her dress and hair.

"Alex, you look absolutely lovely." Charlotte remarked, bending down to adjust the dark green silk skirt over Alex's hoopskirt.

"Will won't be able to keep his eyes off you." Ginny agreed.

"Thank you. I owe the both of you so much. Ginny, the dress turned out absolutely perfect. I love it."

The door opened and Alex's mother came in.

"My dear, you have never looked more beautiful." Tears welled up in her eyes. "I just wish your sister could have been able to come."

"I do too. But Aaron is here, and I have both my parents and my friends. And Will, of course. The day will be perfect." Alex took a deep breath and smiled.

"I cannot believe how you have grown up. You are such a lady. I know you and Will shall do well together." Mrs. Clark held out her arms and Alex rushed into her embrace.

"Oh, this is the happiest day of my life!"

"Come along, let's get you all to the church."

A small carriage took the four women down Carlisle Street to St. James Lutheran Church on York Street. It was the perfect day for a wedding. The sun shone brightly and the skies were clear. There was a slight breeze to keep the air from getting too warm.

As the carriage reached the church they noticed that most of the guests were already inside. Alex's father was there to assist the ladies, as was Alex's brother Aaron, who had recently turned sixteen.

"Everyone is ready and waiting inside." Mr. Clark said with a smile. They walked up the church steps, and he brushed his wife's cheek with a kiss before they entered. Ginny and Charlotte lined up and prepared to proceed down the aisle.

"I can't wait until it is me walking down this aisle to Jack." Ginny whispered to Charlotte.

When Alex entered the church on her father's arm, her eyes focused on where Will stood, flanked by his cousin, Christopher and his friend Daniel. The groom was dressed in a fine black suit with a Union blue shirt underneath and matching cravat. His smile was more radiant than she had ever seen it before. She couldn't help the small tear of happiness forming in the corners of her eyes. They slowly walked down the aisle and her father handed her to Will. She took his arm. As the pastor spoke, Alex lost herself in Will's eyes. She was so focused on him that she almost missed her cue to answer; "I will."

The rest of the ceremony was a blur. When the pastor gave Will permission to kiss his bride, he framed her face with his hands and kissed her gently on the lips, then rested his forehead briefly on hers.

"I love you." He whispered, then pulled her into his arms for a hug. They then turned to the guests as the pastor introduced them for the first time as Mr. and Mrs. Will Sadler.

*****

The Clarks hosted a small gathering after the wedding. As Charlotte wove through the crowd, she couldn't help but notice most of the talk among the guests, especially the male guests, was about the war. Those who had signed up to fight would be leaving for Camp Scott in York, while others would be staying behind to care for family, or to keep their businesses going.

"Miss Turner." Charlotte turned toward the familiar voice of Thomas Culp, her father's right-hand man on the farm. Thomas was tall and lanky, with neatly trimmed blonde hair and the beginning of the popular facial style of hair known as "mutton chops". He looked nothing like his cousin, Wesley. "Alexandria makes a lovely bride, does she not?" Charlotte glanced at her friend with a smile. The newlywed was truly glowing. Will, beaming with pride, could scarcely take his eyes off his new wife to thank the well-wishers who had formed a line to congratulate them.

"Yes, she does." Charlotte agreed. "And Will looks quite happy as well."

"Marriage can do that to a man." Thomas said. An uncomfortable silence followed his statement. Charlotte was about to excuse herself, when Thomas spoke again.

"How do you feel about the war; the men of this town leaving to fight?" Thomas's question stopped her, and puzzled her. In all of her acquaintance with him, he had never asked her opinion on anything. He was never rude, but it wasn't his way.

"I am not sure, truth be told." Charlotte admitted. "I can't say that I would like a war to happen, but I don't believe that the South should keep slaves. Or leave the Union."

"Yes." Thomas said, clasping his hands behind his back. "I would like to stay here and farm, as many others are doing. But I cannot stand by and stay here while my friends and family members go out to defend our nation."

"I believe many men feel that way." Charlotte replied.

"I'm sure they do. Word is that most of the men who moved to Virginia with Hoffman will be returning to Gettysburg. Smart to get away from the traitorous rebels."

Charlotte glanced over to Annie and Julia Culp, Wesley's sisters. She wondered if they had heard from him, as she herself had not in over a month. The last letter she had received led her to feel morose.

"What about Wesley?" Charlotte asked Thomas. "Has anyone in your family heard from him?"

"Wesley." Thomas spoke his name with disdain. "I wouldn't know. I visited him not long ago, when I was doing business in the area for your father. The boy wasn't sure how he felt. If he decides to go against his family and fight for the Rebels, well…let's just say he would never be welcome back home. In fact, he would cease to be a part of the family."

Charlotte was silent, unsure of how to respond. Finally, she spoke softly. "Let's hope that doesn't happen."

"Indeed." Thomas stroked his face as Ginny approached them. She smiled at Thomas, then took Charlotte's arm. "Excuse us, Mr. Culp, but the bride and groom have managed to get a photographer and would like a portrait made of the wedding party."

As they walked, Charlotte leaned close to Ginny and whispered: "I cannot tell you how much I appreciate you saving me."

"I could tell he was making you uncomfortable. But really, we are to be photographed."

The two made their way to where Mr. Isaac Tyson, a local man who had a photography studio on York Street with his brother, had set up his camera. Photography wasn't new, but it was still expensive enough that most citizens only used it for special occasions.

Charlotte and Ginny took their places at Alex's side. The bride hadn't let go of her husband's arm since she had taken it during the ceremony. Mr. Tyson arranged the wedding party, then stepped behind his camera.

"Ladies and gentlemen, please hold your poses as I count to five." He uncapped the camera lens and slowly counted, then recapped the lens. "Thank you very much." Mr. Tyson's brother, Charles began packing the equipment. Charlotte turned to Ginny as Alex and Will went to go greet more guests.

"So what was Thomas talking to you about?" Ginny asked.

"Nothing much. Just small talk. The war. The wedding." Charlotte paused, glancing across the room to where Thomas stood, talking to her father. "He is a big help to father. I sometimes wonder if Father…" she trailed off, lost in thought.

"You wonder if your father what?"

"I know my father would like a son. I know he wants me married. Soon. Father wants someone to take over the farm. I think he feels as though Thomas would be the perfect man to fit all of that criteria."

"You. Married to Thomas Culp?" Ginny shook her head. "I just can't see it."

"I can't either." Charlotte said. "But sometimes, it's not about what we want." She glanced over to Alex and Will. "We can dream of a great relationship like that, but we might not all get one."

April 21
Gettysburg, Pennsylvania

Charlotte crumpled the letter she was reading and tossed it to the end of the table. It was so stiff, so formal. If it had not been in Wesley's familiar handwriting, she would not have believed it had been him writing at all.

"Many of the men who moved here with me are returning home. I need you to know that I will not fight for the Union. I have made a home here in Virginia. I have friends who I cannot fight against. I am sorry if my actions disappoint you. I know we were good friends before, and I will miss your friendship, but I believe that the North should let the South live the way they want to. I believe the South has the right to leave the country if they desire. If the government takes away slavery from the South, what will they take away next? I cannot in good conscience support that. I may have been born a Northerner, but I now consider myself a Virginian. Unfortunately, I do not know where that leaves you and me."

His letters were usually upbeat and happy. This last letter however did not sound like the Wesley Culp she knew and cared about. Charlotte was filled with sorrow. She had hoped and prayed that the country's built-up tensions and then the outbreak of war would bring Wesley home. Instead it was pushing him even further away. She grabbed the letter, then straightened and refolded it and tucked it in her skirt pocket. She sat down, bent her head and thought back to other times.

1856
Gettysburg, Pennsylvania

The sun beat down on Charlotte, but a light breeze swept through the farm. Charlotte picked up an egg and placed it in her basket when a familiar male voice spoke.

"Working hard?"

"Wesley! What brings you out here?"

"I'd like you to come for a walk with me." Wesley begged, flashing the smile that Charlotte found irresistible.

"Wes..."

"Charlotte I need to talk to you. I have something important to tell you. I have made a decision, and since, well, since you made my decision so hard, I thought I should tell you first."

"I'm confused." Charlotte admitted, a sinking feeling forming in her stomach. Still, she looked at him with pure affection. Her feelings for him had grown and changed in the past few months.

"Mr. Hoffman is bringing some of his workers down to Virginia with him."

"I know." Charlotte said, "Charlie Skelley is one of them, according to Jack."

"Yes. Well, I'm going to go with them too." Wesley averted his eyes.

Charlotte stopped dead in her tracks, looking at Wesley in total disbelief.

"You can't go." She said, hoping that what she thought had some bearing on the situation.

He stopped and turned towards her, pushed his hat back off his face a bit and shoved his hands in his pockets. It was a typical look he had when he needed to talk about something he did not want to talk about.

"I have to go, Charlotte. Working at the carriage shop is something I'm good at, and I like it. I'm eighteen years old. My father keeps telling me that I have to be making my own way. He has my brother to help him run the shop here. William will take over the tailoring business. If I don't go now, I don't think I'll ever find something better that I'm suited for. It's a great opportunity for me."

"Couldn't you open your own shop?" She searched her mind, trying to think of a way to make Wesley stay.

"I don't have the money to start a new business, Charlotte. Besides, Mr. Hoffman is moving because he can't find enough work here to make a living. If he can't find the work, I surely can't."

"But you can't leave, Wesley. I don't know what I'd do if you weren't here."

"You've barely seen me these past few months anyways. We're both too busy."

"Yes, but you are still here. I could visit you in the shop, or in the evenings..."

"I know." He paused, and took off his hat, gently slapping it against his leg. *"But I need the money, and the job, Charlotte."* He stepped close to her, and spoke more softly.

As Charlotte looked into his eyes, the world seemed to stop. Would he ask her to come with him? The moment, the timing, everything felt perfect. She lifted her hand and touched his neck, pulling his head down. He circled her waist with his hand. Their lips met, softly and sweetly. As she moved to pull him closer, he opened his eyes and broke away.

"Charlotte, I can't...we can't." He took a deep breath. *"You're like my sister."* Her stomach plummeted. His words were a crushing blow. She felt like a stupid, juvenile, little girl.

"I'm sorry." She mumbled, pulling completely away and backing up. *"I don't know what came over me."* Her foot hit a stone and she stumbled. Wesley moved quickly, catching her and stopping her from falling. His hand remained on her elbow.

"Charlotte, I don't want to hurt you, it's just, you know...you're one of my best friends, and..."

"No, Wes, it's fine, really." Charlotte put on a smile, trying to cover her emotions and what she was really feeling. She wanted the ground beneath her feet to open up and swallow her.

"Are you sure you're okay?" He still gently held her arm, and the look on his face showed true concern.

"I'm sure." She smiled a brave, but false smile. *"You're one of my best friends, Wes. I need that friendship more than anything."*

Charlotte sighed, caught up in her memories. She still cared about Wesley more than any other man. She had hoped and prayed that the relationship between Wesley and her would evolve into a romance the same way Ginny and Jack's relationship had, but it didn't seem like

God had that in mind. It had almost happened during the summer after he left, in late 1859. The summer Charlotte and her father had traveled to Fredericksburg, Virginia to visit family. The family plantation, Turner's Glenn, was not far away. The family, including Charlotte had been invited to a grand ball at Chatham Manor, a Georgian-style home owned by a prominent family, on the Rappahannock River. Wesley, in Fredericksburg on business, had managed to obtain an invitation.

Late Summer, 1859
Fredericksburg, Virginia

The Lacy family had put a lot of time and money into this glorious ball they were hosting in celebration of their niece, America Joan's birthday. Chatham Manor was decorated more beautifully than usual. The great ball room was open and airy. Everywhere one looked, there were beautiful white morning glories, white and purple aster and lavender flowers. The hallway that connected the ball room and the great dining room was immaculate and so well-lit that it seemed to glow. The male house slaves were dressed in elegant black suits that looked as fine as what a footman in the Royal Palace of England would wear. Charlotte mentally noted that their outfits were finer than the ordinary clothes of a Gettysburg citizen. The servants carried trays of champagne filled flutes and small bite sized cakes. The sideboard tables in the dining room were full of an assortment of small snacks. The outside of the manor looked impressive as well. The formal gardens were as breathtaking as always, made more so with hanging lanterns lighting the paths, allowing the guests the ability to stroll the walkways and enjoy the beauty and smells of fresh blooming flowers.

Grand carriages pulled up and dropped off their elegantly dressed passengers. Charlotte had been dressed by a personal servant at Turner's Glenn, a slave by the name of Zipporah. The girl had spent almost an hour styling her plain brown hair. Every strand was curled into ringlets and half the curls were piled on her head while the other half fell gently around her shoulders. Charlotte's dress was a deep maroon with white lace lining the deep décolletage and sleeves that fell low off the arms and left her shoulders bare. All the women wore dresses much like Charlotte's, but unlike Charlotte, they were well-practiced in walking in the newest fashion of very wide hoop skirts, and none seemed as self-conscious as she did wearing the corsets. She felt as though her bosom was going to pop out of the dress. She was so embarrassed that she continually crossed her arms over her chest to cover up, but her cousin Isabelle would promptly yet gently pull her arms back down.

"That's not proper or very ladylike." Belle scolded, once again pushing Charlotte's arms down.

"Well, I'm sorry." Charlotte whispered back. "I feel so exposed."

"With a figure like yours, you should learn to flaunt it. Loosen up a little bit. Get ready to flirt with all the handsome eligible young men that were invited." Belle was calm and at ease as she ran her hands down her own skirt. The ball gown she had on looked gorgeous on her. It was made of satin, with white and pale pink vertical stripes with black lace lining the hem. The bodice with short puffed sleeves and a deep neckline was trimmed in the same black lace. She had matching pale pink gloves to complete the outfit. The dress perfectly complemented her pale complexion, with midnight black hair and piercing green eyes.

"I don't know how to flirt Belle, you know that, I've certainly told you enough times." Charlotte replied briskly.

"Everyone can flirt, Charlotte. You just need to..."

"Belle, leave her alone." Belle's older sister, Beth, spoke up. "Not everyone is as confident in their looks as you are." She turned to Charlotte. "You do look beautiful though, Charlotte." Beth was not as social and outgoing as Belle, but she was kind and patient. She had married a friend of her brother, a blacksmith, even though she could have married someone with wealth and status. She already had one little boy, two-year-old Benjamin, and was expecting another child. Just as Beth finished speaking, her tall, well-built husband approached.

"Mrs. Bennett, would you care to dance?" He smiled. Joshua Bennett looked more of an aristocrat than a blacksmith tonight. He was wearing dark blue pants with a matching vest and jacket, and a maroon undershirt that made his vivid blue eyes stand out. His dark hair was parted to the side, as was the fashion. Charlotte envied Beth. It was clear that Joshua doted on her and that the two belonged together. Even their outfits tonight were complimentary. Beth's gown was the same maroon color of Joshua's shirt, made of embroidered silk taffeta. The dress just covered her shoulders, and the neckline was trimmed with gold lace. An atatched fabric rose with green velvet leaves graced each shoulder. Beth was just beginning to show her condition, but the dress perfectly fit her.

"I would love to, Mr. Bennett." She smiled, took his hand into hers, and followed him onto the dance floor.

"Those two can be perfectly nauseating at times." Belle said as she watched them join others in the waltz. Her demeanor changed as she noticed two young men making their way over to them. They were clean-cut and elegantly dressed. It took Charlotte a few seconds to realize it was Richard Evans and Samuel Gray, two young men she had become acquainted with over the past few weeks. Richard, as always looked unbearably handsome. His light brown hair was parted perfectly down the middle and looked sleek and shiny. He walked tall and proud and his suit coat was perfectly formed to his broad shoulders and chest. He had a perfect smile that showed straight, white teeth, and a dimple on the right side. He approached the girls, bent over slightly and gently lifted Charlotte's gloved hand, bringing it to his lips. Richard had been extremely attentive to Charlotte since the day they met. Why he wanted to spend time with her was beyond Charlotte's imaginings. In the past few days, Richard had let it be known to her that he enjoyed her company immensely.

"Miss Turner, you look even more beautiful today than you did the day we met." His eyes dropped briefly to Charlotte's bosom, and she blushed.

"Thank you, Mr. Evans." Charlotte spoke softly. She gave Samuel a slight nod. "Mr. Gray, how are you faring tonight?"

"Quite well, Miss Charlotte, thank you." He smiled brightly and took Isabelle by the arm. Samuel Gray was Isabelle's beau. He was tall and muscular, with blonde hair that was worn longer than usual and smiling blue eyes. He had a wonderful disposition and doted on Isabelle. "I do say Miss Isabelle, you have truly turned this northern girl into a beautiful southern belle. Well done."

Isabelle smiled. "Why Samuel, don't tell me that I am such a good teacher that you have now fallen in love with my student?"

"Of course not!" He exclaimed. "Never! And to prove it, I am going to invite you to dance with me. I believe I hear my favorite waltz. Shall we?"

Isabelle flashed Samuel a brilliant smile, nodded to the other couple and took his offered arm, leaving Charlotte to entertain Richard on her own.

"Well, Miss Turner, I understand Isabelle taught you some new dances. Do you happen to know this one?"

Charlotte scratched at the seam of her white glove. Her hands were sweaty and she wanted to take them off, but Belle had warned her not to. She listened to the music and watched the dancers for a minute before recognizing it.

"I do know the steps." She looked into his brown eyes and smiled, trying to be coy, but failing miserably. She tried to remember all the things Belle had told her: stand straight but not too rigid, smooth

45

movements, no jerking, don't skip the steps, but walk them, make sure your moves look graceful and easy, not forced. There was so much to remember and then there were the dance steps themselves.

"Will you allow me to escort you to the dance floor?" Richard asked.

"Of course, Mr. Evans. I must warn you, though: I am not terribly proficient quite yet. You may end up with some swollen feet from my stepping on them." He chuckled, took her arm and tucked it into his. Charlotte allowed him to lead her towards the dance floor and it wasn't long until she was confidently dancing and enjoying every move.

After the first dance was finished they shared two more together before she needed to stop and catch her breath

"Not used to this type of activity?" Richard smiled.

"I just need a few minutes to rest." Charlotte explained. "Especially my mind. It's quite difficult to remember all of the steps and rules. I know some simple dances, but we don't have much call for grand balls like this in Gettysburg."

"We do have the advantage there." Richard agreed and escorted her off the dance floor. "We learn all these dances at a very young age. It comes naturally to us." He smiled. "Would you like some champagne?"

Charlotte nodded and accepted his offered arm. He took a glass from a tray being carried by a servant and handed it to her. She gulped it down quickly. By the amused look on Richard's face, Charlotte assumed she had done something improper.

"I'm sorry." Charlotte said. "I was just really parched. It's so warm in here and with all the dancing..." she trailed off lamely.

"Shall we go out and take a stroll in the gardens?" He asked.

"I do enjoy the gardens immensely. However, I prefer the view from the front of the house, especially at this time of night. You know with the river and the town lights."

"Well, walking out there is an option." He smiled and led her outside. This side of the house was much like the back. Elegant lanterns lined the pathways, lighting the way down the first set of steps and the path that ran parallel to both the house and river. The moon was bright, giving off additional light and the reflection it made upon the river was breathtaking.

"Are you enjoying yourself tonight?" Richard asked.

"I actually am." She replied. "However, I don't like being the center of attention and I feel like everyone is staring at me tonight. Even though it's AJ's party, I feel as though everyone wants to keep an eye on the Northern girl. Even out here." They passed another couple enjoying the night air. They nodded in acknowledgement to Charlotte and Richard.

"Well, I could take you someplace that would be a bit more secluded." Richard suggested. "However something of that nature would probably ruin your reputation."

"I'm a Yankee. According to your southern standards I don't have a good reputation to start with." They turned to the left, down a tree-lined path.

"Well, you may be a Yankee, but if all Yankee women are as sweet and beautiful as you, then I just may have to move up North."

"Mr. Evans are you trying to flatter me?"

"I am indeed." He stopped and stepped back, pulling Charlotte into an alcove of sorts. They were almost completely surrounded by trees and dense bushes. He took both of her hands in his.

"Miss Turner, I must confess. From the very moment I met you, I have been intrigued by you."

"Thank you," She said softly, getting mildly concerned by his actions.

"I have never met anyone like you and I find myself thinking of you all the time." He stepped closer, pulled his white glove off and touched her cheek with his bare hand. "I have never felt this way about anyone. I know you are to return to Pennsylvania soon. I would like to ask you to reconsider. I know your Uncle would allow you to stay with him for an extended period of time. I would like to pay formal court to you, Charlotte. Get to know you better." He smiled slyly. "Much, much better." He intimately slid his hand down her arm, pulling off her glove.

"Mr. Evans, I am honored, really, but...I have no intentions of remaining in Virginia past the time I had planned on. I have friends back home and..."

"Another man?" Richard's voice grew harsh.

"No, at least, well, friends." Charlotte stammered. Richard's hands cupped her elbows and he leaned closer.

"Charlotte, you don't have to play the innocent with me."

"Play the innocent? Richard I am not playing. What are you talking about?" Charlotte backed away, but his grip tightened. "I thought that you were a gentleman!" She exclaimed, now quite alarmed. He held her arms tightly. Years ago, Jack and Wesley had taught her how to fight off a man who was attacking her, but she didn't have enough room to maneuver. She pushed at him but he was too strong for her to fight off.

"Richard let me go!" She squirmed and fought as he started to bring his lips towards her.

"Excuse me." A deep voice spoke out and Richard was pulled away from her. "I believe the lady asked you to stop." The man's voice was familiar. Charlotte's eyes adjusted and she couldn't believe who she saw. She blinked again slowly and saw it was indeed Wesley Culp. Before she could say anything to her friend, Richard spoke back.

"Excuse me, no one asked for your interference."

"Oh, I beg to differ." Wesley stated as his eyes darted from Richard to Charlotte, "Does the lady want me to stay?" Wesley's eyes darted back to Richard.

"Yes, please. Wesley stay." She said softly.

"Then I suppose I'll be staying." Wesley said with a smug smile. Richard pulled his arm back and took a swing at him. Wesley expertly blocked the punch and instead of hitting Richard back he simply shoved him aside. Richard lost his balance and fell to the ground.

"You stupid no-account tradesman!" Richard yelled. He was sitting on the ground, his legs sprawled out like a child. He would look comical if it wasn't for the look of pure anger on his face.

"So would you like some satisfaction now?" Wesley asked in a taunting voice.

Richard pushed himself up off the ground and brushed the dirt off his pants. He took a step towards Wesley, but then seemed to think better of it. He looked at Charlotte, anger apparent on his handsome face.

"I should, but she isn't worth the bother." He stalked off, looking like a pouting child.

"You know, I disagree with that." Wesley said, turning to Charlotte. "You are one of the few woman whose honor I would ever consider dueling for." He smiled the crooked smirk she remembered so well from their childhood.

"Thank you." Charlotte replied, and then took a good look at her friend. Wesley appeared very changed. His hair hung a bit longer than it used to, but it was cut clean and neat. He wore a stylish new suit of dark blue colored pants with a matching, finely cut jacket, and a white silk shirt with ruffles at the collar and sleeves that complimented the ensemble. His cravat was the color of red wine. He was tan, and had filled out quite nicely. He had the shadow of a beard that ran from his sideburns to his chin. Wesley looked at Charlotte, his blue eyes intense and warm. The look he gave her made her heart skip a beat.

Wesley maintained his smile as he continued looking at her. She had changed a lot since the last time he had seen her. She had grown into a young women. She had been such a tomboy he thought, with sharp limbs and a skinny figure. The hair that was usually flying loosely from her braided pigtails was now pinned neatly and elegantly upon her head and not a hair was out of place. Her figure, as much as he knew she would like to hide it, was not shapeless anymore. She looked beautiful. He couldn't help but look at her. Stare at her.

"Wesley, you look so different. You're so, uhh, grown up now!"

"You've matured quite a bit too, Charlotte." His gaze teasingly touched the exposed skin above her dress line. *"I wasn't aware you liked dressing so well."* His smile was a bit mischievous. She crossed her arms in front of her chest.

"You know that I hate it." She said indignantly, dropping her arms. He took her forearms and looked into her eyes.

"That may be but I'm not complaining." He chuckled. *"You look absolutely beautiful."*

"Thank you for saying that." Charlotte murmured.

Wesley took her hand and placed it in the crook of his arm, escorting her back to the house.

"What are you doing here anyways?" She asked. *"Shepardstown is nowhere near Fredericksburg."*

"I was in Spotsylvania with a friend on some business. I heard through the grapevine that you and your father were here in Fredericksburg. I have missed you so much that I decided I had to stop and see you. I convinced my friend that we should stop and visit. His family is from this area, so I didn't have much persuading to do."

"So is that how you got an invitation to the ball?"

"An invitation?" He looked surprised. *"I'm here as your guest, am I not?"*

"Wesley." Charlotte laughed. "Come on now, tell the truth."

"Well, fine then. Yes, my friend Rafe grew up in the area and is the one who secured our invitation."

"What a very good friend he must be." She laughed again. "How is the business going and how is everything for you?"

"Quite well." He answered. "We stay very busy. Mr. Hoffman never regrets moving. I have been able to save up a good deal of money."

"No diversions to help you spend it?"

"Well, I am not a gambling man, as you know, and I only have a couple of drinks a week. There are not many other things to divert my attention."

"No girls you're courting?" She asked, hoping he wouldn't notice the slight strain in her voice.

"Nope." He smiled. "Many friends, but no one in particular." They headed up the dimly lit path, strolling leisurely, taking their time. "How is Gettysburg? How is Ginny, Jack, the families?"

"All the same for the most part." She replied. "There is a new girl in town. She's the daughter of a professor at the college. I wrote you about her, remember? Her name is Alex and she has become a good friend to both Ginny and I. Jack is still working and Ginny stays busy helping her mother with chores and picking up side jobs as usual to help pay the bills."

"So no changes with Mr. Wade at all?" He asked. She shook her head. They had finally arrived back at the house. They could hear the music and see the bright lights blazing through the windows. Charlotte noticed Richard right away, in a nearby corner, talking to Miss Buckley, a girl that Belle was constantly gossiping about because of her reputation of allowing men certain liberties.

"Have you learned to dance, Wesley?" Charlotte asked.

"Well, not like this," he said, as they walked into the ballroom, "not if I can help it. I haven't changed that much."

"For me?" She asked and batted her eyes at him in a ridiculously fake flirtation.

His broad chest rose and fell with the deep breath he took.

"You have grown up so much, Charlotte." He said softly.

"That's not an answer, Wes." She said in a sing-song voice. She glanced around and caught the eye of James Spencer, a young man she had met a few days before, a friend of one of the Lacys' nephews. He *was kind, but Charlotte didn't want any interruptions in her time with Wesley.*

"Wesley, come on." She grabbed his arm and pulled him among the other dancers.

"Wait, Charlotte…" Wesley was at a loss for words, something new for him. She grabbed his right hand and put it on her hip then grabbed his other hand in hers.

"Wesley you are the only man here who I want to talk to or even spend time with. Please just humor me." The thin young man who had been approaching stopped in his tracks and turned away. Charlotte breathed a sigh of relief.

"Not used to being the belle of the ball?" Wesley teased. He had relaxed a bit and pulled her closer.

"You know I'm not." She replied. "I really dislike the falsity of it all. I'm not quite sure why. I'm just too foreword and outspoken, I'm not even that pretty, I don't really care a thing about proper etiquette…"

"Have you looked at yourself lately, Charlotte?" Wesley interrupted. "You're beautiful. You have the personality that perfectly complements your looks, you're smart, you're funny, and you're caring. You've grown up as well. When I left, you were a gangly, skinny little girl, but you have grown into a beautiful, desirable young lady." He blushed.

"Desirable?" They moved around the dance floor, effortlessly.

"Well, yes."

"Hmmm." She was a bit surprised at Wesley's admission. She still didn't think that she was beautiful by any means, but Wesley had always been honest with her. He pulled her closer.

"So it's not like I'm just your little sister anymore?" She asked.

"I'm…not…sure." He replied slowly, as if trying to figure out what he did want. Charlotte was hoping one thing for sure: their relationship was changing.

If only the relationship could have continued. Charlotte rubbed her face as she slipped back into her memories...

The day after the ball, Wesley was able to come to Turner's Glen for a visit. The two walked toward the river's edge. The land sloped at a perfect angle to sit and watch the activity on the riverfront. Across the Rappahannock River, the town of Fredericksburg was filled with people moving and trading and going about their business. Behind them, the family home stood tall, stately and utterly impressive. Charlotte sat with her knees pulled to her chest and her arms wrapped around her legs. Wesley had one knee propped up, the other lying flat, with his arm resting comfortably across the raised knee.

"How long does your father plan on staying in Virginia?" He asked.

"I'm not sure. We are here because my Uncle Charles and Uncle Samuel are also here visiting. Father rarely tells me details."

"Who did he leave the farm with? Isn't it getting close to harvest time?"

"It is. He left the farm in the care of Thomas."

"My cousin Thomas? That's interesting."

"Yes, father is always saying that he doesn't trust anyone else with the farm." Charlotte shrugged. "I'm just happy I was able to come along and visit. I always enjoy spending time with my cousins."

"You have always been like that." Wesley smiled. "Easygoing, ready for just about anything." He was silent again and remained so, a troubled frown on his face.

"Wes, what's wrong?" Charlotte asked in a soft voice. Wesley picked up a twig and began twisting it in his hand.

"It's nothing." He said. She knew better, though.

"Wes, I have been your friend for over half my life. I know when something is wrong." She leaned over and put her hand on his wrist, turning her body so she completely faced him. "You can tell me."

"Everything has gotten so complicated, Charlotte." He paused. "Can't you feel the tension? What's going on in our country?"

"You mean between the Northern and Southern states?" Charlotte shrugged. "Only a little. Some people down here gave me some funny looks. But there is no real hostility that I have noticed. I could be wrong. I could be missing it."

"I suppose you have been pretty sheltered while visiting, and your cousin probably keeps you away from certain people." He nodded thoughtfully.

"How do people treat you? Is it bad for you?"

"Some people make comments that are offensive. I usually try to ignore it. I'm part of a military group up in Shepardstown, called the Hamtramck guards. I have made some really good friends."

"A military group? You must be terribly bored for that."

"Yes, but I like it. It is good to break up the monotony of my life. The thing is, I kind of understand where the Southerners are coming from."

Charlotte looked at Wesley, with shock in her face.

"You agree with slavery?" She asked, incredulous.

"No, I still think that's wrong, but not all slaves are terribly mistreated. Have you seen any abuse at Chatham or Turner's Glenn?"

"No, but that doesn't mean it's not happening."

"True, but Charlotte, most of the arguing has little to do about slavery. Keeping slaves is wrong in my mind, but why should I be able to tell others how to think?"

"Because it's wrong? It's inhuman, Wesley." Charlotte couldn't understand where Wesley was coming from.

"I know, I know. It seemed so clear cut before I moved down here. Now it's not just black and white. There are a lot of gray areas." He sighed. "That's the problem. Harry, one of my best friends from Shepardstown, his family owns slaves, a small farm on the outskirts of town. They treat their slaves like family. His family are really good people."

She nodded. There was a small pause in the conversation, as they both reflected on his words.

"And then there is talk of the South forming its own nation, and then that would most likely lead to war. Things are getting messy."

"Well, I'm sure it will all work out before blood is shed." She tried to think positive.

"It won't be that simple, Charlotte. Wounds will run deep. The issues will not be easily resolved. Pride can be terribly destructive. People like me and you will be torn between our friends and our families. If war does come, I don't know what I'll do." He let out a deep breath. "I'm going to have to choose sides."

Charlotte's stomach churned at what Wes was saying. She struggled with her words.

"But if that happens...Wes...you would come home, wouldn't you? Come home to your family and all of us? You couldn't just...not fight against...of course you would fight for the Union."

"I don't know, Charlotte." He avoided her eyes.

"Wesley, you're scaring me with this talk. Seriously. We...I...you need to come home!"

The look of raw pain in Wesley's face made her hurt. He simply stared off, over the river at nothing particular.

"Charlotte, if you could live down here, see what I am seeing...well, you like your cousin, right?"

"Yes, she has always been a good friend."

"So how would you feel, fighting against her in a war? Possibly shoot at her, fight her in hand to hand combat?"

"That would be exceedingly difficult."

Late Summer, 1859
Turner's Glenn, Fredericksburg, Virginia

Two days later, Charlotte was sitting under a tree near the river at the family plantation, buried in "Mansfield Park", the Jane Austen novel, she had borrowed from Beth, who loved reading even more than Charlotte did. The day was crisp and cool, the sun high in the sky, but the air had a bite to it. She ran her hands gently over the blades of grass, reading the words of her favorite author. Men from the docks hailed each other as they worked. Charlotte's social calendar had lessened since the ball, which gave her time to relax. She caught a movement out of the corner of her eye, and looked up to see a figure approaching. The figure neared, and she smiled when she recognized Wesley. She stood, brushing grass and dirt from her skirt.

"Wesley! It's good to see you." In her excitement, she threw her arms around him. She pulled away and looked up into his eyes.

"Your face is flushed." He commented, touching her cheek with his work-hardened hand. She shrugged.

"What brings you here?" She asked eagerly.

"I'll be heading back to Shepardstown soon. Back to work."

"Sounds exciting." Charlotte smiled,

"It is, terribly exciting." He paused, and took off his hat, gently slapping it against his leg. "But I need the money, Charlotte." He stepped close to her, and started speaking softer.

"What is so important to you that you find it necessary to save this money?"

He turned around and sighed. She knew he didn't want to talk about it, but she wasn't giving up so easily. She pulled at his shirt and turned him around.

"Come on, Wesley. You can tell me anything. You have always told me everything. Now, what do you want to save up for that is so secretive?"

Wesley looked into her eyes. His had changed. They were softer than she had ever seen them.

"You." He barely spoke the word and for a moment, Charlotte thought she misheard him. She looked at him, puzzled.

"What do you mean? You can always have me, Wesley."

He touched her face with his work-hardened hands. "I mean you as my wife, Charlotte."

She took in a sharp breath. "Wes, I'm only sixteen." She stepped back. Her heart told her to jump into his arms and kiss him, but her head was more muddled than it had ever been.

"I know that, Charlotte, I don't mean today. Just like I said, I need to plan. I'm not even officially asking you. I need to be able to provide for you first." He grinned boyishly. "I am always amazed at how you can always make me tell you my deepest thoughts."

She smiled back. "Just one of the many talents God gave me."

"Well, since my secret is out, what would you say if I were to ask you officially?" He held both of her hands in his, gripping them loosely.

"Are you?" She asked.

"I told you I can't, Charlotte. You need...you deserve more than what I have to offer right now."

"Well, I will leave you with this thought, Wesley." Charlotte touched his cheek and pulled his head down to whisper in his ear. "I have dreamed of marrying you for years."

His blue eyes sparkled.

"Is that a fact, Miss Turner?" He gently touched his lips to hers. Jolts of electricity flew through her body. She felt it all the way to her toes. When he pulled away, she smiled. His face was still close.

"That is a fact, Mr. Culp."

...That had been the last time she had seen him, even though they had been corresponding routinely. But this last letter... what had changed? Had he met another woman? Had she done something wrong? Charlotte was so absorbed in her thoughts that she jumped when she heard the door open. She looked up to see Thomas Culp, cousin of Wesley and her father's farm hand, his blue eyes inches away, looking at her. Thomas was the man that Charlotte's father wanted her to marry. Lawrence Turner was very clear about that fact. Thomas was in favor of the match as well. He was always hinting at 'getting to know her better.' Charlotte didn't dislike Thomas, but they simply did not have anything in common. He was a second son, so would not take over his family's farm. He was older than her by at least ten years. He was tall and muscular, due to the many hours he spent doing farm work. He had blonde, shaggy hair that usually needed a trim and pale blue eyes. She didn't think he was bad-looking. However, it pained her to spend time with him. Thomas was self-absorbed and had no sense of humor. He was also resentful because he wouldn't inherit the family farm. It was no wonder he and her father got on so well. Other than the fact that he was a hard worker, there was nothing in his personality that endeared him to Charlotte.

"Have you heard?" Thomas asked. Since Charlotte's mind was still stuck on Wesley and his decision to fight for the Confederacy; she nodded. Thomas pulled her up and put his stiff arms around her.

"I know how hard this is. I will miss you terribly. I will write you often."

Charlotte's head flew up as she took a step back. Thomas was not talking about Wes. He was talking about himself. He was leaving. He looked at her.

"Will you write me back?" He asked bluntly.

"Of course, Thomas. You have been such a good friend to me and help to my father."

"A friend. Yes." He repeated. "I am sure that you have realized that my intentions toward you is for us to be more than friends."

Charlotte knew it was what Thomas and her father wanted. Her relationship with her father had always been strained. He was aloof and distant with her. The main reason she was friendly with Thomas was in the hopes that her father would approve of her more.

"Thomas, I am aware of how you feel about me..." Charlotte began, but was unsure about how to continue her thought without hurting his feelings.

"I care for you, Charlotte. I want you to know that I have spoken to your father."

Charlotte groaned inwardly, knowing what Thomas was about to say couldn't be good. Thomas grinned confidently. He had good reason to be confident, she knew. Her father had always approved of Thomas, calling him steady and having a great future ahead of him.

"He gave me permission to do this, to ask you this." He took a deep breath. "Charlotte, will you marry me?" His confidence was clear; he believed she would say yes. She pulled her hands from his, turned her back to him and crossed her arms across her chest.

"I am honored Thomas, really I am. I just…I don't know. I don't know if I am ready for marriage."

"Charlotte, you are almost 20. Most girls your age are already married, some already have children. How can you say that you are not ready?" He grabbed her shoulder and turned her around to face him.

"Marriage is a huge step, Thomas. I know I may be old enough, but I don't feel ready."

"Alexandria is the same age as you, but she and William were just married." His voice was harsh.

"Alex was very sure about Will." She replied.

"You have known me longer than she has known him." He pointed out.

"I know, Thomas." Charlotte was getting flustered. "I am not saying no. I'm just saying not right now. I need more time. I need to be sure."

"Well, I am sure of you, Charlotte. You should be as sure of me." He turned and stalked off. When he reached his horse, he turned and gave her a last look. "My offer still stands. I leave for camp in two days."

"Thomas, wait!" Charlotte cried. He ignored her plea, mounted his horse and rode away. She sat down on the steps, wondering if he wanted her or her farm, and watched as he faded into the distance.

April 23
Thomas Culp's Home

Two days later, Charlotte walked to Thomas's house. She had spent the last two days in misery. Her father wouldn't speak to her after Thomas had informed him of her response to his proposal. She went to visit with Ginny and her friend tried to make her feel welcome, but Charlotte just felt like she was in the way. She wanted to give Ginny and Jack time alone, as Jack had signed up with the 47th Pennsylvania Infantry Regiment. He would be leaving the same time as Thomas and Will. She didn't want to go and talk to Thomas again, but she knew her father would make life miserable for her for the duration of Thomas's absence if she didn't go and try to work things out. When Charlotte arrived at the Culp's, she saw that she had gotten there just in time. Thomas was hugging his mother goodbye. When he turned to mount his horse, he saw Charlotte standing on the path and froze, his smile fading.

"What do you want?" He asked.

"I need to speak with you, Thomas. Please?"

"I suppose I have a few minutes to spare. Let's walk." Instead of mounting, he grabbed the horse's reins and waved to his family. He began walking down the road in strong, sure steps. Charlotte hastened to catch up.

"So what is it that you want, Charlotte?" His voice was cold.

"Thomas, you are a good, decent man. I am just so confused about everything. My feelings for you especially. I can see myself as your wife sometimes, and others I am just not sure. I don't know if I am ready for it yet."

"I suppose I can understand." He nodded. "I have thought about this quite a bit the past few days. This war will be short. We will crush the Rebels within three or four months. Most people are saying this war will be over in one big battle. I have only signed on for three months. I will be back then, regardless. I would expect you to use those three months to prepare yourself. You will be ready when I come back. I know that this is what I want, and I know it is what your father wants. You want it too. You just don't realize it."

"I'm not so sure, Thomas. I don't know if three months would be enough time for me to get ready." Her voice shook. With her father on Thomas's side, she didn't have much of a choice. She wished God would intervene. However, she doubted it. In spite of her friends' beliefs about God, Charlotte didn't feel as though He paid close attention to her.

"You will be." He dropped the reins and stepped close to her. "I love you, Charlotte Turner." His lips touched hers, gently.

Charlotte waited for some spark of passion to arise, something to help her know that marrying Thomas would be okay. It didn't happen. When he pulled away, she forced a smile. Thomas mounted his horse. "Goodbye, Charlotte!" He called as he rode away. She stood still, alone on the road, watching him ride away. A flurry of feelings cascaded over her and she didn't know what to do about any of them.

The Gettysburg Hotel

Alex couldn't help but sigh at the vision of her husband when she entered their hotel room, the room they had shared since their wedding day. Will was such a handsome figure, standing in front of the mirror, with his crisp, newly issued dark blue jacket and light blue trousers. His uniform fit him perfectly after she had Ginny help her alter it. Ginny was a great teacher, and Alex was making progress in her domestic skills. Will adjusted the blue kepi on his dark blonde hair and turned to look at her, a huge smile lighting up his face. He took two steps towards her and she threw her arms around him. He hugged her tightly, his hands rubbing her back. Alex took a deep breath, trying desperately to keep her emotions in check.

"I just don't know...I don't know how I'm going to say goodbye. I have dreaded this day for so long." Alex felt a tear fall down her face. She buried her face in his shoulder.

"Hey, don't worry." Will pulled away and tilted her chin so he could look in her eyes. He kissed a tear from her cheek. "I'll be back here before you can even miss me. Then we'll have the rest of our lives to spend together." He framed her face with his hands and kissed her. She returned the kiss, gripping the collar of his jacket.

"Will, you can't guarantee that, you just can't." Alex leaned her forehead against his.

"I guess you're right." Will pulled her toward the bed and sat down, pulling her next to him. "But remember, if something does happen to me, remember...I'll be in a better place. You can't spend too much time mourning me. You are a beautiful, smart, faithful young woman who has so much to offer. Don't waste your life mourning me. If that happens." He smiled. "Which it won't. I'll be fine, Allie." He kissed her again. "And the war will be over within months, they say."

"Will, you seriously cannot believe that." Alex stood and paced over to the window, looking out. "The South feels like they are defending their homeland. They will fight to the end. And the North will do whatever it takes to win. Neither side is going to give up easily, Will. The North may have more resources and people, but the South, well, I've been reading the papers and a lot of good, West Point-trained officers are leaving the Union army to fight for the Confederacy. They will put up a great fight. And too many men will be killed."

Will came up behind her and slid his arms around her. "Allie, I don't know what will happen in the next few months. But I can promise you that I will write to you as often as I can and I will do everything I can to get back to you as soon as I can." He turned her to face him. "We've talked about this, Allie. I have to go and fight, defend our country." He pushed a strand of hair from her face. "I have to do this."

"I know you do." She cupped his cheek. "I don't have to agree with it, but I do support you." He smiled, kissed her, then pulled away and glanced at the clock. He sighed.

"Time to go." He bent down to pick up his sack of personal belongings, then took her hand in his and started down the stairs and out of the hotel to the town diamond.

Wade Household

Ginny answered the knock at the door, smiling when she saw Jack standing there, his new Uniform making him look more handsome than ever. He took off his hat and smiled.

"I'm heading off to the town diamond. We're leaving soon. Would you like to walk with me?"

"Of course I would." Ginny said, grabbing a shawl. Even though it was the end of April, it was still cool. As they walked, Ginny remained quiet, simply enjoying the time she had left with the man she loved. He broke the silence.

"I expect Charlotte told you about Wesley?"

"About how he is fighting with the Confederacy? Yes, she did." Ginny replied. "She was quite upset about it." She glanced up at him. "As I know you are."

"I'm more disappointed. I was understanding when Wesley left. I didn't want to lose my friend, but I knew he needed to go for his job. But I always expected him to come home eventually. I had hoped we could go and fight together, as comrades. Now, well..." He looked off in the direction of Culp's hill, the place where he and Jack, Ginny and Charlotte had once played as friends. "Now I hope I'll never see him again."

"Surely you don't mean that?" Ginny exclaimed.

"I do. I just don't know what I will do if I ever meet him on the battlefield. The thought scares me."

"What about after the war?"

"If we both survive?" Jack paused. "He'll never be able to come back here, no matter what happens in the war. Too many people are mad at him. That anger won't go away after battle. Too many people consider him a traitor. Even Thomas, his own cousin, has been saying that he would kill Wesley if he ever saw him. Although Thomas says a lot of things that I am not sure are true.

Ginny's thoughts went to Charlotte at the mention of Thomas. "Is Thomas...he's not a terrible person, is he?"

"No, not at all." Jack said. "He is actually a decent man. I believe he just tends to say things just to appear tougher or more intelligent than he actually is."

"That's good to hear."

"Why do you ask?"

"Well, you know that Thomas is Mr. Turner's farm hand." Ginny began.

"Yes, he has been for the past few years. Thomas says that Mr. Turner intends to give him the farm eventually."

"Yes, and apparently, Mr. Turner intends to give Thomas his daughter's hand in marriage. He asked her yesterday."

"Charlotte? And Thomas?" Jack thought for a moment. "Charlie could do worse, I suppose. Thomas will be a good provider, he goes to church, and he doesn't drink much. I just find it hard to believe that he would want her." At Ginny's look, he quickly explained. "You know I care a great deal about Charlotte and she is a wonderful friend and person. But I feel like Thomas wants a girl that will be his perfect housewife, who will listen to him and obey him without question. We both know Charlotte. She will make someone a wonderful wife. But I don't see her as the kind of wife he always talks about wanting."

"I see." Ginny replied. Then, thoughtful and curious, she asked. "What kind of wife did you always want?"

Jack stopped and pulled her aside. They were close to the diamond. He looked into her eyes. "I don't think I ever knew what I wanted in a wife until I knew I wanted to marry you. And then, I realized that all of your qualities were the ones that I wanted in a wife."

Ginny smiled. Jack was always sweet, it was one of the things that she loved about him. He was not always the best with words. But there were times like this when his sweetness showed in his words and made her feel like the most special girl in the world.

"I love you, Jack." She said. "And I promised myself I wouldn't cry, but…" tears welled in her eyes. Jack reached up to her face to wipe at one that had trailed down her face.

"Ginny, you know I wish things could be different. But I will do whatever it takes to serve my country and come home to you. My country needs me, Ginny. I have to go."

She threw her arms around him, unable to hold back her tears. He hugged her back.

"Ginny…" he began when he was interrupted.

"Jack! There you are." Jack's younger brother, Daniel approached the couple. "Mother has been asking where you are. She wants to say some final things to you. Say goodbye."

Jack took an audible breath. "She knew where I was. I told her I would meet her at the diamond. Where is she now?"

"She's down in front of the McClellan Hotel."

"I'll go see her." Jack looked at Ginny. "I love you, Ginny. I need you to remember that."

"I will, Jack. I love you too.

May 6
St. James Lutheran Church
Gettysburg, Pennsylvania

The women of Gettysburg stayed busy, not only in their own homes, but also as a community, working together for the war effort. That evening, many women had gathered. Some of the older women; mothers, grandmothers, were towards the front of the church. Alex, Ginny and Charlotte and some of the younger women had gathered further back, as they usually did.

"I received a letter from Will today." Alex mentioned, her needles moving slowly as they knitted socks for the troops. "He seems so anxious."

"Jack seems to be feeling the same way." Ginny said, then pulled a letter out of her apron and read: *"I understand that rail duty can be important, and why it needs to be done, but it is still quite tedious. After we mustered in, Captain Andrew Fulton, a man from Stewardstown, led us to Cockeysville, Maryland. We had to ride a crowded train, with barely any room. The stench was horrible. We are now guarding the many bridges along the Northern Central Railroad. When it comes down to it, this work is as important as fighting the Rebs. If not for our presence, the railways would be sabotaged, and our troops would be in significant danger. I hope the day soon comes that we can get some real action, though."* She folded the letter and tucked it back into her pocket.

"That's how Will feels." Alex nodded.

"Thomas wrote to me, also saying that rail duty is just as important as fighting." Charlotte said, hoping the disdain she was feeling was kept out of her voice. "He said that, without their work, the Rebel army would surely win."

"Like most of the mothers and wives, I am glad that they are far away from the fighting." Ginny said. "The longer they stay away from the battles, the more likely it will be that they'll make it home. If what townsfolk are saying is true, the war should be over in a few more months."

"As much as I wish that would be so, I just don't know." Alex replied. "I have heard the war may last longer than anyone thinks."

"But we have so many more men!" Ginny pointed out.

At that moment, the door burst open. The sound was so loud that Charlotte jumped and poked her finger with the needle she was using.

"Hello, everyone." The girls cringed at the honey-sweet, yet annoyingly fake voice of Abigail Williams. She looked around and headed for the group of young women much to Charlotte's dismay.

"Oh, guess what, you will never guess what I am about to tell you!"

"I am sure it's very important." Charlotte said, her voice thick with sarcasm.

"Yes, it is, not life or death by any means, but very intriguing." As always, Abigail was talking a mile a minute. She pulled off her brown hat and sat. "A Rebel, a real Southern belle, is coming to stay in Gettysburg. She is the wife of Michael Lewis, you all remember him, and she is coming to stay with his parents while he's fighting in the war. Isn't that exciting? I wonder if she'll end up being a Rebel spy."

"Yes, a Rebel spy would be well-placed here; military secrets are abundant in Gettysburg, Pennsylvania." Alex muttered. Ginny tried not to giggle. Charlotte felt a prick of annoyance at Abigail's assumption about the young Southern woman.

"My father is from Virginia." She said "I have family, cousins especially, that I am close to down around Fredericksburg, Petersburg and Vicksburg. Does that mean I am a Confederate spy?"

"Well of course not, Charlotte." Abigail tittered. "You were born and raised here. Your fiancé is fighting for the Northern cause. Even though you were best friends with that traitor, Wesley Culp." She paused. "But none of that means you'll be a spy."

Abigail was talking loud enough for the whole church to hear. Charlotte quickly glanced at Wesley's sisters, who were sitting not too far away. The sad, longing look in Annie's eyes made Charlotte want to go and give her a hug. Julia, Wesley's other sister, glared at Abigail.

"Well, I highly doubt that Mrs. Lewis will turn out to be a spy." Charlotte said. "Most likely, she'll want to help us help her husband. Besides, a lot of Southerners agree with the Union and what we stand for."

"I still can't imagine Michael Lewis marrying a rebel." Abigail continued. "He is one of the most patriotic men I know. To just up and marry a girl whose father owns slaves!" Charlotte sighed. Why couldn't Abigail just leave them alone?

"You can't help who you fall in love with." Charlotte said, thinking of her feelings for Wesley.

"To be honest I can't imagine Michael Lewis marrying anyone." Ginny spoke to Alex, who had never met Michael.

"Why is that?" Alex asked. "His parents own one of the general stores in town, right?"

"Yes, they do. Oh, Michael Lewis, how do I describe him?" Charlotte thought back, smiling. "He is tall and thin. He always wore thick glasses and was always studying and doing extra school work. He wanted to go to West Point because it could give him the best all-around education."

"So, why would it surprise you that he is married?"

"Like I said, he was always studious, he was almost dull. He never talked to a girl for as long as I knew him. He was six years older than we were, but he always acted so much more mature."

"Was he nice?" Alex asked.

"To be honest, I don't know. He never really talked enough for me to get to know him well."

"Well, then, we shall get to know him through his wife!" Alex said. "We will have to welcome her."

Late June 1861
Gettysburg, Pennsylvania

"Dearest Will;

Spring has faded and summer is upon us. I spend most of my time with Mother helping with things like housework and preparing things for the war effort, but I continue to see my friends as much as possible. Charlotte spends most of her time on the farm. Thomas and some farm hands were around for the planting, but now Charlotte and her father have a lot more work keeping it going. Her father has been considering enlisting when you all come back, if there is still a need for soldiers. How I long for that day, to hold you in my arms again.

Ginny spends most of her days at her home, with her mother, sister and brothers. They keep busy, as it is well-known that the Wades would take in any washing or tailoring they could. Unfortunately, that leaves me with no one to talk to. I occasionally find myself walking to the homes of my friends, and we see each other at Sunday services, but it just isn't like it had been before. I occupy myself by most often going with Mother to help the war effort. It seems as though there is always a gathering of women to tailor uniforms, knit socks and even make bullets for you men.

I long to hear how things are going with you. Please write when you can.

With all my love,
Allie"

Alex was on her way home from one of those gatherings when she stopped at the Lewis's General Store, picking up flour, salt, sugar and other necessities. The door opened and an unfamiliar woman walked in. She appeared to be a few years older than Alex, and tall, with blonde hair and an uncertain, nervous look on her face. She was carrying a carpet bag and wore a brown traveling dress and hat. Her green eyes darted around the shop as if in search of something.

"Hello." Alex approached the woman with a smile. "I don't believe we've met. My name is Alexandria Sadler. Are you just passing through or are you new to town?"

"No, I am here, at least for the duration of the war. I'm staying with Mr. and Mrs. Lewis." The young woman spoke with a soft Southern drawl.

"Augusta!" A voice from behind the counter cried out. Alex turned to see Mrs. Lewis's stout body scurry around the counter towards the newcomer.

"Mrs. Lewis." The girl said with a soft smile.

"Oh, my dear, call me Aideen. Or Mother, if you are so inclined." Mrs. Lewis pulled her into a big hug. Mrs. Aideen Lewis was one of the happiest, most welcoming women in Gettysburg. Her Irish red hair was streaked with gray and pulled up in a simple bun. "I can't believe the wedding was the last time I saw you. Marriage agrees with you; you look wonderful." The woman turned to Alex.

"My dear Mrs. Sadler, I am pleased to present you to my daughter-in-law, my son Michael's wife, Mrs. Augusta Lewis."

Augusta curtsied and smiled at Alex. "It is a pleasure to meet you, Mrs. Sadler."

"The pleasure is all mine." Alex nodded and smiled.

"Augusta, my dear, you arrived early. Michael's letter led us to believe we shouldn't expect you until next week."

"Michael's division had to move out early, so he sent me here when he left. I hope I am not intruding."

"Not at all. We are happy to have you. Mr. Lewis went to Chambersburg for a few days. He should be back at the end of the week. I'll close up early and help you settle in."

"Oh, no. I don't want to be a bother. You don't have to close up early on my account."

"Nonsense! You have probably been on that loud, dirty train all day."

"If I may." Alex spoke up. "Mrs. Lewis, I have time. I can help Michael's wife settle in."

"You would do that?" Augusta asked, a bit unsure.

"Of course I would." Alex smiled. "It would be my pleasure."

"Thank you very much, Alex." Aideen Lewis said.

As Alex and Augusta headed up the stairs, Alex tried to find out more about the new girl in town.

"I have been told you come from South Carolina. It must be difficult, being away from your family?"

"It is." Augusta said, opening the door of the room Mrs. Lewis had described as hers. "However, I think it will be more difficult being away from Michael."

"I can certainly understand that." Alex said. "My husband and I were married about a week before he left to go fight in the Rebs..." Alex regretted the last words as soon as she spoke them. "I beg your pardon. I meant to say he was going to fight for the Union cause."

Augusta set her carpetbag down. "It's all right. I doubt you'll be the only person to say those words to me. I hope I have prepared myself for them."

"That may be true, but that still doesn't excuse my thoughtlessness." Alex's mind flashed to Abigail Williams and others who were already speaking out and spreading rumors against the young Southern woman. "I do apologize."

"I accept your apology." Augusta replied with a smile.

"I do hope you will allow me to show you the town when you get settled in. I can introduce you around. I am sure the Ladies Union Relief Society that was just formed can use your help. They are always looking for women to volunteer."

"That would be nice." Augusta said, happy to have met this young woman. She could not help but feel that this was the start of a good new friendship.

July 1861
Gettysburg, Pennsylvania
"Wesley,

I will keep writing to you, even if you do not welcome the letters. I can only hope that you will read and write back to me. I long to hear from you.

It seems as though the war has been uneventful since the bombing of Fort Sumter. People in town still believe the war will be an easy victory for the Union. Even with the lack of action, war remains on the minds of everyone, and is the talk of the town. Between you and me, I am not looking forward to the end of July. August means that Thomas's three-month stint is up and he will be coming home. I have been able to persuade Father to agree to allow me to wait until the war is over before I get married. However, I dread the thought of telling Thomas that. I know he will be angry and put more pressure on me. He writes me often, and his letters indicate that he is ready to move forward, right when he gets back. Each letter flows with loving verse, Shakespearean sonnets. It's pretty, but feels impersonal and distant. I remember the letters you used to write, especially when you first moved away. You were never good with words, tending to let actions speak for you. Your letters never contained poetry or fancy phrases, but I know they were from your heart. I don't know why I continually compare what Thomas does to what you do. Deep down, I know; it is because it is you that I love, Wesley.

Ever since Alex's marriage, she has been talking nonstop about the joys of matrimony. Ginny and I are happy for her, but she wants to talk about nothing else. However, if I am honest with myself, I can admit I am a little jealous. Alex is able to be with the man she loves. I know deep down that I will not have that opportunity.

Ginny keeps busy, as usual, mending clothes and her family has taken the responsibility of caring for Isaac Brinkerhoff. Isaac is a four-year-old disabled boy from town. I try to help them whenever I can, but with Thomas leaving Father, I am spending even more time helping on the farm. It seems as though there is always something else to do. Father has been talking about joining the regiment when everyone comes home. It worries me. We still don't have the most loving of relationships, but I don't want to lose the only parent I have.

I wish you would write back. I would like to know how things are going with you, to know what you are thinking and feeling. Please write back.
Forever your friend,
Charlotte"

Charlotte stopped at the Post Office to post the letter she had written and pick up the mail for her family. On her way out, she ran into Alex. When her friend saw that she had a letter from Thomas, Alex immediately pulled it out and read it.

"Love's not time's fool, though rosy lips and cheeks..." Alex murmured aloud, reading Charlotte's latest letter from Thomas. "Charlotte, he is quite romantic. 'Love bares it out to the edge of doom.'"

"It's not even his own writing, Alex." Charlotte told her, the edge of annoyance apparent in her voice. "It's superficial and emotionless."

"It's still pretty." Alex replied, handing the letter back to Charlotte. "What's so wrong with Thomas? Sometimes love can grow from respect and common goals."

"I do respect him. And we seem to have common goals. It's just...when we talk, it's like he thinks he knows me so well. That he knows what's best for me. He puts words into my mouth. He is a very likable man most of the time, but when it comes to me and our future, he is so controlling. I just cannot imagine a lifetime of his smothering ways."

"I see." Alex said. "Well, for now, just get to know him best you can. Maybe share your feelings with him. They will be home soon." She was practically singing her words now. "And I will get to be with William!"

"That is wonderful for you." Charlotte smiled for her friend.

"Mrs. Lewis!" Alex smiled, then pulled Charlotte over to a young woman with blonde hair who had been approaching the Post Office. The woman smiled as the two approached.

"Hello, Mrs. Clark. How are you doing?" She spoke in a soft Southern accent.

"I'm doing well. Mrs. Lewis, this is my good friend, Charlotte Turner. Charlotte, this is Michael Lewis's wife, Augusta."

"It's good to meet you, Mrs. Lewis." Charlotte smiled.

"Please, call me Augusta, Miss Turner. It is a pleasure to meet you as well."

"And you must call me Charlotte."

"Where are you headed, Augusta?" Alex asked.

"I was going to stop at the post office, and then head to a house on Breckenridge Street. Mrs. Lewis, Michael's mother, wants me to drop off some mending at a home there. I told her I could do the work, but she said she likes to try and support the family."

"Which family?" Charlotte asked. "If it's the Wade family, I can walk you there. I was heading over that way myself."

"Really? It is the Wades. I would love your company." Augusta smiled.

Charlotte turned to Alex.

"Are you in for a visit? I'm sure Ginny would love to see you. She doesn't get out much, now that they have also taken on caring for Isaac Brinkerhoff."

"That crippled boy?" Alex asked. "Why?"

"His mother has to go to work and since he cannot walk, he needs a place to stay. The Wades need the money." Charlotte said. "So, can you come?"

"I probably could stop by…" Alex's words were cut short as the two girls turned toward a commotion back in the post office. "What is going on in there?"

Elizabeth Thorn, the wife of the cemetery caretaker, exited the building, clutching a newspaper.

"Mrs. Thorn, what's the commotion?" Charlotte asked.

The woman held out a paper. "There has been a battle. Right outside of Washington. They say our troops were crushed by the rebels."

Alex took the paper and scanned it. "Almost five-hundred of our men were killed, over one-thousand were wounded, and about twelve-hundred more of our men are missing in action…those men could be dead, hurt or taken prisoner…Union men proved to be very inexperienced and undisciplined." She continued reading. "It doesn't look like the Gettysburg unit was fighting."

"Well that's good." Charlotte said.

"Oh my goodness!" Alex's hand flew to cover her mouth. "It says that civilians from Washington rode out to watch the battle. They

73

brought picnics, their families, it was just like some social event. They were chased from the field just like our soldiers were."

"My goodness." Charlotte said. "Were any of them killed?"

"I don't believe so." Alex kept reading. "Wait, yes-it says the only civilian who died was an 85-year-old widow who couldn't leave her home, which was hit by cannon."

Charlotte shook her head as Alex handed the paper back to Mrs. Thorn with a nod of thanks.

"Well, that article says it all." Alex said. At Charlotte's questioning look, she explained. "This war will be long, not just a one-battle-fight like everyone was predicting."

*****

Alex and Charlotte waited for Augusta to pick up the mail for the Lewis household, then the three women walked toward the Wade home. As they got closer, a group of men huddled together broke apart. One of them held a newspaper. They gave the women a look, noticing the new town resident.

"You wouldn't be the rebel that's living here now, would you?" One of the men broke away from the group and sidled over to the women. He looked Augusta up and down with his blood-shot eyes. Charlotte knew the man. Nik Braxton was of medium height and had dirty, red-blonde hair and was rarely clean-shaven. He was usually hanging around the saloon, as were most of his friends.

"Excuse us, Mr. Braxton. We have an errand to attend to." Charlotte said, trying to shield Augusta from him.

"Well, then, I reckon I can let you pass." He stepped around Charlotte, close to Augusta. She could smell his putrid breath. "But know this, Reb. We are a Union town. And anyone whose loyalties aren't for the Union, well, I will personally be keeping an eye on them." He sauntered back to his group. His words had left the three women chilled. Augusta's face was pale.

"Don't worry, Augusta." Alex said. "We may have some narrow-minded people here, but we have many good people as well."

"I have met some of both." Augusta assured her. The girls continued their walk to the Wade's.

"I don't want to tell you who to befriend, but if you need any assistance getting to know people, please let me know." Charlotte said.

"Thank you. You two have been so kind."

As they approached the Wade's front door, Charlotte knocked twice and then pushed the door open. Ginny was in the front room, working on a shirtwaist. She looked up and grinned when she saw her friends. She stood when she saw the new young woman with them.

"Hello!"

"Ginny, we have come to visit and bring you some business." Charlotte said. "Augusta, this is seamstress and friend, Ginny Wade. And Ginny, this is Augusta Lewis. She is Michael's wife."

"From the South? I heard you were coming. How are you liking it here?"

"I am liking it very much. Most people have been very kind."

"That's good to hear. Do you have some work for us?"

"Yes." Augusta placed her basket of clothes in Ginny's waiting arms. "A few skirts and some of my father-in-law's shirts."

"I should be able to get started on these by the end of the day." Ginny set the basket down. "Would anyone like some coffee? I put a fresh pot on not too long ago. It should be ready by now."

Charlotte and Alex nodded, but Augusta shook her head.

"I wish I could, Miss Wade, but I have to get back to the Lewis's store."

"It was so nice meeting you, Mrs. Lewis."

"Please, call me Augusta."

"And you must call me Ginny."

Augusta left with a wave. Ginny poured the coffee and sat down, picking up her work.

"Augusta seems nice." She commented.

"I agree." Charlotte said.

"I feel bad for her, though." Alex said. "Up here, away from her family in a town where some people will be hostile towards her. It won't be easy."

"Have people been giving her trouble?" Ginny asked.

"She hasn't said anything specific to that fact, just hinted about it. And on our way over here, Nik Braxton and some of his buddies were giving her a difficult time." Alex replied.

"Nik Braxton is a troublemaker. And drinks too much." Ginny said. "He brings his clothes here when he needs them mended. He is not an easy customer. He makes all sorts of vile comments to Georgia. Luckily, since she has John McClellan's protection, it has stopped."

"Well, let's hope he doesn't go from harassing Georgia to harassing you. Or Augusta." Charlotte said.

"It's not like we can do anything about it." Ginny said. "He is a man, and a paying customer. We need all the help we can get."

"But you shouldn't work at the risk of your safety, Ginny. That's not worth it."

"That may be true." Ginny looked down at her hands. "I wish Jack and I could have made an official announcement, or even better, gotten married. That may have stopped some of my problems."

"What other problems are you having?" Charlotte asked, concern apparent in her voice.

"Nothing, nothing really." Ginny said with a sigh, then changed subjects. "I just miss Jack. I write to him as often as I can. I hope and pray every day that he comes home soon."

"That is something we all wish for." Alex said.

August 18
Turner Farm, Gettysburg, Pennsylvania

"*Wesley,*

I write to you again, but honestly, do not know if I will even send this letter. They say how difficult it is to get mail through. Maybe I will write and send all my letters to you after the war. The Gettysburg boys from the 47th Pennsylvania are due to arrive at any time. I want to see them all, Jack especially. Days in town seem empty without them. The Fourth of July picnic and dance was especially dull this year.

As much as I want to see the men, I am also nervous about their return. I am apprehensive about seeing Thomas again. It isn't that I detest him, but I know he is going to continue pushing me about getting married. I am not quite sure why I am so opposed in my heart to marrying him. He isn't bad looking and he will make a good living once he takes over Father's farm, as is the plan. He is usually polite and he is already like a son to Father. He is a good match. One thing I can't understand is why he wants me. I am not the girl that he wants me to be. You know that I would rather be out of doors than inside, would rather be dancing than sitting in a parlor flirting. Even as a child, Ginny and I would be found playing ball with you boys when all of the other girls were playing dolls. He wants a wife who would be whatever he wants her to be.

I don't know why I write these thoughts to you. You probably don't want to hear it. It's just good to be able to get some of my thoughts out."

Charlotte had the door open to let the light breeze pass through the house. It was a warm day, a bit muggy. In her childhood, Charlotte would spend days like this swimming in the pond by her house with Ginny. However, now, she was stuck inside, baking bread. She thought about the return of the men and the letter she had just written. Her father had made it known that Thomas would have the farm regardless, whether he married her or not. Why did he want to marry her so much?

"I'm not even that attractive." She muttered, pounding the lump of dough.

"On the contrary, Charlotte," a deep male voice startled her from the doorway. "You are quite beautiful." Her head snapped up.

"Thomas." The moment had arrived. He took a step in, looking handsome in his Union uniform. He had started to grow a ridiculous mustache and beard; it was bushy and even though the style was quite popular, Charlotte was not fond of it. He smiled and held out a hand to her. She walked slowly toward him and placed her flour-covered hand in his. Thomas pulled her into his arms. His facial hair tickled her face as he lowered his head and kissed her. She didn't enjoy the kiss any more than she had during the first kiss three months ago.

"I missed you." He whispered.

"How have you been?" She asked, drawing back.

"Good." Thomas said. "We haven't seen any action yet. Mainly marching and training and a good lot of nothing." She remained silent, not quite knowing what else to say. She never quite knew how to carry on a conversation with him.

"I stopped and saw your father first. He gave me permission to come in and visit you."

'*Of course,*' Charlotte thought, '*always following the rules, completely predictable.*'

"How long will you be in Gettysburg?" She asked. "Are you going to go back to war?"

"As much as I would like to stay here, I am going to re-enlist with most of the others. I want to go out and actually be part of a real battle. We have been training enough for it. We will muster into the 87th Pennsylvania at the end of the month."

"Oh." Again, she was stuck with what to say.

Thomas pulled the door shut behind him, pulled her close once and kissed her again.

"Thomas." Charlotte said in a firm voice. He sighed; she could feel the frustration in his voice.

"You will be my wife Charlotte. I would like to think that you would be a little more open to me." He spoke sternly.

"If you have spoken to my father, then I am sure he told you of the condition I have if I will marry you." Charlotte tried not to let her voice shake and show her fear. She had never seen Thomas like this: hard, angry, and hurtful.

"He did mention it." He clenched his jaw. "Although I do not understand why. Are you hoping that I won't come back from the war at all? Is that what you want?" Thomas asked, menacingly, taking a step toward her.

"Thomas, please, it's not that." Charlotte backed up. "I just want to be ready. I want to be sure that this is real, that it is not just the war fever that is causing you to push for marriage. I want us both to be ready."

"You have been keeping your father's house for years. How can you not be ready to have one of your own?"

"I don't know, Thomas."

"Whatever you say, Charlotte." His voice was ice. She grasped for words that she hoped would ease the tension and change the subject.

"Have you heard from your cousin?" She asked softly. Thomas looked at her with daggers in his eyes.

"I have no cousin." The words were cold and calculated. "Wesley Culp is a traitor to all of us. He will never set foot in Gettysburg again if he wants to live. I know I would not hesitate to shoot him on sight."

Charlotte was horrified at Thomas's words. "How can you say that? He just made a choice…"

"And it was the wrong one!" Thomas exploded. "Do not speak to me about that traitor ever again." He threatened.

"Thomas, what is wrong with you?"

"We're in a war, Charlotte! How can you expect tenderness out of all this? We don't have the ability to be kind and loving."

"You said you didn't do any actual fighting." She tried to soften the mood. She hated the tension of argument.

"We haven't, but that is not the point. I am a soldier now, a fighter." His voice softened, but he still spoke with a bit of a condescending tone.

"I understand." Charlotte said. She was grateful that he had started to calm down. She could still see anger in his eyes, but he looked a little more like the old Thomas, the Thomas she could actually consider marrying. Although, the way today's encounter was going, Charlotte wasn't sure she wanted anything to do with Thomas Culp.

******

Alex held her husband's arm as they walked through the campus of college. It was nice to have Will home, but strange living with him at her parents' home.

"I wish I could afford to rent a room for us." Will said. "Although it is nice to have good, home cooked meals every day. And your bed is surely better than what I have been sleeping on." He gave her a grin. "And you are definitely an improvement on my bunkmate."

"I would hope so." She shyly smiled back. "I worry about you. I know you have avoided battle so far, but we have heard that many men die in the camps."

"That's true." Will said. "Men come down with sickness all the time, especially the boys from the country who have spent most of their lives on farms. We all get so crammed together, disease can easily pass from person to person." He pulled her to a bench and sat her down, then pulled her into a kiss. "I miss being able to kiss you whenever I want." He softly kissed her again.

Alex grudgingly pushed his shoulders away. "Will, we're in public." She whispered. "Anyone could walk by and see us, including my father."

"All right." He took off his hat and looked around. "It's strange to me that classes are continuing in the middle of a war."

"I agree." She said. "Honestly, how do you feel about missing the battle in Manassas?" She stroked his hands.

"I wish we could have had a crack at the Rebs. Maybe we could have stopped the craziness. We drill enough to be prepared for battle. And I am glad that I joined with the 87th instead of a regiment from home. I like the boys from Gettysburg. They're good men. I just hope we get a chance soon to prove ourselves in battle."

"Would you be upset if I told you I hope you never see combat?" Alex asked gently.

"No, I wouldn't be upset. You're the woman who loves me, looking out for my safety. I think I would feel the same way if our roles were reversed."

"But is there no chance that I can talk you into staying? You can continue with your studies, we can find a place to rent…"

"How would I pay for that? My father was only helping to pay for my education. The money I am getting from the army isn't much, but it is something I can save and use after the war, to take care of you."

"Father would…"

"You are my wife, Allie. I should be the one to take care of you. It already stings my pride that I can't afford to care for you much now, that I have to depend upon your parents."

"Will, you don't have to…"

He stopped her words with a kiss. "I don't want to argue with you." He said softly. "We don't have time for that."

"I agree. Let's go back to the house. I believe mother is out, visiting or helping the Ladies Union Relief Society. We could…"

"…make up from our fight?" Will suggested.

She stood and pulled him up. "That sounds like a splendid idea."

Wade House

Ginny was disappointed in the amount of time she had been able to spend with Jack. He was spending the bulk of his time with his family; his mother always finding excuses to keep him around. Jack was too kind to tell her no. She saw him when he initially came home, but he had stayed only long enough to talk briefly with her and her family. They hadn't been able to spend any time alone.

"It's a good thing Jack Skelley is staying away." Ginny's mother said. "I like him, but as much as you pine over him when he's not here, if he were around, I wouldn't be able to get any work from you. It is hard enough getting work done with Georgia visiting John every day. With these soldiers back and needing work done, we are way too busy for social calls."

Ginny nodded and lugged a basket of laundry to the back of the house. She enjoyed being out of doors. It was quiet and peaceful. She reached up and began hanging clothes on the line. Her hair was a mess and her dress was wet and grimy with soap suds. 'It's a good thing Jack won't come around, at least he won't see me like this.' She thought as she finished. As she rounded the corner to the front of the house, however, she looked up to see the familiar stride and figure of Jack. He saw her, smiled, and hastened over to her.

"Ginny!" He took the empty basket from her and set it on the ground, then threw his arms around her.

"Oh, Jack!" She hugged him back, then pushed back to look at him. "Of course, you choose the one day I look an absolute mess to come and visit."

"You always look beautiful to me, Gin." He reached up and tucked an errant piece of hair behind her ear. "I was able to talk mother into letting me go this afternoon and evening. Can your mother spare you?"

"Jack, I'm not sure…"Ginny trailed off.

"Of course she can be spared." Ginny turned to the voice of her sister. "I am back now, it's only fair that you two should be able to spend some time together." Georgia bent and picked up the laundry basket. "I'll tell mother. You two go on."

Jack grinned and held out a hand to Ginny. "Devil's Den?" He asked, knowing that she loved the view from the rock formation. She took his hand.

"You do realize how long of a walk that is, right?"

"It's always been long. But I know you love the view, as I do. I have missed it. I have missed you." He tucked her hand around his elbow.

"And I you, Jack." She paused, not knowing what to say to him next. There were so many things, but she didn't know how to start.

"The training, it has changed you a little." She commented, squeezing his arm. "You've never been a weak slouch, but I can tell you've gotten more muscles."

"Yes, those are definitely from training. God knows I haven't put on weight from camp food."

"How is it, cooking for yourself at camp?" Ginny asked.

"Tough to get used to doing any cooking. The Sanitary, or US Sanitary Commission, has come through to help us out. They won't be around once we move out and get on the battlefield, but we are learning."

"What do you have to cook?" Ginny asked. "Do you get your chicken and dumplings?"

"No, unfortunately, we don't. We each get a piece of meat, pork usually, and not cooked at all like you women can prepare. We usually get a potato, a chunk of bread and some coffee. If we want anything else, like milk or butter or sugar, we have to buy it ourselves."

"Sounds like when the war is over and you come home, I will have to make you chicken and dumplings every day."

"I do love your chicken and dumplings. But the cooking isn't all that bad. It breaks up the monotony of the day. When we're not eating, we're drilling. Drilling, drilling, and drilling. I know it's important, but it gets very tedious. Makes a body wish we could just go fight in a battle just to change things up."

"Isn't there anything to cheer you?" Ginny asked.

"Letters from home, and writing home. It's good be around other men, the companionship is good. We'll sit around the campfires and some of the men will bring out jaw harps and harmonicas. Some know how to play the banjo. We can find sticks to use as percussion. We all sing along. That is pretty enjoyable to me."

"You always have enjoyed singing and dancing." Ginny smiled.

"As have you." Jack said, pulling her into his arms and spinning her around. They had walked far enough that they were out of town, away from eyes and gossip. Jack pulled her close and pressed a kiss to her lips. "I have wanted to do that since before I left."

"Since the last time you kissed me?" She asked.

"Yes. Every moment since then." He pulled away and continued walking.

"What was stopping you, Jack? There have been opportunities."

"My family, propriety, it's not in good taste to kiss in public. Even if we were married, it wouldn't be proper."

"That didn't stop Will and Alex." Ginny said, thinking back to when Will had returned. Alex had been waiting for him with other mothers, wives, daughters and sweethearts, Ginny had been with her. When Will saw her, he broke rank and immediately ran to her, then threw his arms around her. There had been some titters from older women and a loud objection from Maime Williams, Abigail's mother, as the two had passionately kissed, but most of the townspeople had been too busy welcoming their loved ones to pay Alex and Will any mind.

"Alex and Will are newlyweds, and neither one of them are shy about expressing their feelings. In public or in private, as Will has mentioned. They seem to get on very well together."

"So Will never speaks of regret for getting married so quickly?"

"No, quite the contrary." Jack paused. "I have spoken to him quite a few times, gotten to know him. He actually suggested I should throw caution to the wind and get married while back here." They arrived at the stone formation known as Devil's Den. Jack helped Ginny climb the slope, then leaned against a boulder as she sat down.

"And why not? You know I would marry you in a heartbeat, Jack."

"I know that, Ginny. But I want to be able to provide for you. And protect you. Once we're married, I want to have our own home, our own place that you can keep and I can work. God willing, you'll never have to take in mending anymore and I can take care of you. You and any children we may have. I don't want to marry you and leave you. I know it worked for Alex and Will, but I just couldn't abandon you like that."

"Sometimes, you are too honorable, Jack."

"It's how I was raised." Jack looked out across the landscape. Farms spread out everywhere. In the distance, he could see the town and a familiar hill, Culp's Hill. One that he could spend hours on with friends when they were younger. He sighed. She followed his gaze.

"Have you heard from Wesley?" She asked.

"No." He sat down next to her. "It's definite that he joined up with the Rebels. Made friends down in Virginia. My brother Edwin said he was really involved with a social and military group."

"The Hamtramck Guards." Ginny said. "Yes, Wes wrote to Charlotte about that."

"Edwin said when they heard the news about Fort Sumter, they were all getting ready to come back home, but Wes was determined to stay, come what may. When we talked in April, it was just rumors that he was joining the Confederates. Now it's a certainty. So now, one of my oldest friends is fighting against me. If I ever see him across the battlefield from me...I don't know what I would do."

Ginny put her arm across his back and laid her head on his shoulder. "I don't think it will come to that."

"I hope not. I'd rather just never see him again, which may be the case. I even heard William, his own brother, call him a traitor. I don't believe he will be coming back, even after the war."

"But why did he stay? Was there a girl down there?"

"I don't think so. Ed said the only girls he ever spoke of were you and Charlotte. So I don't know. Wesley is the only one who knows for sure." Jack looked at Ginny. "Has Charlotte ever mentioned anything? I know they continued to write to one another."

"She said she didn't know a reason either." Ginny said. She looked out across the landscape. "I do love this view. So peaceful. Hard to believe there is even a war going on."

"It shouldn't make it this far." Jack said. "We won't let the Rebs get into Northern territory." He shifted his body, arranging himself and Ginny so that she sat between his outstretched legs, her back against his chest. She leaned into him and he placed his chin on her shoulder and layered his arms over hers.

"Jack..." Ginny began. "I am not opposed to being this close to you, but it is definitely not proper." She turned to look at him and he kissed her lips.

"I know." He said. "This is all the closer I will get, I promise. I just want to be with you."

"And I you." Ginny rested her head against his. "I am yours, Jack. You know that, right?"

"Of course I do." Jack said. "And I am yours."

September

"Wesley,

All of the Gettysburg men have made it through their first enlistment, safe and sound. They are now home for a brief visit before they head back. I have been spending most of my time with Father and Thomas. Father has made his decision. He will be joining the army and leaving me to run the farm. The time with them is not as bad as it could have been. Father is being kind to me. I'm still not sure about my feelings for your cousin. I can't see myself with him for the rest of my life. A positive thing about him is that when he is around, it makes the atmosphere around home better. His family welcomes me and is cordial, even if your aunt is a bit cold toward me. I suspect it is because I am delaying the wedding to Thomas.

I am still missing you. I wish that I could hear from you. I hope you know that I still value your friendship.

Charlotte"

Finally, the day came for the 87th Pennsylvania to leave. Most of the town had gathered to see them off. Jack spoke to his mother, hugging her and his brother while Ginny stood behind him, her hands clasped in front of her and her head down. Will stood with his gun slung over his shoulder, his hands framing Alex's teary face. Their foreheads were pressed together, and they were talking to each other in low tones. Alex's parents stood nearby.

Charlotte stood with her father and Thomas. Thomas held her hand as her father gave her some final instructions.

"Now, remember to keep an eye on the fences. Ask any of the neighbors if you need advice with any of the crops. They will know what to do." He pulled his slouch hat down a little lower and gave her an awkward hug.

"And when I come home, we can finally make our relationship permanent." Thomas smiled.

Across the road, Jack turned to Ginny, a serious look on his face. He bent down to kiss her on the forehead and spoke softly. "I know you are disappointed we didn't get married. But like I said, I cannot marry you when I will not be able to take care of you. I know others have and will, but I cannot do that."

"I understand." Ginny said softly.

"I love you. Write me?" He asked, already knowing the answer.

"Of course." She smiled, tears welling up in her eyes. "I love you too."

Down the road a bit from Ginny and Jack, Alex and Will stood close, still whispering to one another, as close as they could be while still being proper in public.

"I will write you as often as I can and come and see you whenever I get the opportunity." Will murmured.

"I will write you too." Alex reached up and brushed a strand of hair that had fallen in front of his eye. He pressed his lips to hers.

"I love you. I will always love you." Will whispered.

"Let's move out, men!" The call from the road caused the men to line up. Will pulled himself away from his wife, as he, Jack and the rest of the Gettysburg boys boarded the train to go back to war.

September 11
Turner Farm

Charlotte was reading a letter from Thomas one day when Alex and Ginny came for a visit. She hid the letter in her pocket as she stood to greet them. Thomas was the last person she wanted to talk about. Her action wasn't quick enough to escape Alex's attention.

"Charlotte, is that a letter? From your soldier?"

"It is." Charlotte handed her friend the letter. Alex quickly scanned it.

"I'll say it again, Charlotte, he is soo romantic!"

"He is just taking poetry from other men, Alex. I have told you that before." Charlotte told her, the edge of annoyance apparent in her voice. "It is superficial and emotionless."

"I like the letters Thomas Culp sends you." Alex replied, handing the letter back. "He writes some pretty verse."

"I am certain that the words he writes are not original. Besides, I agree with Elizabeth Bennett and what she says about poetry and such."

"What? Who is Elizabeth Bennett?" Alex's look was pure confusion.

Ginny and Charlotte laughed.

"Pride and Prejudice? Jane Austen?" Ginny said. "I thought you were going to read that."

"Oh. I was." Alex shrugged.

"'There has been many a one, I fancy, overcome in the same way. I wonder who first discovered the efficacy of poetry in driving away love!'" Charlotte quoted her favorite literary heroine. Ginny continued the quote.

"I have been used to consider poetry as the FOOD of love,"

"Of a fine, stout, healthy love it may. Everything nourishes what is strong already. But if it be only a slight, thin sort of inclination, I am convinced that one good sonnet will starve it entirely away." Charlotte finished and both she and Ginny dissolved into giggles. Charlotte's sour mood was quickly driven away, something Ginny could always do.

"So have you heard anything at all from Wesley?" Ginny asked when they calmed down.

Charlotte shook her head. "I know it's hard to get letters through from the South, but it still worries me. I wish I knew where he was, how he is doing. The last letter he wrote was so stiff and informal. If it had not been in his handwriting, I would not have believed that it had been him writing it at all. I had hoped and prayed that the tensions and the outbreak of war would bring Wesley home, not tear him away. And I know I shouldn't care, but..." She shrugged her shoulders.

"I understand." Ginny nodded. "He's still our friend."

"What kind of friend would join the enemy's army?" Alex asked. "I don't know how you two can sympathize with him. He's over there trying to kill Union men."

"I'm sure if Wesley came across any Gettysburg boys, he would do anything in his power to keep them out of harm's way. I'm sure, if he and Jack met each other, they would probably want to go and find the nearest pub for a drink." Ginny smiled.

"You may be right." Alex said, sounding unconvinced. "But what about Will? I'm sorry but I cannot feel any empathy towards anyone that could be putting Will in danger."

Charlotte hated it when the talk turned to Wesley's decision to go with the south, so she jumped on the opportunity to change the subject. "How is Will? We really haven't had the chance to talk much since the boys left."

Alex smiled. "He is doing very well. We had a lot of catching up to do, you know, we didn't even get a proper honeymoon. Mother and father tried to give us some privacy, but it's difficult in our house."

Charlotte turned to her other friend. "And Jack? I hardly got to see him at all. He was busy or I was busy. The timing was always off."

"I didn't get a chance to see him as much as I wanted. He spent a lot of time with his family." She smiled a sweet and innocent smile. "We did find some time to be together, though. It's just so good being with him. It's like we were made for one another. I can't imagine being with anyone else. If he dies..." she shuddered. "Well, I just don't know. I want to spend the rest of my life with him. I want to have his children, I want to grow old with him. If he dies..." She took a shaky breath. Charlotte moved over to her and hugged her tightly.

"He'll be fine." She muttered, praying she was right. Her next words were purely for Ginny's benefit. "We all will be. We just have to have faith."

Part Two:

1862

January 16

Gettysburg, Pennsylvania

"Will,

As always I miss you terribly. I long for the days that you return to me for good and we can start our lives together. I eagerly await letters from you, news from you, to hear the words that you want to tell me. I know you are frustrated with the lack of excitement, but I am happy that you are staying safe. I cannot bear the thought of losing you.

The middle of the winter has brought excitement to Gettysburg. The Tenth New York Cavalry has been ordered to the town for training. Boys like Sammy Wade and Paige Pierce spend every available moment climbing trees and looking for the best view of the soldiers as they drill and practice. Aaron is continually telling Mother and Father that he intends to enlist, but so far, they have been able to keep him here. My sister Maria has written to say that her baby boy, Abraham, grows more and more each day. Mother says every day how she longs to go and visit, but it is too expensive, and too dangerous.

Charlotte spends many of her days at the Wade's. The winter leaves very little work to be done at her farm, and there is no one else to feed after her father has marched off to war. We try and get together as much as possible. I have also become quite close with Augusta Lewis, the Southern woman that you met while back in town. She is very kind, and spends most of her time helping her in-laws with the store. Mr. and Mrs. Lewis are well-respected and I believe that helps rumors and anger about her background from reaching Augusta too much. I enjoy spending time with her. She has fit in rather well with my little group of friends.

Your Love,
Alex"

Charlotte trudged through the snow to the Wades, pulling a sled with what little laundry she had. Since she was only washing for herself, she was able to take it elsewhere, making the tedious task a little better with company. As she walked into the house, she saw Mrs. Wade and Ginny sitting at their table, going over what looked like their dreaded monthly budget. Georgia was wiping the breakfast dishes dry.

"Taking care of Isaac helps, but we'll still fall short." Ginny was telling her mother.

"Hello, everyone! Laundry time!" Charlotte said, trying to be upbeat. The melancholy atmosphere was thick in the house. Charlotte shut the door behind her against the wind and blowing snow. The heat of the fire rushed to her, warming her cheeks.

"Hello, Charlotte." Mrs. Wade forced a smile on her stern face. "How is your father doing?"

"I haven't heard from him since the last letter I told you about. I'm sure he's fine." Before Mrs. Wade could say anything else, Harry ran into the room. The boy's clothes were already mussed, and his smooth blonde hair bounced on his head.

"Charlotte!" He exclaimed, throwing himself into her arms. She caught him and hugged him tightly.

"Hey, there. Where are you running off to?"

He leaned back in her arms to look at his mother. "Hey, mama, Sam and Paige and some of the other boys are going to go and watch the soldiers. Can I go?"

Mrs. Wade sighed. "I don't know, Harry. I'm always afraid one of you boys are going to get hurt."

"Mother." Harry looked at her with all seriousness. "No one is going to get hurt. Besides, if we learn some of this stuff now, we won't have to take the time to learn it later. So when it's our turn to fight, we'll be ahead of everyone else."

"Who told you that?" Ginny asked.

"Johnny." Harry said. "Please, mom?"

"Well, as long as you stay far away from the guns and close to Samuel. And make sure you bundle up!"

"Yess!" Harry pumped his fist in the air, and then ran out of the room, yelling. "Thanks, Mother, I'll bundle up tight!"

"All right."

Ginny stood and began to sort through the laundry while Mrs. Wade began to get the rest of the laundry set up. John came in, lugging buckets of water for the women.

Just as soon as they started the laundry, there was a knock on the door. Ginny went to answer it. A Union soldier stood there. The wind had died down and snow was falling gently to the ground.

"Hello, ma'am. Is this the Wade residence?" The soldier was young, about twenty or so, and his face was heavily bearded with the same thick brown hair that covered his head.

"It is." Ginny nodded. "I'm Virginia Wade, and my mother and sister are inside. Please, come in out of the cold."

The man nodded politely as he stepped in. "I'm Second Lieutenant Adam Nelson from the 10th New York Cavalry. My friends and I heard that you ladies have experience mending clothes and such."

"Yes, sir. Is there some way we can be of service?" Mother Wade had dried her hands and joined Ginny near the door. Ginny moved aside to allow the man in and then shut the door.

"Well, we are in need of some repairs to our uniforms. We'd pay you, of course." His brown eyes looked around the front room.

"Of course." Ginny said. "We could use the extra money. And it would be a privilege to help our Union boys in any way we can."

"Thank you, miss." He touched his hat and nodded his head. "Is it all right if we stop by later this evening then?"

"Yes, that would be fine." Ginny said. The man smiled and left.

Ginny shut the door and leaned against it, a small smile on her face. "Well, mother, that will help us make ends meet. The Lord answered our prayers again."

*****

After dinner and when Charlotte had left, there was the expected knock at the door. Ginny answered and found Lieutenant Nelson and three other men outside. The other three were of various ages. The youngest was blonde and pale-faced, with rosy cheeks. He didn't look to be much older than John Wade. The middle soldier was of medium height and build with a full beard and mustache. His dirty black hair passed his shoulders and looked like he hadn't groomed himself or showered since Fort Sumter had been bombarded. The oldest soldier had black hair with some gray streaks, and was distinguished-looking,

92

as though he had been a professor, lawyer or politician before the war. They each held some clothes in their arms.

"Evening, ma'am." Lieutenant Nelson said. "I would like to introduce Lieutenant Michael Stratton, 10th New York." He nodded at the oldest, who saluted. He then gestured toward the young blonde. "This is Private Jacob Warner, and that there," he nodded at the other man, "is Burton Porter."

"Come in and warm yourself by the fire." Ginny said. "I can take a look at what you have and we can figure the pricing out."

The men sat down at the table.

"Would you men care for some coffee?" Ginny called over her shoulder.

A chorus of 'thank-you' sounded from the men. Ginny quickly handed them mugs and filled them with hot coffee. It didn't take long for the men to warm up. As Ginny looked over the clothes, the oldest man spoke up.

"There are many other soldiers who will be in need of a seamstress. I am sure we can keep you busy."

"That would be good." Ginny said, smiling. "Send them over." She named a price. "We have our customers pay half first and then half later. I can send one of my brothers to your camp when they are finished."

"That sounds fair." Burton Porter said.

"We will spread the word." Michael Stratton said, standing. "Thank you again, ma'am.

"I will send one of my brothers over when they are finished." Ginny let them out.

"Thanks again, ma'am, and thanks for the coffee." The men all thanked her and headed into the darkness.

February 23

"*Michael,*

Winter has gone by quickly. I am staying busy, working for your parents at the store. I have made some good friends here. They are younger than you and I, but we still have much in common. Ginny Wade, a seamstress, stays busy with her family, working and mending clothes. You may remember her and Charlotte Turner from your childhood. Charlotte has been running her family farm on her own, and has begun to plan for spring planting. Alexandria Sadler is a newlywed whose husband is fighting for the Union cause. Her father is a professor at Pennsylvania College. She and I are frequently working with the various church groups in town, rolling bandages and such. She writes daily to her husband, Will Sadler, who was a student at the college before fighting broke out.

I miss you more and more each day. I feel as though our marriage was just beginning before this cruel war tore us apart. Please write as often as possible, I long to hear from you and know how you are and how you are doing.

Yours forever,

Augusta"

Augusta reread the letter, tears of worry and loneliness welling in her eyes. She wanted to tell Michael more, to really share with him her fears and feelings, but she knew she couldn't. She knew that Michael, with his kind and caring heart, would worry too much. She didn't want him constantly thinking about her and not his own safety. She didn't want him distracted. She took a deep breath, wiped her eyes, and headed downstairs.

The store was mostly empty. Her father-in-law gave her a smile from behind the counter. The bell by the door rang and Charlotte Turner walked in.

"Augusta, Mr. Lewis! How are you both doing?"

"Very good, Miss Turner. And how are you on this winter day?"

"Quite well. Cold, but well." Charlotte pulled off her brown mittens and came closer to Augusta. She immediately noticed Augusta's slightly puffy eyes. With a glance at Mr. Lewis, who was rearranging the canned goods, Charlotte put a hand on Augusta's arm. "Augusta, what's wrong?" She spoke quietly, so only the two could hear.

"It's nothing. I just wrote a letter to Michael. I miss him and got a little too emotional."

"I can understand that feeling. But I feel like you are upset about more than just that. Would you like to talk? I'm not in any rush right now."

"It's no trouble, Charlotte, really. I will be fine." Augusta forced a smile on her face, but Charlotte could tell right away that it was not genuine.

"Well, what if I wanted to have a chat? I wouldn't want to impose, but I would like to get to know you better."

Augusta smiled for real, touched by the offer of friendship. "Mrs. Lewis put some coffee on a while ago, and I have been saving some coco that we can use to sweeten it. Would you like a cup?"

"That sounds wonderful."

The two girls went into the kitchen. Augusta prepared the drinks, then joined Charlotte at the table.

"So, be honest with me, Augusta. How are you in terms of getting settled?"

"It has been an adjustment." Augusta admitted, curling her hands around the warm coffee mug. "I am constantly worrying about what to say and do so I don't offend anyone. Then, there are times that I wonder if just me speaking, with my accent, offends people."

Charlotte nodded in understanding. "It is hard." She agreed. "I remember visiting my cousin Isabelle in Virginia two summers ago. There are so many differences in our cultures."

"There is!" Augusta exclaimed, glad to have found someone who understood. "I didn't know you had family in Virginia."

"Yes, my father's whole family is from the south. The family plantation is outside Fredericksburg. My father came here on business for my Uncle Matthew who inherited the plantation. He met my grandfather and my mother and never left."

"So you do understand, a little."

"I do. I cannot imagine being in your position. I know men like Nik Braxton can be narrow-minded and judgmental. They can be to me as well. And the Wades, and anyone who doesn't fit their idea of a 'perfect' townsperson." She paused. "Are those men still harassing you?"

"Sometimes." Augusta sighed. "And some days, it doesn't bother me at all. Other days, I can't help but get upset. I knew it would be difficult, falling in love with a man who my family and neighbors consider an enemy." She paused. "But from what I understand, you know that too."

"Not to the degree that you do, but yes. Wesley Culp was one of my best friends. When he left, I realized that I had fallen in love with him. I can't help but think that if it wasn't for the war, we could be together. Maybe things could have worked out. Maybe my father would have been a little more receptive to a relationship between us."

"I am thankful for the time Michael and I were able to spend together." Augusta said. "And I pray every day for an end to this war and for his safety.

"You pray. Are you religious, then?" Charlotte asked.

"I believe in God, yes, and have always considered myself a Christian. I rarely went to church as a child. My family just didn't. Meeting Michael changed that, though. The Lewis family is very devout. We were married in a Catholic service. My family, strangely, didn't seem to mind that much. I realized then that religion wasn't important to them. But Michael's faith, and now the faith of Mr. and Mrs. Lewis, especially Mrs. Lewis, has made me want to learn more. And Mrs. Lewis is a very good teacher." Augusta rose to refill the cups. "What about you?"

"I believe in God and Jesus. I usually go to church at St. James Lutheran with Ginny and Alex. They are more serious about religion than I am. I just can't fathom why an all-powerful and loving God would allow so much suffering in the world. I wondered that even before the war began. My mother believed in God. She read the Bible every day. She went to church every week. But did God save her when she was giving birth to my brother? No. My mother died bringing him into this world. And then he died too. God may be there, but I find it hard to believe that He cares about us.

"I'm not quite sure what to tell you, Charlotte. I have some doubts as well. But when I look at the Lewis's, Michael and his parents, they have such confidence in God. Such peace. Such a deep feeling that all will be well. It's hard not to be inspired by that, surrounded with that every day."

"I know. Alex and Ginny are constantly trying to help me understand. Alex is fully part of the church. Ginny is not yet confirmed Lutheran, but it is only a matter of time." Charlotte sighed. "I wish I could have their blind faith, I really do." She pulled out her watch and chatelaine. "I really have enjoyed our talk, but I should be going." They both stood.

"I'm glad we talked, Charlotte. It's good to know that you can sympathize with me."

"I can and do. It was wonderful getting to know you better. I hope we can talk more."

"As do I." Augusta smiled, grateful for her new friendship.

*****

Charlotte walked quickly down Baltimore Road, heading to Alex's one afternoon when she saw Private Jacob Warner. Warner was one of the youngest members of the "Porter Guards", as the 10th New York was called. He was a frequent customer of the Wades.

"Good afternoon, Private Warner." Charlotte greeted him. In between his drilling and exercises, where he and his fellow soldiers would perfect their use of small arms and sabers, he was spending time with the Wades, especially John Jr. Charlotte suspected that John and Jacob were closer in age than the soldier would have anyone believe.

"Hello to you, Miss Turner." Warner took off his hat and tipped his head. "Are you on your way to the Wades?"

"Eventually." Charlotte smiled. "Were you just there yourself?"

"I was. Miss Ginny invited me and some of the others to services on Sunday."

"That's wonderful." Charlotte said, "Will we see you there?"

"I never was one for church going, but some of the other men probably will. I don't know, maybe I will tag along."

"Well, I hope you decide to come. It's always nice to see our Union boys worshipping."

"Yes, ma'am. Not only that, Miss Ginny says it's a good idea. All the men in our unit really like the family. They've been very kind and hospitable."

"That they are." Charlotte smiled. "I hope to see you Sunday. It was good talking to you."

Charlotte took no more than a few steps toward her destination when Abigail Williams stopped her.

"Charlotte, who was that boy? Is he one of those men visiting the Wade home at all hours, day and night?" Abigail's tone was heavy with insinuation of inappropriate behavior.

"He may be a frequent visitor, but it's not at all what you are making it sound. Private Warner is more friends with John than anything."

"That could be true for that boy, but you have to admit it's quite interesting to see so many of those men over there all the time. It makes you wonder if the Wades are doing more than just laundry."

"Abigail! You cannot be serious. If people heard you say that..."

"People are already saying things, Charlotte."

"Well, I can assure you, people are all wrong."

"I do hope you're right. Ginny and Georgia have already been through enough scandal. What would Jack Skelly say if he thought Ginny was paying special attention to other Union soldiers?"

"I think Jack and Ginny's relationship is stronger than rumors and speculation." With that statement, Charlotte pushed past Abigail and continued on her way to Alex's.

When Charlotte arrived, Alex noticed her friend's mood right away.

"What happened?" She asked.

"It is just so frustrating the way people treat Ginny and the Wades. I know they're poor. I know Mr. Wade made a lot of mistakes and is mentally unstable, and I know her mother can be harsh, but people always just assume the worst about them." Charlotte quickly detailed her run-in with Abigail.

"That is too bad. People really should be more forgiving and understanding." Alex agreed. "It's not as though Ginny or her siblings have ever done anything wrong."

"They're good people." Charlotte brushed a lock of her hair off her face. "Ginny is inviting men from the 10th New York to church services. She is one of the most faithful people that I know."

"Well, to some people, having money and status is more important than being a good person."

"Yes, well, I feel that in the coming years, we will need more faith than anything."

*****

The Lewis's store was busy, full of soldiers from the 10th New York and other townspeople when Ginny stopped in. She immediately spotted Augusta and hurried to her side to talk to her. Before they could start a conversation, one of the soldiers approached.

98

"Evening, Miss Wade." The black-haired man tipped his hat at Ginny. "Will I see you at the dance tomorrow?"

"Yes, Mr. Porter, I was planning on going." Ginny answered with a small smile. From time to time, the townspeople would have parties and dances for the soldiers.

Augusta turned to Ginny as the soldier left. "Who was that?"

"That's Burton Porter. He's from the 10th New York. He is one of my customers. I had to repair his uniform a couple of times. He stops by often to talk. He has been very kind."

"I understand a lot of the New York men are trying to romance local girls."

"Yes. Abigail Williams has two or three on a string."

"I'm sure she enjoys that immensely." Augusta folded some pre-made shirts neatly.

"Yes." Ginny said, picking up the thread she needed and putting it in her basket. "You really should come tomorrow, Augusta."

"No." Augusta shook her head. "I have been to enough dances in my life to keep me more than content."

"But there are always uneven numbers, more men than women. You could help even things out."

"I'm married. What would people say?"

"Alex goes and dances. The men respect the fact that she's married. It's all in good fun."

"Yes, but would they be able to respect the fact that I'm from South Carolina? Would they be able to respect the fact that my brothers and father are fighting against them? For the Confederacy?"

"Oh, Augusta, I didn't think of that. I'm sorry." Ginny gave Augusta's arm a squeeze. "It must be very difficult for you."

"Ginny, I would like to go. Really, I would. It's just...better that I avoid social functions like that."

"But it's probably very lonely for you." Ginny said, grabbing the last item she needed. "Well, know that you are more than welcome to come. I hope to see you there." Ginny held up her basket. "Could you put this on my family's account?"

Augusta nodded, then continued her work as Ginny left.

*****

The next evening, Ginny, Alex and Charlotte stood together and watched as soldiers came in to the dance. The soldiers mingled with the townspeople. Alex, dressed in a white silk gown that was patterned with purple flowers, was her usual, flirtatious self, but never went so far as to make the soldiers believe she wanted more than friendship. It wasn't long before she was escorted onto the dance floor.

"I don't know how she does it, the small talk with anyone she comes across." Charlotte said, wishing she found it as easy to converse with people she barely knew. She brushed her hands down her best dress, made with white and maroon-checked cotton and lined in pink piping.

"It's just the way she is." Ginny said as Burton Porter approached. Ginny had gotten to know Porter well over the past month. He was 29 years old, kind, and well-liked by the other soldiers. He and Ginny could talk for hours about things, mainly religion. He was talking her into becoming fully confirmed into the Lutheran church.

"Miss Wade, you are looking very nice tonight." Porter smiled.

"Thank you, Sgt. Porter." Ginny smiled back, looking down at her plain brown dress lined in blue. She knew it wasn't nearly as nice as any of the other dresses in the room, Burton's words showed how kind he was.

"Would you care to dance?" He offered his arm and she immediately took it. He led her on to the floor.

"I think he fancies her." Augusta's voice sounded from behind Charlotte.

"Augusta! You came!" Charlotte turned and hugged her friend.

"I did. I decided it would be a good thing." Augusta nodded toward Ginny and the Sergeant. "What do you think about the two of them?"

"I think you're right. I know Ginny only cares for him as a friend, but I believe his feelings are stronger. I have mentioned it to her, warned her, but she doesn't agree. She's believes he just wants to be friends with her." Charlotte sighed. "I hope it doesn't cause any problems. Ginny doesn't need any more trouble."

"What if Jack gets word of their friendship? Will he trust her?"

"Oh, I am sure he will get word of it. It's too good of a story for the gossips of this town not to spread. But I do know that Jack won't make any hasty judgements. He'll speak with Ginny or myself before he believes the gossip. He and Ginny are first and foremost best friends."

"That's how it should be." Augusta smiled.

"Why, if it isn't our own little South Carolina belle." Abigail Williams glided up to Charlotte and Augusta. "I'm surprised to see you here, boosting the morale of our Union boys in training."

"My husband is in the Union army, Miss Williams. His side is my side." Augusta said softly.

"But what about your family? Don't you have brothers fighting for the Rebels?"

"I do. And I, above all people, would love to see this war end. I care about too many people on both sides."

"Yes, yes. I am sure it will be over soon." Abigail glanced out at the dance floor, directly at Ginny in the arms of Burton Porter. "I see Ginny Wade wasted no time in getting on the dance floor. With her around, these Union men will be taken care of."

"Abigail, really." Charlotte challenged. "You know that Ginny is doing nothing improper. How many of the men here have you danced with? How many of these soldiers are you leading on?"

"I have my fair share of male friends, but they aren't coming and going to and from my home at all hours of the night like they do at the Wades. Besides, I don't have a beau who is away, fighting for the cause."

"The men visit the Wade home for business, Abigail." Charlotte said.

"And it appears as though business is booming." Abigail said, her words heavy with insinuation. Before either Augusta or Charlotte could respond, a handsome young soldier approached the trio.

"Miss Williams, may I have this dance?"

"Why, yes, of course you may." And with that, Abigail flounced off.

March 30
Turner Farm
"Dear Thomas,
The 10th New York has left and life has slipped back into
normalcy, at least as normal as it can be with the country at war. I
have started to prepare for spring planting. With Father now gone,
and no available men to hire and no money to pay them with, I plan
to be very busy. I know I won't be able to plant nearly as much as we
have in years past. I am trying to find a solution to the problem..."

Charlotte stopped her writing when she heard a knock on the door.
She answered it to find John Wade, a big grin on his face.
"Charlotte. How are you?" John. was tall and gangly for his age of
sixteen, with dark blonde hair and blue eyes. He was a hard worker,
and invaluable to his family for the money he made doing odd jobs in
the town.
"I'm doing well. What brings you out here?" Charlotte ushered
him in.
John. ran a hand through his shaggy hair. "Ginny mentioned you
might need some help with the planting. I wanted to offer my services.
If you still needed help."
"John, that would be an answer to my prayers." Charlotte threw her
arms around the boy. "I could definitely use some help this planting
season. I can't pay you much."
"I understand. I will take whatever you can offer. Maybe fresh
vegetables, I know you have some fruit trees I can help harvest in the
fall." He looked out the window towards her fields. "What are you
planning on planting?"
"I think I am going to focus on wheat, since I have the seeds.
Probably only half of what we usually plant. I am going to grow more
vegetables this year. I think I will be able to get more money in town
for those." She took her lantern and stepped out into the evening,
gesturing for John to follow her.
"That's a good idea." John nodded. Even though he he had been
raised in town, John knew quite a bit about farming. "How are you
doing with your livestock?" They walked toward the barn.
"Father sold off most of the animals before he left. He didn't want
the government to just come and take them during the course of the
war." Charlotte explained.

"I have heard that could happen, although it will probably happen more often in the areas where fighting is actually happening. So what stock do you have left?" He looked around the barn.

"I have one milk cow and a half-dozen pigs, about 10 chickens, a rooster, and Cricket here." She patted the brown and white spotted horse on the neck.

"That's a good number." John nodded. "I can definitely help you out. I can ask around and see if there are any other boys who can help too. But I am sure that together, you and I can make a pretty good go of it."

"You're not going to get war fever and up and leave me with all the work like everyone else, are you?"

"Not this year." He flashed a grin, showing off two dimples. "I promised Mother. Next year is a different story, though."

Charlotte smiled sadly. She couldn't imagine little John going off and fighting, but she knew that boys younger than John had joined the army.

"Well, I will use your help for as long as I can get it, John.. When can you start?"

"How about tomorrow morning?" John asked.

"I will see you then!" Charlotte smiled "I have a list a mile long waiting for us. After John left, Charlotte sank back down into her chair and said a silent prayer of thanks to God for the help.

April 15

"Oh, Georgia, you look absolutely beautiful." Ginny smiled as she pinned a final curl into her sister's perfectly coiffed hair. "John won't be able to take his eyes off you."

"Thank you for saying so, Gin. I can't believe my wedding day is finally here."

"I can't either. I'm going to miss you so much."

"It's not like I'm moving out of town. I will be right down the road. We can visit one another at any time."

"I know that, but it just won't be the same. No more sharing a bedroom. No more sitting and mending before bed. We will see each other often, but everything is changing."

"Things changing isn't a bad thing, Gin. Besides, it won't be long until you are off and married to Jack anyways."

"If his mother ever lets us get married." Ginny spoke before thinking. "I'm sorry. We shouldn't be discussing my problems on your special day."

Georgia stood and hugged her sister. "Jack's mother will eventually realize how good of a wife you will actually be and just how happy you will make her son. Someday."

"Yes, well, your someday is today. Let's get you married."

*****

The wedding was simple, but sweet. There was a small reception at the McClellan Hotel after the vows had been spoken.

"That was a very nice ceremony, wasn't it?" Alex said, gliding up to Ginny and Charlotte. "I feel very fortunate to have been invited."

"Yes, well, Georgia likes you, enjoys your company, even though you don't see each other much. You always have treated our family with kindness and respect."

"Well, I enjoy her company as well. Alex gestured to Ginny's dress, old and outdated, but nicely altered for the occasion. "Ginny, I am always impressed by your talents. Your dress looks absolutely beautiful."

"Thank you, Alex. It's not much." Ginny glanced at Alex's gown with envy. It was a day dress, with thick navy blue and light blue vertical stripes. The blue in the dress made her blue eyes even brighter than usual.

104

"You look beautiful, as always, Alex." Ginny commented.

"Thank you." Alex smiled and looked at her two friends. Ginny's dress was clearly old and repaired. Charlotte's dress was newer, but plain green cotton. The color was good for her, and she looked nice, but Alex finally felt self-conscious about her own outfit. She had both her parents to care for her and support her. Neither of her friends had that luxury. Ginny has an entire family to help support. Charlotte was running herself ragged trying to run the farm in her father's absence. Her friends were fighting battles that she couldn't even dream of.

"I really admire both of you, by the way." Alex said. The comment took both Charlotte and Ginny off guard.

"Thank you for the compliment, Alex. What made you think of that?" Charlotte asked.

"Just...everything you two have done and will do during this war. And before it. And probably after it. You two have so many more skills than I do. Skills to help you survive."

"And yet, of the three of us, you are the only one who is married." Ginny said with a smile.

"Yes, strange world, isn't it?" Alex smiled.

"Alex, you have your own talents and gifts from God." Ginny said. "You're kind, funny, and you always know how to make people feel at ease and good about themselves. I admire you for that."

"Thank you, Ginny. I needed to hear that." She smiled. "And your sister made a most beautiful bride."

"She did, didn't she?" Ginny glanced at her sister, who was making rounds visiting her guests. Charlotte noticed the longing look in Ginny's gaze.

"It won't be long before you're the bride, Gin."

"I hope you're right." Ginny replied. "I am missing Jack, that's true. But I'm also missing Georgia already. Her being married and moving into her own home. She will still be here in town, but it will be different."

"That is true." Alex said. "I remember feeling the same way when my sister was married. She was my closest friend growing up, despite our age differences. It was difficult being without her those first few months. And when I was engaged and first married. There's things that you just can't talk about with your mother and would be nice to talk about with another married woman. Anyways, even though it's different, we learn and change for the better."

"I suppose that's true." Ginny said.

"Besides, now, instead of just one sister, I now feel like I have three. Both of you and Maria."

"I am more thankful for you two than you can even imagine." Charlotte said. "I dislike my lack of siblings so much. I love big families, like yours, Ginny. When I get married, I want to have as many children as possible."

"And does Thomas also want a lot of children?"

"We haven't really discussed...that." Charlotte admitted. "But what man doesn't want a lot of children, especially when you're running a farm?"

"That's a good point." Alex said. "Will told me he wants to have a lot of children."

"Jack and I have never talked about that. He talks about coming back and getting married. But we haven't discussed anything past that."

"I think it can be hard for the soldiers to discuss things like that, especially when there is a chance that they might not return from war. Will doesn't like to." Alex said.

"I hadn't really thought about that." Ginny said.

"However, having faith, praying and keeping positive, that's all important." Alex said.

"I agree." Ginny said with a smile.

April 20
The Wade Home
"Ginny, I am so happy for you." Alex said with a smile.

"Thank you, Alex. I am quite excited myself." After years of worshipping, praying and discerning, Ginny was finally being fully confirmed into the Lutheran church. Alex had been very instrumental in helping Ginny along the way.

"So, confirmation." Charlotte sat down next to her friend. "That is a pretty big deal for you." Charlotte had always admired Ginny's faith. And Alex's. Even Augusta seemed more open to religion than Charlotte.

"It is a big deal." Alex threw her arm around Ginny in a side-hug. "Ginny will be making a personal, public profession of the faith and making a lifelong pledge of faithfulness to Jesus Christ."

"But you've attended a Lutheran church your whole life, right?" Augusta asked.

"I have already been baptized and receive communion, but confirmation is my personal choice to remain Lutheran."

"I see." Augusta said. "I have always believed in God, but never really attended Church on a regular basis. Michael and his parents are devout Catholics. We were married in a Catholic Church, and Mrs. Lewis has been talking to me about their Catechism, their faith. I have even been to Mass with them a few times. It is very traditional and difficult to understand the Latin, but I am enjoying it."

"Good for you." Alex smiled. "I know there are quite a few people who dislike the Catholics, but I feel like that is mostly based on misunderstandings. I have read many books from my father's library on different religions. Catholicism and Lutheranism are actually quite close. In fact, Martin Luther, the founder of Lutheranism, had been a Catholic priest. He had some objections to the Catholic faith, so he broke away. He even married a former nun, Katharina von Bora. However, from what I have read, though, the problems that Lutheran had with the Church have been taken care of. That was all back in the 1500's."

Ginny glanced at the clock. "It's almost time." She turned to her friends. "I really appreciate you all coming to support me today. Alex, your guidance has been invaluable. Augusta, your quiet support and Christian example are wonderful. And Charlotte...I know you are skeptical about some of my beliefs, but you're never negative about it, never judgmental. I just wish you could feel the same way I do. The way we all do. I wish you could learn to rely on God."

"Well, if anyone could convince me that God cares about me, it's you."

May 18
Turner Farm

Alex waved to Charlotte as she walked up the path to her friend's home. Charlotte shielded her eyes with her hand and smiled.

"Alex, what brings you out here?" Charlotte wiped her forehead with a handkerchief and leaned her hoe against the fence.

"I haven't seen you in over two weeks. I wanted to come out and check on you, make sure you're okay."

"I'm fine, just been very busy. Even with John's help, I can barely find time to do much." She looked at her pocket watch. "However, it is about time I started the dinner meal. Would you like to come in?"

"I would." Alex said, following her friend into the house. Charlotte began gathering some vegetables to cut up for soup.

"Would you like something to drink? I have some cool water in the root cellar. I would offer you some tea, but it's a bit too warm for that."

"It is hot." Alex paused and folded her hands in front of her on the table. "Ginny and I both noticed you haven't been around lately. Augusta said that you've been to the store a time or two, but that's it."

"Like I said, Alex, I've been busy. My neighbor, Mr. Bigham comes by to check up on me, but he has his own work to worry about."

Alex paused, hesitant to ask the next question on her mind.

"Charlotte, why haven't you been to church lately? You haven't been in a month."

Charlotte's back stiffened. "I told you. It's not easy being out here all by myself and taking care of things."

"But Charlotte..." Alex hesitated. "You should find time."

"Alex, I admire your blind loyalty to God and I do believe He exists, but...too many things have happened...bad things. I'm finding it hard to believe He's paying attention to us. Why would he allow the war, the battles..."

"But Charlotte, you pray. I've heard you do so."

Charlotte turned. "Yes, and a lot of good it's done me. I've prayed that Wesley would come home. I've prayed that my father stops being so angry. I have prayed for the war to end, for peace to come. I have prayed for the people of this town to give up their prejudices and be kind to the Wades." She paused, tears forming in her eyes. "I prayed that my mother wouldn't have died all those years ago." She took a deep breath. "I have prayed and prayed and none of those prayers have made any impact."

"But going to church could…"

"I am also getting tired of good churchgoing people not acting the way the Bible says they should. Besides, I only went to church so Ginny would have company. She has you for that now."

Alex shook her head. "Charlotte, I really wish you would think harder about this. With your heart. You are one of the best friends I have ever had. I just…I wish I could help you believe."

Charlotte stood and stepped toward the window, staring out across the fields toward town. "I appreciate the thought, Alex, I do. But…how can you…I mean…I know you pray for Will. Don't you pray for him to come home?"

"Of course I do. I pray for him to come home safely. Every night and day."

"But that hasn't happened." Charlotte turned to her friend.

"You're right. It hasn't happened yet. Just because God's not answering my prayers now doesn't mean He doesn't care. His timing is not always what we want. Maybe in order for Will and me to live the life God needs us to live, we need to learn and experience things. Experiences we may never have had if the war and our separation had not happened."

"So hundreds of men have had to die? For that?"

"No, that's not what I'm saying." Alex sighed. She hated this, knowing what she believed and why, but unable to explain it, especially when the other person needed to understand as much as Charlotte did. "I'm sorry I can't explain it any better."

"Don't worry about it." Charlotte said, standing. "I hate to cut this visit short, Alex, but I need to get back to work."

Alex stood. "Will you at least think about what I've said? About coming to church. About God."

"I suppose I can do at least that." Charlotte said.

"Well, that's all I can ask." Alex said, then waved and headed back to town.

June 14
Turner Farm

John Wade's help continued to be invaluable. From time to time, he would bring Jack Skelley's brother, Daniel to help, and they quickly caught up with the work. With farming, however, there was always something new to do to maintain the farm, which included fixing and mending fences, caring for the animals, watering the crops and making sure weeds didn't overtake them.

Charlotte took a break from hoeing in her vegetable garden to drink some water. She brushed back strands of hair that had fallen from her braid and into her face. The late June heat had caused them to stick to her forehead. She looked out to where John was fixing a fence in the far pasture. He had been out there for quite a while with no break. She went into the house, grabbed bread, cheese and an empty canteen and headed out to the boy, filling the canteen at the pump on her way.

"Ready for a break, John?" She asked. He pulled his brown hat off his head and wiped the perspiration from it with his shirt sleeve.

"Sure am. Thanks." He leaned against the fence casually, feet crossed at the ankles. "Good bread." He said, munching. "I was thinking the other day how good a wife you will make some man."

"Is that so?" Charlotte said, humoring him.

"Yeah. You're a good cook, good farm woman, you're easy on the eyes." He grinned.

"Yes, well, John, you know I am...spoken for." Charlotte hated saying the words, despised that they were true.

"Yeah, I know Thomas Culp has spoken for you. I also know you don't really want to marry him."

"Where did you hear that?"

"I overheard you and Ginny and Miss Alex talking about it. And I want you to know that you do have other options."

"Oh, do I?"

"Sure you do. I'll marry you."

"You? John, you're too young, you are more like my brother anyway." Charlotte smiled.

"I'm not too young." He stepped close to her. He was still like a younger brother to her, but the stubble she could see on his cheeks and the muscles he had developed were definitely showing maturity. "I'm sixteen now. Considered a man in almost any society."

"I know all that, John, and I appreciate the offer, I really do and the compliments." She stepped back. "To be completely honest, I'm not sure I am ready to be married to anyone. It's not just Thomas Culp. I don't want to marry anyone." She leaned against the fence. "Sometimes I think there must be something wrong with me."

"There's nothing wrong with you, Charlotte. I understand. Marriage should be something that you know you are ready for. You will be with that person for the rest of your life." He paused, and she knew he was thinking about his parents and their troubled marriage. "You should make sure you are ready and are with the right person." John leaned back against the fence next to her. "Just remember, you have options. And you don't need to feel pressured."

"Thank you. You're very smart, John." She smiled. "What's the news? I don't get into town much anymore."

John swallowed the rest of the cheese and gulped a drink of water. "Nothing too new. Most people are just wondering what Bobby Lee will do now that he's in command of the Army of Northern Virginia. That's what they're calling the main Reb army now. There's been a few skirmishes and a few battles in Virginia. Doesn't look as though our Union boys are any closer to winning. It's kind of disappointing. We have more men and better supply lines, but the men we have just aren't fighting well. And it's been tough for Lincoln to find good leaders. I can't wait until I can join up and maybe help change things."

"And when will that be?" Charlotte asked.

"Next year." He paused. "I'll probably stick around to help you with the planting. Then, in the summer, I'll get my turn."

Charlotte turned and looked at the rolling hills toward the South. "Hopefully by then, the war will be over."

August 13
St. James Lutheran Church

Charlotte was with Alex and Augusta, working on knitting stockings in the back of St. James church.

"How did you meet Michael?" Charlotte asked. "Your marriage seems rather unlikely, an outgoing Southern girl and a quiet Northern soldier." Many of the women in town had gathered, including Abigail Williams and her mother, Maime, Annie and Julia Culp, Wesley's sisters, and Jack Skelley's mother and two sisters.

"My brother, Joseph was in his first year at West Point, so my family and I took a trip up from South Carolina to visit him. While up there, he introduced us to some friends. Michael was one of them." Augusta sat back in her seat, a small smile on her face. "I must admit, I didn't even look twice at him that first meeting. He was tall, thin, and studious. He looked more like a preacher than a soldier. And there were so many other handsome soldiers around that I didn't even consider him." Augusta thought back to the day she had met her best friend and husband:

April 1855
West Point, New York

"Augusta, thank you so much for insisting that I come along." Margaret Wiggs adjusted her bonnet and glanced at her friend.

Augusta, her father, and her oldest brother, Andrew had traveled north to West Point to visit her brother, Joseph. She had convinced her father to allow Margaret, her best friend, to accompany them. The Wiggs were close friends of the family, owning the plantation next to Byron Hill. Margaret also fancied Joseph, and Augusta liked no idea better than her best friend marrying her brother. Both girls hoped this trip would be the beginning of a courtship between Margaret and Joseph.

"I'm glad you could come. It's been so nice having you along."

There was a knock on the door and Andrew entered, a smile on his face. "Ladies." Of average height, Andrew was the picture of a perfect Southern gentleman. He had black hair, the hazel eyes that ran in the Byron family, and a soft, kind smile. Andrew was proper, almost to a fault, and always kind and gentle. Being the oldest brother, he had been raised to take over the family plantation, and at age 24, he was already taking over many responsibilities of the the farm.

"Ladies, if you are ready, Joseph will be meeting us for dinner in half an hour."

"We certainly are ready." Augusta said, smoothing her pink and white dress over her hoopskirt. Andrew offered one arm to each girl, and they headed to the hotel restaurant.

"Joseph!" Augusta exclaimed when she saw him sitting with her father and another man, clearly a student at West Point that she didn't recognize. The men stood and Augusta threw her arms around her brother. "It's so good to see you! Fifteen months is too long! And you barely write." Joseph moved to pull out a seat for his sister while Andrew did the same for Margaret. The men all sat down.

"My apologies, dear sister. They keep us quite busy here, right, Lewis?"

Joseph's friend nodded in affirmation. He was skinny, with dark hair and brown eyes. He averted his eyes, as if too shy to make eye contact with Augusta.

"Augusta, Margaret, this is my good friend and roommate, Mr. Michael Lewis of Gettysburg, Pennsylvania." Joseph introduced his friend.

"A Yankee?" Margaret batted her blue eyes and tossed her black hair. "I didn't think you would befriend a Yankee, Joseph."

"Yankee or not, Michael here has gotten me out of more scrapes than I care to admit. He is smart, and fiercely loyal." Joseph looked at Augusta, then Margaret. "Michael, I am pleased to finally introduce you to my sister, Augusta Byron, and her best friend, a girl who has become like my younger sister, Miss Margaret Wiggs."

Only Augusta seemed to notice Margaret's slight stiffening at Joseph calling her a sister.

"Pleased to meet you both." Mr. Lewis said, still not meeting the girls' eyes. Augusta had to stifle a giggle. This man may have been the shyest man she had ever met....

"He always was shy." Charlotte agreed.

"He was. Is." Augusta grinned a bit wider. "Three years later, we went back to New York for Joseph's graduation. I almost didn't recognize Michael, he had grown up so much. Oh, he was still quiet and studious, but it now struck me as endearing. Granted," her smile dropped. "I wasn't so enamored with the smooth-talking men with the Southern charm anymore. I had learned my lesson. We danced and walked and I waited for him to kiss me, but he never made a move. I was a little disappointed, but I realized he was just shy and respectful. I agreed to write him. He was off to build things, my smart little engineer. I was able to visit him a couple more times, and I knew I was falling in love with him. My family approved, for the most part. My father and other brother, Andrew had liked Michael immensely, and he was one of Joseph's best friends."

"They weren't concerned about the whole "Yankee" thing?" Alex asked.

"They were." Augusta said. "But they knew what I wanted, and the men in my family could never tell me no. My mother died when I was born and they have always wanted to keep me happy." She smiled. "Joseph, of course, was completely in favor of the match. He was always getting into trouble and Michael was always getting him out of it." Augusta took a breath. "Anyways, Michael eventually got up the courage to ask Father permission to marry me, and Father said yes. We were married for a year before Sumter was fired on. I had been with Michael in Washington, and I stayed with him until after Manassas. Then he realized that it would be too dangerous for me to stay with him. I would have gone home to Carolina, but by then it was impossible. Not only traveling South, but my father and brothers were all in the Confederate Army. Father left the plantation in the care of his old overseer, who, even though he was old enough to be my grandfather, would always give me looks that would give me the shivers. With my mother and the men gone, I had no one to watch over me." She smiled. "But I am glad I am here. It has been wonderful getting to know all of you. You two and Ginny have become great friends."

Augusta paused, a puzzled look on her face. "I have a question for you both. I saw Abigail Williams in the store earlier and she made some comments about the Wades. I have heard gossip from her before and I usually ignore it, I realize people look down on the family, I assume because they're poor, but Abigail said that I shouldn't be friends with Ginny and that the Wades should be run out of town. Why is she so harsh to them? Does it have to do with the fact that Ginny's father isn't around? She never wants to talk about him. It seems like a sensitive matter."

"It is." Charlotte answered, then took a deep breath, thinking of where to begin. "Ginny's dad was a tailor. She grew up having to help support her family by doing housework and sewing for her father, and Mr. Skelley, Jack's dad. Jack is Ginny's beau, as you know. The Wades have never been wealthy, but they were able to make a living. About ten years ago, Mr. Wade's health started to get bad. Ginny, Georgia and Mrs. Wade had to do more work as seamstresses so they wouldn't lose their home. It was around that time that Mr. Wade was arrested. He took, I think $300 or so that Mr. Durborow, a man from town, had dropped. Mr. Wade knew who it belonged to, and knew it wasn't right to keep it, but he did. He was convicted of larceny and had to spend two years in a Philadelphia prison."

"That doesn't seem fair. Kind of harsh, actually." Augusta said. "How unfortunate."

"Well, that's not the last of it." Charlotte continued. "Two years later, he started acting strange. Mrs. Wade had the court declare him insane. He was sent to the poorhouse."

"What did he do to deserve that?" Augusta asked.

"Ginny has always been tight-lipped about that. She wouldn't even tell me. The only reason I didn't drag the information out of her was because I knew she was confiding in Jack, and also had her sister as a confidant. Since she had people to talk to and I assume that she would talk to me about it when she was ready, I let it go. However, I don't think that Mrs. Wade would have done something that drastic unless the family was in danger from him. I know my father never wanted me to go over there when he was there. Mr. Wade never did anything untoward when I was there, so I still visited, in spite of what Father said."

"Yes, I have noticed whenever you talk about your father, your respect for him is somewhat lacking. Or nonexistent." Augusta said. "What is the reasoning behind that?"

Charlotte organized her thoughts. "My father was born and raised in Virginia. He was the fourth and youngest son of a wealthy planter. As the fourth son, he had a lot of trouble fitting in and deciding what to do with his future. His oldest brother, Matthew, obviously took over the plantation. He lives near Fredericksburg with my Aunt Miriam and my cousins, James, Beth, Belle, Annie, Meri, Lainie and Max. My uncle Samuel took a West Point appointment and went into the military. He's fighting for the Union and his wife, my Aunt Susanna and cousins Jonah, Rebekah and Jacob are in Petersburg, Virginia, where Aunt Susanna's family is from. I believe Jonah and Jacob are fighting for the Confederacy. Uncle Charles, the third oldest went to Harvard Law school in Massachusetts and became a lawyer He's in Vicksburg Mississippi now with my Aunt Rachel and cousins Jason, Victoria, Gregory and Mary. My father wanted to be a planter, but it was my uncle Matthew who inherited Turner's Glenn, the family plantation. My uncle is a good man, though, and had my father help him with the plantation. I believe he would have given Father a share in the plantation, but Father wanted complete control. Father came to Gettysburg on business once and met my mother. He decided to stay here and help my grandfather, my mother's father, run his farm. Then, when grandpa Billings died, father took over. By then, he had married my mother."

"Well it sounds like your father isn't a bad man. Leaving a life of luxury to be a farmer in Pennsylvania."

"That's partially true. Like I said, my Uncle Matthew would have made sure Father always had an income and work." Charlotte agreed. "I am fairly certain that Father always wanted to prove that he could run a successful farm on his own and part of his marrying my mother was to show his family that he could do something on his own and that he didn't need them or their money. He had always been very interested in the farming aspect of the plantation. He was always upset about how his oldest brother got the whole plantation and he received nothing."

"Well, that's how it works in this world." Alex voiced her opinion. "My father had to branch away from the family business because of his order in the family as well."

"Yes. I think father always harbored jealous feelings toward his brothers. I think my father must have truly loved my mother, though. When I was six, my mother died. I can remember before that, my father was kind and loving. But after Mother died, he changed. He was bitter and unhappy. Folks around here say I remind him too much of my mother, and that pains him. Apparently she was the same height as I am now, with the same blue eyes and blonde hair. I had someone in the street, someone who had grown up with my mother and then moved away and she believed I was my mother. The woman hadn't heard my mother died and started talking to me as if I were her. That's how much I look like my mother."

"If you don't mind my asking, how did she die?" Augusta asked.

"She was with child. The baby came early. Neither survived. I can still remember hearing my mother screaming in pain that night."

"I'm sorry, Charlotte." Augusta, then felt it best to change the subject. "Is Ginny's father still in the ahh...asylum?"

"Yes, he is. I don't believe he will ever get out."

"That's too bad." Augusta said. "I like Ginny and her family. Her mom can be a little cold, but..." Augusta shrugged. "Hopefully, with a little prayer, their situation will improve."

September 19
Wade Home

"An estimated 2100 dead Union soldiers, and 2,000 Confederate." Charlotte shook her head in sorrow. A tear fell down her cheek as she handed Alex the paper. "Our Gettysburg boys may be bored, but at least they're not in the middle of all this fighting."

"That is true." Alex paused, reading. "18,000 Americans total wounded. Injured by other Americans." She sighed. "It hardly seems possible."

"Where did this battle take place?" Ginny asked from the table she was working at. Ginny and Charlotte were working together and Alex had stopped by to talk. She had brought the most recent issue of the *Gettysburg Times* with the report of the recent battle.

"In Maryland, near an Antietam Creek. The closest town is called Sharpsburg." Alex answered. "It has been called the bloodiest day of the war, and the bloodiest battle on American soil."

"Maryland. So their General Lee is trying to move the war north?" Charlotte asked.

"Yes, and our General McClellan doesn't seem to be doing much to stop him." Alex replied.

"Mother is quite worried." Ginny said. "The rebel army, getting so close."

"She has good reason to be worried." Charlotte said. "We all do."

"Alex, are you going to stay for dinner?" Ginny asked, stirring the stew she had on the stove.

"I would but I promised Augusta I would go and roll bandages with her."

"I like Augusta. She is very kind. Although now that I know her, it is even harder for me to believe that she would marry Michael Lewis. They seem like complete opposites." Charlotte smiled.

"Sometimes that's what works." Alex said. "I do need to get going. If you finish what you have here, come on by the schoolhouse. It is where the Ladies' Group is meeting. Hope to see you later!" Alex bounced off. Before she shut the door, Harry darted in.

"Charlotte!" He ran over and threw himself into her arms. "I missed you so much!" She kissed his hair.

"I missed you too." She smiled down at the boy. "I think you get bigger every time I come over."

"Well, not big enough." He sighed dramatically, as only an eight-year-old could. "I really wish I could be like Jack and go off and fight the Rebs."

Charlotte sighed. This war fever was still so strong. John Wade was continually telling her all about how anxious he was to sign up, along with Aaron Clark and all the other local boys, and now Harry.

"John mentioned the harvest is looking good this year." Ginny said.

Charlotte nodded. "Your brother's help has been invaluable. I don't know what I would do without him." She paused. "I wish the war would be over so my father would come home. Running the farm is not easy. So many decisions. I just don't know that I'm cut out for it."

"Well, you seem to be doing a fine job." Ginny nodded. "Have you heard from Thomas?"

"Yes, he writes. Father writes too. It's mostly checking up on the farm. From both of them. What do you hear from Jack?"

"Not as much as I would like. His letters can be strange. Sometimes, they sound as though he is losing interest in me. Others, it sounds as though he can't wait to come home to me. I keep fearing that one day, he'll wake up and realize that I am not good enough for him."

"Ginny, you are good enough. Jack is lucky to have you and your love. What makes him seem distant?"

"Well, for one thing, I write twice as many letters as I receive…"

"That's irrelevant. The mail system is unreliable. Honestly, he is probably sending twice as many letters as what you receive."

"I just get afraid. I'm sorry." Ginny wiped her eyes, tears had formed. "Things are…I just don't know."

Charlotte rose and hugged her. "It will be all right. Jack loves you. You know that. Don't let others bring you down and plant doubt in your mind. I know you have been doing that."

"I have, I know." Ginny pulled back from the hug. "I just cannot wait for this conflict to be over."

October 29
Lewis General Store

Charlotte placed a small sack of sugar in her basket and glanced over to find Augusta heading in her direction looking worried.

"Charlotte, did you walk into town all by yourself?" Her tone was stressed.

"Yes, I do it all the time." Charlotte paused.

"There is a war going on, Charlotte."

"I'm aware of that, Augusta."

Charlotte was puzzled. Augusta never acted like this. The Southerner took a deep breath.

"I'm sorry, Charlotte. It's just...everything is a jumble. We just received word from Michael's aunt and uncle over in Franklin County. They said that there have been some Confederate cavalry raids along the Southern Mountains and into their town. That's only twenty miles away. Some of those raiders got as far as Adams County. Those men steal all they can lay their hands on and they might take advantage of any women they meet up with. You're out there on that farm with no one to protect you." Tears welled in her eyes. "I'm sorry, I just get worried for you." She paused and took a deep breath. "And then, I haven't heard from Michael in weeks and..."

"Oh, Augusta, don't worry about me." Charlotte's stomach churned, as she put a comforting hand on her friend's shoulder. "Tell me, was anyone killed in the raiding?"

"No one was even hurt as far as I know." Augusta said. "It's just the idea that nothing stands in the way of the war. Like I said, Franklin is only 20 miles to the West. That's why we have to be careful. " She sighed. "Not only do we have the Southern Army to worry about, but there are also deserters from both sides. There aren't too many, but all it takes is one lonely deserter to decide to ...well...you know."

"Okay. I understand." Charlotte shuddered. She hated it every time she realized just how much the war had changed their lives and the way they lived. It was hard on them, even though they were far away from all of the battles. She couldn't help but wonder how people like her cousins Isabelle and Elizabeth were coping, being right in the middle of all the fighting. In Gettysburg, they just had the threat of violence; people in Fredericksburg and most of Virginia were in the thick of the fighting.

"Are you heading home after this?" Augusta asked.

121

"I am, by way of the post office. Would you like a walk? Talk?"

"Yes, just a moment." Augusta quickly told her mother-in-law where they were headed. Charlotte paid for her goods and they both headed out into the crisp autumn air. The colors of fall were all around them, and a light, cool breeze blew through Charlotte's shawl.

"Do you hear anything from home?" Charlotte asked.

"No." Augusta's voice cracked. "With the way mail is, I'm lucky to hear from Michael when I do. Getting letters from the south is nearly impossible." She paused. "What about you? Do you hear from Thomas or your father?"

"Too much from Thomas, once in a while from Father." Charlotte answered. "I'm glad to know that Thomas is safe. I just…I'm not too fond of the idea of marrying him, you know that, and he keeps pushing the matter." She spoke softly, not wanting anyone else to hear her.

"You shouldn't rush into marriage, that's true. I have had some friends who did that and they…" She trailed off, looking ahead. Two burly men stepped in front of them, blocking their path. Both girls recognized them right away. Augusta knew them as two troublemakers who had given her a hard time before in the store. Charlotte knew them to be two of the meanest drunkards in town.

"Well, well, well, our own little Southern belle." Garrett Sullivan chuckled at his rhyme. He used to work with Wesley at the harness shop, and other places but had always been fired for drunkenness and fighting. He could never hold any job. When the army had started calling for volunteers, Sullivan had made every excuse not to go to war. He was tall and muscular, with a full red beard and mustache. He was also known to have a mean temper.

"What'chu hear from your Reb family down there, gal?" Jedidiah Smoker, the second man, asked in a fake Southern drawl. Smoker was newer to town, and had quickly gained a reputation of a good-for-nothing who gambled and drank too much, he supposedly was supported by his wealthy family in New York City, but no one knew for sure. He was handsome, with black hair and a charming smile when he chose to bestow it. He had a tendency to act better than others.

"We don't want any trouble, sir. Just let us pass, please." Augusta spoke softly. She grabbed Charlotte's arm and tried to push past. Sullivan grabbed her other arm and spun her around.

"We weren't done talkin' quite yet, girl." He taunted.

"Let go of her!" Charlotte exclaimed, pushing his hands away. "She may be from the South but her husband is off fighting for the Union. That's a whole lot more than what you can say."

"Well you're no better, Miss Turner. You and your family is just a hotbed of Southern sympathizers." Sullivan said with a sneer.

"My father is loyal to the Union! He does more for the cause than you could even dream of doing." She grabbed Augusta's arm and pushed her way past the two oafs. Her arm was roughly pulled back.

"You might be just as bad as this Reb scum. Maybe worse." Sullivan's grimy hand tightly clenched her upper arm and he was so close that she could smell his stale breath. "She at least married a good Union boy. You go along, pretending to be all proper-like with Tom Culp, but some remember how close you used to be with his traitor of a cousin, Wesley. I bet you still hear from that boy. Maybe even writing to him behind Tom's back. Mebbie even more."

"I am doing nothing of the kind!" Charlotte said as she ripped her arm from his grasp. "And my relationship with Thomas or Wesley or any other man is none of your business." She turned and stormed away, Augusta right behind her. The men took two steps towards to follow them, but then thought better of that action, as a small crowd had gathered.

"So why didn't you defend yourself?" Charlotte asked Augusta as they walked briskly away.

"I didn't want to cause a scene. Besides, if I stopped and defended myself every time someone said something about my loyalty, I wouldn't have time to do much of anything else."

"This happens often?" Charlotte was surprised. Augusta was always so positive and upbeat, it was hard to believe she dealt often with that type of hostility.

"Often enough." Augusta sighed. "It's usually not as obvious as those two men. Usually, it's more subtle." The two girls walked into the post office.

"Why haven't you told anyone about it?" Charlotte asked after they had checked for mail. Mr. Lewis had gotten a correspondence, but neither of the girls had received anything.

"I can handle it myself." They exited and headed toward the Lewis home.

Charlotte shook her head. "Augusta you need to tell us about things like this."

"Charlotte, there's nothing you or anyone else can do about it." Charlotte could see the glistening of tears on her friend's face. She put her arm on her shoulder. "Mr. and Mrs. Lewis are well-respected members of the community. I can't bring them into this."

"That may be true, but you don't have to handle it alone. You do have some friends here, whether you think so or not. You don't need to go through everything alone."

"Thank you, Charlotte." Tears began to roll down her cheeks. "It's just, Michael's parents are very good to me, but I still miss him so much, and I'm so worried about the people I left at home."

Charlotte put both arms around Augusta and gave her a squeeze.

"You come and see me any time, Augusta. I know Alex and Ginny feel the same way. You're not alone."

"I will have to do that soon." Augusta smiled. "I need to hear more about this Wesley and what he is to you."

"Yes, well, that will be a story for another day."

November 12
Lewis Household

Aideen Lewis smiled at her daughter-in-law as she came down the stairs.

"Good morning, my dear. Did you sleep well?"

"As well as I usually do, thank you. Yourself?"

"Quite well, thank you."

"That's good to hear." Augusta helped herself to a cup of coffee, then poured her mother-in-law a fresh cup. She noticed that Aideen had started breakfast.

"Is there anything I can help you with for breakfast this morning?"

"No dear, that's fine. I know cooking isn't your greatest talent." She teased kindly.

"It's just that I had no need of cooking knowledge on the plantation." Augusta admitted.

"I'm not trying to make you feel inadequate, my dear. You are a wonderful young lady with many God-given talents. You are a wonderful help in the store, with your ability to help people and make them feel special. I believe most people in town have either forgotten you are from South Carolina or just don't care anymore."

"Most people. Not all." Augusta regretted the words right after she spoke them. Aideen stood, walked to the stove, and mixed the cornmeal mush that was cooking.

"Some folks still giving you trouble?" She asked.

"Not really. I just still get looks and occasionally, I hear whispers that I think are about me. I'm probably overreacting. It's probably nothing. I just get upset and worried sometimes."

"Have you prayed about it, my dear?" Aideen asked.

"Prayed?" Augusta had never even considered that. "No. I haven't. Do you think that's something...do you think that would work?"

"Well, prayer is more than just saying words, Augusta. It's believing and trusting that God has a plan and will always be there to help you. It's asking Him for help and guidance."

"I've never really thought about it. I mean, I enjoy going to Mass with you and I know there is a God, a Creator, but I never really thought about...talking with Him. Like in a...a relationship."

"A relationship is exactly what He wants to have with you, my dear." Aideen said with a smile.

"Now that I think about it, Michael has made similar comments to that effect. Even back before we were officially courting." She smiled. "I think he tried to make it his personal mission to convert my brother."

"Yes, Joseph. Your brother is a good friend to Michael. Have you heard from him?"

"No, not since before coming here. Letters are unreliable, as you know." A tear formed in Augusta's eye as she thought of home.

"That they are." Aideen noticed the homesick look in Augusta's eyes. "I am sure all of your family is okay. I remember you have another brother. How was he the last time you heard from him?"

"Good. He was running the plantation, but right now, he is in the Confederate army. Probably still madly in love with my oldest friend, Margaret, even though she wanted to marry Joseph. She ended up not really deserving either of them."

"Oh, dear. What happened to her? Who did she end up marrying?"

"Neither of my brothers." Augusta thought back to her former friend. "She married a local politician. Broke Andrew's heart."

"And she didn't marry Joseph?"

"No." Augusta hated thinking about how Margaret, a girl she thought was her best friend, had used her, then discarded her…

June 1857
Byron Hill Plantation

"I am so excited to see Joseph." Augusta said, patting her hair. "I cannot believe he has been gone for four years."

"I cannot believe it either." Margaret said, checking her perfect reflection in the mirror. "Maybe now, he will be willing to settle down with me."

Augusta sat on her bed and looked at her friend. "Margaret, it has recently come to my attention that...well, I found out that..."

"Does Joseph have another girl?" Margaret spun around.

"No, I don't think Joseph is ready to settle down at all. Not yet."

"That's too bad." Margaret looked at her friend. "You see, I just....can I confide in you about something?"

"Of course."

Margaret sat on the bed and turned to face her friend. "Father said things are not going well with our family finances. Apparently, he made some poor investments. He needs me to marry, and soon."

"Well, then Joseph is not your man, not if that's your goal. He's not ready to settle down and he is never going to be terribly wealthy."

"Wealth isn't the most important thing. Prestige and power can be good as well, and he will surely get that as an officer."

"That may be true."

"Could you talk to him, Augusta?" Tears appeared in Margaret's eyes. "I need a husband. If I don't, father is likely to arrange a marriage for me."

"I honestly don't know about Joseph. But, Margaret...how do you feel...I mean...what about Andrew?"

"Andrew? He's nice enough, I suppose. A little boring and stuffy, but he's handsome. Why do you ask?"

"I recently learned that Andrew has had feelings for you for years. He just never thought you were ready for marriage. If I were to tell him that you are, well, I'm sure he would speak to your father, maybe even make an offer for your hand."

"Would he, now?" Margaret smiled. "That just might work."

"That's sad, how she could switch from one man to another so easily." Aideen said.

"Well, it was how we were raised to look at marriages. Affection may be a nice addition, but a good match is more important than affection."

"But she didn't end up with either Joseph or Andrew."

"No, she didn't. She actually saved me and my future happiness, even though she didn't know it, nor intend to do it."

"That sounds cryptic. You must explain more, my dear."

"You must remember that I was a different girl back then. I was being courted by a politician, Jeffrey Cullen. He was tall, blonde and smooth talking. Fresh out of law school. Full of promise and everyone said that he would be well-placed in the South Carolina government. In fact, I believe he might now be an aide to Jefferson Davis himself. Anyways, we were having a reception honoring Joseph and his four years of success at West Point. Michael was there as well, visiting. At one point that evening, I went into my father's study to get away from the crowd. I was sitting when the door opened and in came Margaret and Jeffrey, kissing. Apparently, they had been introduced, and she realized that Jeffrey could be a better catch for her than either of my brothers. As for Jeffrey, Margaret's father had better connections in South Carolina politics than our Father did. It was a better match for both of them. I was heartbroken. Margaret had been my closest friend. And I really liked Jeffrey and enjoyed his company. I saw a future with him." Augusta glanced up at Aideen. "I'm sorry. I suppose its strange hearing about my past. My suitor before Michael."

"It's quite all right, my dear."

"But that night, Michael found me, crying in the garden. I had fled there after seeing Jeffrey and Margaret. Michael comforted me. Listened to me. He was so kind, such a gentleman. Such a good friend. At the time, I had no thoughts of him other than a friend and confidant."

"He was very taken with you from the moment he met you Augusta. He knew that he had to become your friend first. He always had faith that things would work out. That things happen for a reason."

"Do you believe that?" Augusta asked.

"Yes, I do. Consider what you just told me. Knowing Margaret and Jeffrey Cullen helped shape you, helped make you who you are. If you hadn't been through that heartbreak, you may not have gotten to know Michael in the way that you did. And you may never have had the opportunity to fall in love with him. The book of Jeremiah says

'For I know well the plans I have in mind for you, says the Lord, plans for your welfare and not for woe, so as to give you a future of hope.' God has a plan. He knows what He is doing. We just have to have faith."

December 16
Lewis General Store

Ginny walked briskly through town, her destination and mission foremost in her mind. She finally reached the store and pulled the door closed behind her.

"Oh, blessed warmth!" She smiled at Augusta, who was wiping down the front counter. Her eyes were red and swollen.

"Augusta! What happened?"

"There has been another battle, a big one. In Virginia." Augusta took a deep breath. "Michael's regiment was part of the fighting. I haven't heard from him in months. It has made me a little weepy. I apologize."

"No apology is needed." Ginny replied. Both girls looked up to see Charlotte walk in. She waved and headed to them.

"Hello," Charlotte said. "What is new?"

"There has been another big battle." Ginny said, picking up the paper on the counter. "In...Fredericksburg, Virginia."

"What!" Charlotte exclaimed, tearing the paper from Ginny's hand. "I have family there, my cousins, Isabelle, Annabeth...." Charlotte quickly scanned the paper. "No civilian casualties were listed, but it doesn't say that there weren't any."

"How many casualties this time?" Ginny asked.

"Around 1,300 dead, 9,600 wounded and 1,800 missing or captured from the Union side. The Confederate lost around 600, 4,000 wounded and 700 missing." Augusta said. "But those are just estimates. It could be worse. It could change. It didn't say if the Gettysburg regiment was there."

Charlotte put down the paper and leaned against the counter. "I just can't believe it. I have been there. My cousins must have been in the middle of the fighting. Their home is so close to the city. I pray to heaven they are safe and that their home is not destroyed. How can you rebuild after all the destruction?"

Augusta spoke up glumly. "I don't think you can."

Ginny set her cloak on the counter. The movement caused the sleeve of her calico dress to pull up, exposing her wrist. Charlotte immediately noticed a dark bruising around the wrist.

"Ginny, what happened?" Charlotte asked. Ginny quickly pulled the sleeve down.

"It's nothing. John and I were playing around and it got a little rougher than we anticipated."

"Oh." Charlotte said, wanting to ask further questions, but was stopped when Abigail Williams and her mother came into the store.

"Well, hello ladies." Abigail said, approaching them. "Charlotte, it's so good to actually see you out and about. You've been cooped up at your farm for so long. Augusta, I do hope no one blames this newest Union loss on you." Then, completely ignoring Ginny, Abigail turned and went to go look at the fabric that was in stock.

"Does she ever stop and realize how impolite she really is?" Augusta said.

"I've known her for too long. And I don't think she cares." Charlotte replied, then turned back to Ginny.

"Are you sure you're okay? John didn't say anything about that injury."

"He felt bad about it when it happened. He probably didn't want to bring it up again." Ginny shrugged. "So when was the last time you heard from your family down there?" She asked Charlotte.

"Before the war." Charlotte sighed. "I can't believe they were in the middle of a battle. I don't know...how can they get through that? With all of that destruction, how can you recover?"

"Well, we can pray for them. Hopefully, we'll never have to find out ourselves." Augusta said.

December 24
The Lewis Home

Augusta put the finishing touches on the table she had set for Christmas Eve dinner. Michael's parents were in Philadelphia and had asked her to join them, but she had already invited Alex, Ginny and Charlotte for the evening and didn't want to break those plans. Christmas would be even less extravagant this year. The Confederate Army had been steadily moving north, as was evidenced by the battle of Fredericksburg. Food and other goods were not as easy to get, and many people were more concerned with their family members at war and surviving than celebrating the holiday.

Two knocks on the door caused Augusta to turn as Alex walked in.

"Alex! Welcome. How are you this wonderful Christmas evening?" Augusta ushered Alex into the parlor and they sat down.

"The same as usual. Missing Will. Trying to keep busy so I don't think of how much I miss Will all the time."

"I understand how that goes."

"I wish I would hear from him soon. I believe he will be okay, that the Lord will watch over him. But...I just think about those whose loved ones will never be coming home. Those wives, mothers, daughters, they prayed for their men. But they still died. It's just...hard."

"It is. Very hard. But...Michael once told me that we have to have faith no matter what. Even if he is...if he doesn't make it, he still needs me to have faith that God has a plan. I didn't think about it much at the time. At least didn't think about it too hard. But Michael's mother, she has been very comforting. Her strength is unbelievable. And her faith is so strong. It has been very helpful to me."

Alex nodded. "This war is strongly testing our faith." She looked at the clock. "Charlotte and Ginny should be here soon. Do you need any help with last minute preparations?"

Augusta smiled. "No. Not only has Mrs. Lewis been helping me with my faith, but she has also been helping me with my domestic skills. I am quite proud of what I have done."

"It sure smells good!"

Down the road, Charlotte and Ginny walked to the Lewis's. A light snow was falling, and it was late enough in the year that it was already dark. The street lamps glowed, showing the way. Instead of wagon wheels creaking, there was the soft sound of bells ringing from passing wagons.

"I keep hoping that Georgia will come home with the news that I am going to be an aunt. It would be so nice to have a baby around." Ginny told Charlotte.

"Well, John was home, what, a month ago?" Charlotte asked, her breath a white cloud in the crisp air. "Maybe you'll get your wish sooner than you think."

"I really believe that Georgia will be a good mother."

"I agree. And you will be a good aunt. And a good wife and mother someday."

"Do you think so?" Ginny asked. "I hope so." She sighed and looked longingly in the direction of the Skelley home. "I cannot wait until Jack comes home and we get married. There are many times I wish we would have said our vows before he left." Ginny paused. "What about you? Have you decided anything with Thomas?"

"There are times when I can see myself with Thomas. It could be an easy life. I know how to be a farmer's wife. I believe he would treat me well. He is a likable enough man. The problem is, I don't love him and don't think I ever will. There are times when I don't think I am the type of woman he really wants to marry. Sometimes I have this feeling that if I settle for what is easy, with Thomas, then someone that I really could fall deeply in love with, would come along and I would miss a chance at a life with true love." She paused. "Sometimes I wonder if I could even have that with Wesley. I do miss him. The talks we would have, his sense of humor."

"You and Wes." Ginny smiled knowingly. "I can see it."

"Yes, and then you can marry Jack and we can have children who will be best friends, and we can own land next to each other."

"That would be ideal." Ginny smiled.

"I wonder what Jack and Wesley would say about all our plans?"

"They know us well enough. They'll most likely expect it."

They reached Augusta's house laughing, their cheeks pink with the cold. A wreath hung on the door, and garland had been twisted around the porch railing. Augusta had really dressed the house up for the holidays.

"Hello, Ladies!" Augusta's smiling face greeted them after they had knocked on the door. "Alex is already here. Dinner should be ready soon. Come on in!"

133

The inside of the house was as decorative as the outside. A fire was blazing, and the mantle and table had been decorated with homemade pine bundles. The smell of roast chicken permeated from the kitchen.

"Charlotte, Ginny!" Alex rose from the chair she had been lounging in. They each hugged one another. With the weather being so cold, it had been a while since they had all been together.

They discussed mundane things, the weather, the latest gossip in town, but tried to stay away from the topic that was really first in their minds: the war. Everyone helped Augusta put the meal on. It was a simple affair, a small roast chicken, some boiled potatoes, biscuits, gravy, beans and cider. After saying Grace, Augusta apologized for the simplicity.

"I know it's not much, but it's the best I could do."

"Augusta, it's wonderful." Charlotte bit into a flaky biscuit.

"Really, it's the best thing to just be together." Alex said. "There is no place I would rather be right now." She glanced down at her wedding ring. "Well, except for with my husband."

"I agree." Ginny added.

"Besides, there are so many people, like my cousin down in Fredericksburg, who have so much less." Charlotte said.

"That battle was disastrous for the Union. We lost over 12,600 men, while the Confederates only lost 5,000." Alex said.

"Only 5,000?" Charlotte asked. "I understand that it is significantly less than the Union losses, but that is still 5,000 men. Men who were fathers, husbands and sons."

"That is true." Alex said. "At least the battles are staying in the south."

Augusta stood and checked in the oven, making sure there was enough wood to keep the fire going and the room warm.

"Everyone in town is talking about how we might be the next town to be invaded." Ginny said. "Prices are going up constantly."

"It's tough for the storekeepers to get meat, spices and other things that we took for granted before the war." Augusta said, sitting back down.

"So many families are struggling." Charlotte said.

"Yes, and our boys. I wonder what they're eating tonight." Ginny spoke softly.

"I don't like thinking about it." Alex admitted. Her usual smile had disappeared, replaced by a look of sorrow and longing. "Just imagining how Will is out there, cold and hungry. I just want him to be warm and safe."

"Has anyone heard from any of the soldiers lately?" Augusta asked, her voice cracking, trying desperately not to cry.

"Other than John visiting Georgia not long ago, no." Ginny said.

The other two all shook their heads.

"Rumors are that General Lee wants to invade the North. Maybe some of the troops will get close enough to Gettysburg and they can visit." Alex said hopefully.

"I would rather not see Michael until this war is over, rather than have him here because there is a battle nearby, or any battle, really." Augusta continued to hold her emotions, but her fear was apparent.

"I agree." Ginny nodded. "I just want this war to be over and have Jack back home."

"It's what we all want." Alex agreed, her voice choked with tears.

Augusta quickly rose from the table and walked briskly into the kitchen, tears in her eyes. Alex bowed her head, hands covering her face, and her shoulders began to shake. Charlotte followed Augusta into the kitchen while Ginny slid over to Alex and put her arms around her.

Augusta was hunched over the water basin, hands gripping the sides. Her hair covered her face and her shoulders hitched with sobs. Charlotte crossed the room and placed a hand on her back, rubbing back and forth.

"It's almost too much to bear sometimes." She spoke softly, not looking up. "I knew it would be hard, I knew it, but…"

"I know." Charlotte wasn't quite sure what to say to her. "I never really knew Michael, but I do know that he is a good man, with strong faith. He'll be fine."

"I miss him so much, Charlotte. But it's not just that." She looked up, shaking her head. "People hate me. You saw that. They're going to hate Michael when he comes back because he married me. There will be a division between the North and South that will last long after the war is over. There will still be hate. Why does there have to be so much hatred?"

"I don't know, Augusta." Charlotte murmured, then thought of her feelings for Wesley. "At least no one here in town wants to kill the man you love."

She let out a sarcastic laugh. "Maybe not the man I love, but they are hell-bent on killing my brothers and friends." She paused. "I'm sorry, that was improper. I suppose you do know how I feel, more than most."

Charlotte shrugged. "My father is from the South, not me. Not that there's anything wrong with being Southern." She quickly said. "And while I do have family that I care for down in Virginia, I mainly worry about Wesley." Augusta turned around and leaned against the basin.

"You love him, don't you?" She asked, wiping the tears from her cheeks with the palm of her hand. Charlotte nodded. "And your feelings toward Thomas?" Augusta asked, a bit hesitantly.

"I don't love him. He has many good qualities, but I don't love him." Charlotte confessed. "When Wesley left, I was miserable. It was a tough time. Thomas was around a lot, working for my father, and my father approves of him...he is just not for me!" Tears fell down her face. Augusta pulled her into a hug. They were both crying. After a few moments, they finally pulled apart.

"I'll bet my dinner is all cold by now. I am such a poor hostess." Augusta said.

"No, you're not. Besides, I'm not hungry anymore anyways." Charlotte admitted. They headed back into the dining room. Alex had pulled herself together by then, and was laughing at something Ginny had said.

"You know what I feel like right now?" Charlotte asked. "Christmas Carols." She pulled Augusta to the piano and looked at Alex. "Come on, Mrs. Sadler. Let's hear you play!" Playing music always put Alex in a good mood, and they all loved singing. Augusta had one of the most powerful beautiful voices in the town. Alex smiled and quickly obliged. They started with an upbeat "Here We Come a Wassailing", and the mood quickly lightened. That was followed by "Deck the Halls". After that, Alex flowed into her favorite Christmas song, "Silent Night".

As the girls sang and looked around at each other, they felt a little more peaceful. War was raging. The loves of their lives were probably hungry and cold and they might never see them again. But they had friends. They could help each other through whatever came their way. As Alex continued to play song after song about peace on earth and goodwill to all men, there was a knock on the door. Augusta hastened to answer. Her heart beat wildly as thoughts flew through her head about who it could be. At the door was a man, a soldier, his head bent low and covered with his hat. His dirty blonde hair was long and shaggy, hanging in waves around his face. In spite of the unkempt look, she knew in a second who it was.

"Michael!" Augusta yelled, jumping into the man's arms. He held her tightly and his lips were on hers in a second. He had lost weight since she had last seen him, but was still solid. She ran her hands over his body, checking for wounds.

"Yes, Augusta, I'm here, I'm whole." He murmured, framing her face with his hands and touching his forehead to hers.

Augusta quickly remembered that the others were there. She pulled away reluctantly, her cheeks flushed and breath heaving. She didn't let her husband go. It was too much to believe he was actually there, with her.

"What are you doing here?" Augusta whispered, stroking her husband's face. It was dirty, and covered in scrapes and he hadn't shaved in what seemed like months.

"My commanding officer gave me and a couple of others leave, so I got here as soon as I could." He smiled brilliantly and stepped into the house. Augusta's hand slid down his arm and she pulled him into the room and shut the door.

"Oh, Michael, here are the girls I have been writing to you about. You might remember Charlotte Turner and Ginny Wade."

"I remember you as young girls, but you're all grown up now." He spoke with a smile.

"Hello." Ginny said, smiling.

"You've grown up too." Charlotte said.

"And this is Alexandria Clark Sadler." Augusta continued. Alex stood from behind the piano bench and curtsied. Michael nodded at her.

"I know of your father. He is a brilliant man." Michael nodded at Alex. "I feel as though I know all of you through Augusta's letters. I thank you all for being so supportive of her."

"Has anyone else from the Gettysburg area returned home for the holidays?" Ginny asked hopefully.

"No." Michael shook his head. "I was lucky. I volunteered for a scouting mission earlier in the month and was rewarded with leave. To be honest, since I'm with the engineers, I rarely see the other

Pennsylvania boys. I'll occasionally meet up with them when I ride with the cavalry, but that's a rarity."

"Oh." Ginny nodded, the disappointment apparent in her face.

"However, I did run into the 87th a month or so ago. Who in particular were you worried about? I spoke with Thomas Culp, who told me of his engagement to you, Miss Turner." He nodded politely to her. "Congratulations." His voice was soothing, Charlotte felt he could read straight from the almanac and she could listen for days.

"Yes." Charlotte answered, struggling not to roll her eyes.

"Did you see Jack Skelley?" Ginny asked.

"I did. Jack looked well, just homesick, a little thinner, like everyone else."

Augusta continued to look at her husband with such longing; it suddenly hit Charlotte how intrusive they were being.

"Well, Michael, it has been wonderful seeing you again. It is getting late though, so we should be going." Charlotte walked towards the door to grab her cloak, Ginny and Alex right behind her. Augusta followed. "I am sorry to cut the evening short. Thank you for understanding."

"Are you okay with cleaning up yourself?" Ginny asked.

"Yes, of course. Thank you for offering, though." Augusta smiled.

"Have a great evening, enjoy the time with your husband." Charlotte grinned.

"It was good seeing you, Michael!" Ginny called over Augusta's shoulder. "Merry Christmas!" The three walked out the door into the crisp evening air. Light snowflakes fell from the sky as Augusta shut the door behind them. She turned to Michael, eyes full of happy tears, and threw herself into his arms.

"Michael, Michael, Michael. I am so glad you're here."

"I am too." He held her tight. "Merry Christmas, Augusta."

Part Three:

1863

January 3
Clark Home

Ginny, Charlotte and Augusta walked up the front steps of Alex's house, carrying small sewing projects. Alex had invited them over for dinner and then time after for visiting and sewing. When Alex opened the door, she smiled sheepishly. The front room smelled faintly of burned food.

"What happened in here?" Charlotte smiled.

"Well, I tried to cook a roast, but it didn't quite work out. Luckily, mother was able to get us some ham. I hope no one minds sandwiches."

"I love ham sandwiches." Ginny smiled.

"Wonderful." Alex said, leading them into the dining room. They sat down and, after prayer, began passing food around.

"Where are your parents tonight, Alex?"

"They are having dinner with another professor and his family. That's why I thought tonight would be a good night to get together. I liked how we did that at Christmas and wish we could do it more often."

"It's a great idea." Charlotte said. "I haven't been to town since that night."

"And so much has happened since then." Ginny said.

"Yes, Alex, what's your take on this Emancipation Proclamation?" Ginny asked. "We briefly discussed it on the way over, but I'm not sure I understand everything about it."

"Well, it is a difficult document to understand." Alex said.

"I thought it was pretty simple." Charlotte said. "Lincoln freed the slaves in the South. He's also turned the war into a fight to end slavery, not just to end the Southern rebellion."

"Well, you're right about that last part, Charlotte. Lincoln has added slavery to the reason the Union is fighting. But it is more complex than that. Lincoln isn't really freeing any slaves. He's basically made a statement saying that the slaves from the ten states in rebellion are free. Delaware, Kentucky, Maryland and Missouri, states that remained in the Union, aren't affected by the Proclamation."

"Lincoln doesn't want to alienate them and push them to secede as well." Charlotte commented.

"Exactly." Alex said, pausing to take a sip of the wine she had persuaded her mother and father to bring up from her father's wine cellar. "And since the Confederate states believe that they are their own country, they don't believe that they need to follow any law or decree that Lincoln sends out."

"So it really didn't do much of anything?" Ginny asked.

"Not the way I see it." Alex replied. "And to add to things, Lincoln recently admitted the Northwestern part of Virginia, the part that broke away from Virginia, Lincoln brought that part to the Union as a new state. Many people believe that's unconstitutional, and many Southerners are upset that Lincoln admitted West Virginia with the condition that they abolish slavery.

"So many politics." Ginny commented.

"Yes, politics play a big role in this war. All wars, really."

"I'm so glad you're so knowledgeable, Alex. It really helps me understand what's going on." Ginny said.

"I'm glad you feel that way. There have been times when I couldn't always speak my mind or show my knowledge. It's off-putting to some people. Men and women."

"What does Will think about it?"

"He is actually the one man who I have never had to hide it from. He actually likes that about me. He encourages me to read and discuss things with him. It's one of the things that he says he loves about me. And I love that he appreciates it." She paused. "I just hope he stays safe. That they can all stay safe."

"And that the war will end soon." Ginny agreed.

February 6
Clark Home

"I get so sick of people picking on the Wades because of their family history!" Charlotte muttered, bursting into Alex's kitchen. Alex looked up from the scarf she was knitting.

"What did Abigail say this time?" Alex asked knowingly.

"It wasn't just Abigail, she had young Tillie Pierce with her too." Charlotte sat down, her anger apparent. "They brought up last year, back when The Wades were taking in mending and work from the New York Division"

Alex looked down at her folded hands, unsure if she should ask the question that had crept into her mind.

"What's wrong?" Charlotte asked,

"Has Ginny ever mentioned anything to you about a Dutchman?" Alex asked.

"Dutchman?" Charlotte was puzzled. "What do you mean?"

"I'm not exactly sure what I mean. I just have bits and pieces from what Harry told me when I was helping at school. When I asked Ginny about it, she told me it was nothing and not to worry about it."

Charlotte sat down. "She can be so secretive sometimes. What happened?"

"Do you remember back in December, when Ginny had those bruises? She claimed they were from John."

"I remember." Charlotte said.

"According to Harry, Mrs. Wade gave her those bruises. She actually hit Ginny. One of the men belonging to the militia apparently took a fancy to Ginny. He spent a lot of time there with the family. Harry said the man even gave Ginny some jewelry, but she wanted nothing to do with him, so she broke it all. Harry said something about the Dutchman giving money to Mrs. Wade if she kicked Ginny out of the house. I'm not sure if Mrs. Wade did or not, but Ginny went to stay with Georgia until things calmed down. It was all confusing and Harry only knew bits and pieces."

"The Wades are very private when it comes to some things. Ginny is one of my best friends and yet there are some things that she refuses to discuss with me. I remember her staying with Georgia, but I thought..." She trailed off.

"When I talked to her, she made me swear not to say anything to anyone about what I already knew."

141

"But still...you're just telling me now?" Charlotte was hurt and felt a little left out.

"She especially didn't want you to know. She said something about a Billy Holtzworth and not wanting to repeat something." Alex shrugged.

"Billy..." Charlotte's mind flew through the many encounters she and Ginny had with Billy growing up. He was a friendly boy from town who got on well with Jack and Wesley. Sometimes, he was too friendly.

"I need to go see her." Charlotte stood. "Come, I will tell you what I know on the way."

"Good." Alex put her knitting down, then grabbed her forest green cloak and knit gloves.

As they walked, Charlotte talked. "When we were younger, maybe thirteen or so, Billy kissed Ginny when she didn't want him to. She was going to tell Jack, but didn't want him to overreact, so she told me. Well, as you know, I have a temper, I just keep it hidden for the most part. I wanted to go after Billy for hurting Ginny, but she and Wesley stopped me. I still don't think that Jack knows what happened. So if she said she didn't want a repeat of that event, the Dutchman must have forced himself on her. She didn't want me to go after him."

"Would you have? You can clearly hold your temper better now."

"I lose my temper when my friends are threatened. If this man hurt Ginny..."

The girls had reached the Wade house. Charlotte didn't knock, she just walked in. Ginny looked up and smiled, her hands covered in bread dough. The smile turned tentative and she saw the expression on Charlotte's face.

"Ginny, where is everyone?" Charlotte asked.

"Sammy is working and Harry is running errands with Mother. Isaac is napping. Why?"

"We need to talk to you. Alone." Charlotte leaned against the table. "Ginny, who is the Dutchman?"

"Wha-what? Who told you?" Ginny sent a betrayed look toward Alex. "Why did you tell her?"

"It just came up, Ginny. She needed to know." Alex defended herself.

"Well, it doesn't matter. He's gone. Out of our lives. He told mother he would come back and marry her, but I am sure it was a lie.

He did write Mother some letters, but I burned them before she could see them. I will do everything I can to keep him away."

"Who was he?" Charlotte persisted.

"He was part of the militia. He was a substitute for Will Tutor, you know Mr. Tutor. He started coming around after we did some mending for him. Mother liked the attention, but he always made me feel uncomfortable. Nervous. He was older, almost Mother's age. I never liked him coming around. He tried giving me jewelry. I didn't accept it. Mother punished me for it. In her eyes, that man could do no wrong. He even tried to get Mother to kick me out of the house. He wanted me out and alone, maybe thinking I would go to him for help." She shook her head. "Little did he know that I would have gone to anyone, even Abigail Williams or old man John Burns before I would go to him."

"Did he hurt you? Who else knows?"

"Mother, of course. I did tell Jack some of the story in a letter. Jack's sister, Nell knows bits and pieces. As for him hurting me..." Ginny looked at her dough-covered hands. "He tried. The one time Mother wasn't home, he almost did, but...John stood up to him and stopped him."

"Why didn't your mother do anything?" Alex asked.

"Mother never believed me. He only tried things when she wasn't around. She didn't believe John either. The Dutchman could be very persuasive." Ginny sighed. "Charlotte, I know you're upset that I didn't tell you. But the man was dangerous. I know you, you would have tried to step in and maybe have gotten hurt yourself. You know you can lose your head when your friends are threatened."

"And yet you have a hard time defending yourself." Alex said thoughtfully.

Charlotte looked over at Alex. "What is that supposed to mean?"

"I mean you are a strong and confident young woman in some circumstances, but not in others. For example, you will stand up for your friends without hesitation. But if it comes to something between you and your father and what he wants, you don't say anything."

"When did this conversation become about me?" Charlotte asked.

"It was just an observation." Alex said.

"But a true one." Ginny agreed.

"Yes it may be true. I'm not sure why." Charlotte sighed. "He's my father, it's hard to stand up to him." She looked at her two friends. "I suppose we all have our problems, our weaknesses."

"Oh, not me." Alex said with a smug smile on her face.

"Oh, you want us to discuss your weaknesses now?" Charlotte asked with a smile.

"I don't have any."

"You do have a weakness." Charlotte said. "And it is a man by the name of Will Sadler."

"How is Will a weakness?"

"He's a weakness because you would do anything for him."

"Well, that is true." Alex paused, getting somber. "And I suppose it's a weakness that I know that if anything ever happened to him...I...I just don't know how I would go on without him."

Ginny spoke, "God willing, we will never have to find out."

April 23

"Michael;

Things are very much the same here as they have been. Work, news of the war and its effects, and worry for you. We have heard reports from Richmond of women and children starving. One of the latest reports said that some women formed a mob and attacked a supply wagon. Those poor souls!

Just over the wire came the news that President Lincoln has brought a new state into the Union: the northwestern part of Virginia will now be known as West Virginia. I am sure you have heard that news.

Michael, there has never been a time during this war that I have wanted to see you more than I do right now. I have so much I want to share with you. First and foremost, I need to tell you: as wonderful as your Christmas visit was, something even more wonderful has come from it. You are going to be a father..."

Augusta looked at the words she had written, then tried to imagine Michael's face when he learned the news. She wanted to tell him as soon as possible, but also wanted to see his face when he found out. But would he live to see his child? She bit her lip as she thought about her options. As she thought, her mother-in-law walked into the study and noticed Augusta's contemplative look.

"You look puzzled, my dear girl." She said, sitting across the desk from her.

"I am. I am writing to Michael and am trying to decide how to tell him something. I am not sure how to word it or if I should even tell him in a letter."

"I see." Mrs. Lewis took a long, knowing look at Augusta. "This wouldn't have anything to do with your sickness in the mornings, your appetite change, and the slight change in your figure?"

Augusta's head shot up and she looked into Mrs. Lewis's smiling face. "You know?"

"A mother knows. It would be hard for me not to at least suspect. A new life in all of this terrible tragedy is a blessing from God indeed. I have been praying for something like this. God did not disappoint."

"Oh, Mrs. Lewis. I'm sorry I didn't tell you. I just didn't know the best way to say it and I wanted Michael to know first, but now I realize that cannot be the case." She paused. "I don't know if I even want to tell him in a letter or wait until I see him."

"The news would do Michael good." Mrs. Lewis said. "But I can see your dilemma."

"What would you do, if you were in my position?"

Mrs. Lewis thought for a moment. "I would wait." She finally said. "When Michael finds out, you two should be together. I know that's what I would have done, had I been in that situation."

Augusta stood and rounded the desk that separated her from her mother-in-law and threw her arms around her.

"Thank you. That is what I was thinking. I just want to let him know."

"That's understandable, my dear." Mrs. Lewis hugged her back. "He will be back soon and you will be able to tell him. I can feel it in my soul."

May 12
Turner Farm

Charlotte looked out across her fields. She and John Wade had been hard at work, planting. It was going to be a smaller harvest than last year. In spite of her best efforts, Charlotte had not been nearly as successful getting everything harvested and sold last year. It was too much.

"Where is that boy?" Charlotte moved her gaze to the road that led into town. She finally saw John's form racing up the road. Charlotte met him at the gate. He was breathing heavily.

"Sorry I'm later than usual. I just got a whole bunch of news."

"Well, come in and get some water and tell me what happened." Charlotte said, pulling him in.

"Well, you heard about the latest battle, right? Chancellorsville?"

"Yes, that was a week or so ago." The battle had led to another Union defeat and 17,197 casualties for the North.

"Well, the latest news is that the Reb general, Stonewall Jackson was shot and killed."

"Jackson? I have heard of him. He was one of their best soldiers."

"He was good." John agreed. "But he was wounded by friendly fire from his own men, the night after the battle. They say he had his arm amputated and then died of pneumonia. Sad as it may be to say, but this can only help us."

"I heard Jackson was a good, religious man." Charlotte recalled.

"That may be true. The last rumors I heard was that Lee wants to move his army north."

"That has been said before, John. The farthest north they've gotten was Sharpsburg." Charlotte pointed out.

"I know, but Lee is a good soldier. If he wants something, he'll stop at nothing to do it and one of these times, the Rebs may make it up here."

"Well, if they ever make it up here, God help us."

"There is one more thing I need to tell you." John said.

"And what is that?" Charlotte asked, her stomach turned.

"I'm signing up. I'm seventeen now. I am going to enlist in Company B of the 21ˢᵗ Cavalry Regiment. I am going to be a bugler. That's where they need me"

"I see." Charlotte tried not to cry. She wasn't upset about losing her farm hand, but she felt as though she was losing a brother. "When do you leave?"

"I won't officially enlist until the end of June. I want to make sure I take care of things here and at home."

Charlotte stood and put her arms around John. "I will miss you so much. You are invaluable, not just to this farm, but to me. You're like family. The brother I never had."

"I care about you too, Charlotte." John hugged her back. "But you will have to put up with my working here for another month and a half. Let's get to work!"

June 10

"My Dearest Will,

Aaron has left. He went to join the Union Army. He left for Philadelphia yesterday morning, instead of going to his classes. Mother is sick with worry and father is furious. Being home is not pleasant right now. I feel if I do or say anything wrong, Father will yell and Mother will burst into tears. Everything is so tense right now. It's the same with the town. Rumors are flying that the Rebels are going to attack nearby.

As I say with every letter, I miss you. I wish you were here. My days seem so tedious without you here. I can't remember what I did with my time before I met you. I suppose you could say that my life truly started when you entered it.

I received your letter dated May 31. It is such a joy to hear from you. To know that you are safe, even if you are bored. I was so glad to hear that you survived your bout of dysentery. So many other men have not.

I pray every night that the Lord will bring you home safe, and soon.

With all my love,
Allie"

St. James Lutheran Church

"The paper says there was another battle, at Brandy Station in Virginia. The Confederates seem to be moving north." Alex said to Charlotte and Augusta. The three were helping the war effort. Ginny had not been able to make it.

"How many casualties this time?" Charlotte asked, placing the bandage she had just rolled in a box.

"1450 total. Only 81 Union men died." Alex replied.

"Only 81 died! How can you be okay with 'only 81' dying?" Augusta snapped, which was uncharacteristic of her. "Even one man dying is a tragedy. Every one of those 81 men had a family. They had friends. They had a story. They had hopes and dreams." Tears rolled down her face. "Michael is one person. One man. To the army, he's just another soldier. But to me? He's my whole world."

Alex moved to hug Augusta. "I'm sorry. I didn't mean it that way. I feel the same way with Will and my brother. Sometimes, I don't know how I can survive another day without Will."

Augusta placed a hand on her slightly rounded stomach. She had been so excited to share the news of her new baby with her friends. "There are days when I wonder if Michael will ever see this child. I haven't heard from him since he was home for Christmas. I suppose there is comfort in the fact that if he doesn't come home, I will have a part of him with me always in the baby. But I can't handle the fact that I might not see him again."

"Have you told Michael about the child?" Charlotte asked.

"Not yet." Augusta sighed. "I want to. But I don't want him worrying about me. I don't want him distracted. I want him to focus on his job so he can get home safely. Besides, I have thought of all the different ways to tell him in a letter, but I can't figure out any good ones. I feel like this is something I need to tell him face to face."

"I can see how you would feel that way." Alex said. "I have to admit, since you told us about the baby, I have been thinking of ways I would tell Will news like that. As much as I would want him to know as soon as possible, I would want to see his face when I told him."

"Yes." Augusta said. "I know he will be excited. I can't wait to tell him and see him." She paused. "How is your mother? Is there any word on Aaron?"

"Not any." Alex frowned. "It makes me so mad that he just up and left without telling anyone, without saying goodbye. I had hoped he would have at least written to let us know that he made it to camp okay. A lot could have happened between now and then."

"I am so scared about John leaving in a few weeks." Charlotte said. "I depend on him so much. I don't know how I will manage the farm without him."

"You'll find some way." Alex said. "We all just have to keep finding ways to get through it and support one another."

June 19
Gettysburg, Pennsylvania

Alex stood outside the Post Office and looked at the letter that had been sent to the family, in the hopes that it was from Will. She frowned: it was from her brother.

"Alex?" Augusta walked in. "What's wrong?"

"I was hoping this was from Will. It's from my brother, which will make Mother happy, and myself, of course. It's good to hear from him, although the way he left still upsets me. It feels like it has been so long since I received a letter from Will, even though it was a few weeks ago. But I worry. You understand, I know."

"You are right. I finally received a letter from Michael last week, but I selfishly want more." She quickly went to the counter to check for mail for the Lewis's, but there was nothing. As the girls walked out of the Postal Office, they overheard two men of the town talking.

"...the captain, both lieutenants, and nearly all the men, killed or captured."

"Excuse me?" Alex asked the man. "What Company are you speaking of?" The man looked at them.

"The 87ᵗʰ, ma'am." He answered somberly.

"Oh, God, no." Alex gasped, putting her hand over her mouth, fear strong in her eyes.

"Yes, ma'am. The word is they were overtaken in Winchester, Virginia. About four days ago."

"No, please, God, no."

"It's okay, Alex. It might not be Will. He could be fine."

"You should talk, little Miss from Carolina. For all we know, it could be your family that attacked our troops."

"Augusta, please, come with me." Alex quickly pulled Augusta towards the Lewis's store. She had to walk, to move. Augusta remained silent, not sure anything she could say would reassure her friend. Once in the store, Alex continued to pace. Augusta immediately got to work, straightening products. She liked Gettysburg, but hated some of the comments the townspeople made. Alex bit at her thumb, not knowing what to say, not knowing what to think.

"Nearly all the men killed or captured..." She repeated, distracted. "Dear God, if anything has happened to Will, I just don't know..."

151

Clark Home

An hour later, Alex was back home, nervously chewing on her fingernail and pacing. Augusta sat paging through a book from Mr. Clark's personal library. The bell to the front door jingled and heavy booted footsteps sounded on the floor. Alex turned and froze. The soldier standing before her was disheveled, covered in mud. His black hair touched his shoulders and a full beard covered his face. He was thin, and fatigue was apparent in the bags under his eyes. But in spite of all that, she knew without a doubt who the man was. She threw herself into his arms. "Will!" She squeezed tight as he hugged her back. His arms ran over her back and arms and he kissed her forehead, then nose, then lips.

"Alex, Alex. How I have missed you." He murmured.

"You're alive and safe, thank God, you're alive." Alex said. "What happened? We just had word…"

"We were in a battle, at Winchester, a pretty bad one. We lost so many men. I was lucky to survive with just some small cuts and bruises. When it was over, those of us who were left were given a short leave." He took a deep breath. "I couldn't get to you fast enough."

Augusta spoke up. "Did you know of anyone who was killed? My husband is not with your regiment, but I know others…"

Will smiled. "You must be Augusta Lewis. Alex has written about you. All good things, of course. It is wonderful to finally meet you."

"It is a pleasure to meet you as well." Augusta smiled.

"Well, of those who are missing, they include Billy Holtzworth and Jack Skelley." He paused. "Charlotte will be happy to know that her father was wounded, but got to safety. He was left at a hospital. She should also know that Thomas Culp missed the whole thing; he was in a hospital with fever. He should be back in town soon. I'm not sure about any of the rest of them."

"Ginny will be crushed to hear about Jack." Alex said, smoothing a strand of hair behind her husband's ear.

"I think he'll be all right. Some of the men most likely got separated and just haven't made it back to camp yet. Hopefully, they'll be back when the rest of us return to our unit."

"I hope so." Augusta said.

Alex touched the hair of Will's beard. "We need to trim this. You look like a mountain man."

"I should leave you two to it." Augusta said, smiling. "Will, it was wonderful meeting you. I can see myself out."

"It was wonderful meeting you as well, Mrs. Lewis. Will smiled.

"Goodbye, Augusta!" Alex said, not looking away from her husband.

June 24
Turner Farm

Charlotte smiled as she looked up the road to see Alex riding toward her. Her friend had been coming out to visit with Charlotte once every few days. Charlotte knew Alex was checking up on her, and she appreciated it.

"Good to see you, Alex." She said once Alex was closer. Her friend dismounted.

"It's good to see you as well. I'm sorry I haven't been out in a few days, I…" Charlotte held up her gloved hand.

"You don't need to explain, Alex. I understand completely."

"I knew you would understand. I just…I could have come out for a little while and talked with you."

"It's really all right. I'm glad you got to spend time with Will."

"Me too." Alex leaned against the fence. "Lots of talk going on in town. People are saying that the Confederates are headed this way and that there could be a battle in the area within the next month or so. Some people say that there are some spies in the area as well."

"I hadn't heard that. I can't believe we've allowed the Confederates to get this far north."

"I know. It's scary." Alex stated. "Did you hear about Jack Skelley?"

Charlotte placed her rake against the fence and hopped up to sit on the fence. "I did. Ginny actually came out to tell me when she heard."

"How was she handling it?" Alex felt like a horrible friend, not being there for Ginny, but she had been too occupied with Will.

"She was upset. We talked. We prayed. Well, she prayed and I listened to her."

"You didn't feel the need to say a prayer yourself?"

Charlotte shrugged. "I'm not sure it would do any good."

Alex sighed. "Charlotte, Charlotte. You are one of the closest friends I have, but your stubbornness on this frustrates me sometimes. What will it take for you to realize that God cares about you and each of us, no matter what?"

"I don't know. The war to end? For my father and Jack to come home safely, along with everyone else who is fighting? For Thomas and I to work things out with our relationship. My mother…" Charlotte hesitated, thinking back all the years ago when her mother died. "I did have faith in prayer once, Alex. When I was a girl, and my mother was with child, but she was sick and the doctor didn't know if Mama and the baby would make it. I prayed and prayed and prayed that God would save them, but He didn't. I prayed to God that my father would love me again, but that prayer went unanswered as well. That is frustrating to me."

"Sometimes, it seems prayers do go unanswered, Charlotte. There have been times when I felt that has happened to me as well. Prayers that we feel go unanswered are not necessarily God saying 'No.' Usually, it's God saying 'Not yet.' or 'I have something better in mind.' Alex looked at her friend. "The Bible never says that we will have an easy life, that nothing bad will ever happen to us. But it does tell us, multiple times, to 'be not afraid', and that God will be with us, no matter what, if we only ask Him. He can help us get through whatever problems we have."

Friday, June 26
Wade House on Breckenridge

Ginny sat near the stove, holding her brother John's new uniform. He had enlisted in Company B of the 21st Pennsylvania Cavalry, as he said he would. The bright-eyed kid who used to tag along with Ginny, Charlotte, Jack and Wesley was going to war. It hardly seemed possible. There were two knocks at the door, and then it opened as Charlotte entered with a smile on her face.

"Charlie!" Harry exclaimed, jumping into her arms. "You haven't visited in so long!"

"I know." She smiled and kissed his mop of unruly brown hair and set him down. "You get heavier every day." She glanced around. Mrs. Wade was nowhere to be found, and John was pacing in front of the fireplace. Isaac was in the corner, sleeping. "I couldn't let my farmhand-turned-soldier leave without saying goodbye." She gave John a quick hug.

"It is good to see you, Charlie." He turned to his sister. "Are you almost done, Ginny?"

"Hold on and be patient, Johnny. Your commanding officer knows the situation."

"They've already rode out?" Charlotte asked, sitting down.

"The Rebs have invaded Pennsylvania, you know." John told her. "My unit has already left to do some scouting."

"I see. I didn't know that." Charlotte looked at John, again wondering just when he had grown up. He now stood close to six feet, with dark hair that curled in small ringlets around his head. He had become strong and muscular while working on her farm over the past two years. She would miss him. His brown eyes shown with the excitement of finally being off to war. "So, Bugler Wade, do you really think you are ready for this?"

John broke into a wide grin, his dimple showing in his left cheek. "Charlotte, I was born ready!"

Charlotte heard a small sigh of despair from where Ginny sat. She understood how her friend felt. It seemed as though all the men in their lives were leaving, one way or another. Even Sam, at age 12, was in the Gettysburg Zouaves, a semi-military organization in town.

"Where are Sam and your mother?" Charlotte asked. She glanced at Harry, who was sitting in a chair, his elbows on his knees and his chin sitting in his hands.

"Sam's over working at the Pierce's butchering shop and Mama's over at Georgia's." Harry's face broke into a wide grin. "Hey, Charlotte, guess what! I'm an uncle!"

Charlotte looked at Ginny. She had a smile on her face.

"Georgia had the baby?" She asked.

"Yes, A little boy. He is so tiny and perfect, the cutest thing! She named him Louis." Her eyes never left her work. She finished the last few stitches.

"Here you go, Johnny." She handed him the coat. He threw it on.

"Well, I'll be off, then." He hugged Ginny. "Thanks, Ginny. You're the best!"

"Be careful, little brother." She said, holding back tears. "Make sure you stop by and say goodbye to Mother and Georgia."

"I will." John turned. "See you later, Charlotte. I'll come back from this war a hero and we can get married." Charlotte hugged him tight, smiling.

"Yeah, we'll see about that." Charlotte struggled to hold back her own tears. "Take care of yourself."

"See you later, kiddo." John ruffled Harry's hair and he was gone. Ginny moved to the open door and leaned against the doorframe. Her arms crossed, she watched her little brother mount his horse and leave. Harry stood and ran to join her. With a wave, John was gone, hurriedly trying to catch up with his new comrades.

*****

Before going home, Charlotte stopped by the Lewis's shop to pick up a few supplies and to see Augusta. The bell jingled as she opened the door. The store had a few other patrons, but Augusta smiled and approached Charlotte right away.

"How may I help you today?" She said in her light, Southern accent and a smile.

"I just wanted to stop by, say hello, and check out some supplies." Charlotte smiled back. "Beeswax? Maybe some cloth?"

"We moved our cloth, it's over here now." Augusta led Charlotte to the far side of the store. "What we have left of it, that is."

Charlotte held up a bolt of pink and dark green checked cloth and looked at the price. "Is your father-in-law really charging this much for cloth?"

Augusta sighed. "He is. He has to. Prices are high for us too. Farms aren't producing as much, and factories are only producing war materials." Augusta gestured toward the South. "You understand that. You make just enough surplus to sell or trade for meat and other necessities. You said not too long ago that your crop will be even smaller this year. Other families are in the same situation. And trying to get items from cities? Almost impossible. We are lucky we sell groceries here. It is what is keeping us in business."

"I suppose that's true." Charlotte said. "I do want to try to grow more. I depended on John so much last year, but now he's off and gone."

"It is hard to find help." A voice from behind the girls said. They turned and saw Aideen Lewis, Augusta's mother-in-law. "I would suggest asking some of the Negroes around here to help, but they're skedaddling out of town, with the Confederates right at our back door."

"I don't blame them." Charlotte said, setting down the cloth and moving to the counter, resting her hands on empty glass containers that once held candy. "You hear stories all the time of Confederates capturing Negroes and sending them back into slavery, whether they were born slave or born free."

Augusta looked down at her folded hands, clearly uncomfortable. Charlotte put her arm around her friend's shoulder.

"I didn't mean to offend you at all."

"I know." Augusta replied. "You have a point, though. Marrying Michael and coming up here has opened my eyes a bit about slavery." She spoke softly. "Growing up, it was just a part of life. I never knew any different. I never saw it as a negative thing. We never mistreated our people that I knew of. I liked my personal servant; Emmy was my confidant. She never complained to me about anything. In my own narrow world, she was happy, and I thought that everything was good." As she spoke, she began twisting her wedding ring around her finger. "Michael showed me why I was wrong. He opened my eyes. I would still be naive about slavery had it not been for him. I cannot honestly say that I believe they are completely equal, but I also cannot say that they should just be treated as property." Tears began to shimmer in her eyes.

"Augusta?" Charlotte tightened her arm around Augusta.

"I'm sorry." Augusta wiped her eyes. "I just...I miss Michael so much. And being away from my own home..." Charlotte pulled

Augusta into a full hug. Aideen came around the counter and joined the embrace.

"I know, Augusta, I miss him too." Augusta's mother-in-law murmured.

The door crashed open. Harry Wade dashed in and grabbed Charlotte's hand.

"Charlotte! Mrs. Lewis! You gotta come see." He pulled Charlotte toward the door. "The Rebs are here in town! They're walking down the street. Come on!" He let go, then dashed out again.

"The Rebels? Here?" Aideen put her hand over her stomach.

"The rumors must be true this time." Charlotte said, her voice shaking. Some of the other patrons in the store gathered around the counter.

"What does this mean?" Sallie Meyers, the schoolteacher, asked.

"It means our virtue and that of our daughters are in danger." Margaret Pierce, wife of the butcher said, pulling her daughters Margaret and Tillie close.

"Those wild and crazy Rebs will kill us all!" Tillie whimpered.

Augusta backed further and further away from the venomous tongues. Charlotte reached out and pulled her back, then spoke. "You're all worrying for nothing. The Confederates are gentlemen. They will treat us like ladies unless we give them reason not to."

"That's easy for you to say." Abigail Williams' mother, Maime spoke up. "Your father is from the South. And you, Mrs. Augusta Lewis. You are a Reb yourself..."

Charlotte stiffened and was about to speak out, but Augusta gently pulled her back.

"Now just hold on Maimie Williams." Aideen Lewis spoke up. "John Turner may be from the South, but he is fighting for the Union. And my daughter-in-law is a wonderful young woman who was just crying for the safety of her husband. I shouldn't have to remind you that her husband is a West Point graduate and is out there fighting to preserve the Union. There are no traitors in this room."

Augusta gave Aideen a small smile and squeezed Charlotte's arm. Just as Maimie Williams opened her mouth to argue, the door crashed open again. This time, instead of Harry dashing in, the women all gasped as a dirty Confederate officer strode in. His gray uniform was caked with mud. He was tall and thin, with blonde hair that almost touched his shoulders. A full beard covered his face and a rifle was gripped in his right hand. He quickly looked around the store. Falling in behind him were four other men, their uniforms showing they were privates, as unkempt as he was.

"Ladies." The first soldier greeted them. "We are here to buy supplies." He had a thick accent from the Deep South, from Georgia, maybe Alabama. He stomped in and signaled to his men. Not a word was spoken by the citizens. Tillie Pierce cowered behind her mother. All the women trembled. The four privates spread out to look for some food.

"That should be just fine, officer." Aideen said calmly. As soon as the path to the door had cleared, Sallie, the Pierces, and Mrs. Williams, quickly cleared out. Augusta, Aideen and Charlotte were left with the men.

"Are you planning on paying for those supplies? Sir." Charlotte asked.

"You gotta sharp mouth on you, eh Yankee girl?" One of the privates sneered, dropping a sack of flour on the counter.

"Burnett." The officer spoke sharply. "These are ladies, and they deserve our respect, even if they are...Yankees." He pulled out a wad of paper money and tossed it on the counter. "This should cover everything." He began to lead his men outside. Aideen picked up the bills.

"Sir, these are Confederate dollars. I can't take them. They aren't any good."

The man turned and gave an arrogant smile. "Ma'am," he drawled, "By the end of the week, those bills will be good." He then walked out, slamming the door behind him.

*****

Charlotte left the store shortly after, bringing Harry with her. When they were a block from the Wade's house, they ran into Ginny, carrying Isaac.

"Harry, there you are!" She said, pulling her brother close to her. "You need to stay closer to home. It's dangerous." From the direction of Chambersburg Street, they heard shouts.

"Rebels!" Harry exclaimed. "Coming down the street!" Ginny took a deep breath and threw Charlotte a worried glance. Sure enough, Confederates were marching down the road. Shots rang out as they fired in the air. Other townspeople began lining the street, watching the procession. Charlotte scanned the men for the familiar face of Wesley Culp.

"Any sign of him?" Ginny asked softly, as if reading her mind. Charlotte shook her head.

"No, not yet at least."

"Why would you be looking for a Rebel?" Harry asked, looking up at the two.

"Mr. Culp. Wesley, who went South long before the war." Charlotte knelt down and put her arm around his shoulders.

"Why would you care about him? Everyone around here knows he's a traitor. Some folks say if he ever comes back, they'll shoot him." Harry sounded as if he had heard that statement a few times.

"He's still our friend, Harry." Ginny said.

"He's not my friend." The boy replied.

Charlotte's stomach plummeted. She cared deeply about Wesley and there were some, such as Wesley's sisters and Ginny who had forgiven him for fighting for the South, but what about the rest of Gettysburg? Would Wesley ever be able to return to his hometown?

After the troops had passed through, a tow-headed youth with dirt-stained cheeks and dirty clothes ran up to Ginny. He bent over and was breathing heavily, as though he had run miles.

"What's happened, Page?" Ginny asked the boy. It was Page Pierce, the nephew of the butcher that Sam worked for.

"The Rebs arrested Sam." He panted.

"What?" Ginny exclaimed, pulling Page to the sidewalk.

"Uncle James had Sam take our best horse out of town so the troops wouldn't take him. So he rode off, down the Baltimore Turnpike. The Rebs caught up with him and brought him back to town. When he put up a fight, they arrested him."

"How could they? He's just a boy!" Charlotte asked.

"Said it didn't matter." Page replied.

"I need to get him out of there." Ginny said, handing Isaac to her friend. "Stay with Charlotte." She told Harry. "I'm going to help Samuel."

"But I want to help." Harry said.

"Stay with Charlotte!" Ginny ordered.

As she started down the street, Charlotte turned to Page. "Why don't you come stay with us? You boys can play a while, and then I can get some food ready."

Page shook his head. "Naw. Thanks, I am supposed to go right home." He turned and headed back. Charlotte took Harry's hand and quickly walked to the Wade's house.

****

Ginny raced through the street, heart hammering. She had to get Sammy back. Page said he had been placed under arrest and taken into town. She headed to the center of town, where Confederate General Early and his men were reported to have gathered. Once she arrived, she pushed her way through the crowd. She saw Sammy being guarded by soldiers. Fearful, but needing to help her brother, she rushed toward them. When Sammy saw her, he stood.

"Ginny!" He called. Before he could get to her, a gray-coated soldier grabbed him and yanked him back.

"Please, sir, he's only a boy. He can't do any harm!"

"He is a prisoner of the Confederate Army, ma'am." Another soldier said.

"He's twelve years old! What could he have done?"

"Well, he was riding out of town on a good looking horse. He claimed he was just sent to hide the horse." The second soldier explained.

"It's the truth, it's what Mr. Pierce asked me to do!" Samuel cried out.

"How is that grounds for arrest?" Ginny asked.

"We need horses, for one thing, and he wouldn't turn it over. Besides, who's to say he's not a Federal scout, trying to get information about our position to the enemy?"

"He's twelve years old!" Ginny pleaded. "He is no more a Federal scout than I am. You have to let him go."

"We're in charge, ma'am." The first man spoke again, still holding Sam back. "We don't have to do anything."

"Please. I beg you. Please let him go."

"Ma'am, even if we could let him go, we have orders to hold him and anyone else who opposes us." The set of the man's chin told Ginny that she wouldn't get anywhere with these men.

162

"Samuel, I will get you out of here. Just be patient." She turned and headed back toward her sister's house. Once she reached the McClellan home, she poked her head in the door, not wanting to disturb Georgia.

"Mother, the Rebs have Samuel."

"What?"

"They arrested him, they have him down at the Diamond. He was trying to hide the Pierce's horse and wouldn't give it to them. They wouldn't let him go, no matter what I said."

"Oh, Ginny, you should have come to me straightaway." Mrs. Wade looked toward the town center. "Where are Harry and Isaac?"

"They are at the house, with Charlotte."

"I will go and bring Samuel back. You stay here with Georgia and the baby."

Ginny watched her mother go down the street until she heard baby Louis crying out. She quickly walked into the house and turned right into the sitting room. When it had been time for Georgia to have the baby, John and Samuel had brought Georgia's bed down to the main room to make things easier. Ginny reached into the bassinet and picked the newborn up.

"Hello, there." She cuddled the baby close to her chest and sat in the rocker in the corner. Louis looked up at her with big brown eyes. As soon as she started rocking, he stopped fussing. She touched his tiny hand and it curled around her finger. "You're gonna be a strong one." She said.

"Like his papa." Georgia's voice came from the bed. "What are you doing here, Ginny?"

"Mother had to run some errands. I'm staying in case you need something. Do you need anything?"

"Not right now, no." Georgia said. "But thank you."

"It's no problem." Ginny continued rocking her nephew. He was so tiny, so perfect. A good mix of both Georgia and John in looks. She could only imagine what her own child would look like. Would it favor her or Jack? "He's perfect, Georgia. Just perfect."

"Thank you." Georgia gave Ginny a thoughtful look.

"What?" Ginny asked.

"I know what you're thinking. I know that look. You're wondering what your child will look like and if you'll ever have a chance to find out if you'll be a good mother."

"Am I that easy to read?" Ginny smiled. "I was thinking about my own future children, although my mind hadn't gotten to wondering if I will be a good mother or not. I can only hope and pray."

"You will be." Georgia reassured her.

"Did...did giving birth hurt?" Ginny asked tentatively.

"Yes. But it was worth it." Georgia had a wistful look fall across her face. "I just wish John could have been here. He will be so happy and proud to have a son."

"You did well, Georgia. I can only hope that one day I can have a child as perfect as this little one." Ginny's face was full of longing. "And I hope Jack..." she couldn't finish the thought.

"Have you heard any more news about him lately?"

"No, not since way before Will and the others came back and told us what happened in Winchester. I don't know if Jack is dead, wounded, a prisoner, or safely back with the regiment. I don't know if I'm not getting mail because his letters aren't getting through or if he's stopped writing because his feelings have changed or if he can't write because he could be..." She trailed off, again unable to put her thought into words.

"It'll be all right, Ginny. We'll get through this. You'll hear from Jack soon."

Ginny looked down again at the tiny baby in her arms. She had never before felt as intense of longing to have her own child. As she was about to speak again to her sister, the door opened and Mrs. Wade stepped in.

"Mother, what happened? Did you get everything taken care of?"

"I did." Mrs. Wade turned to the fireplace to stoke the fire to get ready for dinner.

Ginny handed the baby back to Georgia and joined Mrs. Wade in the small kitchen. With a smile at Georgia, she shut the door leading from room to room. "How did you free him? Where is he now? At home?"

"One question at a time, Ginny." Mrs. Wade began pulling out supplies to make a small dinner. "I got to the Diamond and appeared before General Early. I talked to him and pleaded with him and he finally agreed to let Samuel go. He allowed me to take him. I left him with the Pierces. They'll be able to keep an eye on him until all this blows over. The Confederates kept the horse, which is really what they wanted anyway." She sighed. "Everything is well. Go tell your sister goodbye and get on home. I'll stay here until tomorrow."

"Yes, ma'am." Ginny did as her mother asked, said goodbye to her sister and headed home.

****

Once home, Ginny fell into a chair, exhausted.

"There is some stew left over, Gin. I can put on some coffee, too." Charlotte said.

She shook her head and rubbed her temples. "I just want this to be over." She groaned.

"Did you get Sammy back?" Charlotte asked.

"They refused to let him go at first." She muttered, then told her friend what happened. "He is going to stay with the Pierces for now." She buried her face in her hands. "Dear God, Charlotte, what more can happen to us?" Charlotte knelt beside her.

"You know, it's like you always say, Gin. We just need to have faith in God. He'll bring us through this trial."

"I know, Charlotte. I just have a feeling we'll need a lot of prayers within the next few days."

Charlotte stood and put her hands on her waist. "Well, you've always been better at that than I have."

"You could be good at it too, you know." Ginny looked at her friend. "I can tell you, I am so afraid about what the next few days may bring. But my faith in God, in knowing that He will be there for me, helps a lot."

Charlotte sat down. "I wish I had the strong faith that you do, Ginny, I really do. I try. You know I believe in God and Jesus and all that. But what I can't understand is why, if God is so all-powerful, why is He allowing bad things to happen? Why does He allow the war? Why is he letting people kill others?"

"God doesn't make those things happen, Charlie, nor does He want them to happen. Those things happen because of humans. God gave us free will, the ability to make our own choices. And humans often do the wrong thing. But God allows us to choose. We are not His puppets. We can make our own decisions."

"Then if God isn't going to do anything about our problems because of free will, what is the point of prayer? Why ask if He won't answer?"

Ginny sat in silence for a moment. "Do you remember when we met?" She asked finally.

"Of course. I had just lost my mother and we were just starting school. I was so jealous that you had brothers and sisters to play with."

"Yes, and I was lonely in spite of having my siblings. I specifically remember praying in the months before school started, praying that God would send me a best friend, someone I could talk to, spend time with, share secrets with. Someone who would look past the fact that I was poor. Having Georgia around was great, but she always had friends of her own. And then, that second day of school, Abigail Williams started to make fun of me and you jumped in to defend me. I will never forget that. I can't. You were an answer to my prayers. God does answer prayers, Charlotte. Not always the way we want Him to and sometimes not as quickly as we want, but He will. God knows what's best for us, even better than we do and He can take anything that we do or anything that happens to us and make it work for good if we let Him."

"That makes sense, I suppose." Charlotte said. "I still have my doubts, but what you say makes a lot of sense." She stood. "I had better be going. It's been a long day."

"The Confederates are all over the town and countryside, Charlotte. You should stay here."

"No, I need to get home and get some chores taken care of. I'll be fine. Are you still doing wash tomorrow?"

Ginny nodded and walked her friend to the door. "Yes, and you are welcome to join."

"I think I will. I despise washing clothes, but it is tolerable to do with others, and that's one of the chores I have been putting off, so really need to do. See you tomorrow."

"See you then."

June 27

"Dear Michael:

Confederate troops came through Gettysburg yesterday. The town is in a panic. Even though the division has already left, the experience altered the town severely. Everyone is worried and on edge, trying to get ready just in case there is a battle. I wish I could go and help others, but your mother insists that I stay with her. She wants to make sure I stay safe, especially with the animosity some of the townspeople feel toward me.

The Wade family needs extra help more than ever, as Georgia is bedridden and there is a new baby to take care of. It seems as though Charlotte has taken it upon herself to help them. It is probably best that she stays in town anyway, around other people and not all alone at her farm.

The store is quite busy, as many people want to get supplies before being stuck inside their homes. People are panicking at the threat of a battle in our backyard. Mr. Charles Will and his son JC, remember, the owners of the Globe Hotel, spent an entire day moving supplies from the hotel to the loft of their hostelry on York Street. They even buried bottles of liquor in the garden, fearful of losing it to troops. Mr. Fahnestock shipped a stock of his goods to Philadelphia in a freight car that he leased specifically for that purpose. Everyone is hiding their horses and livestock, valuables and food anyplace they can find. I worry about the possibility of a battle here, and have mixed feelings about your involvement in it. On one hand, if you were a part of this battle, you would be nearby, and I would be able to see you. However, I cannot bring myself to wish you part of any battle, regardless of being able to see you. Your safety, and you getting through this war alive is of utmost importance, and is at the forefront of all my thoughts and prayers.

Your parents are doing well. We are trying to stock as much as we can in the cellar in case we are raided. They miss you and give their love.

I long to see you, and cannot wait for the day you return home for good.

Your loving wife and best friend,
Augusta"

Charlotte returned to the Wade house the next morning. She was washing clothes with Ginny when Alex rushed around the house, waving a newspaper.

"The Rebels are still near! Not far away at all. A lot of them." She was breathing heavily, as if she had run all the way from her house. Ginny took the *Compiler* and read the article.

"A force of 13,000 Confederate soldiers with thirty-three cannon and a long wagon train." Alex continued.

Ginny's eyes widened as she read. "They're camped out near Mummasburg, not far from here at all!"

"So what do you think? Will we have a battle around here soon?" Charlotte asked.

"I suppose our great fear is about to become a reality. We always knew this would be a possibility." Alex answered.

"Ohh, I just can't believe it. It doesn't seem real." Ginny handed the paper back to Alex. "What are we going to do?"

"We're just going to have to get through it the best we can, I guess." Charlotte shrugged. "We just hope and pray, as you two would say, that this battle won't come to pass. And if it does, that it doesn't affect the people of Gettysburg that much."

"I don't think it will." Alex said. "The armies are still a long way off. And if there is fighting, it should happen far away from the actual town."

Alex, Ginny and Charlotte said their goodbyes to each other and headed to their respective homes.

All through the night, Charlotte could see the flicker of enemy campfires, dotting the Eastern slopes of South Mountain. It was hard to believe that the army was only a mere nine miles away.

June 28
Turner Farm

Charlotte woke the next day and quickly remembered the events of the preceding day. She dressed and put together a breakfast before heading to the garden. With John gone, she had to work even harder to take care of things. She knew her vegetable garden was most important, as it would be the most useful, for herself and selling in town. Although, now, with the armies nearby, she was concerned about them simply confiscating her crops without her getting anything in return. She would gladly give what she could to support the troops and feed hungry men, but she also knew she had to take care of herself.

Charlotte glanced up at the sound of a horse approaching and smiled when she saw Alex.

"Charlotte!" Alex smiled and dismounted.

"Alex, what are you doing out here? I just saw you yesterday." Charlotte took a good look at Alex's appearance. "And looking like that?" Alex was usually perfectly put together in the nicest, newest fashion possible, but today, she was dressed in a plain green skirt and old brown shirtwaist that looked two sizes too big for her. Her dark hair, usually perfectly styled, was in a simple braid that hung down her back.

"I came to help." Alex said, "What can I do?" She reached over to grab a rake. "What is this for?"

Charlotte looked at her friend in disbelief. "You? Help? No offense, but…"

"What do I know about farming? I will admit: nothing. But I know you need help and I can take direction. I won't be able to do nearly as much as John, but I should be able to do something. So," She looked at the vegetables. "Where do we start?"

Charlotte smiled. "You, Philadelphia-raised Alexandra Clark-Sadler, wants to be a farm hand?"

"I just want to help. Please, let me help." Alex set the rake down and picked up an empty wooden pail. "I can at least pump water."

Charlotte laughed. "I'm sure we can find some things for you to do. And I appreciate the help. And the company."

The two friends discussed many things as they worked. Charlotte appreciated the companionship and conversation much more than the actual help. It was clear that Alex had never worked a day of physical labor in her life. But she made up for her inexperience in enthusiasm and a positive attitude.

"What do you make of the Southern army coming through here?" Charlotte asked, hacking at the dirt in between her rows of vegetables. Alex followed behind her, picking up the weeds.

"It's probably a variety of things. They need supplies and felt the need to come up here, where the land is untouched by war. They need to win a battle or two on northern soil to try and convince foreign nations like Britain to help them."

"Do you really think they'll have one? A battle here, I mean."

"It's likely. Somewhere around here, maybe in our own Gettysburg fields. It's hard to predict exactly where. But it will most likely happen."

"It's so hard to believe. We've discussed the possibility, but I never imagined it would actually be so close to us."

"I wonder." Alex paused. "I wonder if the 87th will be part of the fighting. If they will be able to visit if they are part of the Union troops headed this way? It would be nice to see them."

"You did see them, at least the one you wanted to see, not long ago." Charlotte reminded her.

"I know." Alex smiled at the memory of being in Will's arms again. "Was Thomas with them? I was so preoccupied with Will that I didn't even ask."

"No, he is, or was, sick. In a hospital. He'll make it, he'll pull through."

"That's good, right?"

"It is good. In spite of my personal feelings for Thomas, he is a good man. He will be a good husband and provider. There are a lot of men out there who would make worse husbands."

"But will he be the best husband for you?" Alex asked.

"Maybe." Charlotte stopped and looked out over the fields. "I just don't know. I wish there was some way that I could look into the future and know what decisions to make. I hate the feeling of...I don't know how to describe it...kind of just floating around."

"You mean you wish there was some...master of the universe, watching over us with a master plan and a plan for each of us?" Alex stood, brushed her hands on the apron Charlotte had given her and took a drink from the bucket of water.

"Yes, I suppose that's what I am saying. Why?"

"Oh, Charlotte. You mean to tell me that after all the talk about faith and God and His love, you don't understand that there is a great master plan that God has for each of us. He's there for us. He wants to help us find a beautiful life."

"What about all those good, Christian men who have died horrible, painful deaths. How is that a beautiful ending?"

"Their earthly ending may not have been beautiful, but where are they now? It's paradise."

"But how do you know?" Charlotte asked.

"I'm not sure that anyone can know for absolute certainty. That's why it's called faith." Alex said.

Charlotte looked at the sun, which was creeping toward the horizon. "It's getting late. You should start heading back soon."

"Oh, didn't I tell you?" Alex grinned. "I planned on spending the night."

"No, you didn't mention that." Charlotte said. "You think I don't know what you're doing? Staying with me, keeping me company."

"Mama wanted me to try and talk you into staying with us, but I knew you wouldn't. So I decided to come out here. Either you come to town with me or you're stuck out here with me. At least until the danger passes."

"I don't deserve a friend like you, Alex. You really didn't have to do this."

"I know." Alex said. "But what are friends for?"

June 29
Lewis General Store

Augusta folded a bolt of gingham on its display table. She placed a hand on her stomach and looked up as the door to the store opened. Augusta smiled as Ginny walked in.

"Ginny! How are you? How is your new nephew?"

"I am good. Louis is doing very well. How are things here?"

"Kind of crazy. Some people are doing everything they can to pack up and get out of town. Then, there are those who are preparing to stay in their homes if the worst happens. They have been hiding belongings, buying goods, stocking up."

"That's what I am here for. I'm bringing some supplies over to mother at Georgia's house. She's been staying there since before Louis was born. She'll probably stay there for a few weeks more, at least."

"That makes sense." Augusta said, rubbing her stomach. "I'm glad I am going to be here, with Michael's parents when my child comes. It's a scary thing to face alone.

"Yes, and I understand why Mother is there. It's just...it makes things difficult for me, tending to Harry and Isaac. At least the Pierces have been watching out for Sammy. I am considering going over to Georgia's as well. Space is just so tight there."

"It is good to have options, though. If one place isn't safe, perhaps the other one will be."

"Yes." Ginny said. "And you? Will you stay here?"

"I will. Mr. and Mrs. Lewis have been preparing the store. Unfortunately, as we saw a few days ago, the stores will be one of the first places the soldiers go if they want food or supplies. Either side. And they may or may not decide to pay us for the supplies."

"And you wouldn't be able to do anything about it."

"No, we wouldn't." Augusta said. "But we've been lucky so far. I think about family and friends down south. What they must have been going through. This fear, every day. Armies marching through and destroying things."

"War is horrible. So much more so than we could have imagined." Ginny said.

"And now, I fear the horror will be right in our fields."

June 30

The town was abuzz with excitement and fear, anxiety and trepidation. They had just received word that Union troops were marching to town. A group of townspeople had gathered to welcome the men, who were from General John Buford's cavalry.

"I think just about every young, single woman of marriageable age is out here." Alex noted. The soldiers who marched by looked only slightly better than the Confederates. Their uniforms were dirty and torn. Their faces were unshaven and muddy. Some limped. Some weren't wearing shoes. Some looked old enough to be Charlotte's grandfather. Others looked younger than John Wade. The way they carried themselves was much different than the Confederates. Their eyes were averted to the ground, and the only sound they made came from the marching feet and jangling gear.

Many of the young women in the crowd waved and tried to catch the attention of the young men. Abigail Williams looked like she had gotten dressed for a party. Her maroon ball gown was made of silk, and her hair was perfectly coiffed.

The Union men continued to march through town and when they were gone, Charlotte, Alex and Augusta tried pushing through the crowd to meet Ginny.

"Isn't this exciting, ladies?" Abigail asked, gliding up to them. "Those soldiers coming to protect us and all?"

"Abigail, in all likelihood, there will be a battle here. I don't know about you, but I don't want fighting, especially anywhere near town." Charlotte said.

"Yes, but all of those young, handsome, brave men. It's kind of romantic."

Alex took a deep breath, holding back from letting her temper loose. "Abigail, I hardly think that they'll be in the mood for romance. This isn't like last winter, when the New Yorkers had a lot of spare time for socializing."

"I know." Abigail smiled meanly. "Although I am sure Ginny will find time to...make them happy."

"What are you talking about?" Charlotte asked, irritated. "Abigail, you are not making sense."

"Well, I'm sure that, you Charlotte, being her best friend and all, you know how she is. Talk about town is that she'll boost the morale of these Union boys straight away, if you know what I mean."

Charlotte clenched her teeth, wishing desperately she could knock Abigail down with her fist. Alex took a step forward, but Augusta gently held her back. "I don't know what you mean, Abigail." Charlotte said. "What are you insinuating?" Unfortunately, Charlotte did know exactly what Abigail was talking about. People were still gossiping and saying that Ginny had loose morals. Charlotte wasn't quite sure who had started the rumors, but she fervently hoped that Jack would not get wind of them, or that if he did, he would know better than to believe them.

"Well, I would think that you, being her best friends, you would know all about it." Abigail smiled at her patronizingly.

"Oh, we know more about it than you can ever guess." Alex said.

"We know that Mary Virginia Wade is one of the sweetest, kindest girls we know." Charlotte added.

"And the only man that she has ever cared about is Jack Skelley and you know it." Augusta added, then turned and strode away. Alex and Charlotte quickly followed.

"Who does she think she is, saying things like that?" Alex said. "If I wasn't a lady, I would show her just what I think of her and her rumors."

"She's not the only one who says those things, just the only one saying things right to us." Charlotte said. "I'm not sure if that's better or worse than speaking of it behind our backs."

"The sad thing is, Ginny doesn't deserve it. The only reason people are so merciless against her is because of her lack of wealth and family history. She is an easy target when they need someone to be cruel to." Augusta commented.

"Yes, her mother and family background do not help the situation." Charlotte sighed. "I hate this, her being treated like that. And it will not stop after the war. Maybe a marriage to a 'respectable man' like Jack will help. I can only hope."

They met Ginny at the corner of Baltimore and Breckinridge. A few of the Union soldiers had broken away and were talking to the townspeople.

"I wonder if any of them know anything about our Pennsylvania soldiers." Alex said.

"Let's ask." Ginny said. As they asked around, they were disappointed. None of the soldiers knew anything about the 87th. Charlotte approached one final soldier. He was taller than she, with light brown hair that brushed broad shoulders and he had kind, brown eyes. He looked as though he hadn't been able to shave in a few days.

"Excuse me, sir." She said softly. He turned and gave her a shy smile, a dimple showing in his left cheek.

"How can I help you?" His voice was deep and soothing.

"My friends and I are trying to find information about the 87th Pennsylvania. It is our hometown regiment."

"The 87th?" The man thought for a moment. "I don't believe they are here. There's no way to be sure, of course, but last I heard, they were still in Virginia. I'm sorry I can't be of more help."

"No, thank you." Charlotte smiled. "I appreciate your assistance." She turned back to her friends.

"No one seems to know for sure." Alex said.

"It doesn't sound like they are here, or going to be here." Charlotte said.

"I'm not sure if that makes me happy or disappointed." Alex said. "I would love to see Will, but if he were here, he would be in danger. Not that he's not in danger wherever he is, but…" She shrugged, not finishing her thought. It was unnecessary: all the girls shared a constant fear for their loved ones.

"I would love to see Jack. See that he's safe. Talk with him. It's been so long. I would do just about anything to get him back."

Charlotte put her arm around Ginny and hugged her. "He will be fine. I promise. I feel it in my heart. You will be with Jack before the year is out."

"Oh, I do hope so."

The girls headed towards the Wades home.

"Ginny, I think I am going to stay home, at least for tonight. I need to check on things at the farm. "

Alex turned to Charlotte. "You know if you need a place to stay over the next few days, you are more than welcome at my house. I don't like the thought of you out on that farm all by yourself. I know you have work to catch up on, but it's not worth putting yourself in danger."

"I know," Charlotte said. "I will be careful."

"You know you will never wear out your welcome here." Ginny said. "Or you can stay at Georgia's. I know she could use help with the baby."

"I know." Charlotte said. Before Augusta could speak, Charlotte stopped her. "And I know I am welcome at the Lewis's as well. You are all wonderful friends. But I'll be fine. If I feel any danger, I will come into town. I might come in tomorrow after morning chores." As the girls talked, two men in dusty Union uniforms approached them. They were young, boys really. Both were very thin and weary-looking.

"Excuse me, missus." One said. He was taller, with shaggy red hair and tired green eyes. "We were wondering if you had any food to spare."

Ginny knew they didn't have much in the pantry, but didn't have the heart to turn the boys away. "I am sure we can find you something. Please wait here." She went in the house, then came out with some bread and cheese.

"Where are you boys from?" Alex asked.

"Massachusetts, ma'am." They bit into their snack. "We'd best be getting back to our division. Thank you for the food, ma'am." And with that, the two were gone.

The four young women spent the remainder of the afternoon at the Wades. They worked and talked, mainly about the prospect of battle. Finally, Charlotte said her goodbyes and headed home, tired from her long day. She was not looking forward to the chores that awaited her. Dusk was falling, the sun setting and only a glow of sunlight could be seen peeking from beyond the horizon. As she neared the fence, she noticed unfamiliar shadows around her house. As she went nearer, she realized they were Union soldiers. She quickly ducked behind a tree. She knew they were on her side, but also knew that no soldier was one-hundred-percent trustworthy. Her heart hammered in her chest as she peeked out from around the tree, her eyes open wide. From the horses that were standing around, she knew the men had to be cavalry. They were laughing and joking around, but it didn't seem like good humor. She saw them approach the door to her house, but before they could do any damage, Charlotte summoned her courage and yelled out, stepping around the tree and striding towards them.

"Hey you men!" She challenged them, her heart pounding and her palms sweating.

"Well, hello, there!" One called back, taking a few steps closer to her. He was short, shorter than her, and had a high-pitched whiny voice. His once white shirt, was dirtied to the point that it was brown and his hair hung loosely to his shoulders. A scraggly beard covered most of his face. "Come on, now, be nice to us Union boys. We're just hungry, looking for some food."

"Maybe a warm fire and a soft bed, too." A second soldier chuckled wickedly. He was unkempt as well, and had a mop of unruly blonde hair. He looked too young to even be shaving. The two of them walked towards her. Charlotte stepped back, thinking of the closest place she could run to that would be safe. Before she could assemble a plan in her head, she bumped into a soft, but solid body behind her. Strong hands gripped her forearms tightly.

"So, boys," the man behind her had a deep, gruff voice. "Looks like we will get both food and some good company." Charlotte struggled against the man, but he held her tightly. The man spun her around. He was heavier, with a pudgy face and squinty little eyes. He had a mean-looking smile, and began pulling her toward the house. The other two soldiers followed.

"Let me go!" Charlotte used all her strength to fight him, but it was no use. She tried desperately to think of something to do, a way to escape. 'Oh, why couldn't I have just kept my mouth shut?' She thought. They had almost reached the door of her house when a sturdy male voice barked out a command.

"McGary, Burke, Morgan!" The three men immediately turned and Charlotte was jerked around with them. Their right hands flew to their foreheads in a salute as she was let free.

"Sorry there, Captain." The pudgy soldier chuckled nervously. "Did you want to join us?"

"You were told there was to be no looting, or contact of any kind with the citizens." The officer said sharply. "You will be disciplined for this. Get back to camp. Now. We have other things we need to worry about."

"Yes sir." As the three troublemakers mounted their horses and rode off, the officer stepped closer. He was a few inches taller than Charlotte, with broad shoulders. Dark blonde hair poked out from underneath his Union slouch hat. While he didn't have a full beard, it was apparent he had not shaven in days, as stubble covered his face. He had sharp brown eyes and had an air of kindness about him. There was something about this man that put her at ease, and also seemed familiar to her. Charlotte immediately relaxed as he spoke to her, his voice softening.

"I'd like to apologize for my men's behavior, ma'am. They're tired and anxious, and that's no excuse, but I suppose it's an explanation." He took his hat off and bowed slightly, like a gentleman.

"Well, thanks to your timing, no harm was done." Charlotte said. "I'm Charlotte." She offered him her hand, and he gave her a small but warm smile. "Charlotte Turner"

"I believe we are acquainted." James said, smiling and shaking her hand. "James Spencer. Well, actually, Captain James Spencer. I'm still not used to being called Captain. It's a fairly new promotion."

"Well, congratulations. And again, thanks, for coming to my aid." Charlotte turned toward the house, and looked at him over her shoulder. "Would you like some coffee? I can put on a pot quickly and you can explain to me when we were acquainted. You do seem familiar"

"I wouldn't want to cause any trouble."

"It would be no trouble at all." Charlotte opened the door, then turned and smiled. "You did just come to my rescue."

"Coffee would be great Ma'am." He followed her into the house and took off his hat.

"Oh, it's Miss. I'm not married." She gestured to him to take a seat, and quickly lit a few lanterns. She then lit a fire in the stove and began preparing the coffee.

"I see." He paused.

"Now, where did we meet?" She sat down across the table from him.

"In Fredericksburg. Before the war. I believe you were with your cousin. I was with a friend, Nathaniel. We were introduced at a ball, but you had many other admirers."

"I do recall, slightly." Charlotte said. "Much of that time was a blur, especially at the dance."

"If I may be so bold to ask, are you living here alone?"

Charlotte hesitated. Captain Spencer might not be a complete stranger, but she still didn't want him to know that she was alone. However, the Captain had behaved honorably so far, and she felt that she could trust him.

"Yes. My father is away, fighting for the cause." She got up to check the coffee, then sat back down. "And my farm boy enlisted just this week."

"I see. What about your mother?"

"She died when I was six." She clasped her hands in front of her on the table. "I don't really remember her."

"I'm sorry." He paused. "Has that led to you and your father being close?"

Charlotte gave a short laugh and shook her head. "No, not really. Not at all. To be honest, we don't really get along. When he's here, I do his laundry, cook his meals, and keep his house." She shrugged. "It's not really a big deal."

"Sounds to me like you're a maid to him, not a daughter." Captain Spencer said thoughtfully.

"Yes, that's how I feel. My Aunt Miriam told me that I remind him too much of my mother, and it makes him sad." She rose again to check the coffee. "Tell me about yourself, since we never had the opportunity to talk in Virginia"

"I'm from the 3rd Michigan. I signed up at the beginning of the war, even though I probably could have stayed home and used my farm as a justification for exemption. I just didn't want to let all my friends go without me."

"That's understandable." Charlotte nodded, knowing that there were many men who used any excuse possible not to fight. The coffee was hot, and she poured him a cup.

"I received my education from the Michigan Agricultural College. I was fortunate to travel a bit before taking over the family farm, if you call Virginia traveling." When he smiled his whole face brightened. Charlotte thought she had never seen such a handsome and infectious smile.

"I would call Virginia traveling. It's the only place I have traveled to." Charlotte couldn't help but smile herself. "Its beautiful land."

"I agree, when I joined up, I was elected Lieutenant, and a few weeks ago, I was promoted to Captain."

"Good for you." She sat down and wrapped her hands around her warm coffee cup. "So what do you like better, being a soldier or a farmer?"

"I prefer farming..." Captain Spencer was interrupted by a knock on the front door. The soldier quickly stood. Charlotte headed towards the door to open it, the Captain right behind her. Another Union soldier stood there.

"Captain." The man saluted. From the corner of her eye, Charlotte saw Captain Spencer salute back. "Captain, the Colonel sent me to find you. He wants to meet with you and some of the other officers. General Buford is coming in, will probably be here in the early morning."

"Thank you, Lieutenant Dantonio." Spencer said. Charlotte turned to him. "And thank you for the warm coffee and conversation, ma'am. I appreciate it more than you know."

"It was my pleasure, Captain." Charlotte nodded. "And thank you, again, for your assistance."

"It was no problem at all." He smiled, again that smile that seemed to light up his whole face. Charlotte smiled back.

"Good luck with everything. And stay safe. If you can, you may want to move to town for a few days."

July 1
Wade Home on Breckenridge

Ginny turned the key in the door, gave the house a last look and dropped the key in her skirt pocket. In spite of it being very early in the morning, it was quite busy.

"Why are we leaving, Ginny?" Harry asked, clutching the beat-up carpetbag Ginny had filled for him. She picked up the basket of supplies she had packed for herself. She had already carried Isaac over to her sister's.

"Mother says Georgia's house will be safer. Let's go."

The two headed to Georgia's house.

"We have quite a bit to do when we get there, Harry. I am going to need you to be my big helper, especially with Isaac." Ginny told her brother.

"Of course, Ginny." Harry said with a small smile.

Union soldiers mulled around the house Georgia shared with the McClain family. It was a paired home, where the two homes shared a wall and had opposite side entries. The building looked like one large home. Ginny and Harry walked into the north entrance of the house. Once inside, Ginny immediately began preparing to bake bread. Georgia lay on her bed in the next room, stitching some shirts. Louis lay in his bassinet. Isaac sat under the window, playing quietly with a toy train. Her mother was working on some needlework in the rocker in the corner.

A knock sounded at the door. Ginny, hands covered in flour paste, hurried to answer the door. A Union soldier stood there.

"Ma'am, do you have any food to spare?" He asked.

Ginny looked at her mother.

"We can spare some bread." Mrs. Wade nodded. Ginny went to cut some bread that had been baked the day before.

"Here you are. I know it's not much. I'm sorry it can't be more." Ginny said to the man.

"Thank you, ma'am." He said. "You wouldn't happen to have fresh water, would you?"

"Yes, of course." She led him to the east side of the house to the windlass well. She quickly filled a bucket to fill the soldier's canteen.

"Thank you for everything, Ma'am." The soldier tipped his hat and continued on his way. Ginny put her hands on her hips and looked toward the northwest. Gun smoke rose from the area and she could hear what sounded like hundreds of guns firing.

"Lord, please be with Charlotte and Alex and Augusta."

Clark Home

It was still morning when cannon and gunfire exploded all around the house. Alex peered out the window.

"Alexandria, come away from that window right now." Her mother scolded, pushing a strand of blonde hair from her face.

"I'm sorry, mother. I can see the Union men fighting."

"Well, if you can see them, they can see you and possibly shoot you." Mrs. Clark continued stitching the light blue jacket she held. "Besides, the 87th is not here. If they were here, you know Will would have found any excuse possible to come and see you."

"I know he would if he could." Alex sat back down and continued her knitting. She was working on a new scarf for Will for Christmas. It was only July, but at the rate she knitted, she would only get it done just in time. "Mama, how do you really feel about my marrying Will?"

"Two years later and you're just asking me now?" Mrs. Clark smiled. "I see how much you care for him. I was unsure at first, but seeing you two together, and how dedicated you have both stayed to each other during the war, I am sure that you did the right thing. You don't regret what you did, do you?"

"No, not at all." Alex paused. "I love Will. I know I can be flirtatious and love to socialize with anyone, even bachelors, but I never cared for anyone except him."

"There were times when I wondered if you would ever fall in love." Her mother added.

"I know. The moment I met Will, I knew I was ready to be serious, to settle down." Her eyes welled with tears. "Oh, Mama, I miss him so much." She fingered the scarf, wishing she could be holding her husband.

"Oh, Alexandria." Her mother put down her work and moved to sit next to her on the chaise. "My dear." She held her daughter's hands.

"I miss him so much and I worry about him every moment. I don't know how I will survive if anything happens to him."

Mrs. Clark pulled her daughter into her arms and hugged her tightly. They were interrupted by a knock at the front door, then the door burst open and a tall man with shaggy blonde hair and a week's worth of stubble in a Confederate uniform came in. Mrs. Clark shot to her feet.

"What is the meaning of this?"

"I'm sorry ma'am, but this house is needed." The man gestured to someone outside.

"Needed? For what?" Alex asked, standing next to her mother.

"We need a place to take the wounded." Two other soldiers came in, carrying a moaning man on a stretcher. "Put him on the table." The soldier pointed. More men crowded into the dining room, more soldiers carrying wounded in.

"The table?" Mrs. Clark's eyes went wide. "Sir…"

"Ma'am. I am sorry, but we need the house. You can either stay here and help or you can find someplace else to stay, but we will be using the house." He turned and went outside. A tall, thin, man came in, pulling white coverings over his shirt sleeves.

"Ladies, I am Dr. Knightly. Do either of you have experience nursing?"

"No, but I would like to help." Alex stepped forward. "What can I do?"

"Follow me." The doctor said.

Mrs. Clark pulled Alex back. "Are you sure, Alexandria?"

"Of course, Mama. I have to. If Will or Aaron was wounded, I would want someone to help them. I can only do the same for someone else's husband." She pulled away and followed the doctor.

Lewis General Store, Baltimore Street

"Augusta, dear." Michael's mother walked in from the store and looked out the window.

"Yes, ma'am." Augusta was in the kitchen, where she had just finished cleaning up after the noon meal. The morning had been spent cleaning and trying not to think of the fighting outside. She joined her mother-in-law at the window. Union men were racing by, as if they were being chased.

"What do you make of this?" Mrs. Lewis asked.

"They must have been fighting and their lines broke."

"Jesus, Mary and Joseph be with us. Do you think the Confederates will overrun the town?"

"I'm not sure what to think." Augusta said.

"Oh, I do wish Mr. Lewis was back." Mrs. Lewis said. Earlier that week, Michael's father had ridden out of town to Emmetsburg to meet with suppliers and hadn't returned.

"I'm sure he's just staying where it is safe." Augusta said. "Although, who really knows where safe is. Alex told me yesterday that a Union private named Thomas Smith captured a Confederate spy here in town."

"I have heard many reports and rumors of spies for the past few months." Mrs. Lewis said.

"I'm surprised that no one has accused me of being a spy." Augusta said.

"Well, you've been here since way before this town was of military significance." Mrs. Lewis pointed out.

"That's true." Augusta sighed.

"Have people been saying things to you again, my dear?"

"No more than usual." Augusta said. "I just hope and pray we all stay safe during this battle and the war ends soon."

Turner Farm

Charlotte had been able to get most of her work done, but gunfire popped and she could see a cloud of smoke from the town.

"Oh, I hope that is gun smoke and not homes on fire." She said to herself. It was a hot day. Charlotte pushed a strand of sweaty hair behind her ear. She sighed and headed inside where she began to prepare the dinner meal. She poured some fresh water from the bucket into her pitcher bowl, splashed the cool liquid on her face and then blotted it dry with a towel. As she began to prepare for chicken stew, there was a knock at the door. She glanced at the clock, heart hammering. A quarter after one. She wiped her hands and hastened to the door. A Union soldier stood outside.

"Begging your pardon, miss, but do you have any food to spare?" The man looked gaunt, as if he hadn't slept properly for days.

"Yes, please stay here." She hurried inside, grabbed some bread and peach preserves and went back outside.

"Thank you, miss." He nodded.

"Would you like water or coffee?" She asked.

"Water would be nice." He nodded. She quickly got him a cup.

"What...news of the battle is there?" She asked.

"Rebels are chasing Union troops through town as we speak. I am one of the first through. We want to take positions south of town."

"Do you think there will be fighting around here?"

"Most probably." The man looked over toward Cemetery Hill. "Our forces will want to take position there, or on the high ground." He tipped his hat. "Thank you for the food, miss. If you have any family or any other place to go, I'd go there if I was you."

With that, the man turned and headed to join the rest of the Union army.

Clark Home

Alex quickly learned what she could do to help although the stench soon grew overwhelming. She gagged often as she moved from man to man. Dr. Knightly had been a big help, letting her know what she could do and had her help him often. Alex's main job consisted of carrying water to the doctors for surgery and brought drinking water to wounded men. The injuries were horrifying. Men had arms and legs missing before they even came through the door. The doctor spent most of his time in the dining room, performing surgery. Screams of pain came often from that part of the house. Alex's mother had also decided to help. There was much to be done.

"Will the incoming wounded ever stop?" Alex asked Dr. Knightly as a young stretcher-bearer came by.

"Not anytime soon, Ma'am. The Confederates have started pushing through town. We are getting more and more wounded." He ran a hand through his mussed hair. Alex looked at the packed entryway. Almost every available space had been filled. She walked outside, pail in hand to fill with more water. Men had been laid on the porch as well as the lawn in front. She looked over towards the window off the parlor. What she saw caused her to rush to the side of the house and retch over the railing.

"First time seeing the results of an amputation?"

Alex turned. A soldier sat slumped in a porch chair. His head was wrapped in bandages and he held his left arm against his chest. Alex's eyes watered, then glanced again at the severed limbs on her porch.

"That's what they've been doing in there? That is why there are screams?"

"Yes, ma'am." The man looked over to a sweating soldier who was shaking and muttering. The boy's leg ended at the knee. "Most men would rather be dead than lose a limb."

"I am sorry to hear that." She looked back to the soldier who had spoken. "Can I get you something?" Alex asked.

"Water would be nice." He said.

"I will return straightaway." Alex grabbed the pail and headed to the back. As she looked toward the main road, she saw Union soldiers retreating to the south. Not far behind them, the Confederates gave chase.

"Dear God." Alex said. "And on top of all this, are we to lose our town to the rebels?"

McClellan Home

Ginny bent and filled a pail with water from the well. Soldiers continued to pass by in front of the house. She carried the pail and a dipper to the sidewalk and set it down, then went back inside. Her mother had taken over the bread-baking. Over the next few hours, Ginny and her mother continued to bake, repeatedly answering knocks at the door and giving Union men fresh bread and water.

She was outside, refilling the pail with water when she heard a commotion from the north. What seemed like hundreds of Union soldiers came, hurrying, fleeing down the road. Ginny took a spot on the edge of Baltimore Street, trying to hear what the men were saying

"...right flank broke..."

"...retreating to the south side of town..."

One soldier fell in front of her, exhausted. Ginny reached down to help him, but he was too heavy. She looked down at his leg. His thigh to his ankle was covered in blood.

"Water..." he whispered. Ginny quickly filled the dipper and helped the man drink. "Thank you, ma'am." He said, then closed his eyes. Other men dashed by, some taking water and all too soon, the pail was empty again. Ginny quickly stood and hurried back to the well to fill the bucket. The sun beat down, high in the sky. Ginny looked down the road. Other men had fallen. Some of those men were still, lifeless. Others crawled down the road. Ginny looked again at the now-empty pail. She let out a breath and refilled it.

Ginny continued to refill the pail and help the soldiers for what felt like hours. The soldiers were constantly emptying the water pail. They were so thirsty. She had given out quite a bit of bread as well, bread that her mother was busy baking and bringing out. Ginny's skirt was drenched from the waist down from hauling water. She looked at the seemingly endless stream of men.

As evening came, Ginny looked north to see gray-clad men instead of Union soldiers. Her heart dropped. The rebels had taken over the town. Union men had stationed themselves beyond Georgia's house. Shots rang out, it seemed from everywhere.

"Mary Virginia Wade, you come in here right now!" Mrs. Wade called.

"Yes, mother." Ginny entered the house. She was exhausted from the day's ordeal.

"Have some bread. There's cheese too." Mrs. Wade gestured to the food. Ginny grabbed some strawberry preserves and spread them on the slice of bread. She could still hear gunfire from outside.

"Do you know who is doing all the shooting?" Mrs. Wade asked calmly.

"Mostly Rebels." Ginny answered with a hoarse, cracked voice. She quickly took a drink of water. "It looks like they've taken over buildings just south of town. Some Union men surrounding our house are shooting back at them." She sighed. "And to think we believed staying here would be safer."

"We couldn't have known." Mrs. Wade said. "I am sure our own home has been taken over by the Rebels."

Gunfire continued sporadically. Ginny glanced through the window. It was getting darker. She could see that soldiers had fallen in the side yard. One was trying to crawl to safety. Another had hidden behind a rock, clutching his bloody arm.

"Mother, hand me a fresh loaf of bread. I have to go out and help."

"Ginny, it's too dangerous." Mrs. Wade protested.

"I know it's dangerous, but I have to. What if it were John out there hurt? Wouldn't you want someone to help him?"

Mrs. Wade nodded and handed Ginny a loaf of bread and some biscuits.

"Thank you." Ginny hurried out into the night, the bread and biscuits wrapped in her skirt. She grabbed the pail, filled it with water and stopped at the first form she came upon. He was wounded, looked like he had taken a bullet to the shoulder.

"Hello. Would you like some water?" She asked. The man nodded, and Ginny carefully poured some water into his mouth. She moved and knelt by another wounded man.

"Would you like some food or water, soldier?" She asked.

"Thank you, ma'am. Thank you." He took part of the bread she offered. "You must be an angel from heaven." He said. She gave him a smile and hurried to the next fallen man.

"Hello, soldier." She said. "What's your name?"

"William O. Kahlar, 94th New York, ma'am." He took the biscuits she offered. "Thank you." She quickly moved from one man to the

189

other, staying low to the ground, giving the men what food, water and comfort she could.

Ginny approached a man whose eyes were closed and whose chest was moving slowly up and down. She placed a hand on his shoulder, unsure if he was awake or unconscious. "Sir?" She said. He opened his tired eyes. His face was caked with dirt mixed with blood. His lips were cracked and bloody. "Can I get some water for you?"

The man tried to speak, but nothing came out. Tears in her eyes with compassion for his obvious pain, Ginny filled the dipper with water and dripped it into his mouth. His breaths were coming out, short and shallow. "Is there anything I can do for you, sir?" Ginny asked.

With what seemed like all his effort, he finally spoke. "I know I'm gonna die here." He said, his voice barely audible. "Just…don't let me die alone."

Tears fell from Ginny's eyes. She arranged herself so his head was in her lap and she held his hand. "I'll stay with you. What is your name?"

"Derek Moore, from New York. Are you a Christian, ma'am." The soldier whispered.

"I am." She said.

"Will you pray for me?" His eyes closed again.

"Of course, I will." Ginny racked her brain, trying to think of a Bible verse she could say with him. A combination of Psalms and Joshua came to her almost immediately. "And though I walk through the valley of the shadow of death, I shall fear no evil, for the Lord is with me. Be strong and courageous, and do not be afraid or discouraged for the Lord, your God, is with you wherever you go. The Lord is my light and salvation. Whom shall I fear? The Lord is my rock, of whom should I be afraid. When wicked go against me, they shall fall. Though an army attacks me, I will not fear. Though war shall rise against me, I will still be confident…"

The soldier smiled at her efforts. "Well, miss, that is a good mix of scripture there." He took a deep breath. "In my pocket, miss, is a picture of my gal, Martha. Her address is on the back. If it's not too much trouble, could you write her and tell her I loved her and died fighting for my country? It would be of great comfort to me."

"It would be my honor, Mr. Moore." Ginny brushed scraggly hair out of the soldier's face. He wasn't a handsome man; his nose was crooked and his face was full of scars. But he seemed like a kind, loving man. "Your Miss Martha is a lucky woman to have you in her life."

"It is I who was lucky." Ginny could barely hear his words. Then, he took one last breath, and lay completely silent and still. She didn't want to move. Tears continued to fall from her face. But the cries and moans from other men quickly jarred her from her thoughts. She reached into the pocket of Derek Moore and pulled out the tintype. She pocketed it and moved on.

Ginny knelt by another soldier.

"Miss, you'd best be careful." A bullet whizzed by and hit a fencepost, not far from where Ginny knelt. Her heart hammered as the man she was feeding spoke again. "The Rebs don't much care who they hit."

"I am only doing what I can to help." Ginny said. When her bread was gone she headed back into the house.

"Is all the bread gone?" Mrs. Wade asked.

"Yes." Ginny replied. "But I feel like I helped a good deal of men". She collapsed into a chair. "It's so horrible. They're dying painful, lonely deaths out there."

Her mother pulled a chair next to her daughter and draped an arm around her shoulder. "I was looking out the window, checking on you, and saw you with that man who died. Are you all right?"

"I'll be fine. I don't ever want to go through this again, but I have a bad feeling. We will get more than our fill of death before this is all over."

Bullets continued to hit the house and areas around it. "Do you think they will ever stop shooting?" Mrs. Wade asked.

"They'll have to sometime." Ginny answered, making her way to Georgia's bed. Louis lay sleeping in her arms.

"I suppose we should try to rest." Mrs. Wade said, brushing her hands on her apron and entering the front room.

"I suppose so." Ginny looked around the room. Harry and Isaac lay on piles of blankets on the floor. Her mother, still wearing her day dress, climbed into bed with Georgia and Louis. Ginny took the lounge that was under the north window. She tried to sleep, but it was not easy. So much had happened in one day. It had felt like a week. It was hard for Ginny to comprehend and process all that had happened in such a short time. And the battle wasn't over yet.

Lewis General Store, Baltimore Street

Darkness had just fallen when the door of the Lewis's home slammed open. Augusta jumped from her seat and dropped her mending on the floor. A Confederate soldier burst into the room, rifle in hand.

"Sorry for bursting in like this, ma'am, but your home is needed."

Mrs. Lewis entered the room and froze at the sight of the young soldier.

"What for?" Augusta asked.

"None of your concern." He headed upstairs, while six men followed, crowding in, and taking places at the windows.

"What are you doing?" Augusta asked again. One final man walked in and stopped once he saw her face.

"Audge?" He asked in disbelief. "It can't be you."

Augusta recognized his voice. The body build and face were unfamiliar. This man was thin and his hair hung in messy curls to his shoulders. A beard covered most of his face. Augusta finally got a look at his eyes. She would know those eyes anywhere.

"Andrew!" She ran and threw her arms around him. Still holding his rifle, he hugged her tightly back.

"What are the chances? I can't believe it." Her brother exclaimed, pulling back to look at her.

"Lt. Byron!" One of the men at the window took a break from firing to look at the two. "What are you doing?"

"My apologies, I know the orders but I had no idea my sister would be here."

"Sister?" One of the men approached the two. "Lt. Byron, what is your sister doing here in Pennsylvania?"

"Apparently her husband thought it would be safer here than having her stay in Washington or at home in South Carolina." Andrew said. "That's the reason, isn't it?"

Augusta nodded, still taking in her brother. He was safe! He was alive! But he was also in the middle of battle. He had changed. Andrew was always the brother who was proper to a fault. Perfectly trimmed and styled black hair and mustache. Clothes always perfectly pressed and tidy. He was the perfect example of a southern gentleman. He had been trained and ready to take over the family plantation when war broke out. Had it not been for his voice and those eyes, she would not have recognized him. She reached up and touched a streak of gray in his hair.

"Oh, Andrew."

He looked down at her, concern on his face as he looked at her slightly rounded belly. The men around them continued to shoot out the windows.

"We need to get you someplace safe." He looked at Mrs. Lewis. "You must be Michael's mother." She nodded. "Glad to finally meet you. I am Augusta's brother, Andrew." He looked at his sister.

"Where is the cellar? Or a back room? Someplace I can put you to stay safe?"

"There is a cellar. But couldn't we just stay…"

"No." He interrupted sternly. "The cellar is the safest place for you. We need to get you down there. Union pickets will be shooting back at us, and you could accidentally be hit. Let's go."

Augusta grabbed Mrs. Lewis's hand and a lantern and followed her brother toward the hatch to the cellar. He pulled open the trapdoor and held it as the two women descended.

"You two stay there. I'll let you know when it's safe." He closed the door above.

"Well, that happened fast." Augusta said. She turned up the lantern and quickly found some blankets and candles. "Luckily we use this cellar for storage and have moved a lot of goods down here. We will be well-supplied." She turned to her mother-in-law, who still hadn't spoken. It was unusual for Mrs. Lewis to remain silent for this long.

"Mother, what's wrong?"

Mrs. Lewis sat on a crate. "Oh, I can't believe what just happened. Our home taken over by Rebels...they were shooting, Augusta. Using our home as protection as they shoot our Union boys. It could be Michael they are shooting at." Her face was ashen white, her eyes staring ahead.

"Yes, but Michael isn't here. He would have come by." Augusta pointed out. The whole day seemed surreal. She couldn't believe what was happening.

"I feel like we need to go up there, to tell them to stop, get them out. This is our home."

"We cannot do that." Augusta said. "There were more of them than us. They won't harm us if we just stay out of their way." She looked around the room and found a flat, open space. She piled the blankets there. "Come on, let's try to rest, maybe even get some sleep. Maybe they'll be gone in the morning. Although I hope I can see Andrew one more time."

"Oh, Augusta." Mrs. Lewis said as she lay down, placing her spectacles on a barrel. "How much more will we have to endure? I am not as worried about the store and house as I am the townspeople. And Mr. Lewis. I never expected this to happen, not in a million years."

Morning, July 2
Turner Farm, Taneytown Road

Musket fire popped early the next morning. Charlotte glanced at her pocket watch as she straightened the blue and brown checked muslin day dress she had fallen asleep in. It was 6:30. She carefully drew back the curtain to peek outside. From the vantage point of her upper room, she could see gunsmoke rising from the direction of the Peach Orchard, all the way along the ridge towards the Lutheran Theological Seminary. All night long, she had heard gunfire and voices. They sounded close. Campfires could be seen on the hills around her.

"Well, here it is again." Charlotte muttered to herself. "I wonder if I even dare go out to work today. Or if I should risk going into town and taking shelter there." After eating an apple, she quickly braided her hair and tied a straw hat to her head. Once outside, she fed the few animals that were left, then grabbed a hoe and began weeding the area where she had planted her small crop of vegetables. She glanced up as gunfire continued.

"Excuse me, Miss Turner?" A slightly familiar male voice spoke behind her and she quickly turned around.

"Captain Spencer!" She brushed a stray strand of hair off her face as he dismounted from his horse. The man looked just as handsome in the full light of day as he had by the light of the candles. He had shaven since he rescued her, and his hair had been combed.

"I remembered you were out here, alone. I have come to escort you someplace safer, if you'll allow me."

"Safer." Charlotte gave a quick, short laugh. "And where would that even be, Captain Spencer?"

"Well, for one thing, miss, it's not out here, tending to your garden, alone." He stepped toward her, his deep brown eyes filled with concern. He stepped even closer. Her heart beat quickly.

"Please tell me you have a friend or family member or someone in town that you can go and stay with. I don't like the thought of you out here alone."

Charlotte's feelings were torn. On one hand, she was touched at this man's concerns, but her stubbornness pushed to the front.

"With all due respect, Captain, what I do and where I stay is none of your concern." She surprised herself with the way she was talking to this man. She seldom argued with anyone. She set her hoe against the

195

split rail fence that lined her garden. "What are you doing out here anyhow? Shouldn't you be with your troops?"

"I was sent to do some scouting. Heavy fighting will happen here today. I decided since I was out here, I would make sure you were all right." He stepped closer. She could smell the soap and shaving cream he had used to wash with, combined with a smell she had always connected with horses. "I am sorry. I don't mean to be...improper. I'm not quite sure why I feel so protective of you. Please, allow me to escort you elsewhere. A woman out here alone...it's way too dangerous. You should not be here, especially not alone."

Charlotte looked again toward the sounds of battle. She sighed. As much as she didn't want to run and leave her home completely unprotected, she knew what the captain said was true. She would be much safer in town, with Ginny or Alex or Augusta.

"I suppose you're right, Captain. Do you have a moment to spare so I can pack some supplies?"

"If you hurry." He nodded. "Do you ride? Is there a horse I can saddle for you?" He followed her as she headed into the house.

"I do ride, but no horse." She quickly threw some clothes and various supplies into a carpet bag. "My father gave them to the Union army back in '61. 'For the cause', you know."

He nodded. "Can you ride double with me?"

"Captain," She turned to him, bag in hand, ready to go. "I have been riding for as long as I can remember. As of right now, one of the greatest losses I have suffered in this war is the loss of my own horse, Breslin."

"I'm sorry to hear that." He said, leading her outside. He mounted his horse, then took her bag and hooked it over his pommel. He then reached down to help pull her up behind him. She quickly settled in and wrapped her arms around his abdomen. As he curved his hand around her forearm, she couldn't help but note how improper this act would be considered, but since they were on the verge of a battle, it couldn't be helped. 'War changes things.' She thought as they headed into town.

"Most of the fighting will happen south of town today. It was mostly in the north and west yesterday. The Rebels pushed us right through town, but we dug in over here." The Captain explained.

"What about by the college? My friend lives over there, she is the daughter of one of the professors. Do you think she's okay?"

"As long as they kept to their house and stayed together, they should be okay." He paused. Let me know where to go."

"How do you expect to get through town if the Confederates have taken control of the town?" Charlotte asked.

"We have pockets in town that we hold. If this house is under Rebel control, I will take you elsewhere."

Charlotte was quiet the rest of the ride, speaking only to give Captain Spencer directions to the Wade home. When they came close to town, nearing the McClellan house, Ginny was outside, giving water to wounded soldiers.

"Here, Captain, here." She tried to jump down, but he held her arm tightly. He dismounted, then reached up to help her down. His hands gripped her waist, her hands on his arms, and looked into her eyes. Ginny had waved to Charlotte, then continued with her work.

"Thank you, Captain, for everything. The other night, and now. I do appreciate it."

"It's no trouble." Captain Spencer said. "I'm just...doing what I can to help." He paused, as if thinking of something. They were so close, he bent his head slightly. Before he could make any further move, gunfire broke out. Captain Spencer dove to the ground, pulling Charlotte down and covering her body with his. Ginny also flung herself to the ground.

"Charlotte, are you okay?" Ginny crawled over to them.

Captain Spencer looked down at Charlotte. "Are you all right?"

Charlotte sat up and nodded. "I'm fine." She turned to Ginny and threw her arms around her. "Ginny! You're okay. I was so worried."

"I was worried about you too." As the two girls spoke, Captain Spencer mounted his horse.

"Captain!" Charlotte called. He turned to her.

"Thank you again for everything. Take care of yourself."

He nodded. "Goodbye, Miss Turner." He saluted and rode away, leaving Charlotte's heart pounding and stomach fluttering.

Lewis Cellar

Augusta and Mrs. Lewis stayed in the cellar for what seemed like days, but had only been overnight.

"Should we go up and see what's going on?" Augusta asked, anxious.

"I can still hear gunfire." Mrs. Lewis said. "We'd best stay here. For now, at least."

The trapdoor above opened.

"Audge?" Her brother's voice came down. "It's me." He climbed down the ladder, a bit shakily as he still carried his rifle.

"Andrew!" She stood and hugged him. "How are you? What's going on up there? How many days have passed?" She paused and looked at him.

"One question at a time." Andrew sat on a crate. "Good afternoon, Mrs. Lewis." He nodded and tipped his hat. She gave him a stiff smile. "It's only Tuesday, we haven't even been here a full day. From what we can tell, the Yanks have gone south of town and taken positions. We've taken over most of the town. The big fight is shaping up to the South of town."

"Oh, Lord, please watch over Charlotte." Augusta prayed.

"Who is Charlotte?" Andrew asked.

"A friend of mine. She is living alone right now on a farm just south of town. Her father is fighting and her mother passed away years ago."

"I am glad to hear you're making friends with the Yankees." In spite of his positive words, his voice sounded disappointed.

"You have friends from the North as well." Augusta said.

"Had." Andrew corrected her, a bit of anger in his voice.

"What do you mean, *had*?" Augusta asked.

"I mean I'm not too fond of any Yankees these days. You wouldn't be either if you'd seen what I had to see."

"That's a horrible thing to say." Augusta said. "Perhaps you have forgotten who my very best friend is." She paused. "Who the father of my child is. The father of your future nephew or niece."

"I haven't forgotten. And I don't understand now any more than I did back then why you married him. And then, coming up here to live, to help the Yanks, instead of going home where you belong!" Andrew's voice was angry, hurtful words coming out of his mouth.

Augusta couldn't believe it. He had always been the kinder, gentler brother. He rarely spoke out of anger.

"It may be difficult for you to understand, but I am where I belong." Augusta touched her brother's hands. They were chapped and dirty. A long scar traveled from his right index finger and continued under his shirt sleeve. "Drew, what has happened to you? You're never this angry."

"I have lost too many good friends to the Yankees." He said. "Beau Obenauf was killed by a sniper. Sam London was killed at Sharpsburg. He was right next to me as he fell."

Tears began to fall from Augusta's eyes. She knew both boys well, and had even fancied Beau for a time. "Do you hear from Joey?"

When Andrew's eyes turned stone cold, Augusta wished that she hadn't asked.

"Joey was hit by a Yankee bullet in the leg during the battle of Fredericksburg. They had to amputate to save his life. They'll send him home, but as you know, there is no one left there to care for him."

"Oh, Lord." Augusta sat back and put her hand over her mouth. "Not Joey, no."

"Yes. He was shot by a Yankee. Could have been the brother or father or husband of one of your Yankee friends." Andrew stood. "I need to get back up there. I have my duty to attend to. I'll let you know when it is safe to come out." He gave her one more hug before climbing the ladder. "I don't agree with what you've done, but you're still my sister. I still love you. Always will." He climbed up and the trap door slammed shut.

Clark Home, off the Mummasburg Road

Alex woke up slowly, then blinked and took in her surroundings. She was in her parent's room, in the same bloody dress she had been wearing the day before.

"Alexandria?" Her mother came in, looking around. "Oh, here you are."

"Yes, mother. I only wanted to lay down for a moment." Alex looked at the pocketwatch she had left on the nightstand. "I had not meant to sleep so long."

"You needed to rest." Her mother said. "Do you wish to stay up here?"

"No." Alex stood and looked in the mirror, patting her hair.

"I have never looked so disheveled." She said, quickly pinning some locks back, then straightening her wrinkled dress as best she could. "Did we have any new men come in?"

"Not new, we can't take any more. We have lost some." Mrs. Clark looked down. "So much suffering and death. What a waste."

Mother and daughter walked out of the room. Soldiers lay in the hallway, some with a blanket, a pillow or quilt, some with nothing. Mr. and Mrs. Clark's room was the only one that hadn't been overrun with injured men. Alex knelt down and tucked the blanket around a man who had tossed it off, then continued down the stairs to find Dr. Knightly. She found him going from soldier to soldier, checking their wounds.

"Dr. Knightly, how can I help today?"

"I can use your help right now, if you could go and get me some water and cloths." Alex did, and quickly returned to the doctor's side. "When you're finished helping me here, there are many more things you can do. You can make sure they have water. You can see if any of them would like to have you write a letter, if you can round up paper and something to write with. That can help keep their spirits up. I noticed that you have every extensive library in this house. You could read to them. One of the most important things you can do is let us, the doctors, know if any of them need any specific medical assistance. Most of the fighting has moved south of town, so I can't see us getting a lot of new wounded. We'll get some, but we're pretty full." The doctor ran his hand through his hair and rubbed his head. "By the way, I would like to make sure you know that I appreciate your help. I've had to take over more houses than I would like to have during this war.

Not all of the occupants are as willing to help. And from what I have noticed, you don't seem to treat the Confederate soldiers any different from your own Union men."

"I just keep thinking about my husband, Will. How I would hope any woman would help him if, God forbid, he was wounded."

"That's a good way of looking at things." Dr. Knightly stopped at a soldier and peeled back the bloody bandage around the soldier's shoulder.

"Well, I haven't seen you discriminate against Union soldiers." Alex replied.

Dr. Knightly gestured for Alex to kneel next to him. He cleaned the wound, using the water that Alex held. "I try not to." He replied. "I met a very compassionate woman who was in a similar situation as you. Married, her husband fighting in the war on the Confederate side. Her own home had been destroyed in battle and she was living in her parent's house. We took over the family home and she quickly took to nursing. She showed so much compassion to all of the wounded. So much Christian charity. She helped me see all men as patients, not soldiers. She taught me to look past the uniform and not pick a side." He stood and Alex followed him to the next wounded soldier. "I've tried to remember what I learned from her. She was such a good friend in the short time that I knew her."

Alex smiled. "Do you always befriend those whose homes you work at?"

Dr. Knightly stood and frowned. "No. In fact, there are many things I wish I could have done differently. Things I wish I would have said and things that I wish I could take back." He moved to the next patient. "But I suppose that's part of life. Making mistakes and learning from them."

"Those are very wise words, Dr. Knightly. And so true."

McClellan Home, Baltimore Street

"I still can't believe you came into town this morning." Ginny said, kneading a loaf of bread. Charlotte pounded down another loaf, preparing it to put in the oven.

"I wasn't planning on it, but Captain Spencer insisted and what he said made sense." She sighed. "I shudder to think about what my home will look like when I return."

"Captain Spencer seems like quite the hero to you. Saving you from his own men and then bringing you in today."

"I'm not quite sure why he took such an interest in me. We have met before, in Fredericksburg when I was visiting my cousin. He's quite different now than he was then."

"Quite handsome, too." Ginny smiled.

"I would have to be blind not to notice that." Charlotte smiled back. "But I am promised to another."

"Have you resigned yourself to that fact?"

"I have. I don't know what else to do. He's a good man for the most part. He seems to care for me. I could do a lot worse than Thomas Culp."

"You could do better, too." Ginny said, disapproval apparent in her voice. "After all the resisting, you're just giving up."

"What else can I do, Ginny?" Charlotte asked.

"What happened to your dreams of marrying Wesley?"

"That's all they are. Dreams. I know that now." Charlotte punched the bread dough as if it were responsible for her troubles. "Ginny, I haven't heard from Wesley since before the war. Even if he lives, there is no reason to believe I will ever see him again. And just because I want him to come back doesn't mean he wants to come back. Just because I love him doesn't mean he loves me. Just because I want to marry him doesn't mean he wants to marry me. No one else in the town, save his sisters and you, and of course, me, want him to come back. Most of the town hates him." Charlotte looked at her friend. "If the war has taught me anything, it's that I need to grow up and take responsibility. I can still be Wesley's friend and hope for his safety, but I see now that a relationship with him is no more than a dream."

"But you still love him." Ginny said quietly, pulling a loaf out of the oven.

"Yes, I do. But we don't always get what we want."

Gunfire continued to sound from outside, occasionally peppering the house.

"Doesn't that drive you crazy?" Charlotte asked.

"It did at first, but I suppose now I am used..." her words were interrupted by a screaming sound and a crash from upstairs. The whole house shook as if an earthquake was happening. The two girls could hear falling bricks clinking against one another. Baby Louis started wailing, and Harry dove under a dresser in fear.

"What was that?" Mrs. Wade asked, coming in from the sitting room.

"I'll go see what happened." Ginny said, turning to go up the stairs.

"I'll come with you." Charlotte said, quickly coming up behind her and following her up the narrow staircase. The sight that greeted them at the top was fallen brick, plaster and wood on the floor. There was a hole in the north side of the roof, where a shell had torn through, then had smashed through the wall that had divided the two homes of the building.

"Where did it go?" Charlotte asked.

Ginny peered through the hole in the wall. The missile had embedded itself in the brick wall at the south side of the house.

"Shouldn't it have exploded?" Charlotte asked.

"I would think so. I suppose we should consider ourselves lucky." Ginny answered. "And thank God."

Clark Home, off the Mummasburg Road

Alex continued to move from wounded man to wounded man.

"I can't believe human beings could do this to one another." She muttered to herself.

"Mrs. Sadler." Dr. Knightly called.

"Yes, doctor."

"I was wondering if I could prevail upon you to check and change dressings on some of the men. I can show you how. Even though you've been helping me and I wouldn't be surprised if you have already figured out how.

"If it will help." Alex nodded. She had learned a lot in the short time that the wounded had been at her home. Her neighbors, Ellen and Emma Aughinbaugh, had briefly stopped by with some news. Most of the homes around the college, along with many of the college's buildings, were being used as hospitals. Many of the town's doctors were helping, including Dr. William Crapster O'Neil and the brothers, Robert and Charles Horner. However, many other men of the town had fled, and only a few had made any attempt to defend their homes.

Dr. Knightly led her to what used to be the parlor. Like all the rooms of the house, men lay everywhere. He knelt down next to an older soldier. His arm was wrapped in bloody bandages. The doctor explained the proper methods for changing the dressings and putting new ones on. Alex recognized the new bandages right away. They were strips from a Christmas tablecloth that had been stored away. She knew that bed sheets had been torn up and used also. It seemed as though all they had would be used and destroyed during this devastating battle.

"Do you think you can handle this on your own?" Dr. Knightly asked.

"I do." Alex nodded and went to work. As the afternoon turned to evening, she visited with the men, read to them and wrote letters for them. Dr. Knightly checked on her often, and asked for her help at times. She quickly grew to respect him, but couldn't help notice a sadness that hung over him. She wondered what had happened in his life to cause it.

Lewis Cellar

"I just cannot believe Andrew would act like that." Augusta said, in between bites of an apple she had found in one of the barrels. "He has always been supportive. He was always the one to comfort me. Even when he was hurting, he would be there for me. He was the perfect gentleman. Proper to a fault. I just can't believe he's become so bitter and angry."

"War has a way of changing people." Mrs. Lewis said. "Did Michael ever tell you about his Uncle Carlton?"

"He mentioned an Uncle Carlton who fought in the war with Mexico." Augusta said. "It seems like all of Michael's ancestors have a military background."

"Well, many of the Lewis's have, but Carlton is my brother. When he went away to fight, he was a happy, optimistic young man. He had always wanted to be a soldier, went to West Point, made some good friends, including Mr. Lewis's brother, and then, after a few years of serving in peacetime, went off to fight against the Mexicans. I remember he even mentioned a classmate named Robert Lee. I am sure it is the same man now in command of the Southern Army. At any rate, Carlton fought and was wounded badly at the first battle of Tobasco in '46. He came back with an arm that would never be useful again and a melancholy, depressed disposition. He lost himself to drinking and ended up breaking his neck when he fell from his horse." Mrs. Lewis was now tearful. "I try to remember him as my loving, kind brother, and not as the man he turned into."

"I hope and pray that Andrew and Joey don't end up like that." Augusta said, holding her mother-in-law's hands. Then, a horrible thought occurred to her. "Michael. Michael could never change that much. Not Michael."

"It could happen, dear. But I believe that, even if it does, your love for him, and mine, might be able to help him through. Love can be very powerful."

Augusta shrank back. She had considered Michael being wounded and worry for his life was constantly on her mind. But now, she had a new worry to think about. Not only were soldier's lives at stake, but their minds were as well.

McClellan Home

As the day went on, Ginny and Charlotte continued to bake and give the bread and water to soldiers that came and went.

"How are we doing for flour?" Mrs. Wade asked as the afternoon turned into evening.

"Getting low." Ginny replied. "But hungry men just keep coming…" As if on cue, there was a knock on the door. Ginny opened it to find yet another soldier. Pardon me, miss, but do you have any food to spare?"

"Here. Take some bread." Ginny said, handing the soldier some of the last of what was left.

"Thank you, ma'am." He turned, taking a bite of what she had given him.

Louis fussed in his bassinet. Georgia had fallen asleep, so Charlotte crossed into the front room and picked the boy up. Isaac and Harry sat on the floor, looking at picture books.

"We could really use more flour and cheese." Ginny remarked.

"There's still some at the house, isn't there?" Mrs. Wade asked.

"Yes, there is." Ginny sighed tiredly. "If it hasn't been ransacked and taken already. I can go over there and get some."

Charlotte placed Louis in his bassinet and crossed into the kitchen.

"Ginny, you are dead on your feet. I'll go."

"Charlotte, you can't risk that." Ginny said.

"You were about to go yourself." Charlotte insisted. "I will go. If it's too dangerous to come back tonight, I'll sleep there and come back in the morning."

Ginny looked at her mother, who nodded.

"I'll be fine." Charlotte said. "Now, hand me the key."

Ginny did so and Charlotte slipped into the night.

*****

Charlotte made it to the Wade's house and quickly got to work. There were soldiers everywhere around the house and she wanted to get back to the comfort of the McClellan house as soon as she could. She had almost packed up all of the supplies and was ready to head back when there was a faint knock on the door. Her heart raced. She quickly grabbed the ancient hunting shotgun from beside the fireplace.

She took a deep breath and leaned against the door. She knew the gun wasn't loaded, but whoever was at the door didn't.

"Whoever is there, I don't have any food." She called as loudly as she dared, her voice choked with fear. "I have a rifle and I do know how to shoot!"

"Charlotte? Is that you? I know you might be mad at me, but would you really shoot the boy who taught you how to handle a gun in the first place?"

She tore the door open and smiled brilliantly. There stood Wesley Culp. She threw herself into his arms.

"Oh, Wesley!" She squealed. He buried his face in her hair. Charlotte pulled back, gripping his shoulders and taking a good look at him. He was dirty, but alive. He was still stocky, but that was better than a lot of the malnourished soldiers she had seen the past few days. His skin was dark from the sun, a beard covered his face, and his hair hung almost to his shoulders. Dust covered his face and his uniform. His butternut coat had only three buttons and was full of tears and holes but in spite of everything, his smile was the same as she remembered.

"What are you doing here? How? Why? What? Oh, Wesley it has been so long! Way too long!" He pulled her tight. She hugged him for a minute longer and then looked up at him. "How have you been? I have written you often, but…"

"I got a few letters before the war, but nothing since." He touched her cheek. "And there were some things you should have written but didn't." He looked down at her, hurt apparent in his eyes.

"Do you mean Thomas?" She asked. He nodded. "Wesley, I am so sorry. I didn't want to tell you because I don't even want it to happen. Please believe me."

"I do." He smiled sadly. "I saw my sisters just before coming here. To be honest, I had no intention of seeing you at all. But they told me how you were doing everything possible to reject him and it gave me hope. It made me realize I couldn't stay away. I had to see you. I came here to give a message to Ginny and ask her where I could find you. Your home is smack in the middle of the fight."

He held her hands in his, and rubbed them with his thumbs. His touch, as innocent as it was, sent shivers up her spine. "What kind of message do you have to deliver?"

"It's from Jack."

"Jack! Where did you see Jack?" He pulled her to a trunk and they both sat down.

"It was in early June. We were marching north and captured a town called Winchester, in Virginia. I got a look at the prisoners. Billy Holtzworth first." Wesley stared ahead, his eyes blank as he recalled his tale. "I called out to him, asked if there was anything I could do to help. I wasn't quite sure how he would react to seeing me. He immediately asked me to get some medical help for Jack Skelley."

"Jack's hurt?"

Wesley stood and strode to the window, his hands palm down on the sill.

"Jack had been hit in the upper arm." His voice cracked. "He was bleeding really badly."

Charlotte stood and walked to him, placing her hand on his back, rubbing back and forth between his shoulder blades.

"It was terrible, seeing him like that, Charlotte. I talked to my superior immediately. Got him transferred to the nearby Taylor House Hospital." He took a shaky breath. Charlotte looked into his face, and could see tears forming in his eyes. She wrapped her arms around him, hugging his back and laying her head on his shoulder.

"I went and visited him a bit later, before we moved on. He gave me the message in case I ever got back here."

"For Ginny?" She asked softly.

"Mmhmm. And one for his mother." He nodded. "Jack was all right when I left him. Hopefully, he'll be back soon. Get wounded and eventually get to come home. There's no shame in that." He paused. Charlotte gently pulled and turned him around.

"And you? Will you come home when this is all over?" Charlotte gently grasped his mustard-colored collar. He averted his eyes.

"When this is all over, I doubt anyone will want me back, Charlotte."

She touched his bearded cheek and turned his face to look into her eyes.

"I want you back." She whispered. "I love you, Wesley."

"I would come back to you, Charlotte." He said, bending his head down. Her lips met his and he pulled her close.

"I love you too, Charlotte." He murmured between kisses. "I love you so much."

"I don't want to be with anyone else but you, ever." She said. "Not Thomas, not anyone."

"I might not come back, Charlotte." He ran a hand through his scruffy hair. "Every day I am at this terrible risk to never come back. It's luck that I have made it through without dying so far. So many of my friends…" he took a deep breath. "Even if I were to come out of it alive, I might not be whole. So many have lost arms and legs. You know Jack could still lose his arm."

Charlotte took his hands and looked into his face. "And you and I both know that Ginny and his mother and everyone will love him no matter what. Just like I would love you no matter what." She took a deep breath and softened her tone. He reached up and tucked a strand of hair behind her ear that had fallen across her face.

"I'm sorry. It might be the gentleman in me or I just love you too much…I want to make you my wife, promise that for the future, but I can't. And we cannot do anything here tonight that could ruin your reputation."

"You are right." She looked up at him. "Will you at least sleep here tonight? You must be exhausted." Wesley smiled.

"I can do that."

Wesley fell asleep in John's bed while Charlotte tried to sleep in Ginny's, but she couldn't find rest. As she thought about what tomorrow would hold, she heard Wesley crying out. She hurried into the other room and knelt down. Wesley's face was scrunched in pain, and he began to sweat.

"No, no." He muttered. She tried to shake him awake.

"Wesley!"

He continued shaking and tossing and suddenly sat bolt upright, finally awaking. He was still breathing hard.

"Wesley, are you alright?"

"It was, it was…the killing, the war." He rubbed his forehead. "It's all so stupid, so pointless, Charlotte. At Manassas, our officers had us stand in straight lines. We would take turns firing at the Union lines, and they would fire back at us. We would just stand there. Men fell all around me, blood was everywhere. I have been shot, punched, slashed with a sword. I have killed men. I don't keep track, not like some men. I don't want to know. After each victory, when we go through to bury the dead and find the wounded, I am afraid to find the body of a friend or relative, from either side. When I sleep, I have nightmares. Even now, in the dead of the night, I can hear cannon and gunfire in my head." He rubbed his temples. Charlotte began rubbing his shoulders. He sighed and continued unloading his thoughts. "It's not just soldiers either, Charlotte. I have seen drummer boys, no older than ten or eleven, charging into battle. Some of them have more guts and courage than grown men. Women and children have fallen as well, to disease, starvation, even battle wounds." He buried his head in his hands. She slid her hands around to his chest and laid her head on his shoulders, hugging him tightly. "I don't know how many people will have to die before we cease this madness." He pulled her into his lap, laying his chin on her head.

"You are a good man, Wesley and I love you. If you..." She choked on the words she was about to say and looked down at his chest. "If you do fall in battle, I suppose it's just God calling you home."

"Charlotte, I'm not used to you talking about God."

"I am a little more now. Ginny's faith is having a positive effect on me, along with two of my other friends. A lot of what they say makes sense. I still have some doubts and fears, but I am praying more." A tear fell down her cheek but her voice remained strong. "If you don't fall in battle, Wesley, if you make it through, just send me word and I will be at your side the first moment I can. I would go to the Orient to be with you, if that's what you wanted.

Wesley tipped her head up and kissed the tear that had fallen.

"I wish I could marry you and run away with you, with no one around but us and no war or fighting going on around us" He kissed her again, then paused, something occurring to him. "By the way...where are the Wades?"

"At the McClellan's house. Georgia married John and she had a baby boy just days ago." Charlotte smiled, and changed the subject again. "I just want to be with you. Why can't we just run away together?"

"It wouldn't be right. We both have things to take care of first. I wouldn't want you to leave and have people think badly of you." He pulled her close, letting her use his shoulder as a pillow. They were, for a moment, both in total peace. All too soon though, dawn began to break, and they both knew that their time together was at an end. Gunshots popped sporadically again. Wesley sighed and broke the silence.

"As much as it kills me, I must go."

"Must you?" Charlotte turned towards him as they stood.

"Yes."

"Come back to me." She whispered. He smiled sadly at her, then clasped her hand in his, interlocking their fingers. As they headed toward the door, a thought flew through her head.

"Wesley, wait." She stopped and pulled him close. "I need to know one thing."

"Anything." He whispered, leaning close.

"Why didn't you come home with Charlie and the others before the war? We could have been together for a while. Are you really that sympathetic to the Southern cause?"

He kissed her lips, then her temple. "It doesn't matter." He murmured. Charlotte pulled away and looked into his eyes.

"It does to me, Wesley."

He sighed. "Thomas came to visit me the Christmas before the war, do you remember?"

"Yes. I was glad to be free of Thomas's company for a while."

Wesley smiled, then continued. "Well, he told me that he had been courting you. I was upset by it and he knew it. So he continued to rub it in. He told me that you would be his wife before he left for the war. Said that you were very excited and couldn't wait to become Mrs. Thomas Culp. Now, I realize he was lying to me, but I did believe him, Charlotte. It upset me. I felt betrayed by Thomas for going after the girl that he knew I wanted. I felt betrayed by you for stepping out with Thomas, especially when you never told me anything about a relationship with him."

"I was embarrassed and I never wanted his attentions. You are the only man I have ever had feelings for." Charlotte kissed him again. They broke apart at the loud boom of cannon fire. He glanced in the direction of Culp's hill.

"I need to get back to my unit." He was reluctant, she could tell by the look in his eyes. "And you need to get back to Georgia's. You'll be safer there, with others." They began walking down the steps, keeping a sharp eye for anyone. Their fingers were still laced tightly together and Charlotte's shoulder brushed Wesley's with every step. All too soon, they came to the juncture where they had to part ways.

"I will find you when this war is over, Charlotte." He promised, gently kissing her forehead. "I love you."

"I love you too." Charlotte reached around her neck and undid the clasp on her mother's cross necklace. "I want you to keep this." She placed it into his hand. "I will be praying for you to stay safe."

Wesley slipped the necklace around his neck and tucked it inside his shirt. "Thank you. I will wear it with pride." They kissed one more time, and amid the sounds of battle, they parted. It was only after he was out of sigh that Charlotte realized that he had never given her the message from Jack to give to Ginny.

July 3
Clark House

Alex woke up to the sounds and smells that she had become accustomed to over the past two days. She dragged herself out of the bed carefully, so as not to wake her mother. She slipped on the day dress she had brought in from her own room the night before. She then opened the door that led to the balcony outside her parent's room. It was still the only place in the house that wasn't overrun with wounded. She looked out around the landscape. This early in the morning, the guns were, for the most part, quiet. She could see bodies still littering the streets and the farms further out. The stench of rotting corpses filled the air. The past days had been hot and most folks were so preoccupied helping the wounded or hiding that they couldn't be bothered with the dead. In spite of the carnage around her, Alex couldn't help but notice the beauty of the morning. The sun was just rising over the mountains in the distance.

Suddenly, to the south, cannon fire thundered, breaking the tranquility. Alex looked east to see smoke rising from the area of Culp's Hill. It was apparent there would be another day of fighting.

"Water!" Alex could hear cries from wounded men on the porch below and in the yard, men waking up in pain and hungry and thirsty. She took a deep breath, mentally preparing herself for another day of nursing, then headed downstairs.

She moved through the wounded men, doing what she could for them. She was beginning to learn some of the names of the men, as well as some information about them. She had always enjoyed socializing with people, and Dr. Knightly had told her that visiting with the soldiers would help keep their spirits up. He said that it was sometimes just as important as helping them physically.

"How are you doing today, Lieutenant West?" Alex approached one of the young men she had been helping. He had been shot in the wrist and to stop the wound from becoming infected, the doctors had amputated part of his arm. The young man, from New York, reminded her of her brother. Same black hair, same brown eyes. He was about Aaron's age as well.

"I'm all right today, Mrs. Sadler." He said weakly. Alex knelt next to him, holding a bowl of chicken broth.

"Do you think you can stand to eat a little?" Alex asked.

"I can try." He unsuccessfully tried to lift his head, so Alex gently cupped the back of his head to help him.

"Mrs. Sadler." Alex looked up to see Dr. Knightly, a grim look on his face. "Can I speak to you when you are finished there?"

"Of course, Dr. Knightly." Alex finished with Lieutenant West, who barely ate anything, and went to find Dr. Knightly. He was in the dining room-turned-operating room speaking with some of the other doctors. When he saw her approach, he excused himself.

"How can I help you, doctor?" Alex asked.

"Walk with me, Mrs. Sadler, as we talk." She followed him back toward the patients. "I just wanted to touch base with you on some of the patients you have been working with for the past few days. How did Lieutenant West eat?"

"He didn't really eat a lot. He actually ate more yesterday than today."

"I was afraid you would say that." Dr. Knightly ran a hand through his hair and rubbed his head.

"Is something wrong?" Alex asked.

"Yes. No…Probably, yes." He sighed. "He's been getting weaker and weaker every time I see him. I'm just not sure if he will make it."

Alex nodded sadly. She had witnessed more death and destruction in the past two days than she had ever dreamed possible. "Is there anything I can do to help?" She asked.

"No more than you're already doing. Keep a close watch on him. Let me know how he's doing." Dr. Knightly rubbed his eyes. Alex wondered how much sleep the man had gotten since the battle began.

"I can do that. Do you doctors hear much from the front?"

"Bits and pieces. There was a lot of devastation yesterday south of town. It sounds like there will be more bloodshed today."

"Three days of fighting? I wouldn't have though it possible." Alex commented.

"I agree." Dr. Knightly replied. "Thank you again, Mrs. Sadler, for your assistance. I will check in with you later." He gave her a small smile. "You're a good nurse. Your help has been invaluable."

"I only want to help." Alex said. "Just like you."

Lewis Store

Augusta took a new candle and pushed it on top of the candle that had almost burned out. Her mother-in-law turned a page in the book she was reading. Augusta picked up the stitching she had been working on, glad for the distraction. The worst part of the whole ordeal was the waiting, the boredom, the anticipation and wondering what would happen next. From upstairs, they could still hear occasional gunshots, so they did not dare go upstairs. Andrew hadn't come back down. Augusta worried about him. She couldn't stop worrying about him and Joe and Michael. Especially Michael. Worrying about Alex and Charlotte and Ginny. Worrying about her family and friends back home. It was suddenly too much. She threw her stitching on the floor and stood, pacing back and forth.

"Augusta, my dear, whatever is the matter?"

"I am so sick of this!" She exclaimed. "Sitting down here just waiting, while my brother is up there, shooting and being shot at. And my husband is God-knows-where. He could be wounded or dead or in prison. I don't know what I would do without him and I am so sick of waiting and wondering and I'm just...so...so scared." Exhausted, she collapsed back on the crate, buried her face in her hands, and sobbed. Her shoulders shook.

"Oh, Augusta." Mrs. Lewis knelt before her daughter-in-law and hugged her tightly.

"I'm sorry, so sorry. It's just...without sleep, it's just...all catching up with me." Augusta choked out. "I try so hard to be strong, but I miss home. I miss my brothers and father. I miss Michael more than I ever imagined possible. I'm sick of trying to pretend that the whispers and stares and hostility don't bother me. They do. And now the war has come to our back door, my new home, which negates the very reason Michael wanted me here in the first place." Augusta wiped at her eyes.

"My dear, it is good to let your feelings out. You have been so strong to try and fight all these demons by yourself. And in your condition, no less. I had no idea it had gotten this bad. Have you been completely keeping this to yourself? Have you told no one?"

"Charlotte knows a little. She was with me once when some men were harassing me. And I talk some to Ginny and Alex. I write to Michael and tell him things. Not everything, but I probably tell him more than I should, but he is my best friend. I don't want him to worry."

"He is a good boy." Mrs. Lewis remarked.

"He is a wonderful man." Augusta said. "You and Mr. Lewis did such a good job raising him. He's funny, kind, loving, stubborn, passionate…" She trailed off with memories of him. "So many memories. I wish I could share all of them with you, Mother, well…" she trailed off with a blush. "Almost all of them."

Mrs. Lewis smiled. "You don't know how glad I am that Michael found you. I was very unsure about the match at first, but he chose well with you."

Before Augusta could speak, the trapdoor opened and Andrew's voice came down. "Augusta, Mrs. Lewis, it's safe to come up."

The two women quickly ascended the ladder.

"I don't have much time. I have to join my unit."

"Andrew…"

"I'm sorry if I upset you. I wasn't kind. I still love you, though." He pulled her into a quick hug.

"I love you too, Andrew. Please take care of yourself."

"I will. You too." He glanced again at her stomach. "And that little Yankee-Rebel you're carrying." He grinned for a second. "If it's a boy, you should name him Billy John." He chuckled.

Augusta smiled back. Andrew nodded to Mrs. Lewis, then left.

McClellan Home

Charlotte reached the McClellan house just as the sun rose. Ginny and Harry were up and outside already, collecting firewood.

"At it again?" She asked as she approached them. Ginny's hair was slightly mussed, and it looked as though she had gotten very little sleep. She was wearing the same dress as she had been the day before.

"Of course we are." Ginny nodded.

"Is everyone else still asleep?"

"As asleep as they can be with all of this commotion."

The three quickly made their way into the house. It was still warm from the day before. The fire in the stove must have been going all night. Ginny got a good look at Charlotte.

"What took you so long?" She reached out and flicked some stray hair from Charlotte's loose bun.

"I fell asleep at your house." Charlotte explained, then glanced towards Harry, who had finished stoking the fire and had curled up with a blanket, closing his eyes.

"Fell asleep?" Ginny looked at her and noticed the blush on Charlotte's cheeks. "Come on, I know there is more to this story. Tell me." She asked in a hushed tone. Even breathing from Harry told her the boy had drifted off to sleep again. Charlotte pulled her best friend towards the kitchen table, where the bread dough that Ginny had prepared the night before was rising. Ginny began kneading the dough as Charlotte stared toward the Wade home as she unpacked the supplies she had brought back.

"Wesley." Charlotte finally whispered, so that only Ginny could hear her.

"What?" She looked at her, disbelief covering her face.

"He came to see you last night. He had a letter..." Charlotte explained. A soft rapping at the door interrupted Ginny from asking any further questions. She opened the door to a ragged Union soldier. Like every soldier they had met, his face was thin and gaunt and he was covered in dirt and sweat.

"Mornin', miss. I just got pushed back from my post and I'm powerful hungry. I heard that you been giving out bread to Union boys and would really be obliged if you had some to spare."

"We are baking more right now, sir. You may come back in a bit for a share." Ginny explained gently.

"Thank you, ma'am." The boy looked disappointed, but continued on his way.

"What time did you go to bed last night, Ginny?" Charlotte asked as she returned to the table.

"At least I got some sleep." She said, looking at her friend slyly.

"I slept." Charlotte murmured, "And that isn't answering my question."

"I fed my last soldier at around ten. I gave him all the food we could spare. They are all so weak and hungry. It makes me angry that some people around here are charging them for food."

"It's only right that you would be giving bread away for free, but Ginny, you can't afford that."

"Can we afford to let our Union men go hungry? I can only imagine what Gettysburg will be like if the Rebels take it over."

"That's true." Charlotte agreed.

"So. Wesley." Ginny said, continuing to work on the bread. "Tell me, what did he have to say?"

Charlotte gave her a brief description of what had happened the night before.

"And" Charlotte grinned. "He did say that he met up with Jack."

Ginny's hand flew to her apron pocket, the pocket that held the photograph of Jack that she always carried. As Charlotte explained Jack's injuries, Ginny's breathing got heavy and her face turned an ashen white.

"Will he be all right?" She whispered, fear and tears in her eyes.

"Wes believes that Jack will pull through." Charlotte didn't mention how Wesley had said that Jack could lose his arm. Ginny had enough to worry about.

"Well, what a blessing. And I am glad that he is not here to see what has become of our town." Ginny closed her eyes and breathed a sigh of relief. She quickly regrouped, resilient as always.

"How about some breakfast?" Ginny asked, moving to the stove. As she began to make coffee, Charlotte went to the pantry to get the last of yesterday's ham and butter. It was a meager supply. Soon, the smell of fresh coffee began to permeate through the house. Within a few minutes, Mrs. Wade, Isaac and Georgia awoke and little Louis began to fuss. Harry rolled over and rubbed his eyes, awaking from his nap.

"There is some applesauce here too." Ginny said, pulling the jar from a shelf. The six ate their small meal. Charlotte would have declined her share, but she was hungry, and had a feeling that it would be a long day.

After breakfast, they sat down for a while as they waited for the bread. They could hear the occasional sounds of battle, and the room was filled with tension. Ginny pulled out her bible.

"Devotions?" Charlotte asked her.

"Every day." She smiled. "Today is one of my favorites, Psalm 27. *The Lord is my light and my salvation; whom should I fear? The Lord is the strength of my life, of whom should I be afraid?* How appropriate." Ginny continued to read silently, absorbed in the Word. Charlotte knew the verse. Ginny had often read it over the past two years. Charlotte sat back and closed her eyes, praying for the safety of Wesley and Jack and everyone else fighting. Georgia was feeding Louis, and Mrs. Wade was knitting some socks. Harry and Isaac were playing with some toy soldiers in the corner.

"*Though war should rise against me, in this I will be confident.*" Ginny read quietly. "*I had fainted unless I had believed to see the goodness of the Lord...Wait on the Lord, be of good courage and He shall strengthen thine heart.*"

"Ginny, stop." Georgia suddenly cried, her face uneasy and her voice unsteady. Ginny looked up in surprise.

"Why? What's wrong Georgia?"

"Mother, make her stop. She's making everything feel worse." Charlotte and Ginny could tell that Georgia was uneasy about the undeniable danger they were in. No one wanted to make the situation worse.

"I'm sorry Georgia. I didn't mean to upset you." Ginny closed the Bible and looked out the window. Charlotte followed her gaze and saw Confederate soldiers across Breckenridge Street, running, shooting, and taking up positions. Mr. Pierces' home, where Sam was staying, was not far from there. Ginny could only hope that the butcher would be able to keep Sam safe.

Georgia finished feeding Louis and had calmed down a little bit. Gunfire was steady, closer to the house. Ginny sighed.

The clock had just struck seven when a barrage of gunfire came from the North. The windows shattered with a deafening crash. Harry ducked into a ball on the floor as Charlotte dove to the floor. Ginny fell on top of Harry and Isaac, covering them as best she could. Georgia curled around her son. One bullet whirled through the air and they heard a sharp splintering of wood. Mother Wade moved to the head of the bed where Georgia and Louis were huddled, and picked up something small off of the pillow. Ginny, Harry and Charlotte picked themselves off the floor. Ginny took a look at what her mother held.

"A bullet." She stated.

"It's still warm." Mrs. Wade murmured.

They remained in that room for close to an hour. No one spoke; all were praying silently. Bullets continued to fly everywhere outside. Charlotte couldn't help but wonder why Captain Spencer had thought it would be safer in town.

****

Ginny had finally had enough of sitting in the room. She stood and headed into the kitchen.

"Ginny Wade, what are you doing?" Charlotte asked standing and following her.

"Well, I have bread waiting to be baked and soldiers outside needing to be fed." By the determination in her voice, Charlotte knew it would be pointless to argue with her. She prepared herself mentally for another day just like yesterday.

"Fine, I'll help." Charlotte said, "But I still think if we're not careful, someone is going to get shot."

"Well, if there is anyone in this house to be killed today, I hope it is me." She replied.

"Must you always be so selfless?" Charlotte asked her.

"Well, Georgia has the little baby, and..."

"You don't need to explain anything to me, Gin." Charlotte smiled. They began working on another batch of bread. They slowly blended together the flour and baking soda. After all the baking they had done in the past few days, this was becoming routine. Soon, their hands were full of dough.

"Mama!" Ginny called to the other room. "Could you please get the stove ready? We are almost ready."

The gunfire continued as they put the bread in to bake.

"Why in heaven's name are they shooting at our house?" Mrs. Wade wondered aloud.

"Probably just shooting to keep the Union men down. I saw some soldiers of ours along the North slope of Cemetery Hill." Charlotte answered.

"Do you think the shooters are Confederate, then?" Ginny asked.

"Most probably." Charlotte nodded. "When I came in this morning, I had to avoid a bunch of them. They're crawling along Baltimore Street and the South side of town. It looks like some have even gone into homes."

"Why did you come back here?" Mother Wade asked. "Not that we are not happy for your company, but it seems like a huge risk. You should have just stayed at our house."

"Alone? How boring." Charlotte smiled. "Besides, I wanted to spend time with you all. And you needed the flour."

Without warning, a sharp crack rocked through the house. Charlotte threw her hands over her head. Ginny fell to the ground, pain ripping through her shoulder. Charlotte looked at her friend. Blood soaked from a hole just below her left shoulder blade. Without thought, Charlotte fell beside Ginny and pulled her in her arms. Ginny's eyes were open, but all life had vanished from them. As Charlotte gasped for air, her heart tore through her chest. She couldn't control her breathing. She tried to scream, but no sound came out. She tried to fill her lungs with air but a pit feeling deep in her stomach was making it difficult. She did not want to believe what just happened, yet knew what she saw. Mrs. Wade knelt beside the two girls, her own heart hammering and a feeling of emptiness coursing through her. She read the pain in Charlotte's face. She stood, with a calmness Charlotte couldn't fathom, and walked into the front room. Tears streamed down Charlotte's cheeks and she hiccupped, still trying to catch her breath. Her vision blurred as she heard the muffled voice of Mrs. Wade.

"Georgia, your sister is dead."

A wave of dizziness passed over Charlotte's head as Georgia's scream ripped through the air. Before Charlotte could do anything else, the door burst open and Federal soldiers surrounded her and Ginny. The men were battle weary, famished and broken. Charlotte struggled to focus on their faces, but her vision was so blurred that she couldn't see any features. She felt strong hands lift her up. She fought, trying to get back to her best friend. Sobs racked her body as the soldiers took charge of the tragedy, one holding her tightly. Charlotte could hear them talking to Mrs. Wade, but she couldn't make out any words. She finally stopped struggling as her legs turned to gelatin and gave out underneath her. Not knowing what else to do, she threw her arms around the soldier, buried her head on his chest and sobbed. She started to distinguish some words of the conversation.

"We need to get to the cellar." A nasally private said. "The south side would be best."

"How do we do that?" Another voice asked. "Look outside, man."

The north wall of Georgia's home was dangerously exposed, and Rebels were still firing bullets in the direction of the house. One wrong move and someone else could die. Mrs. Wade spoke, still unbelievably calm. She described an escape route, going upstairs and over to the other side of the house. Charlotte barely heard her. There was one thing going through her head, over and over, that wouldn't stop, *Ginny. Gin. Virginia Wade. Not dead. Can't be dead.* Her tears continued to soak the uniform of the soldier who held her. How she wished it was Wesley holding her, comforting her. She clung to the man as if her life depended on it.

"Come on Miss Turner." Charlotte felt the soldier turn and begin to lead her. As she went to take a step, her legs turned to jelly again. She couldn't walk. She allowed the man holding her to bend and lift her into his arms and began carrying her up the stairs to the rooms, the room where the cannonball had crashed through the upstairs the day before. Georgia was ahead of her, the baby in her arms. A soldier carried Isaac and Harry followed quietly. Men following behind carried Ginny's lifeless body. They reached the top rooms, and the men began ripping, tearing and kicking at the hole left from the cannonball, making it big enough to crawl through. Georgia and Louis went through first, followed by a soldier who carried a rocking chair. As the soldier carried Charlotte through the hole, she couldn't help but remember the day before when she and Ginny had laughed at their wild escape from death when the cannon ball had ripped the hole in the house. She choked back tears and buried her face in the soldier's jacket. She would never laugh with Ginny again.

They continued on, through to the McLean side of the house. Charlotte glanced back to see Mrs. Wade and the boys. Mrs. Wade's face was sullen. Harry's eyes were wide with fear and sorrow. They tramped down the stairs, out the door and quickly headed into the cellar. Once in the cellar, the soldiers gently placed Ginny's body on a wooden bench that the McLeans usually used for milk pails and crocks.

The soldier carrying Charlotte set her down. Her legs held her, but were still unsteady. She looked solemnly at Ginny's figure. She had been wrapped in a colorful quilt. Charlotte recognized it as one that Georgia had patched together when she was ten years old. Charlotte leaned her back against the cold stone wall. Her knees gave way as she slid down. She thought she had cried out all her tears in the short span since Ginny had been shot. However, as she leaned her elbows on her knees, more tears came. A little bit of light peeked through a window high in the wall. Mrs. Wade sat next to Ginny's head. Her hand caressed the quilt absentmindedly. Harry and Isaac huddled on the floor. It seemed almost unnatural for Harry to be so still. Georgia held her baby close; tears fell unchecked down her face. The soldiers who had helped were spread around the cellar. Charlotte caught the eye of one, standing close to her, a familiar face. He sat down next to her. She hadn't realized it was Captain Spencer that had held her earlier.

"She is with the Lord now, Charlotte." The captain spoke softly. He looked like he had been to hell and back since the last time she had seen him just yesterday morning.

"Yes, well, I don't care about what the Lord wants." She replied coldly. He tentatively placed his arm around her shoulders. "I want her to be with me."

"I know. She was special." He spoke softly.

"You don't know the half of it."

"I do know, believe me. You're still in shock. And pain, the pain will last a long while. It will never go away completely. I have seen a lot of men die. Good men. But it's for a good cause. Seeing Miss Wade die like this, it really took something out of me. I'm not used to seeing a woman shot down." He paused. Charlotte's face was expressionless.

"How could you possibly know anything about what I have just lost?" Her voice was flat as she spoke. "It's because of you and this war that I lost my best friend." She felt numb, a pit had formed in her stomach and seemed like it would never leave. Captain Spencer continued.

"When someone close to you dies, you can't die with them. You need to remember the best parts of her and keep the memory alive. Bring her best assets out in yourself."

"It's never going to be the same." She whispered.

"No, it won't. But it will get better. Miss Wade had a loving and caring heart. Don't let that be forgotten. Don't let it go to waste."

"Waste. Ginny's death is a waste." Charlotte was getting angry. "She was killed! And for what? A stupid war? War is a waste." She looked to the corner where the Wade family huddled. "I am never going to laugh with my best friend again, never hear her laugh or see her smile." She looked at the Captain. "We were supposed to marry the men we loved and have children that would grow up to be best friends and we were supposed to share adjoining plots of lands. How can you tell me that it is going to be all right?" Her voice cracked. "It's all a cold, cruel stupid waste. And what do you know about losing a loved one? Who have you ever loved who has died? I mean, known, known, not just a comrade or someone. Who have you ever just loved and lost?" Charlotte was angry, not thinking straight. The soldier was there, available to yell at, and Charlotte needed to take advantage of it. When he sat there not speaking, she threw his arm off her. "I asked you a question!"

"My wife." He answered calmly. Charlotte immediately averted her eyes, feeling guilty about her outburst.

"Oh." She looked down.

"It was in childbirth, three years ago. All I could do was sit there, unable to do anything. I lost both my wife and the baby." He smiled sadly, remembering. "You know, you remind me a lot of her. It's one of the reasons that I left my farm to fight in this war. There were a lot of memories at home. Too many."

"I'm sorry." Charlotte suddenly just wanted to be alone. Her best friend was dead. They were all still in danger. She had no idea where the rest of her friends and loved ones were. Alex, Augusta, Wesley, her father. She sighed and leaned her head back against the wall, closing her eyes. Maybe she would fall asleep and wake up and find that this was all just a dream.

Lewis Store, 3:00pm

Augusta and Mrs. Lewis worked the rest of the day to straighten the store and house and they were nowhere near done. It seemed as though everything had been broken. Glass lay everywhere, pillows had been torn apart. Blood and mud and dirt covered every surface. Bullet holes dotted the wood of the store front. There was a dead body on the parlor rug. Other dead bodies littered the road outside, bloated and rotting in the sun. They dared not go outside yet.

"Dear God." Augusta could still hear the blast of guns and cannon firing from the direction of Seminary Ridge and Cemetery Ridge. For the past two hours or so, the artillery had been firing so heavily that the ground was shaking. Finally, the noise ended. It was almost eerie.

"It sounds like it may be over." Mrs. Lewis remarked, standing next to Augusta in the doorway.

Augusta looked at the destruction around her.

"I don't know that it will ever be over."

July 4, 1863
McLean Cellar

Charlotte and the Wades waited in the cellar for what seemed like an eternity. Time dragged on. Charlotte fell in and out of sleep. When she was awake, she just wanted to sleep, her thoughts plagued with memories and visions of what had happened. She couldn't get the images out of her head. When she was asleep, she had nightmares of Ginny, Wesley, Jack, Alex, Augusta, Thomas, her father and even her mother, dying in many terrible ways. Sounds of war still raged in her head. The cellar was cool, but the air was stale. The Wade family and Charlotte kept a vigil, waiting for the gunfire to cease. Captain Spencer had left not long after telling Charlotte about his wife. He had to get back to his unit. Some of the other soldiers had stayed behind. After the streets outside were quiet for a while, one of the soldiers pulled out a pocket watch.

"It's one in the afternoon." He said. "It sounds like it should be safe outside." The others agreed and began filing out of the cellar. Georgia with Louis, Harry and Isaac, carried by a soldier, followed closely behind them. Charlotte took a few steps toward the exit, then turned to find Mrs. Wade. She hadn't moved, still sitting next to Ginny's body. Charlotte walked over and knelt in front of her and took her hands. "Mrs. Wade, you have to come up with us. Ginny wouldn't want us to just mourn her." She spoke halfheartedly. "She would want us to go up and take care of the soldiers who are hurt up there. She can't do it, so we need to do it for her."

"Oh, Charlotte." Tears filled her eyes. "My girl." Charlotte pulled her up and hugged her tightly. She clung to her, and she could feel the woman's whole weight on her. When her body had stopped hitching with sobs, Charlotte patted her back. She couldn't ever recall a time that Mrs. Wade had shown emotions.

"Let's go finish Ginny's work." Charlotte said. They walked, arm and arm up the stairs. When they got outside, it was lightly raining. They walked around the house and into the kitchen. Charlotte couldn't help but notice a pool of Ginny's blood stained the floor. Mrs. Wade kept her head turned from the red and began working on the bread. Charlotte glanced around the small room, but the memories were too strong.

"I'm going to go out and help some of the wounded." Charlotte said. Mrs. Wade nodded. Charlotte walked out the door and leaned against the fencepost, taking in the town in front of her.

Parts of Gettysburg had been destroyed. Pieces of building littered the road and yards. Dead horses and soldiers lay in the streets. The stench of the dead caused her stomach to churn. She ran to a bush and vomited. Union soldiers and people from town moved from body to body, trying to do what they could for the wounded and dead. Charlotte overheard some of the people saying that Elizabeth Thorn, was burying the dead at Evergreen Cemetery. Even though she was six months into her pregnancy, she was stepping into her husband's role of taking care of the cemetery while he was fighting for the Union. Charlotte took a deep breath. It would take so long to get the town back to normal. If it ever could get back to normal.

Clark Home

Alex woke again in her mother's room. All other rooms in the house were still filled with the wounded. Alex quickly got dressed and went downstairs, then began going about the rooms, checking on the men, giving them water, re-bandaging their wounds and easing the pain of the sweating men with cool cloths like Dr. Knightly had taught her.

"Mrs. Sadler." She looked up as the doctor approached her. "I wanted to let you know that the battle is officially over. We received word that Lee and his men started to retreat south this morning. Southern sharpshooters are covering the retreat."

"It's over?" Alex sighed in relief. She couldn't believe it. "The Union won the battle?"

"Yes, ma'am. I may have to leave soon, but your help will be needed. The wounded will be here for a while."

"Of course I'll help. Thank you for the information, doctor." Alex said. "There will be quite a lot of work to do, cleaning up and such, won't there?"

"Yes. There will be." Dr. Knightly ran a hand through his hair and rubbed his head. Alex had noticed that he had done that a lot over the past couple of days, usually when he was agitated.

"Was there something else you wanted to tell me?" She asked.

"It's...its Lieutenant Davis West. He passed away late last night."

Tears began forming in Alex's eyes. She had helped many men since her home had been turned into a hospital, some hadn't made it and some were still fighting. But for some reason, her heart had gone out to Lieutenant West.

"I know you spent a lot of time with him since he was brought in. I'm sorry."

"Does losing your patients ever get any easier?" She asked.

"No. It never does."

McClellan Home

It took until early evening before Charlotte realized that it was Independence Day. That reminder brought back memories of Independence Days of the past, of the dances with Ginny, Jack, Wesley, Alex. Her stomach clenched at the thought of Wesley. Had he survived the battle? She had lost Ginny, surely God would not take away Wesley as well. Had her home survived? What about Alex and Augusta? Who had survived this nightmare? Would Charlotte be left alone in her grief? Why had this happened? She couldn't help but wonder where God was in all of this mess. The rain had stopped, but the sky was still overcast.

"Charlotte?" She turned to the small voice behind her. It was Harry. Charlotte sat down on a fallen fence post and pulled him into her lap, hugging him tightly.

"Is Ginny gone forever? Sam just came home from the Pierces' and that's what Mama said." He asked in a small voice.

So Sam had been told. Charlotte was glad that she had missed that emotional exchange.

"Yes, Harry, she is." She motherly stroked his hair. "She is with Jesus, though."

"But it's Georgia's birthday! Something this bad can't happen on her birthday."

"We can't control when bad things happen, Harry. They just happen."

"Mr. Comfort brought over a box to put her in. Said some Rebs started building it, but it's ours now that we ran them out of town, and Ginny gets it."

"That's very nice of him." Her throat tightened up and tears threatened again, but Charlotte felt she had to be strong for the sake of Harry. Sam walked around from the back of the house.

"Hey, Charlotte. Mama said that we're going to get Ginny buried right now. There are some soldiers who are gonna help us." His voice was strained. The young boy was heavy with grief, but she knew he was trying to act tough, like the man of the house. She felt a wave of guilt for not helping the family prepare for the funeral. She just couldn't do it. Holding Harry's hand she went around to the back of the house to say goodbye to her friend. The garden had been trampled, and a muddy hole had been dug, a grave for Charlotte's twenty-year-old best friend.

Ginny's coffin lay at the side of the grave, her body already nailed inside. Georgia held Louis, and Mrs. Wade stood at the head of the grave, stoic. Charlotte knew that underneath her strong front, Mrs. Wade wanted to crumble.

"Let's get started." Mrs. Wade said.

"Wait." Charlotte spoke up in a shaky voice. "What about Alex and Augusta and everyone else? Can we find out where John is; he can't be far. More people are going to want to be here." Harry clung to her hand as if his life depended on it.

"We can't wait for everyone, Charlotte." Mrs. Wade said softly. "We don't even know where everyone is or whether they are even..." She stopped, not wanting to finish her thoughts. Charlotte's eyes brimmed over with tears as she nodded.

It was a quick affair. It was as though Mrs. Wade wanted it done as soon and quietly as possible.

Oh, Ginny. Charlotte thought. *Why did this happen? Why did you leave us?* Charlotte kept glancing over her shoulder, waiting for a familiar person to come around the corner. She needed a friend: Augusta, Alex, someone. The person she really wanted to see was Wesley, but she knew deep down he would not be there for her. He had retreated. A lump formed in her throat and she sniffed. They all stood silently, heads bowed, as the Union soldiers laid Ginny's coffin in the hole, then began filling it with clods of mud. She kept her head down.

The Lord is my light and my salvation, whom should I fear? Ginny's words from the morning before rang in her ears. It seemed like forever ago. Why had this happened to Ginny, of all people? Why her? She was good, Godfearing, kind. The best friend a person could have. She had tremendous faith that God would always be there for her. Why had He let this happen?

After the short burial, Charlotte walked away. She needed to do something. Something to take her mind off of everything that had happened, but all around her were reminders. Broken buildings, dead bodies. She needed to talk to her friends. She would see Augusta on her way to Alex's. After all of the artillery pounding and gunshots that had been constant for the past three days, Gettysburg seemed eerily quiet and she cringed at the number of blue and gray clad bodies that littered the ground. She tried not to look at their faces. There was just too much death. She hurried to the side of the road, afraid that she was going to be sick to her stomach.

Lewis Home

"Mother?" Augusta walked into the front room where Mrs. Lewis was scrubbing at the rug, trying to get the blood stain out of it. They had moved the dead Confederate to the porch, not sure what else to do. The upstairs living area was finally in order, but the store's supplies had been wiped out, taken by Andrew and his comrades.

"Yes, dear?" Mrs. Lewis sat up and wiped her forehead with her arm.

"I am going to go out, over to the church, to see what I can do to help."

"Are you sure?" Mrs. Lewis asked. "It will not be a pleasant sight."

"I know, but I have to help." Augusta left and headed toward St. Francis Xavier Catholic Church. Not only was it the closest church, it was the church she usually attended with her in-laws. As she arrived, she saw Sallie Meyers, the schoolteacher and a close acquaintance. Sallie sat on the stone steps, head in hands.

"Sallie, what is it? What is wrong?"

"Augusta! I am so glad you made it through okay! How is the store, the Lewis's?"

"Everything is fine. The Confederates took over our home and store and we were stuck in the cellar for most of the battle. Mr. Lewis is out of town, so it was just me and Mrs. Lewis. I'm glad you made it through." The two women hugged. "I'm here to help. What happened to you? What has made you so upset?"

"I have been here since the start of the battle. I am just getting tired and overrun." She led Augusta inside.

"What can I do to help?"

"We have hundreds of men here. The Sisters of Charity from Emmetsburg have arrived and are helping. Many of the townspeople are as well. There are just so many wounded men."

Augusta looked around. Wounded men lay everywhere, on pews, under pews, and in every aisle.

"We even have wounded in the sanctuary." Sallie commented.

Sun shone through the stained glass windows of the building, windows that depicted the Beatitudes. Augusta had not been raised

Catholic, but Mrs. Lewis, being a strict Irish Catholic, had explained many of the traditions, so Augusta was familiar with her surroundings.

"Lord, bless all of these people and be with them, please help to heal them." Augusta murmured a prayer as she followed Sallie.

"There is much to do. Changing bandages is usually a task for the trained staff. But you can help bring water to the wounded and there will be soup available soon. Talk to the men, keep their spirits up. Let one of the orderlies know if you come across a man who didn't make it. If you can find paper, you could write letters for the men. Just talk to them, pray with them. That should be manageable in your condition. Can you do that?"

"Of course." Augusta immediately went to work.

Hours later, she came upon a young man whose head was wrapped in bandages and whose face was clean, but covered in sweat.

"Miss...what can I call you, Miss?" He gasped out.

"You can call me Mrs. Lewis." She offered him some water, and he drank, some dribbled down his chin. He then lay back, his eyes closed. Augusta began to move on to another man when he spoke again.

"Mrs. Lewis, eh?" He groaned. "So I suppose you wouldn't want to become my girl, then? You sure are one of the prettiest gals I've ever met, even though you speak like a Reb."

"Yes, I am married. Happily married. My husband, Michael is an officer with the Union Corps of Engineers. I have been staying with his family since the start of the war."

A man behind her reached out and gently touched her arm. "Lewis? Michael Lewis is your husband?"

"Yes, yes he is." Augusta's heart dropped in her stomach as she turned to the man. "Do you know him?"

"Sure do. He's not with us on this campaign, but I was with him earlier this year. He's a good man. Talked about his wife quite a bit. Nothing but good things to say. How lucky he was to have you." The man speaking was about Michael's age. His face had cuts and scrapes, but Augusta could see no other signs of injury. Until she looked down his body to where his left leg ended abruptly below his knee. "Talked about you all the time, but Ma'am, you sure are prettier in person."

"Thank you." Augusta replied. "May I ask, when you last saw Michael? Is he alright? I haven't heard from him in months."

"Last I saw Lewis was back in April, where he was doing okay, I think. Other than his shoulder, of course."

"Shoulder? What do you mean? I haven't heard from him since last Christmas. What happened?"

"I'm sorry ma'am, I thought you would have known. Lewis was shot in the shoulder."

"What...where..." Augusta sat back on her haunches, face ashen. She didn't even know what to say. "Oh, Lord...is he..." A tear fell down her cheek.

"It happened in early spring, I believe, but he was patched up and fine in no time. It was just a small wound."

Augusta closed her eyes, whispered her thanks to God, prayed that Michael would stay safe, and gathered her strength. "Thank you, sir, for the information." She gave the man some water and a smile. "Let me know if there is anything I can do for you." He nodded, and she moved on. She didn't have time to dwell on her husband now. She was needed here.

Clark Home

After stopping to check on Augusta and hearing from Mrs. Lewis that Augusta was all right and helping at the church, Charlotte found Alex outside of her parent's house. She was walking from soldier to soldier, giving them water if needed, and any other help she could. Charlotte had never seen Alex so disheveled. Her hair was coming out of her usually neat bun, and her plain calico dress was covered in dirt, blood and water. When Alex saw her, she immediately stood and rushed over.

"Charlotte!" She gave her a hug, pulling her close. "How are you, how is everything in town, have you seen Ginny?" Alex looked at her friend. "What's wrong? You don't look well at all."

"You don't know?" Charlotte choked out. She would have thought or rather hoped, that she wouldn't have had to tell anyone what happened to her friend.

"Know what?" Alex looked puzzled.

She took a shaky breath. Alex was the first person that she had to tell. She wasn't quite sure how to do it. "Ginny...was...she is ...she's dead."

"What?" All of the color left Alex's face in a second and she stumbled back a step. "What do you mean? What happened?"

Charlotte quickly told her, struggling to keep her voice steady. The tears threatened once again. "She was killed, shot by some stray Reb bullet, came from the tannery, we think."

"Oh, no...Dear God, no." Alex slunk to the steps of her porch, a dazed look on her face. "I can't...can't believe it. What was she doing? Was she outside? Was she walking around?"

"No, she was inside Georgia's house, baking bread for soldiers. She had been outside earlier; I had also. Nothing had happened. She just was standing at the side table in the kitchen, kneading dough yesterday morning and a bullet came right through the side door and then the open door that goes between Georgia's sitting room and kitchen." Charlotte tried to hold back her tears, but failed. She sat down next to Alex. Soldiers and civilians rushed around them, helping the wounded. Wounded soldiers moaned in pain. "It was so quick, Alex. One second we were talking and laughing and the next, she was on the floor, dead."

"You were with her?" Alex asked, tears streaming down her face.

"Yes. I didn't think it would be safe to stay at my farm alone. So many soldiers around. I never imagined that my place of refuge would be more dangerous? At least...at least I got to spend time with Ginny..." Charlotte closed her eyes to the sight of wounded men around her. But when she closed them, all she could see was Ginny. "We already buried her. Her mother wanted it done as soon as possible. I wanted to wait for you and Augusta, but..." Charlotte buried her face in her hands, not wanting to relive the horrors of the past few days. She suddenly stood. "I need to get out of here. I need to walk. I know I should go check on the farm, but I am afraid to see what it looks like. I can't go back yet."

"I'll walk with you." Alex said. She ducked into the house and spoke to someone Charlotte couldn't see, then rejoined her.

The two friends walked in silence, heading nowhere in particular. Charlotte wanted to get away from the death, the carnage, but it was inescapable. It was everywhere. The stench was overwhelming. Alex let Charlotte lead as they headed east on York Street, then took a path along Rock Creek. Before they knew it, they were at the base of Culp's Hill.

The hill looked nothing like the place they had all played on as children. Charlotte remembered when Wesley and Jack would play their war games. It wasn't just a game anymore. Soldiers and animals were dead, and dying. The stench and sound were things that Charlotte knew she would never forget.

Alex linked her arm with Charlotte's. Both civilians and Union soldiers walked through the bodies that littered the land. She again could not fathom what could be so important that would waste so much human life. She knew why they were fighting but there was too much to lose. Was it all worth it?

"Dear God, why did You allow this to happen?" Charlotte murmured again.

"Now is not the time to dwell, Charlotte. We need to do what we can to help." Alex said.

"I wanted to get away from this. I thought if we came out here, it wouldn't be so bad." Charlotte said.

"There is no getting away from it. It will be a long time before it's cleaned up." Alex replied. "We have to help, and now."

Alex and Charlotte walked through the fallen men, looking for any survivors they could help. Alex had a canteen slung over her shoulder and some bandages. At first, the Union officers tried to keep them away from the death and injuries. Alex had told them they were both married and only wanted to help.

Charlotte worked vigorously, pouring all of her efforts into helping the soldiers, trying to forget what had happened. Uninjured Union soldiers and older boys from town were loading wounded soldiers onto wagons, or carried them on stretchers to nearby homes and barns, which had all turned into field hospitals. The dead were left where they had fallen, to be taken care of later. Not much care was being taken to document who had fallen. In fact, many of the faces were so disfigured; it would be hard to recognize them even if they were known.

Charlotte felt a tap on her shoulder. Alex stood there, a puzzled look on her face. She held out her hand to show her a familiar piece of jewelry. Charlotte's heart skipped a beat.

"Your house must have been looted. It's your mother's necklace. You never take this off. How else would a Rebel get it?" Alex asked.

Charlotte's heart was crushed at her words and the sight of her cross necklace. She felt as though she couldn't breathe. No. This could not be happening. She tried to catch her breath.

"Where...where did you find it?" Charlotte steadied herself on Alex's arm.

"A dead Rebel just up the hill there. The man was actually wearing it. I don't know why, but it caught my eye. I suppose God wanted you to have it back."

"I don't think God had anything to do with this." Charlotte said. Alex looked at her friend's face, angry and cold. "Show me." Charlotte's voice was harsh. She stumbled behind Alex and she stopped at a memorable spot. The spot where she had first met Wesley, back so many years before. The spot where she had fallen in love with him years later. What was happening to her world?

Alex stood over a body, then turned and motioned to her friend. Charlotte was afraid. She didn't want to look. To see his body and know for sure. Know that it was over. Wesley's life, her possible future with him.

"Charlotte, what's wrong? Do you know him?" Alex asked.

Charlotte came closer and knelt down. The man's dark hair was wet and caked with mud. His undershirt was in tatters. His gear was gone. His gray pants were full of holes. Charlotte could see bruises, cuts and scrapes that had not been on Wesley two nights ago. She looked into the man's face, touching his hair and cheek. Through the dirt and grime and blood, she recognized the features.

"It's Wesley." She sobbed. "No, Wesley, no!" She threw her body over his. First Ginny died in her arms and now Wesley was gone? It was too much to bear. What had she done to deserve this? Why was this happening? "Why?" Charlotte growled through clenched teeth. She felt Alex grab her shoulders, pulling her up.

"Charlotte, come away." A few soldiers and townspeople were looking at them. "Let's go over here and talk. You need to talk to me."

"No!" Charlotte cried, her teeth still clenched. "Not Wes, no!" The lack of sleep and food, the emotional stress of the past few days caught up with her. She was overcome with exhaustion, and her body wanted to give up. Alex pulled her away, to a more secluded spot between some trees.

"Charlotte." She spoke softly, but with authority. "You need to pull yourself together. If anyone were to find out or realize that it's Wesley Culp laying there, it could be very bad. He is considered a traitor here in Gettysburg. You know even his own family hates him. They could take the body and make a mockery of it. It's better to just leave him and hopefully no one will recognize him."

Charlotte tried breathing normal but her emotions were making it difficult.

"Come on, Charlie." Alex continued her voice low. "What would Ginny say if she saw you acting like this? And Wesley. I know he was your friend, but…"

"He was more than just a friend, Alex." Charlotte whispered intensely. She was calming down from the initial shock. Her anger was beginning to rise, though. "I gave him that necklace. Two nights ago." She took a deep breath.

A look of confusion crossed Alex's face.

"The night of the second day of battle, Wesley came to the Wade's house to see Ginny and I was there picking up supplies. We talked, we made promises to each other. He was supposed to come back to me." Charlotte took a deep breath. "I love him, Alex. I always have." She fought the tears that had formed yet again. Where did they keep coming from?

"Oh, Charlotte." Alex hugged her tightly, shaking a little, crying herself. After they had held each other for several minutes, Alex pulled back and wiped her eyes with her hands. "Sorry, it's just...I'm fine." Alex said, trying to smile. "Here is what we will do. We'll let the Union soldiers take care of his body. I imagine it is hard to tell exactly who it is."

Charlotte nodded. "I barely recognized him myself. I may not have recognized him at all if I hadn't seen him a few days ago." She tried to hold back another sob.

"Then, later, we can come back to the place he fell and you can say goodbye."

"I don't know...Alex...It might be days before they bury the Confederates...I just..."

"Ladies." Charlotte turned to find, once again, Captain Spencer. He was even more disheveled than the last time she had seen him. He had given his blue jacket to another soldier for warmth, so all he wore was was a dirty undershirt. An area around his right thigh was covered in the crimson of blood. Captain Spencer touched her arm. "Miss Turner, I am surprised to see you out and about."

"I am stronger than you may think, Captain Spencer. Besides, since my best friend..." she almost choked on the words, "since she cannot help, I feel as though I need to." She looked at him, concern on her face. "What happened to you?"

"It's nothing." His face was sweaty. He looked around the carnage that surrounded them. "It's quite admirable that you want to help." He sighed. "If you have had enough of this for one day, I should escort you back into town. You really shouldn't be out here."

"Are you worried about the Rebels coming back?" Alex asked.

"No, we beat them pretty soundly. They tried a charge over at Cemetery Ridge as a last-ditch effort but we held them and they lost a lot of men. The Confederates are heading back toward Richmond as fast as they can go. We should follow Lee's army and catch them before they cross the Potomac, and just end this war once and for all. Our commander thinks the army is way too tired." The soldier sighed again, a little agitated. "Like the Rebs aren't just as tired as we are."

"You should be tired. You all fought so hard." Alex said. Charlotte remained quiet. She wasn't good at small talk even when she was perfectly coherent, much less when her world was falling apart.

238

"True enough, but again, Lee's army is too. We should chase them, we want to chase them. We want to finish this. But our commander, General Meade refuses to move."

"Maybe you'll give them chase in a few days." Charlotte said hollowly.

"Possibly, but by then, it'll be too late." He shook his head in frustration. "The fighting here was brutal. So many lost their lives."

"You are so right." Charlotte muttered.

"And we could stop it and go on the offensive, but we won't. I don't understand what our generals and the men in Washington are doing most of the time. I feel as though I could run this war better myself."

"You? You're just a farmer." Charlotte stated, a bit of sarcasm in her voice.

"Yes, a farmer. An educated farmer with only two years of military experience. I wish things were going differently." He sighed again and rubbed his temples. His hand dropped to the bloodstain on his leg. "I apologize, ladies. I'm just venting my feelings. I am sure you don't care about all this."

"On the contrary, we do." Alex assured him. "The sooner the war ends, the sooner everyone comes…home." She glanced at Charlotte, afraid that she would once again break down into tears. Instead, Charlotte looked angry.

"Yeah, so when Jack comes home we can tell him that Ginny is dead and when Thomas comes back I'll be forced to marry him." Charlotte babbled, not caring that Alex and the soldier were listening. Alex was one of her best friends, but Captain Spencer, well, she would never see him again. "I really don't want to marry him, but he believes he has some claim to me. And the one person, the one man who might have stood up to Thomas and my father is gone as well."

"Charlotte, I think you should stay with me. At least for now, at least for the rest of the night. I would feel better." Alex said as she held the inside of her friend's elbow, concern apparent in her face.

"I would feel better too." Captain Spencer threw his opinion out as well.

"I'll be fine." Charlotte said giving a weak smile. "I just need to go home and get some sleep." As she turned the other way, Captain Spencer turned to go with her. Before he could take another step, he moaned and fell. Charlotte fell to her knees and looked at the Captain's thigh. Fresh blood seeped from the wound. She looked into his face.

"Captain, this looks serious!"

"I just took a piece of shrapnel. I should be fine. There are many others who need help more than I do. Don't worry..." His voice trailed off and his eyes closed and he lay silent.

"Oh, Lord, is he..." Alex rushed to the two.

"He's breathing." Charlotte said, looking around for help. There was no one. "Can we get him to your house? Is there a place we can take him?"

"We still have a good ten-minute walk to my house." Alex looked around and spotted a man carrying soldiers to a wagon.

"Sir!" She called out. The man turned and Charlotte and Alex saw that it was none other than Jedidiah Smoker, the man who spent his days drinking and gambling. On more than one occasion, he had harassed Augusta for being Southern.

"Mr. Smoker, please! We need help! Could you bring this soldier to my house?" Alex asked, walking towards him.

The man looked them up and down. "It will cost you."

"Cost us? What? How much?" Charlotte said, still kneeling down beside Captain Spencer.

"I would say One Hundred dollars should do it." He smiled from his perch on the wagon seat.

"One Hundred dollars??" Alex gasped.

"You cannot be serious." Charlotte said angrily. Mr. Smoker looked at her.

"Well, now, Miss Turner, maybe you and I could make another arrangement..."

"That won't be necessary." Charlotte and Alex turned to see Abigail Williams, standing next to her father. Charlotte tried not to stare. Abigail's blonde hair was up in a practical chignon, with none of the curls and ribbons she usually wore. She wore a black cotton gown that, for once, looked more serviceable than fashionable. "We will take you. Father, can you help them get that man into the wagon?" Mr. Williams gestured to a soldier who was helping carry fallen soldiers.

The two men carried Captain Spencer to the William's wagon, which already held wounded soldiers. Charlotte looked at Abigail, puzzled and not sure what to say.

"Thank you, Abigail." Alex said, walking toward the girl. "Thank you so much."

"You're welcome." Abigail nodded. "I'm just trying to do what I can to help."

Charlotte and Alex got into the wagon, kneeling next to Captain Spencer. It didn't take them long to get to the Clark home.

"We can put him in my mother's room for now." Alex said. The soldier and Mr. Williams carried the captain up the stairs. When they had him laying down, Charlotte looked at the wound. It was still bleeding.

"If that is all, we need to go transport more of the wounded." Mr. Williams said.

"Yes, thank you, we can take it from here." Alex said. The two men left.

"We need bandages, something to stop the blood." Charlotte said.

Alex quickly left the room and came back with a blanket, sheets and sewing scissors.

"I couldn't find any bandages." She tossed the blanket on the bed and began cutting and ripping the sheets. "This will have to do.

Charlotte took one of the pieces of sheet and pressed it to Captain Spencer's leg. She sat on the side of the bed. "We need a doctor. Where is the doctor?"

"I asked downstairs. They said he was in surgery." Alex continued ripping the sheet into strips. "I told an orderly to tell him when he is done that he is needed up here."

"Has the bleeding stopped?" Alex asked.

"It has slowed down. I'll keep the pressure on the wound." Charlotte said, brushing a strand of her hair out of her face with a bloody hand.

"I will go and check on the doctor and see if I can get some soup for the captain for when he wakes up." Alex said.

"Yes, that is a good idea. I will stay here with him."

As soon as Alex left the room, Captain Spencer groaned and opened his eyes.

"Miss Turner. I am so sorry." He spoke weakly.

"Don't worry about talking, Captain. Save your strength to get better." Charlotte reached for the pieces of torn sheets and used them to tie the other sheet onto his thigh. "Let me get you some water." She rose to get some, but his bloody hand grabbed her arm.

241

"I need to show you, I have something that you may want." He reached into his pocket, the opposite side that had been wounded and pulled out a small, leather book that was almost falling apart. "I found this on a fallen Rebel soldier. I usually bury their valuables with them or try to send them home, unlike other soldiers I know. Well, when I found this, I knew you should have it."

Charlotte took the book from him and paged through it. It was a prayer journal, with Wesley's name written on the inside cover. As she flipped through the pages, a photograph fell out.

"I thought you might want that especially." He looked at her, struggling to stay awake.

Charlotte looked at the picture with tears blurring her eyes. It was a photograph of her and Wesley, taken years ago, when she had visited Chatham at the Lacy ball. She tried to fight the tears, but of course, they decided to come back.

Charlotte felt Captain Spencer's hand holding hers.

"Thank you." Charlotte whispered. "For everything you have done for me."

"It was a pleasure to help you." He said. Then, he laid back and closed his eyes. His breathing was shallow, but regular. He looked so young, calm and innocent. Charlotte brushed back a piece of hair that had fallen in his face. Her thoughts drifted to the time she had first met him.

Fall, 1859,
Fredericksburg, Virginia

Charlotte sat in the parlor of America Joan Prentiss, a young woman whom Belle spoke very highly of. Belle was with her, as was Charlotte's other cousins, Victoria and Rebekah. Charlotte enjoyed being able to spend time with her family and liked the young woman who insisted on being called AJ as well. She was a year older than Charlotte, with straight, blonde hair and a pale complexion. She was a bit overweight, and her blue eyes always seemed to be observing what was happening around her. She was one of the most sensible young ladies of Charlotte's new acquaintance, even though she was shy and socially awkward.

"AJ, how is your brother doing?" Belle asked after the initial small talk.

"Oh, he's doing well, I suppose." AJ answered with a smile. She turned to the visitors. "My brother Nathaniel is attending an agricultural school in the north, out in Michigan. He has been forever interested in farming, always experimenting with plants and growing them."

Charlotte nodded. Belle had told her a little about the young Mr. Prentiss.

"He will actually be visiting us this week, and I believe he is bringing a friend."

"How wonderful!" Belle exclaimed. She sounded genuinely excited, but also a bit like she was trying to hide just how excited she was. Belle's reaction gave Charlotte pause. Belle usually talked about Nathaniel Prentiss as though he was beneath her because of his dream of becoming a farmer. But underneath her pretension, she seemed excited to meet him again.

"Will they be here in time for your dance at Chatham?" Charlotte asked, keeping a close eye on her cousin.

"That is one of the reasons that Nathaniel is coming home.. They could be here as soon as this evening." AJ smiled a delightful, pretty smile, obvious that she couldn't wait to see her brother.

"Really? As in, today?" Belle exclaimed. "Why we didn't mean to intrude!"

"Isabelle, you know you are never an intrusion!" A deep male voice spoke from the parlor entryway. Belle spun around in surprise. Charlotte followed her gaze to a young man, about twenty years old.

America's brother, had black hair and deep blue eyes. He was short and thin, and had a much darker complexion than his sister.

"Nate!" AJ stood, unable to hold back her excitement and threw herself into his arms. Charlotte stole a glance at Belle, who quickly looked away from Nathaniel. Charlotte wasn't quick enough to catch her cousin's expression.

"Hello, AJ!" He smiled brightly and embraced her.

"Nate, you know Isabelle, of course, and these are her cousins, Miss Charlotte Turner, visiting from Pennsylvania, Miss Victoria Turner from Vicksburg, Mississippi and Miss Rebekah Turner from down in Petersburg."

"A great pleasure to meet you all." He smiled and turned to his side, where Charlotte finally noticed that Mr. Prentiss was not alone. Standing next to him was a tall, lanky young man who almost blended in with the wall. His dark brown hair was an unruly mop on the top of his head, and his blue eyes were looking around, as if he was trying to take in everything he saw. He may have had a handsome face if it wasn't for the marks that dotted his face. He may have been twelve or twenty, it was quite difficult to tell.

"Ladies, may I present my very good friend from college, Mr. James Spencer." The young man stepped forward and nodded in their direction. He looked uncomfortable in his good, pressed suit.

"Hello, ladies." His voice was soft and polite, but he kept his eyes to the ground. Charlotte smiled at his shyness.

"Well, come in and join us, gentlemen." AJ said. They did, and conversation continued. Charlotte soon learned that both men attended the Agricultural College in Michigan that had recently been established. Nathaniel had plans to buy land in Virginia and farm when he was finished with school. James Spencer, who was from a small Michigan town, would take over his family farm once he graduated. Conversation flowed from one topic to another. AJ and Belle dominated the conversation, and Nathaniel would speak often as well. James Spencer remained quiet, except for the times he was spoken to. When asked a question, he answered quickly and in a good manner. He even smiled and laughed a few times. Charlotte found his laugh to be pleasant and his smile showed off a dimple in his right cheek. It was still difficult to determine his age, and she didn't know how to ask the question tactfully.

Before long, it was time for the Turner cousins to leave. Belle wanted to stop at the milliner's shop on the way back to Turner's Glenn, and it would close soon.

"It was great meeting you, Mr. Spencer." Belle said as they left. She gave Nathaniel a short nod. "Mr. Prentiss, nice to see you again." She then gave AJ a hug and they left with the promise of seeing one another at Chatham for the dance.

Charlotte looked down at James's face. As pale and sickly as he was now, he was more handsome than he was all those years ago, more confident. He was a part of her past, her family in the south, a kind, good man, who had helped her many times without the expectation of anything in return. He had been there for her when she most needed it. Not knowing what else to do, she bowed her head and whispered a prayer.

"Lord, please. If you're up there, please, spare this man. You already have Ginny and Wesley and so many others. Please help me to save Captain Spencer."

July 5
Clark Home

Charlotte spent the night in the rocking chair, next to Captain Spencer. She was avoiding going home, doing whatever she could to keep from thinking about the friends she had lost and the fact that her world had been turned upside down. The Sanitation Commission had arrived, which was a blessing, because food had been hard to come by until they arrived in town. With their house still taken over by the US Army as a field hospital, Alex and her parents had spent the night at Professor Jacobs' home, a house that hadn't been overrun by soldiers. Professor Michael Jacobs taught with Alex's father at Pennsylvania College. Alex's father had returned while Charlotte and Alex were at Culp's Hill yesterday. He was safe, but appalled at what had happened. The college dormitories were filled with wounded. So many homes were full of wounded. Dead bodies were still lying around the city, no one knowing quite where to put them all.

Stories from the battle came from everywhere. Some homes had been completely destroyed, including the home of William Comfort, the man who had donated Ginny's coffin to the Wade family. In order to stay safe, nineteen women and children had hidden in one of the bank's vaults. Some Union officers had criticized the Gettysburg men who ran and hid instead of defending their homes and families. Those who had helped were being recognized. John Burns, a veteran of the War of 1812, had picked up a weapon and fought. Julia Culp, Wesley's sister, and Daniel Skelley, Jack's brother, along with many others, had given water to soldiers at the courthouse. Women like Alex had nursed soldiers. But Ginny was the only civilian who had died.

Captain Spencer's leg had been examined by both of the doctors at the Clark house. One had taken a quick look at it and sent an orderly to get his instrument bag.

"What are you going to do?" Asked the second doctor, a man Alex had introduced as Dr. Knightly.

"We have to take the leg." The first doctor replied. "It will get infected."

Knightly examined the wound closely and ran a hand through his hair, then rubbed his head. "I'm not so sure, Bartlett. Let's give it a little time. I think we can save it." He looked at Charlotte. "He will need constant care. Do you know the man?"

"I know he is a farmer. I know he needs his leg. I'll do what I can. I will watch over him, anything to help him." *Anything to stay busy and not have to think about the past few days.*

"I'll do what I can. I really think he can survive without amputation. It appears to have missed the bone." Dr. Knightly stated.

Dr. Bartlett sighed and rubbed his sweaty face with both hands. "I do hope you're right, Knightly." He looked at Charlotte. "Keep the wound clean, change the dressings often. Mrs. Clark can show you how if you don't know."

Charlotte nodded, determined to save Captain Spencer's life. "I can do that."

******

Charlotte woke to a soft touch on her hair and raised her head, looking into the eyes and smiling face of Captain Spencer. She blushed at the realization that she had fallen asleep with her head next to his arm.

"Captain. I apologize." She said. "I was just so tired..."

He touched her hand and held it to his chest. "Miss Turner, please. It's quite all right."

"How does your leg feel?"

"It feels much better. I am surprised it's still there, to be honest. I have seen too many instances where limbs get amputated almost without thought."

"Well, the two doctors here did discuss it, although I don't think either one really wanted to. I told them I would watch over you. They said the wound wasn't too ragged and it missed the bone." She babbled. "Luckily, infection hasn't set in. You should be okay, Captain."

"Thanks to you." He said in a raspy voice.

"Well, you have helped me enough times." She smiled. "I can only return the favor." She leaned forward and cupped the back of his head with her hand and offered him a dipper of water. He held her hand and drank deeply.

"Thank you." He smiled, then lay back down and closed his eyes.

July 7
Clark Home

"How is he doing?" Alex asked, peeking in the room. Charlotte had just changed his dressing. The wound looked like the doctor had said it should. No infection so far. The Captain woke up often, but had just fallen asleep again. One of the male orderlies, a young man named Billy who reminded Charlotte of John Wade, had given him a thorough sponge bath.

"He just fell asleep a bit ago. Charlotte replied. He's getting stronger all the time."

"That's good." Alex said, then stepped aside to let someone else in.

"Charlotte!" Augusta immediately went to Charlotte and hugged her tightly.

"Oh, Augusta! Where have you been? I am so glad you are all right." Charlotte said a quick prayer of thanks for the safety of her friend. "What have you been doing?"

"I have been helping the wounded, like most everyone in town. Mostly at St. Francis. Sallie Meyers is there too. It's...unbelievable out there. I just can't comprehend it." A tear fell down her face. "I couldn't believe the news when I was told what happened. To Ginny." She wiped her cheek. "I still cannot believe it. I haven't yet processed the fact that I will never see her again."

"I still wake up every morning and hope that it was just a dream. It never is, though. It's just a nightmare that won't go away." Charlotte looked at her two friends. "Captain Spencer is doing well, though. They say he is out of danger. He should be back on his feet in no time. And then they will probably send him back to battle. I think it's time to head to my farm and see how it fared."

"Alone?" Alex asked.

"I have been there alone hundreds of times. Most of the soldiers have gone. I will be fine." She tried to slip out of the room, but Augusta stopped her.

"That doesn't matter. We're going with you."

As they walked to the Turner farm, the three women could not believe the carnage that remained.

"The stench is just not getting better." Alex commented, trying not to gag.

"Maybe we can carry around rose water or peppermint oil to cover the smell." Augusta suggested.

"All of the fences have been torn down as well." Charlotte noticed. "Easy firewood or whatever else they needed wood for."

"So many homes destroyed." Augusta said. "I heard that Elizabeth Thorn, you both know her, her husband runs the cemetery. She has been burying the dead as quickly as she can, even though she is only a couple of months away from giving birth."

"Her husband was with the 138th Pennsylvania Infantry. I heard that her young children and elderly parents are helping her as much as they can. But even with their helping others, their house was looted. Everything was stolen except for some mattresses that were damaged beyond use."

"I can't believe humans would treat other humans like this." Alex said. "Even though our home was taken over, we were lucky to be able to stay there. I heard that Mr. Nathaniel Lightner's home was taken over and he was made to sleep outside."

"My father-in-law said that a lot of men are going to ask the federal government for reimbursement for the things they lost." Augusta said. "As if the government can afford that. And many are also planning on charging money to those who come into town, even if the visitors are going to help."

"Why is money the most important thing to people?" Charlotte asked. "And that." She gestured to a man who was putting a padlock on his water pump so that no one could use it without his permission. "That is not the first time I've seen that. It disgusts me."

"It's extremely unchristianlike behavior." Alex agreed.

They passed the Bigham home, one of Charlotte's neighbors. Charlotte saw Cassie, one of the daughters, bringing bread to the barn.

"Cassie!" Charlotte waved and approached the young woman.

"Charlotte! I'm so glad to see you're okay. Papa stopped by to check up on you a couple of times, but he never saw you."

"I've been staying in town." Charlotte explained. "How is your family?"

"Surviving." The girl said. "We have many wounded men out here in the barn. I've been helping Mary feed them as much as we can."

"Do you happen to know how my farm is looking?"

"Papa didn't go into details. Probably a lot like it looks here. No soldiers over there any more, though. He did say that much." Cassie looked at the three visitors, realizing for the first time that Charlotte's closest friend wasn't with them. "Where's Ginny? How did the Wades fare in this disaster?"

"They didn't fare well at all." Charlotte replied. "Ginny was killed by a stray Confederate bullet on the third day of the battle."

Cassie's hand flew to her mouth. "Oh, my goodness! I can't believe it. How horrible. Charlotte, I am so sorry. I know how close you two were. If there's anything I can do…"

"Thank you." Charlotte said. "Well, I suppose I should go see the damage to my home. I will talk to you later."

*****

When they reached their destination, all Charlotte could do was stare in disbelief. Bodies of animals and men littered the ground. The smell of rotting flesh made her gag. The rain earlier had made everything damp, and now, the combination of rain and humidity made the stench almost unbearable.

"Dear God." Augusta said.

"It's...destroyed." Alex said. The three women looked out at the landscape that had completely changed since the first of July. "What is the town going to do?"

"I'll tell you what we're going to do." Augusta said. "We will survive. But Charlotte, you cannot stay here. You are going to come and stay with me. My in-laws will take you in."

"No." Charlotte said firmly. "I appreciate the offer, but no. I'm not homeless." They continued to walk to her house. The door was gone, torn off the hinges and the inside of the house looked only slightly better than the outside.

"The house is still livable." Charlotte said. "I can fix it up, make it work."

"It's barely livable." Alex said. "Charlotte, you're talking crazy. You cannot stay here. Look at this place!" She threw her hand out, gesturing to the mess. Pots and pans had been thrown everywhere. The table had been hacked up and thrown into the fireplace.

Charlotte ascended the stairs. One glance into her father's bedroom showed even more of a mess. The bed was gone, and what was left of the torn up bed sheets were piled in a bloody heap in the corner.

"They even took the headboard, Charlotte." Alex shook her head. "You cannot stay here. Especially not alone."

"Headboard is out back." Charlotte murmured, staring out the window. "Looks like they used it as a grave marker."

"I wonder how your bedroom is." Augusta asked. "And the dining room? The sitting room? I wonder if they are livable."

"Let's go look." Charlotte walked the short distance to her own room. It looked much the same as her father's. The bedframe had been torn apart, leaving a ripped, dirty mattress on the floor. The headboard and sheets and other bedding was gone. Her porcelain pitcher was shattered on the ground. Muddy footprints were everywhere.

"You may not be homeless, Charlotte, that is true." Alex insisted. "But you need to be practical. We can help you clean up. But it would be best if, for the duration, you stay with one of us."

"There isn't room in your house for you, Alex, much less me."

"But we can still use your help. I know you want to fix up this place as soon as possible. We can start to help you now and then go back to town and you can help at my house."

"I can help in a good many places, Alex. The whole town needs help."

"But..."

"Maybe I just want to be alone, Alex!" Charlotte snapped, a bit harsher than she intended. Alex stepped back as if Charlotte had slapped her. Charlotte immediately regretted her actions. "I'm sorry! I...I just..." She sank onto the dirty, smelly mattress, buried her head in her lap and sobbed. Everything from the past few days again caught up with her. The emotions, the physical strain. She felt someone sit next to her.

"Go ahead and cry, Charlotte." Augusta's soft voice spoke as she rubbed Charlotte's back. Tears fell down her own cheek. Alex crossed her arms, trying to hold back her tears. She was unsuccessful. Charlotte threw her arms around Augusta, still sobbing. Alex wiped her face and joined her friends, hugging them both.

"We just don't want to lose you too, Charlotte. We can't lose you too."

Charlotte sighed. She knew that her friends were right. It would take time and money and especially energy that she didn't have to make the house livable again. She could stay with the Clarks or the Lewis's, help out in town, get her energy back, and then come home and take care of things. She knew the house and outbuildings still stood, and she knew the work that would have to be done.

"Let's head back to town." She sighed.

July 14

The days passed by and blended together. Most of the hospitals were getting organized and the wounded were being moved to Camp Letterman, a large, temporary hospital that was being set up east of the town along York Pike on part of George Wolf's farm. Other wounded were at the Seminary hospital on the ridge. Alex, Augusta and Charlotte spent most of their time at Camp Letterman, visiting with patients, writing letters home for them, and doing whatever the doctors needed them to do. Camp Letterman, named after surgeon Jonathan Letterman, was located in a good spot. It was on high ground and had many trees. This allowed the patients to have fresh air, cool breezes and shade. The railroad was not too far away, which made it easy to transport the wounded. There was also a spring that gave the patients and doctors freshwater. The hospital was comprised of hundreds of tents. The girls wondered what would happen to the patients once fall and winter came. Many other soldiers were being shipped on trains to big hospitals in Washington and New York. Dr. Knightly had left to follow the Confederate army, who had quickly retreated across the Potomac.

Horse carcasses and their stench still remained throughout the town. A new problem was also developing. Some of the wells in the area were going bad, as dead soldiers were being found in them. It was hard to tell if they had fallen in or been dumped in.

Charlotte found herself frequently visiting Captain Spencer, who stayed at the Clark's home. He continued to improve daily, and insisted the reason for it was Charlotte's care. When the girls weren't helping the soldiers, they were at Charlotte's farm, cleaning the wreckage of what was once her home.

Visitors began to pour into the town. Some had loved ones who had fought in the battle and were trying to find information about them. Others came to see where the great battle had taken place. Still others came to find relics. Inns and hotels were filled to capacity. Some residents of the town opened their homes to boarders. Organizations like the US Christian Commission sent volunteers and supplies, such as food and medicine, to help those in need. The Union army had left, leaving the wounded and dead for the town to care for.

"How are things looking out there?" Captain Spencer asked.

"It is still extremely chaotic, but improving. The smell is rancid. We are still finding dead soldiers. Those who are burying them having a tough time keeping up." Charlotte looked at the Captain's wounds, checking as the doctor had taught her, for signs of infection and gangrene. The wound looked good. "Doctor Robertson said you should start walking, with help of course. Would you like to go and sit outside for a while?"

"I would like that very much, Miss Turner."

"Here, let me help you." Charlotte put her arm under the Captain's shoulder and helped pull him up. She then walked him over to the balcony. He could smell the stench of rotting corpses still permeating the air. He gripped the railing and looked out across the land. As Charlotte had described, it was still an atrocity. Horses littered the ground. Rain and wind had washed dirt away from some of the shallow graves and body parts poked out.

"I see what you mean about the carnage."

"The aftermath of battle is almost as horrible as the battle itself." Charlotte commented.

"That is true." Replied Captain Spencer. "And it never gets any easier. Not to me. None of it."

"It must be easy to some. Or else we wouldn't still be in the middle of this war."

James didn't know what to say to that.

"This town is so different now. So much different than it was a week ago. The battle has changed it forever." Charlotte ran her finger over the railing. "Not only are there still men's bodies being found, along with dead animals, homes and farms have been destroyed. Crops are ruined, water is tainted. Guns, ammunition, cannon shells all still litter the land. And now, outsiders are pouring in to gawk or find loved ones. I can't help but feel our small town will never be the same. I know I will never be the same."

"How are you doing emotionally, in regards to losing your friend, Miss Wade?" James hesitated to bring the topic up, but felt as though he had to.

"What do you mean? She's still dead. I still miss her terribly. I try not to think about her, but it's hard when some of the townspeople are trying to tarnish her name even worse than before. Men like old John Burns and busybody women like Mamie Williams."

"I recognize the name of John Burns. Isn't he the civilian who took up arms against the Confederates? They say he's a hero."

"He's a crotchety old man who is jealous of the attention 'Poor Ginny Wade' is receiving. He's upset that a lot of townsfolk and soldiers are calling Ginny a hero, like they should. The issue is, Ginny was a girl from a poor family, a girl who has always been second class to men like John Burns. Folks like him don't like the fact that a poor girl like Ginny could be called a hero. So they continue to say nasty things about her. I actually heard someone say she was "entertaining" soldiers in Georgia's house when she was shot."

"Surely people know that wasn't the case."

"There was gossip about her and her family long before the war even started. Like I said, there are certain townspeople who like to make sure that the poor keep their place." A tear slipped down Charlotte's face. She quickly tried to wipe it away before he saw.

"That's too bad." Captain Spencer said. He shuffled closer and put an arm around her shoulder.

"It is." Her voice was almost a whisper. She looked up. James Spencer was close to her, so close she could see a month-old scar on his face that she hadn't noticed before. His eyes were looking deeply into hers as he reached up to touch her face. Charlotte's heart beat quickly and she stepped away. He began to speak. "Miss Turner..." His face had grown pale and he was beginning to glisten in sweat.

"Captain, we should get you back to bed. She pushed a strand of hair out of her face and stepped away.

"I'm fine." He insisted.

"Well, I believe you are just trying too hard to be strong. How about if you try to be smart? You don't want to overdo it on your first trip out of bed."

James sighed. "That is true." He turned and tried to take a step by himself, but stumbled. Charlotte caught him before he fell.

"Come. There's no shame in needing help, Captain."

He allowed her to help him back to his bed and once she had him tucked in, he looked at her with a weak smile. "I think it's best that you remember those words yourself."

"What do you mean?"

"I mean, the way I see it, you are a strong, fairly independent and extremely determined woman. But you don't want help from anyone. Why is that?"

"I don't know what you're referring to. I just do what I have to."

"You have been through so much, Miss Turner. And I really admire the way that you have handled it."

Charlotte looked at the Captain. She wanted to believe what he said was true, but it wasn't. She wasn't strong. She cried herself to sleep every night. She wondered every day how she would ever survive. She wasn't independent. She couldn't wait for the war to end so that her father would come back and work the farm. She just wanted everything to be the way it was before the war. And she was now afraid of losing someone else. She looked at James Spencer. She was afraid of the way she felt when she was with him. He was kind, handsome, and easy to talk to...and he would be going back to war soon, as he appeared to be recovering so well. She needed to keep her feelings in the right perspective with him, not get too attached.

"Well, I thank you for the compliment." Charlotte stood. "But I really must be going. I will check in on you later."

July 21
Turner Farm

Charlotte was alone at her house, scrubbing her makeshift table, which was a broken bedroom door laid across two empty crates the Lewis's had given her. Most of her crops had been ruined and her cellar storage had been raided. Even though she had been able to plant a late garden and some of the crops had survived, there would be little food for the winter. She was lucky that her father had some money safely put in the bank. Once the stores were back in order, she would be able to replace some of what had been lost, but she would have to be frugal. Mr. Clark and Mr. Lewis had teamed up and made her a new front door and helped her put it up. The home was starting to look better.

She turned and caught a glimpse of herself in the cracked mirror. Her hair was falling in her face and was covered in sweat and dirt. Her dress was damp and clingy. She had been working outside when it had started sprinkling and she hadn't bothered to change.

"I suppose it only makes sense that I look as bad as I feel." She muttered. Even though her home was looking better, her spirit was not. The past few days had been bad, and the nights had been worse. Nothing she did could make her feel better. She jumped in surprise at the knock on the door. She opened it to find James Spencer at the door, a clean uniform on and hat in hand, mist dampening his hair.

"Captain! Do come in." She grabbed a towel and gave it to him. "What brings you here?" Charlotte had been distancing herself from Captain Spencer over the past few days. She knew he was healing and he would be returning to the battlefield soon. She had enjoyed spending time with him, but she found herself wanting to be with him more and more. It had to stop. She could not lose someone else.

"I wanted to see you before I left." He said, wiping his face, hair and hands with the towel.

"I see you are looking well. And I suppose this means you are heading back to your unit."

"I am. I don't want to go, but I am healed enough and I gave my word. I am going to see this through. The Union has the upper hand now. The war shouldn't last much longer."

"But there will still be more battles. More death." Charlotte insisted. A part of her was tempted to ask him to stay with her. He could help her run the farm. But she was afraid, and so she could not ask him that.

"That is true, Miss Turner." James stepped closer. "Miss Turner, I know you have lost much, and I have no real right to ask you this but...could I write you? I have come to care for you and I consider you to be a good friend. I hope that you also care for me. As a friend."

"Captain..." Charlotte backed up. "I can't."

"Why?" James asked.

"I'm...sorry if I led you to believe...but I can't. I can't write to you, can't get too close, don't want to get too close to you. I have lost too much, my best friend and the man that I loved, not even a month ago."

"Charlotte..."

"It's Miss Turner." Charlotte tried to think of something to say. Her mind flashed to things that could happen. He could die. He could live. He could live and come back to her. But she was still torn up inside. If he came to care for her as more than a friend, she wouldn't deserve him. He was a good man. She was realizing how broken she was inside. He deserved better than her. He deserved a woman who could love him with everything she had. Charlotte wasn't sure if she would ever be able to love again. James stepped back and ran his hand through damp dark brown hair.

"Miss Turner. I apologize if I have spoken out of turn. I thought...maybe I was wrong, but..."

"Captain, among other things, I am promised to marry someone else." Charlotte wasn't sure what made her admit that to him. Maybe it would be easier for both of them if he knew.

"Yes, but I thought..." James gave her a puzzled and slightly hurt look. "You said before that you didn't care for the man. I know you were in love with the Confederate soldier who was killed. I was in pain when you said all that but I know I heard it."

"I know. I was upset. I said a lot of things that I didn't really mean. I did love Wesley, the man who was killed. But I am engaged to another. My future husband works for my father and will inherit the farm. He's in the 87th Pennsylvania right now."

"None of that matters to me. You don't love this man." James said, stepping close again. "Look me in the eye and tell me you feel nothing for me."

Tears filled her eyes. "Captain, if you care for me as you say you do, you will please just let me go."

He searched her eyes. She felt sure he would kiss her and a huge part of her wanted him to. She averted her eyes.

"I could never care for you." She said, knowing it wasn't true. He leaned forward.

"You could." He murmured. "You're just scared." And with that, he turned and strode away, outside and into the rain. She followed him out.

"Captain...James!" He turned. "Wait!" She stood on the porch, gripping the porch column. He strode back to her, cupped her face and kissed her. She gripped his wet jacket, not wanting him to leave, wanting him to stay with her. She had never before been kissed like James was kissing her. He finally pulled away, breathing hard.

"I have to go." He said, rainwater dripping down his face. "But remember that I do care for you. I feel something between us. I know you're hurting over the loss of so many loved ones. I know you don't love your father's farm hand. I am willing to fight for you. I was raised to be a gentleman but I will fight for your heart." And with that, he turned and walked out of her yard.

July 26

"Dearest Will,

I hope this letter finds you well. It is difficult to know where to start writing. I know I wrote you a letter after the battle, but not sure if you received it, as I have not heard from you. That is no surprise, of course, as I rarely receive your letters. But I wanted to write to you again and reassure you that, while the town is still picking up after the battle, our house still stands and our family is still alive and well.

I still miss Ginny. As I mentioned in my other letter, she was the only civilian to die during the battle but lately a few local boys have been injured or killed by what the armies left behind. Townspeople and visitors alike go through the battlefield, looking for souvenirs, as it looks as though this will be a decisive battle and has swung the war in favor of the Union. Unexploded shells and loaded rifles can still be found littering the land. Three days after the battle ended, the little McPhereson boy was killed when his brother found a loaded gun and started playing with it. The gun went off and three-year-old Edward was hit. The Star and Banner wrote a piece on it, hoping to alert others to the dangers.

Cannonballs and shrapnel can still be found embedded in buildings, both in town and in the surrounding farmhouses. Farmers, like Charlotte, are struggling to get their homes cleaned up, trying to salvage any crops that may have survived. Dead soldiers are still being found daily. Most of them are disfigured beyond recognition. Wild pigs got to some of them before they were properly buried. It is truly horrible.

In spite of all of this, I remain hopeful that you will return to me soon, safe and sound. I love you more than life itself, and pray for you, your unit and an end to this terrible conflict.

With all the love I possess,
Allie"

August 11
Taneytown Road

Alex dragged her feet down the road. She didn't know how she would tell Charlotte the news she had just heard. She had to, though. Charlotte rarely came into town anymore, so she couldn't possibly know the news that Alex had. She had stopped by the Bigham farm, where Cassie had informed her that Southerners were still at her house and had been entranced when Mr. Bigham had brought out the reaper to prepare for the harvest. They had never seen that type of machinery before.

As Alex approached, she saw Charlotte working in the field closest to the house. Most of her crops had been destroyed, but she had been finding some root vegetables that had survived, as well as patches of wheat. Charlotte paused in her work and watched Alex walk to her.

"What brings you out here, Alex?" She asked, setting her hoe down.

"Charlotte! You haven't been to town in so long. I wanted to make sure you were okay." Alex said, looking down; not able to meet her friend's eyes. Charlotte immediately knew something was wrong.

"You're not a very good liar, Alex. At least not to me. Now, what is this visit really about? You want to scold me some more for not coming and visiting? You want me to stop working so hard? You don't want me out here alone."

Alex hesitated. "Let's go sit on the porch. You look ready for a rest." Alex sat on the porch steps. Charlotte looked at her warily, then sat down. She knew that Alex was out here to tell her bad news.

"Charlotte, the Skellys received word today. It was about Jack."

"He's dead, isn't he?" Charlotte stared straight ahead.

"He didn't survive his wounds from Winchester." Alex said, her eyes starting to water.

"Well, that just figures." Charlotte said, slowly.

"Charlotte, I am so sorry. I know how much he meant to you. If there's anything I can do…"

"Alex, just stop. There is nothing you can do. There is nothing anyone can do." Charlotte stood and crossed her arms, looking toward the town. Alex stood and put a hand on Charlotte's back, tears falling down her face.

"I wish I could say something or do something."

"But you can't. I wish I could say I'm surprised about Jack, but I'm not. I just have to wonder who is going to die next. This is all so stupid. Such a waste."

"Is that why you've been scarce? Why you have been distancing yourself? Because you've been waiting for someone else to die?"

"I haven't been distancing myself. I have had a lot of work to do." Charlotte spun and pointed to the fields. "My home and farm are in shambles, and when I am not busy fixing things here, I am over at Camp Letterman, helping the wounded men."

"And I admire that about you, Charlotte, I do. But do you allow yourself to get even remotely close to any of those patients? You don't visit the Wades, you never ask about Georgia and the baby, you never ask about Augusta or Michael or Will. It seems as though you don't care about anyone!"

"No. Why would I? Why would I do that to myself?" Charlotte paced to the other end of the porch, away from Alex. "You don't understand, Alex, how could you? You barely knew Jack. You didn't know Wesley. You have lost one friend to my three. And, no offense, I was a lot closer to Ginny than you were." Her voice was flat and emotionless. Alex tried to be empathetic and hold her temper, but she couldn't.

"So that means I don't mourn her death? I miss her too. And I miss all of the things that could have been. I regret not spending more time with her when I could. I have always admired the closeness that you two had. You were like sisters, more so than you and I or I and she ever were. But you want to know something? The way you have been acting lately, I lost two friends that day. Because you haven't been a very good one! I know you are busy. I know you have suffered losses in your life of late. Augusta and I? We know how you feel. You need to get on with your life. You need to get out and socialize again. Because a life without friends? It's no life worth living. You have a lot to live for. " With that, Alex walked away, leaving Charlotte.

August 30
Lewis Store

Augusta placed a hand on her still-growing belly. It would only be another month or so until the child was born. She still hadn't heard from Michael since Christmas. She was appreciative of what she had heard from the Union soldiers during the battle, but she wanted to hear directly from him, see a letter come that was in his handwriting. Mr. Lewis entered the store from the door that connected to the home. He went to the front door, turned the lock, and flipped the sign to *Closed*. Augusta glanced at the clock. It was still an hour or so before his usual closing time.

"Mr. Lewis. What's wrong?"

Her father-in-law gave her a grim look. "Augusta, my dear. I need to speak with you. Come into the sitting room."

Augusta's stomach dropped. The look on his face and his request could only mean one thing. Her mind immediately flew to the worst-case scenario. Michael was dead.

Somehow, she managed to carry herself into the room and sat on the settee. She twisted her hands together as Mr. Lewis sat across from her, a small paper in his hand.

"Michael. He's dead, isn't he?" Augusta choked out her words.

"No. He's not." Mr. Lewis said. Augusta's heart leapt with hope.

"But he is missing. It is believed that he has been captured. We received a telegram today."

"Missing?" Tears fell down her face. Missing could still mean dead. And if he was in prison, prisons had horrible reputations, men died every day from disease and infection. "Lord, please be with him." She prayed, then stood, needing to walk around. She couldn't just sit.

"Mrs. Lewis, does she know?"

"She does." Mr. Lewis nodded. "She is in her room now. She didn't take the news well."

Augusta wiped her tear-stained cheeks with one hand and placed her other hand on her stomach.

"How could anyone take this news well?" Augusta said. She didn't want to talk to anyone, she just wanted to see Michael safely home. "I'll write to my family and friends, see if any of them have any word of him, in a hospital or prison, but I'm not sure if the letters will even get through. I will try." Tears fell down her face. "I will do everything I can to locate him."

September 15
Lewis Home

Augusta sat in her bed, knitting, Alex in the rocker next to her. The time for Augusta to have her child was close and Mrs. Lewis had insisted that she rest often. Augusta was getting quite bored with nothing to do. After the bustle of the past few months, she didn't like just lying around. Alex came by for visits, but neither girl had visited with Charlotte in a while. They would see her in passing, but she rarely said much more than standard pleasantries. She stayed secluded on her farm. One day when Alex was helping at the Camp Letterman hospital, she saw Charlotte helping. Neither had time to talk, and when Alex had gone looking for her later, Charlotte had already left.

"Have you heard anything from Michael?" Alex asked.

"No. I have written letters to anyone I can think of, but have heard no reply. If I wasn't about to have Michael's child, I would go down to Virginia and try to find him myself."

"Well, I will keep praying. I wonder if Charlotte knows anyone who can help. What did she say when she found out?"

"I'm not sure that she even knows." Augusta said. "It's been weeks since I saw her last. It's like she's pushing people away so she can't get hurt anymore." Augusta remarked.

"I agree. It makes sense. She was okay until she realized that Captain Spencer would be going back to his unit."

"Do you think she developed feelings for him?" Augusta asked.

"I think she could have. Maybe she did and got scared. Maybe she felt as though she was insulting Wesley's memory. I saw her briefly on my way over here. I told her you and I would be working together. Asked her to come, but she declined. She said she had things to take care of."

"Does she ever visit the Wades?"

"No, not at all. I saw Georgia the other day. She said they are all having an especially hard time dealing with Ginny's death. Some people, especially John Burns, are talking bad about Ginny."

"That is so awful." Augusta paused, placing her hand on her belly. "I just had a thought. About Charlotte distancing herself. Her mother died in childbirth."

"That's true." Alex said. "She could very well be afraid of losing you the same way that she lost her mother."

"I just wish she wasn't so scared...ahhh..." Augusta groaned, then clutched her stomach. "Umm...Alex? I would like to discuss this more and I really do miss Charlotte, but could you go and get my mother-in-law? I think it's time."

*****

Alex knocked on the Turner's door, a bit disheveled from helping Mrs. Lewis and Augusta, but she had wanted to bring the news to Charlotte right away. The door opened.

"Alex, what is it?" Charlotte looked tired, as if she hadn't slept in days. Alex was unable to hide her smile.

"I couldn't wait to tell you the news! Augusta had her baby! It's a little boy. She and Baby Michael are doing very well."

A flash of excitement showed in Charlotte's eyes, but it was gone just as quickly.

"That's wonderful, Alex. Tell her I congratulate her."

"Charlotte, one of your good friends has had a child, and that is all you say?" Alex was once again getting frustrated with her friend.

"What do you expect me to say? I have things to do. Sorry to not be able to talk more." Charlotte began to shut the door, but Alex held it open.

"Charlotte, you need to snap out of this! I am tired of you feeling so sorry for yourself. I know you have lost people you care about. We all have! We are in the middle of a war! But it has been months since the battle. The town is rebuilding. We are trying to move on. Because we have to. We get up and move on. We become stronger for it. That's what you have to do when tragedy strikes."

"And I suppose you are going to spout some nonsense about God now." Charlotte retorted. "God's will or some other such hogwash."

"I don't know what to say to you anymore! You are so focused on your own problems and only your sorrows that you don't see other people's pain"

"How can you say that? I help at the hospital ..."

"Yes, you do. A hollow shell of you does. Augusta and I are going through our own issues. Do you even care? I haven't heard from Will in months. He could be dead for all I know. But I can't just hide away. I have to keep busy. Were you even aware that Michael is missing, most likely dead or imprisoned? Augusta is completely torn up about it, but there is nothing she can do about it. Even with all her connections in the South, all she can do is pray. The Wades continue to struggle with Ginny's death. The Skelley's have lost Jack and people throughout the town are having problems. You are not the only one suffering, Charlotte." Alex took a deep breath. "Please come back to us. You don't have to forget Ginny or Wesley or Jack. No one expects you to. They were a part of you. But you have to...stop ruining your life and the relationships you still have. Please be our friend again. Don't shut us out."

Charlotte paused. Everything Alex said made sense. She knew it, had known it, but it was hard.

"So...I heard David Wills is trying to get a National Cemetery here. Probably trying to make as much money as he can. Lots of people, important people, coming into town. It would be a shame to miss it."

Alex smiled. "That it would." She threw her arms around Charlotte and hugged her tight.

"I'm not saying I'm completely over what happened." Charlotte said. "But I'll try to get out and, as you would say, live more."

"That's all we can ask for."

September 16
The Lewis Home

Charlotte paused before knocking on the door of the Lewis home. She waited for the door to be answered, trying to think of what to say. She knew she had hurt both Augusta and Alex. Alex had forgiven her, and she suspected that the sweet Augusta would as well. Charlotte just didn't know how she would forgive herself.

The door opened to Aideen Lewis's smiling face. "Good morning, Miss Turner. How are you doing?"

"I'm fine, just fine. I came to see Augusta. Is she awake, is she receiving visitors?"

"I am sure she will be happy to see you." Aideen let Charlotte into the house and ushered her up the stairs.

"How is she doing?" Charlotte asked.

"She is doing well. Her son is also doing well. Such a sweet, happy baby boy."

"I'm glad to hear that."

Aideen opened the door to Augusta's bedroom. "Augusta, my dear, you have a visitor."

Augusta sat up in her bed, wearing a light blue nightgown, her blonde hair braided and slightly messy as if she had just woken up. She looked tired, but healthy.

"Charlotte! How are you doing?" Charlotte sat down on a chair next to her friend's bed. Aideen went to the bassinet and took out a light green bundle.

"Who would like to hold our new little man?" She asked. Augusta glanced at Charlotte, who nodded.

"I would love to." Charlotte held her arms out, took the child and cuddled him tightly to her chest. "He is beautiful, Augusta. Absolutely perfect."

"Thank you. I named him Michael Joseph, after his father and my brother, Joseph. During the battle when I spoke with my brother, Andrew, he told me that my brother Joseph was badly wounded."

"I'm sorry to hear that. Have you heard anything from Michael or your family lately?"

"No. Nothing from Michael. Nothing from home. Of course, I saw Andrew during the battle, but...."

"Who?" Charlotte looked up.

"Andrew, my oldest brother. I didn't tell you about seeing him?"

"No. Although it's hardly your fault. I've not been a very good friend since the battle. I know that, and I am truly sorry." Charlotte looked down at the baby again, so innocent. "You asked me how I was doing. I am doing better. Not great, not even really good, but better. I spoke with Alex. She talked some sense into me. Told me that what I was doing needed to stop. She actually scolded me pretty good. But it needed to be said." A tear fell down Charlotte's cheek. "I'm so sorry."

"Oh, Charlotte, it's all right. You went through a lot. You saw Ginny...I mean, you were there with her when...you were the last to be with her. That can't be easy."

"I still have nightmares about that day. That morning. What happened?"

"I imagine anyone would. I still have bad dreams about that day as well. I expect we all will for a while."

"I just don't know what to do about it."

"Have you considered praying? Taking your problems to the Lord? Talking with Him?"

"What would it help? Why would a great and powerful Lord listen to the problems that I have?"

"Have you ever wondered how Alex and I get through each day? Its faith. It's all you really need. God cares about you. He cares about all of us."

"Why? What have I done to be worthy of that? I mean, look at you and Alex and Ginny. You are all such good people. And then there's me. Some of the things that I think and say and do...they are not very Christian-like at all."

"None of us are perfect, Charlie and none of us are really worthy of God's love. It's not something we can earn, it's a free gift. God offers it to us and wants us to take it. He wants us to talk with him."

"If he cares so much about us and how we feel then why does He let bad things happen? Why is He allowing this horrid war? I'm sure He could stop it if He wanted to."

"Sure He could. He could also make you a perfect person and make you believe in Him but it wouldn't mean anything. You have to make that choice. He gave us free will so we can choose what's right."

Charlotte sighed. Ginny and Alex had spoken with her so many times about God. She never really understood it. What Augusta was saying, it was starting to make sense.

"So you think, if I pray, that God will make me a better person."

"No. I KNOW if you pray and really want to change, God will help you be a better person. I promise." She reached over and grabbed a small, leather-bound book from her bedside table.

"That looks like Ginny's bible." Charlotte commented.

"It is." Augusta said. "Georgia gave it to me, guessing that I would be more likely to see you before she did, as you would have to stop in the store at some point. She wanted you to have it."

"Why me?" Charlotte took the book and flipped through it.

"Because you were Ginny's best friend. Ginny would have wanted you to have it. I looked through it. It wasn't just a book to Ginny."

Charlotte nodded as she noticed the underlined passages and notes written in the margins of the book. Ginny had truly made the book her own. She looked closely at a Psalm that Ginny had seemed to underline multiple times: "Delight yourself in the Lord; and He will give you the desires of your heart." Next to it, Ginny had written: 'It may not be when we ask, but He will lead us to great things. Everything happens for a reason.' Charlotte glanced at Augusta.

"Thank you, for this. And for everything you have done to try and help me."

"You can thank me by reading through that. Ginny makes some very good points. And know that I am always here to help you, should you need it."

Wednesday, November 18
Gettysburg Town Diamond

It was past dusk when Augusta and Charlotte left Alex's house after another evening of talking, needlework and dinner. Augusta was grateful that her mother-in-law was always happy to watch Michael Joseph. It allowed her to socialize with her friends, and the three women were getting closer and closer every day.

As they walked, the two noticed a small group of people had gathered around the Wills house. Among them was Samuel and Harry Wade, Abigail Williams and several people the girls didn't even recognize. Everyone was preparing for the dedication of the National Cemetery. People had been coming to town in droves since Monday, when the key speaker Edward Everett, politician, pastor, educator, diplomat, and orator from Massachusetts, had arrived. So many trains had arrived that there was very little room for new trains near the station. Some visitors had even ridden in freight cars. Among the visitors were hundreds of reporters, intent on getting a good story.

"I'll bet the President has finally arrived for the ceremony tomorrow." Augusta said.

"You're probably right." Charlotte agreed. "I wonder if anyone has actually seen him."

"Mother said that once the president arrived, no other trains will be allowed to leave until he is gone."

David Wills, a local lawyer, had organized a Soldier's National Cemetery to bury all the Union dead of Gettysburg. He had most recently organized a ceremony for the opening of the cemetery. He had invited several famous speakers and, almost as an afterthought, he had invited President Lincoln, never thinking this important man would come. But the president did accept and it appeared as though he had arrived.

Samuel and Harry hurried over.

"Charlotte, Mrs. Lewis, the president is in there! Word is, he might come out and say something if we wait out here long enough." Harry said, excitement apparent in his voice. Charlotte doubted the eight-year-old really understood what was really going on.

"Not only that, thousands of people are expected to be at the program tomorrow." Samuel said he was now 11, and had grown so much he was almost as tall as Charlotte.

"People have been coming out long before this." Charlotte muttered. Recalling all the people who flocked to the town just after the battle.

"They say 38 people are staying in the Wills house tonight." Augusta said

"And poor Catherine Wills is in her eighth month of pregnancy." Charlotte added. "That cannot be easy on her."

A murmur ran through the crowd, and Augusta and Charlotte immediately looked toward the Wills house. There, on the porch, stood a tall, gangly man. His dark brown hair sat neatly on his head and his beard was nicely trimmed.

"I don't believe I have ever seen anyone so tall." Augusta leaned toward Charlotte and spoke softly. Charlotte nodded. They had never seen anyone quite like him. He did not look elegant enough to be the leader of the Union. She could easily see why he had been referred to as a back-woods rail-splitter. He didn't look impressive at all. But there was something about his mannerisms, the way he held himself that fascinated the crowd. He spoke a few words, words that Charlotte and Augusta could barely hear. Some people in the crowd grumbled that he didn't have a speech to give. But when a line began to form, they quickly fell into it. They knew without being told that they would be able to shake hands with the president of the United States that very night.

"I cannot believe this!" Sammy said, excitement undeniable in his voice. "Mama will be so jealous! And Johnny too, after he comes home."

"If he comes home." Charlotte whispered so that only Augusta could hear.

"Charlotte…" Augusta said in a quiet voice.

"Sorry."

Although the line seemed long, it moved quickly. Soon, the Wade boys, Charlotte and Augusta were in the parlor, the president getting closer and closer. When Charlotte was right in front of him, she found it hard to look away from his face, although she knew it was improper. His eyes looked so sad and tired. She was again amazed at how tall and thin he was. Even his fingers were long and skinny as sticks. She was afraid that too strong a handshake might cause his hand to break.

"Miss." He gave her a small, thin, barely there smile.

"Mr. Lincoln." Charlotte replied in what she hoped was a strong response and then moved on. As she walked out into the crisp, fall evening, she pulled her shawl tighter and looked up into the sky. Ever since the battle, she had needed someone to blame, someone to hate. At first, she felt she could blame God, but her faith was growing strong. And Ginny would never have approved of blaming God. So she had blamed Lincoln and the southern politicians. But the man she had just met was so sad and despondent. She found that she couldn't hate or blame him anymore. A pat on her back interrupted her thoughts.

"Ready?" Augusta asked, pulling her friend close to her side. They continued walking, dodging hundreds of people.

"I can't believe how many people are here." Charlotte said. The crowd continued to grow.

"I heard that all the churches, houses, just about everything will be used for lodging the visitors."

"I heard that as well. I seriously considered taking in boarders for a fee, but I figured it wouldn't be the best of ideas, seeing as though I am a woman alone."

"That was a smart decision."

"Any word about Michael? I never asked earlier." Charlotte still felt guilty that it had taken her so long to come back to her friends. She was glad that Alex had been so persistent.

"No." Augusta replied. "No word from anyone. I feel as though not knowing makes it even harder. If I knew he was dead, I would be...it would be unimaginable. But at least I would know he was in a better place. With him missing...we just don't know."

"He'll be fine. The war can't last that much longer, and then he will be home."

"That's what I keep hoping and praying for." Augusta said. "Do you ever hear from Thomas or your father?"

"Not lately. I feel as though Thomas is distancing himself from me. Even when he does write, they are less emotional than before."

"Do you ever hear from Captain Spencer?" Augusta asked.

"He did write, once. He apologized for being so forward, but said he wasn't sorry for telling me his feelings." Charlotte couldn't help but sigh. "He was right, the day he left. I was scared to admit that I could have feelings for him. I wrote back to him, telling him that. Telling him I would like it if he would write back. I haven't heard since."

"Mail can be unpredictable." Augusta said. The two reached the Lewis's store. The crowd had thinned. "Are you sure you are okay staying alone at your place?"

"Yes. And we can meet tomorrow as planned." Charlotte hugged her friend goodbye and headed home.

As Charlotte walked, she noticed a lot of the visitors didn't seem like they were planning on sleeping. As she walked past Breckenridge Street, wondering what Ginny would say about Charlotte's feelings for Captain Spencer, she saw a young women, holding two children against her while two men, clearly drunk, appeared to be harassing her. Charlotte immediately went to aid the family. She didn't recognize the troublemakers. As she approached, a third man appeared.

"You men should leave." The third man said. Charlotte recognized him immediately as Daniel Skelly, Jack's younger brother.

"What are you gonna do, boy?" One of the drunks leered.

"I won't do anything if you leave them alone. If you continue to harass them, I will be forced to get the authorities."

"C'mon, Jake." Said the second drunk man. "Let's go. There's gotta be easier sport elsewhere." The two men stumbled away. Daniel turned to Charlotte and the woman.

"Hello, Danny." Charlotte said with a smile.

"Thank you so much, sir." The young woman said. "My name is Annie Potter. These are my two children. My husband died here during the battle, and I came here from Pittsburgh to witness the ceremony. I had no idea there would be so many people."

"Mrs. Potter. Charlotte." Daniel said.

Looking at the young man, Charlotte felt a pang of sadness. Daniel looked a lot like Jack. He was only eighteen years old, and hadn't left to fight. Instead, he worked as a clerk at a dry goods company. Daniel looked again at the young widow, who didn't look like she was much older than him. "Where are you staying? I can walk you there."

"I...I'm not sure. I couldn't find any place." The widow looked down at her children.

"I wish I could offer you a place to stay, ma'am, but everywhere I know is full." Daniel said.

"You can come stay with me." Charlotte said. "I live just outside of town, down the road apiece. I don't have much to offer, but I have some blankets and a roof."

"Would you really do that, ma'am?" The woman asked.

"Of course. You and your children need a place to stay, and I have room."

"We would be most grateful." The woman said, hefting her younger child on her hip. The boy looked to be around a year and a half. The girl clutching her mother's skirts appeared to be around three years old.

"I can walk you there." Daniel said. "I wouldn't feel right if something happened to you again."

"Thank you, Danny." Charlotte said. The small group began walking out of town toward the Turner farm. Daniel smiled.

"No one has called me Danny in years. Not since before the war. Really, the only ones who ever did were you and..." He trailed off.

"Jack and Ginny and Wesley." Charlotte finished.

"Yes." Daniel paused and looked at the young widow and explained. "Jack, my older brother, was wounded and died just before the battle here. His fiancé, Ginny, was killed during the battle, the only civilian killed. Their other friend, Wesley...well, I don't know, about him. He ended up fighting for the Confederacy. No one talks about him anymore, unless it's calling him a traitor."

"I'm sorry to hear that." The woman said.

It was on the tip of Charlotte's tongue to tell Daniel about Wesley. As a boy, Daniel had idolized Wesley and Jack. But Charlotte didn't know how he currently felt about Wesley and didn't want to bring it up.

Daniel and Charlotte made small talk, catching up on news. The widow walked in silence. By the time they had reached the house, the boy had fallen asleep on his mother's shoulder.

"I will put some coffee on." Charlotte said, lighting a lantern. "Daniel, would you care for a cup?"

"Thank you, but no. I should be getting back. Ever since Jack...well...Mother is hovering over me more than usual." He gave a quick bow and left, not hearing Charlotte's comment: "Is that even possible?" At Mrs. Potter's confused look, Charlotte quickly explained that Daniel's mother always seemed to be overly involved in her sons' lives.

"She tried to keep my friends Ginny and Jack from being together just because Ginny was of a lower class."

"I've heard of this Ginny. Ginny Wade? Is it true what they say about her?" Charlotte grabbed some blankets and a damaged mattress that had once been in her father's room. She motioned to the young mother to lay her children down. The two children immediately fell asleep, clearly exhausted.

"Some of it is." Charlotte said, stoking the fire in the stove and putting some coffee on. "It depends on what you have heard." She lit some additional candles and sat at the table. Annie Potter joined her.

"I heard she gave wounded Union men food and water at the risk of her own life. And was killed while baking bread for them."

"That is all true. Ginny was a wonderful, caring person. She helped a good many men."

"Were you very close to her?" The young woman asked.

"She was my best friend." Charlotte looked out the window. Campfires could be seen across the land. It brought back sad memories.

"I am sorry for your loss."

"And I for yours." Charlotte said, standing and getting two cups for the coffee. "What do you know of your husband's time here?"

"Not much, I am afraid. A nurse from a field hospital wrote me. Said Ronald fell at a place called Cemetery Hill. He was wounded and then died a month later from infection. He was at Camp Letterman." Tears shown in her eyes. "He never really wanted to go to war, but all of his brothers were going and he didn't want to be left behind."

Charlotte reached across the table and held the woman's hands. "I spoke with many wounded soldiers after the battle. They were all very brave. I expect your husband was very brave as well."

"Thank you." The girl reached into her pocket and drew out a letter. "The nurse that wrote me was named Miss C. Turner. You don't happen to know anyone by that name?"

"I might." Charlotte smiled. "Could I see the letter?" Annie handed it to her, and Charlotte immediately recognized her own handwriting. "It is such a small world." Charlotte skimmed the letter, recalling the young man who she had written it for. "I wrote this letter, Mrs. Potter."

"You?" Mrs. Potter sat up straighter. "You were with Ronald when he died. Do you remember him?"

"I wrote for quite a few men after the battle. There were so many wounded." Charlotte thought back. "But I do believe I remember Ronald. He reminded me of a friend. Young, with red hair. He was quite good-natured, even at the end. Does that sound like your Ronald?

275

Annie smiled, tears welling in her eyes. "That does sound like Ronald." She looked again at the letter. "Do you...do you remember anything else?"

"I remember him for his kind temperament, as well as his faith. We actually had some good conversations about the Lord before he died. Rest assured, Mrs. Potter, your Ronald is in heaven."

"Thank you." She whispered. "We were both so young when the war broke out. He delayed enlisting, instead, did a lot of work at home, ministering to others. He always wanted to become a preacher. We married in '60 when I was only 16, he was a year older. I have always loved him, since I was a young girl. We grew up together. Our first child, Ruth, was born soon after we were married. He went with his brothers and enlisted after the second call to arms. He came home a year later when his term was up. He could have stayed home, but felt the need to re-enlist, he felt a calling. So he did. He never met his son, Ronald Jr. Ronnie." She glanced at the sleeping children.

"I have a friend, she lives in town with her husband's parents. She had a son not long ago. Her husband doesn't even know he's a father. She hasn't gotten the chance to tell him that she was even with child. He's missing right now."

"How awful. It seems as though no one can escape this terrible war." Mrs. Potter yawned. "I can't tell you how much I appreciate you letting us stay here, Miss Turner. I can't pay much..."

"You won't pay me at all. I insist. If you wish, you can accompany me tomorrow to the ceremony. We will have to get an early start. I am meeting up with some friends, but you and your children are more than welcome to join us."

"Thank you. You are so kind."

"Don't mention it." Charlotte said standing. "Will there be enough room for you on the mattress there?" The woman nodded. Charlotte continued "I'm sorry I have no bed frame. The troops passing through destroyed a lot of the furniture. If you need anything, my room is at the top of the stairs. Don't hesitate to ask for anything."

"We'll be fine. It is so much more than I could have hoped." Annie lay down with her children and Charlotte went up the stairs, knowing tomorrow would be a tiring day.

Thursday, November 19
Near the Town Diamond

Alex couldn't believe the amount of people that had come to town. Thousands had lined up along Baltimore Road to watch the procession to the cemetery. Buggies blocked many of the roads. The procession was supposed to start at 10:00 in the morning, but it was already later. Alex looked at her pocket watch and then looked down the road. There were so many people, it would take a good hour for her to get to where she had told Augusta and Charlotte she would meet them. She glanced at the center of town. People were still gathering. She recognized the Governor of Pennsylvania, Andrew Curtin as one of the dignitaries. He was next to a group of girls, one of them Alex recognized as sixteen-year-old Liberty Hollinger. The governor was going around the group and kissing each young girl on the cheek. It was apparent the day would be interesting.

*****

Charlotte and Annie Potter arrived at the new cemetery early. They got a good look at what had been taking weeks to build. A large platform had been built along the ridge of the cemetery. Hundreds of bodies had already been moved and buried in the new cemetery. Bands had begun to assemble and were warming up for the ceremony. As Charlotte walked to her designated meeting place with Alex and Augusta, she passed many booths and tables where people were selling souvenirs. She tried not to get upset when she saw John Burns selling photographs of himself. Charlotte saw Augusta approaching, gently pushing her way through the growing crowd.

"Good morning!" Charlotte greeted her friend, then quickly introduced Augusta to Annie.

"I thought for sure Alex would be here by now." Charlotte commented.

"Trying to get through the crowd in town is almost impossible, and she does have the farthest way to come." Augusta explained. "She'll be here. We just need to be patient." Gunfire sounded from the direction of town. Annie's son began to cry and hold his ears and her daughter whined and pulled at her mother's skirts. Charlotte bent down and picked her up. She looked at Augusta. "You didn't want to bring little Michael?"

"No, Mrs. Lewis is watching him. She didn't care to come to the ceremony. She was just going to mind the store and watch the procession."

Gunfire sounded again, and again. It seemed as though every minute, the artillery fired. Finally, at around 11:30, the procession reached the cemetery, just as Alex arrived and joined the group. She smiled, quickly introduced herself to Annie, and turned to watch the procession enter the cemetery grounds. President Lincoln looked very strange atop his horse, his long legs hanging down awkwardly. He looked pale and a little ill. Music played, then the Reverend Thomas Stockton, the US Congressional Chaplain stood and delivered a prayer. The band played again, and the key speaker, Edward Everett took the podium.

"He's supposed to be one of the best speakers in the country." Alex said.

Alex, Augusta and Charlotte could barely hear the words he spoke. The crowd was getting restless as the speech went on and on. A girl in the crowd, not a local, fainted and had to be carried up to the platform until she woke back up. Finally, two hours later, the man finished his speech. After he sat down, and the applause had died down, President Abraham Lincoln took the podium.

"I hope his speech isn't as long." Alex whispered to her friends.

The girls could barely hear the words, but they could hear them nonetheless, words they doubted they would ever forget.

"Four score and seven years ago our fathers brought forth on this continent, a new nation, conceived in Liberty, and dedicated to the proposition that all men are created equal.

Now we are engaged in a great civil war, testing whether that nation, or any nation so conceived and so dedicated, can long endure. We are met on a great battle-field of that war. We have come to dedicate a portion of that field, as a final resting place for those who here gave their lives that that nation might live. It is altogether fitting and proper that we should do this."

Alex nodded in agreement at the man's words and Charlotte put her arm around Annie. The president continued. The girls were spellbound.

"But, in a larger sense, we cannot dedicate...we cannot consecrate...we cannot hallow...this ground. The brave men, living and dead, who struggled here, have consecrated it, far above our poor

power to add or detract. The world will little note, nor long remember what we say here, but it can never forget what they did here. It is for us the living, rather, to be dedicated here to the unfinished work which they who fought here have thus far so nobly advanced. It is rather for us to be here dedicated to the great task remaining before us...that from these honored dead we take increased devotion to that cause for which they gave the last full measure of devotion...that we here highly resolve that these dead shall not have died in vain...that this nation, under God, shall have a new birth of freedom...and that government of the people, by the people, for the people, shall not perish from the earth."

"Amen." Augusta whispered.

The crowd was silent as the president walked back to his seat.

"Is that it?" Alex asked quietly.

"There doesn't need to be more." Charlotte said. "He summed everything up very well in that short speech."

It appeared as though it was. Another man stepped forward and spoke some words, a benediction. And with that, the ceremony was over.

November 26
Lewis General Store

Alex held baby Michael Lewis tightly to her chest, touching his soft cheeks.

"He is so, absolutely beautiful, Augusta." She said to her friend. Augusta folded a bolt of cloth and smiled.

"Thank you. I cannot wait until his father can see him. Until I can see Michael again"

"I understand what you mean. Did you hear that the president has proclaimed today to be a national day of 'Thanksgiving and Praise to our beneficent Father who dwelleth in the Heavens'."

"I think I like the idea of a national day to give thanks." Charlotte said, leaning over Michael and running her finger down his smooth arm.

"They say it's to be an annual celebration, but I don't think it will last." Alex said.

"But it's a wonderful idea. Even though we are all struggling, it's good to be reminded that we also have a lot to be thankful for." Augusta said, coming to stand in front of her friends and her son. "Because in spite of everything, we do have a lot to be thankful for. The president is a smart man."

"I feel thankful I got to shake his hand." Charlotte grinned.

"Yes, and you are lucky you didn't get sick from it." Alex said. "I heard he had smallpox when he returned to the Capitol."

"How unfortunate." Augusta said. "It's hard to believe he was here for so short a time. Did anyone hear what he did after his speech?"

"He spoke to grumpy John Burns who, by the way, had his picture on the cover of Harper's Weekly, but who didn't even want to meet with the president, crazy old man. Then, Lincoln went to a meeting at the Presbyterian Church."

"Yes, I heard that too." Charlotte said. "Republicans from Ohio held a political rally there."

"From Ohio? Why would they hold an Ohio rally in Pennsylvania?" Augusta asked.

"I'm not sure." Alex said, then gave Michael a kiss and handed him back to Augusta. "As much as I would like to stay and cuddle with your son, I must go home. Mother is hosting a Ladies Aid gathering tomorrow and we need to prepare for it. If either of you are free, please come by."

"I may stop over." Charlotte said. "I have some fences that I want to repair in the hope that someday, we have livestock to contain again. I would love to help out, though."

"I cannot believe all of the physical work you have to do." Alex said.

"I have to keep the farm going. Who knows, when this is all over, it may be all I have left."

"I thought you were through talking negatively like that, Miss Turner." Augusta said, rocking her son.

"I wasn't trying to be negative, I was just stating a fact." Charlotte said. She picked up the basket of supplies she had purchased from the store. "I will hopefully see you tomorrow. Have a happy day of thanks."

After her two friends left, Augusta went into the parlor and rocked Michael to sleep. Just as he nodded off, the bell above the door jingled. With her in-laws gone for the afternoon, she was in charge of the store. She quickly lay her son down in the bassinet Mr. Lewis had made especially for the parlor and went into the store.

"I am so sorry to keep you waiting, what can I get for you?" She asked. A Union soldier stood with his back to her. His hair hung past his shoulders and when he turned around, she could not tell any distinguishing features of his face because of his long beard and mustache. The man was in desperate need of a bath.

"Sir, how can I help you?" The man looked at her with tired eyes. He was thin and malnourished, and looked as though he hadn't slept properly in months.

"Augusta…" His voice was hoarse, but familiar. Her heart hammered in her chest.

"It can't be…" She looked at the man in front of her, wanting to believe it was who she thought it was. "…you're…you were missing…" She quickly walked to him and threw her arms around him. "Michael! Is it you? Are you really here?"

He hugged her tightly and buried his face in her hair. "Yes, Augusta, it's me. It really is me." She pulled back and kissed every part of his face she could reach, then hugged him again.

"How did you get here? I have been trying to contact anyone I could to find you and I was ready to go down there and find you myself, but...some...things...came up."

"I was in prison. A prison in Richmond."

"Prison? How did you escape?"

"I didn't escape, I didn't have to." He turned, locked the door and flipped the sign to 'Closed'. He then pulled her into the parlor where the curtains were drawn and kissed her like he had been dreaming of for the past year. When he pulled away, she spoke again.

"Then how are you here? What happened?"

"I was lucky enough to be a part of a prisoner exchange. I had always thought them a little counter-intuitive, but I am glad for them now." He held her face in his hands, still gazing deeply into her eyes.

"I thought the president wasn't exchanging prisoners anymore." Augusta said, gripping his waist. It was so thin; he needed some good, home cooked meals.

"They aren't doing nearly as many and they will probably stop completely very soon. Like I said, I was lucky."

"Thank you, thank you, thank you Lord." Augusta said, hugging him tightly again. "Oh, Michael, I have so much to tell you."

"I can see. Michael said, nodding to the street. "I hardly recognized the town. The farms are in disarray, cannon and bullet marks all over the buildings. The amount of people here. When I heard about the battle here, I was so worried, wondering if you and my parents had survived. But they said only one civilian was killed, an unmarried woman..."

"Yes." Tears of joy mixed with tears of relief and sadness fell down Augusta's cheek. "It was Ginny. Ginny Wade."

"No." Michael wiped the tears from her eyes. "I am so sorry. I know she was a good friend to you."

"She was, but Michael that is not the biggest news I have to tell you."

"The battle isn't the biggest news? Augusta, what could be bigger than that? Did you hear from home, did something happen to Joey?"

"No, well, yes, I did hear from home, but that is another story. What I need to tell you..." a small wail came from the corner of the parlor. Michael's head spun around to look in that direction.

"What in the world..."

Augusta took his hand and pulled him over to the rocker next to the bassinet.

"You might want to sit down, Michael." He did, and she reached down to pick up their son. "I would like you to meet Michael Joseph Lewis. He's your son."

"My son." Michael looked at the boy, with wonder and a little fear in his eyes. When Augusta bent to hand the baby over, Michael hesitated. "I don't know if I can. I'm dirty, I need a bath…"

"We can take care of that later." Augusta said with a smile. "Michael Joseph is washable too." She placed the baby in the arms of his father. Michael looked down on the boy, touching his tiny hands. "Augusta, you are the most amazing woman...you did this...he's...he's ours…"

"We did it together, Michael, although I will admit, I have done the bulk of the work so far."

"I don't know what to say." Michael was still stunned. "He's perfect." He reached up and grabbed her arm, gently pulling her so she was on his lap and he could hold both of them. "I don't think this day can get much better than this." He smiled. She bent down to kiss him.

"Happy day of thanks, Michael."

December 6
Lewis Home

Augusta crossed the parlor to where Michael knelt in front of the fire. He had just added some logs and was staring into the flames. He looked so much healthier in just the week and a half he had been home. Good food and good sleep had worked wonders for him. She knelt down next to him and slid her arm around his back and placed her head on his shoulders.

"What's on your mind?" She asked.

"How nice it has been being home." He stood, took her hand and pulled her to the chair where they both sat. "How blessed I am to be with you. How happy I am that I was able to be here to see Michael Joseph and be here to see his baptism."

"I'm glad that worked out too." Augusta smiled. That morning, during Sunday mass, Michael Joseph had been baptized into the Catholic Church. Augusta was going to wait until he was three months, as was the tradition, but when Michael had come home, they decided to do it sooner. "And I'm also happy that you are considering Catholicism for yourself." Michael tightened his arms around her and set his chin on Augusta's shoulder.

"I really am, Michael. I thought about it when we were first married. But staying here and going to church with your parents every week. It has made me very serious about being confirmed." Michael was quiet.

"What else is on your mind, Michael?"

"I have to go back, Augusta. I don't want to but I have to. I have to finish this."

"I know you do. I wish you didn't have to either. Some days, I wish you would just up and leave the army. But then, I realize your dedication and loyalty and your desire to do what's right, those traits are the things that I love best about you." She sighed. "I feel like it could be so easy for you to take me and Michael and just head west."

"It would be. But I just can't do it. It's not how I was raised." Michael replied.

"Well, then, we'll just have to keep writing to one another and keep praying for your safety and a quick end to this war." Augusta said. "When do you have to go back?"

"I need to head back tomorrow. I received a telegram with my orders and need to get back. I've recovered enough and they need as

284

many men with my background and skills to prepare for the army's movements in the spring."

Augusta was quiet. She knew he would be going back soon, but tomorrow just seemed too soon.

"It's been so nice having you around, Michael. I just don't know how I'm going to say goodbye." She finally said.

"We've said goodbye to each other before. We can do it again. This war can't last much longer. We just need a good, competent leader. I heard that Lincoln has a good man in mind, Grant is his name. He's been doing well in the West. In my opinion, he's the type of man we've needed all along."

"But I've heard that many men die in his command." Augusta commented.

"That's true, but I still think we need a man like him and he can bring this war to an end. He'll fight Lee and I believe he'll be able to win."

"But at what cost?" Augusta asked.

"I don't know, Augusta. I just don't know."

December 30
Lewis House

"I can't believe this is Michael. He is so big!" Alex, who had stopped by to visit, smiled at her friend.

"Yes, Michael is growing like a weed. He's smiling now, and even though his sleeping is still irregular, he will roll over to his stomach if I place him on his back. I know that sounds unimpressive, but I think it's exciting. He's also starting to babble a little bit. I know he can't understand me, but I find myself talking to him often. And I sing to him all the time. It really seems to soothe him."

"And well it should. Augusta, you have one of the most beautiful voices I have ever heard."

"Thank you." Augusta blushed. "Mrs. Lewis says the same thing. She keeps encouraging me to sing on Sundays in church. It was so wonderful having Michael here for our son's baptism. I am actually thinking of becoming a full member of the Catholic Church myself."

"Good for you, Augusta. That's wonderful. That will be great for your family."

"Thank you." Augusta smiled at her son. "So, what news do you have?"

"There's not much going on at the battle front. The Confederates have some new leaders in Mississippi and Georgia, but no real battles to speak of. The Star Sentinel did report that Mr. Phineas Branson fought against the Southern army back during the battle. He wasn't injured, but he did attempt to protect his home."

"That report is about six months overdue." Augusta commented.

"Yes. But there were so many negative reports about the men of our town that they want to make sure the men who did act valiantly get recognition."

"I guess it's better late than never." Augusta said.

"I suppose." Alex replied. "So, did Michael have any inside information about the war?"

"Not really. At least nothing that he told me. He did say that Lincoln may choose this new man, Grant, to lead the Army of the Potomac instead of the Union army in the West."

"Really? Good. That would be a smart move. Grant's been doing a lot of good fighting out West. They refer to him as a bulldog of a fighter. Very tough. Although it does seem like he loses a lot of men.

I'm not sure I like that about him. But if he brings the war to an end sooner..."

"I agree. It was so nice having Michael home and so difficult for me to watch him leave again. I can only pray that he will return for good soon."

"That they all will." Alex agreed.

Part Four:

1864

March 30
Dear Will,
Things continue to be busy here. We still have some wounded men, and are finding more bodies all the time, especially in the woods surrounding the town. Townspeople, especially kids, are finding used weapons littering the land. Last month, the Star Sentinel *reported that 28,000 muskets had been found around the town. 24,000 of them were still loaded. A few days ago, some 15-year-old boys were playing with a loaded gun and they accidently killed a 7-year-old black girl. Its so sad.*
Many people are still coming in to visit the "great battlefield". The Cemetery is quite a popular place. At the beginning of February, the Adams County Sentinel *had an editorial looking for Southerners to purchase land for the Confederates fallen to be buried on. It's a nice gesture, since they were buried wherever there was room and there are very few markers for them. However, I cannot see anyone stepping up to do it. There is a rumor that Dr. O'Neil is a southern sympathizer who might try to do something about the southern graves, but I am not sure how that will all work out. It's been very interesting here with all of the visitors. I feel as though this town will never be the small, quiet town that it used to be. Many people believe that this battle will turn the tide of the war in favor of the Union. If that is the case, we might be a popular town for years to come.*
I miss you so much. I can hardly wait until I have you back home.
With All My Love,
Allie

Lewis General Store
Augusta looked longingly at her son, lying in his bassinet, and touched his downy, brown hair.

"You look so much like your father." She murmured. The bell to the store jingled and Sallie Meyers walked in. When she saw Augusta, she smiled.

"Mrs. Lewis! It's so good to see you! How are you doing? How is your new son?"

"Michael Joseph is right here." Augusta smiled and picked up her son. "And we are doing well."

"It must have been so nice to have your husband home, even if it was only for a while."

"It was." Augusta handed her son to Sallie. "I wish Michael could have stayed here forever. I wish that he could forget his loyalties and forget about this war."

"It's hard to forget about the war." Sallie said, cuddling Michael Joseph close to her.

"That's true enough." Augusta replied. "It's hard to believe it's been nine months since the battle. Sometimes, it feels like it was only yesterday."

"It does." Sallie agreed.

"How are you holding up? Everything getting back to normal?"

"As normal as it can be, with all of the visitors coming to see the great battlefield." Sallie looked outside. Gettysburg was busier than ever.

"Yes. Some of the visitors seem so sad, looking for loved ones, coming here with hopes of information and being disappointed with what they do or don't find." Augusta said somberly. "Although I heard from Abigail Williams that you will soon be having a very special visitor."

Sallie blushed. "Abigail Williams is not making up tales. It's true."

"That sounds promising. Tell me about it."

"He is the brother of a soldier I tended at St. Francis Xavier. The patient was Alexander Stewart, the first soldier I met when going to help the wounded. I went to care for him, but he was so selfless that he told me to go and help someone else. I feel he knew he was going to die."

"I remember you mentioning him." Augusta nodded. "You said you read to him and wrote home for him."

"Yes. His younger brother, Harry, wrote back. He is a preacher. He is bringing his mother here the end of June, if all works out the way it should. They want to see where Alexander spent his last days."

"So you have been writing back and forth to this Harry Stewart?"

"Yes. I feel as though we are becoming quite close. I like him a lot." Sallie smiled.

"It is good to see something positive come out of all this. The horrors of the past year." Augusta smoothed her finger over her son's head.

"I agree. Especially after the battle." Sallie paused. "How are the Wades? Do you see them ever?"

"I don't, actually." Augusta shook her head. "I see Georgia here in the store on occasion. I know they are still grieving Ginny."

"I can hardly imagine. It must be unbearable. I knew Ginny in passing, just never got to know her very well. I can't imagine how Charlotte Turner is feeling. She and Ginny were as close as sisters."

"Christmas was hard for Charlotte. I am sorry to say I was a little preoccupied during the holidays with Michael home recovering and with Michael Joseph. I was in my own world for a few weeks. I do know that Charlotte will occasionally visit with the Wades, but she spent Christmas with Alex and her parents."

"I don't think anyone could believe that the war could last this long." Sallie said

"I know. Alex Sadler was telling me that Lincoln's new commander, Ulysses S. Grant, might be the man we need to end this. Michael mentioned him too, back in December. Alex said that he was doing such a good job fighting in the West that Lincoln moved him to fight Lee."

"Mrs. Sadler seems to be quite knowledgeable." Sallie commented.

"Alex is one of the smartest women I have ever met. She doesn't make it obvious, but when you hold a conversation with her, you can tell. She loves to read the news and keep up with current events."

"That's good for her." Sallie said.

Michael Joseph began to fuss and Augusta took her son. "It's about time for his feeding. Is there anything I can get you?"

Mrs. Lewis came into the storefront. "Augusta, dear, let me take over the duties here while you go and feed Michael. Miss Meyers, how are you?"

"I am very well, Mrs. Lewis, thank you. I just came in for some sugar and flour." She smiled at Augusta. "It was wonderful talking with you again."

April 25
Lewis Store

Augusta smiled as Alex walked into the store. She always liked when her friends stopped by to catch up. The planting season had kept Charlotte on her farm, while Alex spent her time working for the war effort, in whatever capacity she could.

"Hello, Alex! How are things going this week for you?"

"Things are going well. Trying to stay busy and trying not to miss Will too much, as usual. How about yourself?"

"Nothing out of the ordinary. Michael Joseph is keeping me busy, he's crawling everywhere and I wouldn't be shocked is he started walking soon."

"I bet..." Alex began to speak when the door banged open and Jedidiah Smoker strode in, followed by Garrett Sullivan.

"Thought I would find you here, Mrs. Rebel." He slapped a day-old edition of the *New York Times* on the counter. "What do you have to say about your troops this time?"

Augusta's heart beat heavily as she looked down. The headline-*"Attack on Fort Pillow: Indiscriminate Slaughter of the Prisoners"*-screamed at her.

"Whatever happened, you cannot possibly put any blame on Augusta." Alex said calmly.

"Oh, I'm not blaming Mrs. Lewis. She's loyal to her husband. I'm just curious what she thinks about her Confederates and their massacre of surrendering Federal forces." Smoker said.

Augusta scanned the article and was appalled to see that what the man said was true.

"Massacre?" Alex asked. "What are you talking about?"

"Some Reb named Forest was raiding towns in Tennessee and Kentucky, capturing Union prisoners and supplies and demolishing our military posts and fortifications. They decided to attack Fort Pillow, 40 miles north of Memphis." Smoker explained. "Just thought our little lady from Charleston should know." Smoker then turned and walked out the door, followed by Sullivan.

Alex watched him, puzzled. "What was that all about? He's usually nastier, more threatening and lewd. Why wasn't he?"

"He knew just what to say that would cut me the deepest." Augusta said softly, looking at the newspaper. It tore at her to see what men were capable of doing. Alex stepped next to her friend. And looked at the article.

"Fort Pillow had 600 Federals protecting it. Confederate Nathan Bedford Forest and his troops arrived on April 12 in the morning. Even though Union troops surrendered, the Confederates massacred them in cold blood." Augusta spoke softly. "They killed 80 percent of the Negro troops stationed there, 350 Union men killed in all. Sixty wounded. 164 taken prisoner. I can hardly believe it possible, that Southern gentlemen could do something that atrocious."

"War can make people do horrible things, Augusta." Alex said, continuing to read the article. "And the Confederates evacuated the fort the next day."

"This whole war seems more and more gruesome as time goes on. I just don't know if anyone will get out completely untouched." Augusta said, tears in her eyes.

"I don't think anyone will." Alex looked at her friend. "You said that Jed Smoker knows just what to say to hurt you. Is he doing that often?"

Augusta brushed tears from her cheeks. "Sometimes. He's a cruel man. It's like he knows how conflicted I am. I feel guilty every time the Southern army does something, like win a big battle or something like this." She gestured to the paper. "But then I feel like I'm being disloyal to the place that I was born and raised. But if I don't feel bad about Confederate victories, then I feel like I am being disloyal to my husband." She sighed. "Alex, I just feel so torn by this war."

"I can hardly imagine what you've been going through, Augusta. You are one of the strongest women that I know."

"I don't feel like it. There are days when I'm just not sure what to do or how I can get through the day." She gave a small smile. "But then, I remember everything that I know about God and how much support I have from my new family and friends."

"We do care about you, Augusta, and we're happy that you're here with us."

May 9
Turner Farm

Charlotte stretched her arms above her head after she hung some sheets on the drying line. Days had almost returned to normal as much as it could after the battle.

"Charlotte, are you back here?" Alex's voice came from around the corner of the house seconds before she did.

"Yes, I am." Charlotte picked up her now empty laundry basket and pushed her brown braid over her shoulder. "What brings you out here?"

"Just wanted to check up on you. It's been a couple of weeks. You missed services last weekend."

"I know. I didn't really mean to this time. I lost track of the time. I'm planning on coming into town this coming weekend." Charlotte gestured toward the door and Alex followed her into the house.

"I'm glad you'll be coming." Alex smiled and sat down at the table. Charlotte set the basket down and moved to the stove.

"Can I get you anything? What's the news from town?"

"You don't need to get me anything, Charlotte. I do have some news, though. We just received word that there was another battle in northern Virginia, just a few miles from Fredericksburg."

"Near Fredericksburg? Where?"

"Spotsylvania County and Orange County."

"That's not far from Fredericksburg at all." Charlotte sat next to her friend. "What happened? Who won?"

"Well, it's inconclusive who won. From a tactical standpoint, the Confederates were victorious, but the Union could consider it a strategic victory. This new leader, Grant, he is just the kind of man we've needed in charge of the army. He withdrew from the battlefield, they are calling it the Wilderness, but he didn't retreat to D.C. like all of our other leaders have. I'm not quite sure where they're headed next."

"I can't believe it. I hope they clear out of Virginia"

"And go where?" Alex asked.

"That's a good point. I don't know. End the war and send the men home." Charlotte paused. "How many men were killed?"

"Around two-thousand Union and around 1500 Confederate. Around 12,000 Union wounded and around 800 Confederates."

"That's so many!" Charlotte exclaimed. "So many lives destroyed." She sighed. "How can you always remember those facts?"

"I've just always had a good mind for numbers and remembering facts." Alex shrugged. "How are things here? Have you heard from Captain Spencer?"

"Things are settling into a routine here. I haven't heard from the Captain, not since he left."

"Do you want to hear from him?"

Charlotte took a deep breath, unsure of how to answer. "I'm not sure. I don't know if he will write. I didn't give him much hope when we parted."

"Well, I'm sure you didn't completely ruin a friendship with him."

"I told him about Thomas. Told him that I was engaged to someone else."

"Why did you do that?"

"I don't know, Alex. My feelings for James...I'm not sure about them. I feel like I could fall in love with him. He's a nice man and there's something about him that really pulled me toward him. And when we kissed...I hadn't ever felt that way, ever."

"You never told me that you two kissed!" Alex exclaimed.

"It never really came up in conversation."

"So why did you push him away by telling him about Thomas?"

"I don't exactly know. My feelings for him...they scared me. I had just lost Ginny and Wesley. James is a soldier. He was heading back to war. You know how bad I got after that. I don't know what would happen if I gave my heart away to someone else and they died. I don't know how I would handle it."

"Well, you seem to be doing better, coming to church. How is the bible reading going?"

"Good. Reading Ginny's bible and reading through her notes makes me feel like I'm able to spend time with her."

"That's good." Alex smiled. "I'm so glad."

June 2
Gettysburg Post Office
"Charlotte!" Augusta smiled at her friend and hurried across the street to join her. Charlotte turned and smiled back.

"Augusta! Where is that beautiful baby boy of yours?"

"I left him with Michael's mother. She is so wonderful with him"

"It's good that you have them around to help." Charlotte commented.

"I know. I am very blessed." She smiled. "I heard there was another battle right around the Fredericksburg area. That's two in the past couple of months. You have family there, right?"

"I do. The family plantation is right on the Rappahannock River. They are so close to all the fighting right now. It's so scary. I pray my cousin, Tory is safe. She lives in Vicksburg. I wish I could receive or send them some letters. I only met them a few times, but we formed a great bond. I hope I can see them all again when this is all over."

"I know what you mean. I can't wait until I can go home and visit my family and friends. One of my greatest fears is that the feelings will be so harsh and strong after everything that I won't be welcome."

"I'm sure it won't come to that." Charlotte said. "At least, I hope it won't."

"I don't see how people will be able to easily forgive. Not after all the recent casualties. It's just unbelievable."

"It is." Augusta pulled the door to the post office open and the two women walked inside. The clerk smiled, then turned to see if they had any mail.

"Here is some correspondence for Mr. Samuel Lewis." He handed Augusta some papers. "And here is a letter for you, Miss Turner."

"Thank you." Charlotte smiled, surprised that she actually had a letter.

"Who wrote to you?" Augusta asked.

"I'm not sure." Charlotte said, opening the envelope.

Dear Miss Turner

This is a very difficult letter to write. I hope it finds you in good health and safe from the war surrounding us. I need you to know that you have had a piece of my heart from the very moment I met you all those years ago in Virginia. I feel blessed to have met you again and to have been able to renew our acquaintance. I enjoyed every moment I spent with you. I had hoped to continue our friendship, even if you never cared for me the way I cared for you. Unfortunately, God has called me home...

Augusta watched as her friend's face went from happy to sorrow. "Charlotte, what is it?"

Charlotte somberly handed Augusta the letter. Augusta quickly read it. Apparently, James Spencer had written the letter and then asked his fellow soldiers to mail the letter if anything happened to him.

"I should have expected this." Charlotte said "Just as I was getting through things, just as things were getting back to normal, I find this out."

Augusta put her arms around Charlotte and felt her friend hug her back. Charlotte sniffled. "Why, Augusta? How much more of this are we going to have to go through?"

"I don't know, Charlotte. I just don't know."

July 11

Michael,

If we believed things would calm down after a few months, we were very wrong. It seems like every day the train brings more visitors. People still want to see where the great battle took place. People who come looking for lost loved ones, even though most of the wounded have been sent home or to big city hospitals. Some people come to see where their loved ones passed away. Some people are quite depressed, others seem to be relieved.

People are still finding weapons around town. A few weeks ago, little Adam Taney Jr. found a shell and tried to open it and it exploded. It was very sad.

I miss you dearly. Things have changed so much, but my love for you never will. I pray for the day when this war will end and we can be together. Not just for a few days, but for the rest of our lives. I pray for your safety, comfort and health. Please take care of yourself, and I know we'll be together soon.

With all the love I possess,

Augusta

Lewis Home

"It's hard to believe that a year has passed since the battle." Alex said, leaning against the counter. Ten-month old Michael sat up on a quilt set in the corner, playing with blocks of wood.

"This is a strange thought." Augusta said. "Have you heard from Charlotte? Any news about Captain Spencer?"

Ever since she had received the letter from James, Charlotte had slipped back into her depressed mood. She was somber and quiet most of the time and Augusta and Alex were again beginning to fear for her health. She was getting dangerously thin and shadows under her eyes told that she wasn't getting much sleep.

"It's quite difficult seeing her changed attitude about God." Alex said. "She had made so much progress with her faith. Now, I think she is worse than ever. She was getting so strong, but it seems like she has just forgotten it."

"What she needs is something to live for." Augusta said. "I mean, she has us, and I know she occasionally spends time with the Wade family. She will stop and play with Michael. But she needs something more permanent, something for herself."

"And also, not that lingering fear that she will have to marry Thomas when he comes back." Alex added. "I really thought she had a chance to make it work with Captain Spencer."

"I did too." The girls turned to the door as the bell jingled, signaling a customer coming in. An unfamiliar woman walked in. She was middle-aged, maybe in her early 30's, with brown hair and wrinkled clothes. She appeared quite unhealthy and clutched a tattered case and reticule and looked around nervously.

"Hello, is there something I can help you with, ma'am?" Augusta asked. The woman looked surprised at the accent coming from Augusta.

"There is, actually." The woman replied, shocking Augusta and Alex with a slight Virginian accent of her own. "I am looking for the home of Hiram Turner."

"The Turner family lives on a farm on the outskirts of town." Alex said. "Mr. Turner is away, fighting. His daughter is at the house, though." Alex smiled. "I can walk you out there. I wish I could offer you a ride, but horses are hard to come by."

"I understand and I would be much obliged." The woman nodded. Alex walked out the door, leading the woman toward the Turner home, waving goodbye to Augusta.

As they walked, Alex tried to find out more about the woman without being too forward. She discovered her name was Mary Wilson, and she was from Williamsburg, Virginia. She wondered if this woman was one of the Virginia cousins. Alex quickly discovered that the woman was not very talkative.

They finally arrived at the Turner farmhouse.

"Here we are!" Alex said. She approached the door, knocked twice and opened the door. "Charlotte!" She called out, walking across the threshold. "I have someone who would like to meet you!"

Charlotte came from her bedroom, her hair askew and clothes wrinkled, making her look as though she had just woken up. The bags under her eyes told a different story. It looked to Alex as though her friend were ten years older than she really was.

"Alex." She nodded, and then froze when she noticed Mary. She tucked a stray strand of hair into her messy bun.

"Charlotte, may I introduce you to Mrs. Mary Wilson." Mary Wilson looked at Alex and then corrected her.

"It's...actually, it's Mrs. Mary Wilson Turner..."

"How can I help you, Mrs. Turner?"

"I feel as though I must get right to the point, Miss Turner. I'm with child, and the child I am carrying...his father...his father is your father."

Alex tried to hide her reaction, but she was lucky that no one was paying attention to her. Charlotte could not mask her astonishment.

"You...my father...how...when..."

"I was visiting family near where his unit was stationed. We became friendly, talked a lot, then one thing led to another. We were married by a preacher and spent time together until he left. I know this may come as a shock. But what I say is true." Mary pulled a crumpled envelope from her reticule. "This letter and marriage license should prove to you that I'm speaking the truth." Charlotte took the paper and quickly scanned the letter. It was written in her father's hand, and clearly stated that he acknowledged that the child Mary carried belonged to him, and that they were married. It also suggested to go north to Gettysburg to stay with Charlotte and wait for him.

"I...he...well, of course you are welcome to stay here." Charlotte said. "I have more than enough room."

"Thank you," Mary said. "I will pull my own weight. I'm a good cook. I can help with a lot of things." She placed her hand on her stomach. "My child will probably be born around the first of the year. But I can help around here. Even in my condition."

"I believe you." Charlotte said. She gave Mary a hollow smile. "And we will wait for my father to return together."

August 2
Lewis Home

"Any news on Mr. Lewis?" Augusta asked her mother-in-law. Samuel Lewis had been in Chambersburg, meeting with business contacts and associates. The day before, reports had come that Confederate forces had burned and looted the town. The citizens of Gettysburg knew few details, and many were terrified that the Confederates would once again invade their homes.

"No, not yet." Aideen replied. "I'm sure we will hear from him soon." She had barely finished her sentence when the side door opened and Samuel walked in.

"Sam!" Aideen rushed to her husband and hugged him." We were so worried! What happened?"

"I would have been here sooner, but I was stopped by many people who knew I was in Chambersburg and wanted details."

"Are the Confederates coming here again?"

"No, dear, we're safe." He crossed the room to sit down. Augusta sat as well, Michael in her arms, and Aideen sat next to her husband.

"What happened? We heard there was burning and looting, but that's all we know."

"I was with J.W. Douglass, the attorney that I always meet up with when I am there. He was given an order from Confederate General Early demanding money. $100,000 in gold or $500,000 in greenbacks. Douglass warned everyone he met on Market Street that the confederates were coming and what their demands were, but few believed him."

"Why was the General demanding money? Did he give a reason?" Augusta asked softly.

"Said it was payment to compensate the citizens of the Shenandoah Valley who lost homes and property to our Union troops."

"I am not sure I believe those farmers in the valley would have ever seen that money." Aideen said.

"I'm not so sure either." Samuel said.

"Weren't there any Union troops in the town?" Augusta asked. "I thought the officers in charge of Pennsylvania's defense were located in Chambersburg."

"They were, but Major Couch had sent many men to Washington earlier to reinforce the capital and when he was told the Confederates were coming, he abandoned the town." Samuel took a breath. "The

Confederates attacked severely when they were told there was no money available. They set fire to any building, private, public, it didn't matter. Townsfolk who were not able to leave their homes were just left to burn. Able citizens followed the destruction and were able to save everyone except one, an elderly African American. That is the only civilian that was lost. Five Confederates were killed. Some people tried to pay the soldiers to spare their homes and leave them alone. The Southerners took the money and then burned the homes anyways. Soldiers were breaking into houses, evicting residents, smashing furniture and then throwing broken pieces into piles and burning those. It was all done early that day, I think by 8:00 in the morning the city was in flames."

"How horrible!" Aideen exclaimed. Augusta felt sick. Again, she couldn't believe the destruction that humans could inflict on each other.

"Not all Confederates went along with the looting and burning." Samuel said. "It looked like some of the Confederates were refusing to carry out their orders. Others seemed to be helping the citizens get to safety and move their goods." He glanced at Augusta. "Unfortunately, those acts will probably be overshadowed by the destruction of the town. Many of our townspeople here in Gettysburg are already calling for revenge."

"But this was done in retaliation for that Union general Hunter allowing his men to loot and burn the private property in the Valley, isn't it? When will this all end?"

"When the war ends." Samuel said.

"Maybe not even then." Aideen muttered. "It will take years after the war for the nation to be healed." She turned to her husband. "Should we be worried about any repercussions?"

Augusta looked down at her son, sleeping peacefully in her arms.

"No, I don't think so." Samuel said.

"No more than usual, you mean." Augusta said.

"Augusta, my dear. You know Aideen and I care for you. You are truly like our daughter. I wish I could stop the hatred and comments that the townspeople feel and make toward you. I wish they would all see in you what I do: a wonderful, caring girl with a big heart. I know things haven't been easy for you for a number of reasons."

Tears began to form in Augusta's eyes.

"But you need to know that we care for you, you are a permanent part of our family, and someday, hopefully soon, this war will be over."

Augusta nodded. "I know, and that helps. Knowing Michael is out of prison helps, though I wish he could have stayed here to recuperate longer. Having Alex and Charlotte and my other friends helps. It just gets...frustrating when people make me feel like the enemy."

"Is it still only a small number of people?" Aideen asked.

"Yes, only a minority, and really just some of the men when they've been drinking." Augusta smiled slightly. "You two are making me feel like I'm a schoolgirl dealing with a schoolyard bully. I'm fine."

"It's never okay to be treated like that, Augusta, I don't care if you were Jeff Davis's daughter."

"I'm glad you feel that way. I don't know how I would have survived these three years without you too, and your support."

"You would have survived. You're stronger than you think." Samuel rose, crossed the room to Augusta and kissed her on the head like a father would. "Even if it's just through marriage, you are a Lewis, and we are proud to have you in our family."

"Thank you." Augusta smiled, then headed upstairs for the evening.

Saturday, September 3
Lewis Store

Charlotte entered the Lewis Store to find Alex and Augusta talking. Eleven-month-old Michael Joseph sat in the corner playing with some blocks.

"Hello, ladies." She said. Her friends smiled and gestured her over.

"Charlotte, it is so good to see you. How is your...mother?" Alex asked.

"Mary is doing well." Charlotte answered. "It's quite strange to have a stepmother. Especially one who is not that much older than I am." She looked at the counter, where a newspaper sat. "What's the news?"

"There's actually been quite a bit of news." Alex replied. "Grant, Meade, and Butler still have Petersburg under siege. They're trying to get up to Richmond and end the war."

"Finally. It's been so long." Charlotte said. "What other news is there?"

"A Union general named Sherman's been laying siege to Atlanta since July. Confederate General Hood finally abandoned the city on Thursday." Alex explained. "It looks like the end is quite near. Father says no more than a year, which seems like a while, but when you think about how long it's been, well, hopefully, it won't seem like too much longer.

"A year does seem long." Augusta said. "By then, Michael Joseph will be two years old. That will be so much time that his father will miss."

"Well, then, the two of you will just have to have another one so he can experience it all." Charlotte said.

Augusta's eyes began to water. "We almost did." She whispered.

"What? Augusta, what do you mean?" Charlotte felt horrible.

"After Michael came home, we...I...became pregnant again. But before I was far along, maybe two months or so, I...lost the baby. I was going to tell you two, but I didn't want to burden you. Mr. and Mrs. Lewis are the only ones who knew. Mrs. Lewis is the one who helped me get through it."

"Oh, Augusta! I am so sorry." Charlotte threw her arms around her friend. "I'm so sorry that you had to go through that."

"I wondered if something happened." Alex commented. "You had a glow about you one week, then the next time I saw you, you looked ill. Nothing ever came of my suspicions that you were with child. I just thought I had been wrong."

"No, you were correct. I feel like I should have told you two, but I just didn't know. I didn't want you to feel sorry for me. Besides, what could you have done?"

"We could have been there for you; supported you." Alex said.

"Well, you guys were there. You're always there for me. You just didn't know specifics." Augusta shrugged.

"I suppose." Alex said.

"We should talk about something else." Augusta suggested.

"How about the new attitude of Abigail Williams?" Charlotte said. "She's actually been kind to me the last few times I have seen her. She even sounded genuinely sorry for Ginny's death."

"I've noticed that too. Not nearly as condescending as before the war." Augusta agreed.

"Well," Alex said, "war changes people. Perhaps it has changed Abigail for the better.

October 21
Lewis Store

Alex opened the door to the Lewis Store. Augusta smiled at her from behind the counter.

"How are you doing, Alex? What brings you in today?"

"I was getting bored sitting around the house, working on more sewing projects with mother." She placed a newspaper on the counter. "Where's that little boy of yours?"

"I finally got him down for a nap." Augusta replied. "That child definitely keeps me going. Walking everywhere, falling down all the time, but bouncing right back up again. He loves putting things in a basket and taking them out. He's even starting to feed himself. And he is coming very close to talking."

"That's great. I was hoping to see him."

"He could wake up at any time, now. If you stick around for a while, you might get to."

"Well, then, I guess you and I should have a good, long chat."

"I always enjoy a good talk. I feel like I learn so much from talking to you."

"Well, I am glad to be helpful. I can teach you about world affairs, and I can watch and learn from you about how to be a good mother. Hopefully, this war will end soon and Will and I can start our own family."

"You'll make a good mother," Augusta said. "You're so good with Michael Joseph, and Georgia Wade was just telling me the other day how good you are with Louis when you see them at church."

"I have found that I do love children." Alex smiled. "But, let's see what new news we can find." She picked up the paper and skimmed it. "Hmmm, this is interesting. Apparently, a group of Confederates raided the Vermont city of St. Albans."

"Vermont? How did they get up there?"

"This says they came in from Canada." Alex answered, still reading. "It looks like former prisoner and Confederate Bennett Young from Kentucky escaped to Canada a year ago and returned south. He proposed invading and raiding the Union, coming from Canada."

"Canada? How could that even work?"

"I'm not sure how it could have worked large-scale, but they were able to bring some men in."

"What happened?" Augusta asked.

"It looks like this Young person claimed that they were in Vermont for a vacation. By October 19, twenty-one Confederate cavalry were in town. The men staged robberies of the city's three banks, taking a total of $208,000. Villagers were held at gunpoint on their village green. Several armed villagers tried to resist and one was killed. Another was wounded. They were going to burn the city, luckily, only one shed was destroyed."

"Oh my goodness." Augusta said. "Did they catch the men?"

"The raiders escaped to Canada, where they were arrested, but then freed when the Canadians ruled that they were soldiers under military orders. They Canadians did return the money they found on the raiders."

"Wow. Even Canada is being bought into this conflict."

"Well, at least now, Canada should turn against the Confederacy. They were staying neutral, but with the Confederacy bringing them into the conflict, Canadians won't like that."

"It's unbelievable what has happened these past four years. I can only hope it will be over soon."

December 5
Lewis Store

Alex opened the door to the Lewis store and smiled at Augusta's father-in-law.

"Mrs. Sadler, how are you?" Mr. Lewis asked.

"I'm doing just fine, thank you. I've come to visit with Augusta, if she's available."

"She's just rocking Junior to sleep." Mr. Lewis said, using the nickname that he had given to Michael Joseph. "And I'm sure she would love to see you. Go right into the parlor."

"Thank you." Alex smiled and walked through the door that led into the Lewis home. Augusta was sitting in a rocker, Michael Joseph snuggled against her chest. Alex felt a longing in her heart, something she often felt recently whenever she saw Augusta with Michael Joseph, Georgia Wade-McClellan with 17-month-old Louis, or any mother with a young child. She couldn't wait until Will came home for many reasons, but her growing desire to start a family with him was a big one.

Augusta opened her eyes and smiled, then quietly stood.

"Be right back." She whispered, then slowly walked upstairs. She quickly came back and the two girls sat down.

"Alex, it's so good to see you."

"Likewise. It's been a few weeks, so I thought I would stop in. How are things going?"

"Things are going well. Helping at the store and taking care of MJ helps pass the time and keeps me busy."

"You're calling him MJ now?" Alex smiled.

"Yes, well, it's not as much of a mouthful as Michael Joseph." Especially now that he is starting to understand when I address him."

"I can't believe he is over a year old, already." Alex commented.

"I know. He's just growing so quickly. I blink and he's doing something new. He's smart too. Takes after his father in that way." She looked down, thoughtful. "So what news do you have? Any reports on the war? You're always so good about explaining current events."

"I enjoy keeping up with them." Alex remarked. "Well, there's no real news about the war between the Union and Confederacy. But there has been a battle, a tragedy, really, far out west in the Colorado Territory."

"Colorado Territory? I didn't realize there was fighting out there too."

"Yes, we have troops fighting against Cheyenne and Arapaho Indian tribes. 700 militia men, led by a Colonel John Chivington, attacked and pretty much destroyed a peaceful village. They killed over 100 of the Indians. Two-thirds of those killed were women and children."

"Oh my goodness." Augusta gasped. "How could that have happened?"

"It happened because men like violence and fighting wars." Alex replied, bitterness apparent in her voice.

"Alex, you know that's not true."

"Augusta, look around! You know it's true! We're in the middle of a war, our husbands in danger every moment!" Alex stood and moved to the window, looking out. "If men, on some level, didn't like fighting, we wouldn't be in this mess!"

"Alex, I don't believe that. I just can't. I know of so many men who aren't fighting because they like fighting, but because they feel a sense of duty. Both of my brothers are that way. Joseph, the one who attended West Point, felt that with his education and military background, that he had to enlist, or all of his talents would be wasted. My older brother, Andrew, enlisted, in spite of being ready to take over the family plantation. He felt like he had to fight for his home. And Michael is one of the gentlest men that I know. He's fighting because of his military background and training, but also because he felt as though it was his duty and heritage to do so. His father's family has been in America since before we were a country. He's had ancestors who have fought in every major war that we've had: the Seven Years War, the American War for Independence, even the war with Mexico. He never really wanted to go to West Point. He knew it would be a great education, but he also felt that it was his duty. He never wanted to fight, but he felt he had to. You can't make a generalization that all men want to fight. Do you really believe that Will would rather be fighting than with you?"

"Sometimes I wonder, Augusta." Alex sat down. "Sometimes I wonder. He was so excited to go to war, to fight. He could have stayed in school. Many students did. If he really wanted to be with me...I think he could have."

"Alex, you told me before why Will joined. You said he felt that he needed to do this. And now, he has to follow through and finish it."

Tears fell down Alex's cheeks. "I know, Augusta. I know. I'm sorry to dump all of this on you. I'm just...so worried. I haven't heard from him since before the battle happened here. I miss him so much and just want him home. I'm so tired of this war. I know you feel the same way, but I just want this to be over."

"I know. I do too. I don't know what else to say. Except for what I usually say." Augusta struggled to hold back tears herself.

Alex gave a weak smile. "Yes. We just need to pray."

Part Five:

1865

Hiram Turner would never return. Charlotte sank down in a kitchen chair as she re-read the letter from a chaplain at a field hospital in Virginia. She was shocked. Another death in her life. And yet, she was void of emotion. She felt no tears well up. Her father had been lost to her so long ago, to hear of his physical death was almost a relief. She was ashamed by her lack of emotions, but the knowledge that her father was at peace and would not come back to ignore her or force her to marry anyone, made her feel as though a huge boulder had been lifted off her shoulders.

"I am such a terrible person..." She muttered to herself, crumpling the letter.

"I don't believe that for a moment, Charlotte Turner." Charlotte jerked her head up at the sound of Augusta's voice. "What have you done to make you say that?" She walked into the room

"Oh, Augusta." Charlotte rose and crossed the room to hug her friend. "I just received word...my father is dead."

"You can't be serious. Oh, Charlotte, I am so sorry." Augusta clutched her tighter.

"That's not the worst part, though." Charlotte pulled away from the hug and looked at her friend. "The worst part is the emotions I am feeling about this. Or the lack thereof. When I read the letter, what I felt was...relief." Charlotte cast a quick glance up the stairs to her father's room where Mary was sleeping. The time for her to have her child was quickly approaching and she was growing weaker and weaker. Charlotte was worried about her and the child, and the news about Hiram would not help matters.

"Relief?" Augusta repeated. "I can actually believe that. From what I understand, you and your father have never had a good relationship."

"To me, he's been gone for years, ever since my mother died. I just can't believe he is gone for good." Charlotte let a deep breath go. "My father is dead."

"Hiram...dead?" A voice sounded from the stairs. Augusta and Charlotte turned to see Mary, ashen faced.

"Mary, I'm sorry. We just received a letter..." Charlotte was cut off as the woman crumpled to the ground, tumbling down the last stairs. Augusta and Charlotte rushed to her, and were horrified to see blood stains on her skirts.

"Oh, my!" Charlotte said. "We need a doctor, a midwife, someone!" Together, they moved Mary to a bed and Augusta quickly headed to town to get help.

****

The next day, Alex arrived at Charlotte's house to find her sitting in front of the fire, hunched over and head in her hands. Alex knew right away...someone else had died.

"Charlotte?" She asked softly. Charlotte looked up, her eyes puffy from crying. "What happened?" She glance into the parlor and saw Augusta, seated in a chair, a small bundle in her arms.

"We lost her." Charlotte said softly. "Mary didn't make it. It's as if the death of my father was too much for her. She was already so weak. She just...gave up. And now she's dead. My father is dead. And that little girl in there has nobody."

"That's not true." Alex said. "That little girl has you. And you have me and Augusta and our families and so many others. You have friends that love you."

"I am in no position to take care of a child, Alex. You know that. I can barely take care of myself..."

"I know nothing of the sort." Alex spoke softly, trying not to get frustrated with her friend. "Charlotte, you need to stop acting like this. It's like after the battle all over again. I had hoped Mary being here would help, but even that and the prospect of new life couldn't get you out of your self-pity. We are all going through our own issues. But we can't just hide away. We have to keep busy. We have to get through this together, helping each other out."

Alex quickly pulled Charlotte outside, out of the range of Augusta's hearing. "Were you even aware that Michael is now in a hospital?

Augusta received word three weeks ago. He was hit with debris when a cannonball hit a building he was near. And you know the Wades continue to struggle. You haven't visited them in so long. Did you know Georgia wants to move away when John comes home from the war?" Alex took a deep breath. "I have said this before, I will say it again. In spite of how it feels, God does have a plan with all this horror. We don't know what it is, or what mission He has for us. But Charlotte, I have been praying for something to happen that would bring you back to us, give you something to live for. And now God has dropped that little girl into your life. She needs you, she has no other family. Augusta and I need our friend back." Alex stopped, gathering her thoughts and letting her words sink in. Charlotte looked at her friend, astonished. As it had a year ago, what she said made sense. Charlotte sighed and looked into the house where Augusta sat, rocking the still unnamed baby girl. Her little sister. Charlotte looked back at Alex, and for the first time in a year, she noticed someone else's pain, and she knew deep down that Alex was right again.

March 7

Turner Farm

Charlotte sat in a rocker that she had found in the barn, gently rocking her sister. She had named her Mary Elizabeth, after the baby's mother and Charlotte's own mother. Charlotte loved the times when she could just cuddle and rock the baby girl. Taking care of her had given her life more meaning than she could have imagined. She didn't know if she could ever love a person as much as she loved Mary Elizabeth, and the child was only three months old.

There was a knock on the door. Charlotte softly laid Mary in the bassinet, another piece of furniture she had found hidden in the barn, and went to open the door.

Alex stood there and held up a newspaper. "I thought you might want to read this." She handed Charlotte the paper, then crossed the room and picked up the baby. "The paper printed President Lincoln's new Inaugural address. If you liked the speech he gave here last November, I think you will like this one even better." Charlotte sat at the table and looked at the words on the page. As Alex had said, the words were good, but the last part really grabbed Charlotte's attention.

"With malice toward none, with charity for all, with firmness in the right as God gives us to see the right, let us strive on to finish the work we are in, to bind up the nation's wounds, to care for him who shall have borne the battle and for his widow and his orphan, to do all which may achieve and cherish a just and lasting peace among ourselves and with all nations."

"It sounds like he wants to forgive the South for the war. That can't be a popular opinion." Charlotte commented.

"I agree, it can't be popular, but I also agree with what he is saying. I know we won't be able to just forget the past four years. No one in this country will be able to. There will be hatred and distrust between the north and the south for years."

"If not decades." Charlotte said. She glanced at another article. Petersburg, the city where her cousin Rebekah lived with her mother and brothers, was still under siege. "Petersburg still hasn't fallen. I hope my family is okay down there."

"Do you hear anything from any of your Turner relatives?"

"My Uncle Samuel wrote me after Father died. He's the one fighting for the Union, but his wife and children are the ones in Petersburg. Through his contacts, he was able to find out that my cousins from Fredericksburg survived that battle, although Turner's Glenn, the family plantation, was nearly destroyed. He is also confident that everyone in my Uncle Charles's family is okay. They are the ones in Vicksburg."

"I heard that families there suffered a great deal from that siege."

"Yes, I heard that too. I was too preoccupied with the aftermath of the battle here, I didn't even think about the fall of Vicksburg. It was so close after our tragedy."

"What about any uncles or cousins fighting for the Confederacy?" Alex asked.

"Uncle Samuel didn't really say. He just offered his condolences and sorrow for Father dying. He told me if I needed any help to let him know and he would do what he could. He said all my cousins were surviving as well as could be expected." She looked at the words of the president's speech. "I really do miss them all. Belle, Tori, Bekah, Beth. I hope this war ends soon so I can see them all again. I'm glad the President is working on a peaceful end to this chaos."

"And I hope the peace comes soon."

April 11
Turner Farm

"How much longer will this war drag on?" Charlotte asked, stirring the chicken stew she had on the stove. Mary Elizabeth, lay in a bassinet next to a napping Michael Joseph. Augusta sat next to the children, darning some socks for her constantly growing son.

"I don't think it will be much longer. They say the Union army was able to capture Richmond fairly easily after Petersburg fell, and I hear of terrible atrocities in Georgia. A Union General by the name of Sherman is burning everything in his way from the city of Atlanta to the Atlantic Ocean."

"How brutal." Charlotte said.

"Alex said it was to help end the war, to finish it sooner and make the South suffer."

"That sounds inhumane." Charlotte shivered. "But this whole war has been inhumane."

"I agree." Augusta said. She looked toward the door. "I wonder what's keeping Alex."

"She most likely wanted to stop at the post office and check the mail. It has been so long since she has heard from Will." Charlotte checked Mary and Michael, then sat and picked up her knitting. "How is your husband?"

"He is doing much better. He'll be released soon. He may be able to come home and spend the rest of the war with us. Have you heard from Thomas? I know you don't want to marry him, but..."

"Not in a while. He hasn't written in some time and his letters were getting less personal when he was writing."

"Have you decided what you are going to do about Mr. Thomas Culp?"

"I have been doing a lot of thinking and praying about that. I don't think it's fair to either him or me for us to marry without love. But maybe the war has changed things. I will speak to him and see if..."

Without warning, the door crashed open and Alex burst in.

"It's over!" She yelled, then quieted when she saw the sleeping babies and repeated her message. "The war is over!"

Augusta and Charlotte flew out of their seats and rushed to Alex. The three hugged each other tightly.

"When? How did you hear?" Augusta asked.

316

"I heard it at the post office, the whole town is buzzing with the news. It just came over the wires. General Lee surrendered to General Grant in a private home near Appomattox Court House, Virginia. The men will be home before we know it!" Alex's eyes sparkled in anticipation. "I am so unbelievably happy I can hardly stand it!"

April 15
Gettysburg Town

Charlotte walked towards the Lewis store to pick up some supplies and visit with Augusta. Ever since Alex had talked to her about raising her half-sister, Charlotte had been reading Ginny's bible and praying more. Ginny's notes were extremely helpful, and there were times when Charlotte felt that they were written especially for her. She attended church with Alex weekly, bringing her sister. She now loved to have discussions on faith with her friends. Mrs. Lewis was always happy to answer questions and Charlotte had even had a two-hour conversation with Professor Duncan Clark, Alex's father. She was hungry for more knowledge and understanding. She still had some moments of doubt and feelings of worthlessness, but her attitude was improving every day.

"Charlotte! How are you doing?"

Charlotte turned to the voice of Abigail Williams. She sighed, not wanting to deal with the drama that always seemed to follow Abigail.

"Abigail. Hello. I am doing as well as can be expected. What can I help you with?"

Charlotte had noticed before that Abigail's demeanor was different after the battle. She hadn't spoken directly to her, but where Abigail had gone out of her way to be rude in the past, now she wouldn't. She was also more reserved. Not as dramatic.

"Where is your darling new sister? I heard about your troubles. I'm very sorry for your losses."

"Abigail... Why are you asking? You've never cared before."

Abigail looked down at her feet. "I know. I am truly sorry for everything. Everything I put you and...Ginny...through."

"Are you serious, Abigail?"

"I am. I know you might not believe me. It may take time for me to earn your respect. You may never forgive me for what I have said and done. But I just wanted to say...I'm sorry. I hope you can accept my apology." Abigail turned to leave, but Charlotte grabbed the sleeve of her maroon shirtwaist.

"Abigail, wait." Abigail faced Charlotte. "I do forgive you and I accept your apology. But I can't help but wonder...why the change of heart? What happened?"

"The battle. The war. It has altered my way of thinking. I saw a man shot down, dead. I heard the cries of the dying. And then I heard about Ginny. I'm not sure why that affected me so much. I think it's because I realized that the war wasn't just about the soldiers. Anyone could be hurt. So many lives destroyed."

"Well, it's over now." Charlotte said. "And hopefully, soon, we can have our men home and our town will be back to normal."

"Yes." Abigail agreed. A shout from the Post Office drew the attention of both girls. "What in the world?"

"The President's been shot!"

Abigail and Charlotte hastened toward the crowd that had gathered. Charlotte immediately found Alex in the crowd. As she approached her friend, she saw tears welled up in Alex's brown eyes.

"Alex, what happened?"

"President Lincoln was shot last night. He was watching a play in Washington and was shot by a Southern actor. Lincoln died this morning. The actor is still being chased."

"What? You cannot be serious!" Charlotte's hand flew to her mouth.

"It's what everyone is talking about." Alex said.

"But...the war is over. Why would someone do that?"

"Maybe the man didn't know or didn't accept that it was over. Maybe because he was mad that the south lost. No one knows for sure."

"Who did it? What will happen to him?"

"I'm not sure of the man's name, like I said, he was some actor. I am sure he will be caught soon."

"But...the president...dead?" Charlotte thought back to the president, the tall, gangly man, stoic, but with an air of kindness about him. The man who had stood for hours, shaking the hands of those who had gathered for the cemetery dedication. The man who had given the short, but incredibly moving speech about honoring the fallen men, the man who had led the Union to victory and kept the nation together. How unfair for him to not be able to finish what he started. Who would lead the country now?

"What is going to happen next?" Charlotte murmured.

"I don't know, Charlotte. I just don't know."

April 29
Turner Farm

Charlotte hacked at the weeds surrounding her vegetables. She glanced at Mary, who was lying in the shade, napping on a quilt. She turned toward the road, shading the sun with her hand. Her heart sped up when she saw the figure of a Union soldier approaching. He was clean-shaven, but gaunt and pale. Charlotte didn't recognize him until he came closer.

"Charlotte." The man didn't smile, but he usually did not.

"Thomas. It is so good to see you." Charlotte racked her brain, trying to think of how she would tell him of her decision: she could not marry him.

"It is good to see you as well, Charlotte. Can we talk?"

"Yes, of course." Charlotte said. Thomas was as straightforward as ever. She set her hoe against the fence, then went and picked up Mary. Thomas's eyes narrowed a bit and Charlotte quickly explained.

"This is my half-sister, Mary. Her mother died in childbirth after she received word that my father had been killed."

"Yes, of course I knew her mother. I forgot she was going to come here. Sad thing, about your father. I was wounded in the same battle. Cedar Creek." They walked into the house.

"I hadn't heard that. You never wrote about it." Charlotte placed Mary in her cradle.

"There are many things I didn't, couldn't write to you about, Charlotte."

Charlotte gestured to Thomas to sit down, then poured him coffee. "There are some things I need to say to you as well, Thomas." She sat. "What was it you needed to tell me?"

"Charlotte, there is no way to do what I need to do without causing you pain. I cannot marry you. I fell in love with another woman during the war."

Charlotte couldn't have been more surprised. After all her worries about turning Thomas away, she wasn't the one to break things off.

"I know this may come as a shock to you, Charlotte, a disappointing one at that. I know you staked your future on my coming back and running this farm, but I cannot do it. The woman I fell in love with nursed me back to health when I was in Washington recovering from wounds. Her father owns a farm in Maryland. I will be moving there and marrying her. I apologize for breaking our engagement."

"Thomas. You should know...I understand. I wouldn't want to hold you back. I know you will make a good husband, but you need to know that I probably would not have made you the best of wives. I like you, you are a good man, but I never really loved you."

"You will make a good wife to someone, someday. I am sorry to say that it cannot be me. I wish I could stay and help you here, but I am needed in Maryland." He stood. "Thank you for the coffee. I should be going." She stood and he neared her, giving her a kiss on the cheek. "Good-bye, Charlotte."

Saturday, July 1
Turner Farm

Charlotte was making cheesy chicken and potatoes, one of her favorite dishes for dinner. As she worked, she spoke, as she often did to the child, as if Mary could understand her.

"Women in the town keep pestering me about our future, Mary. They say you need a father figure. I wonder what they expect me to do. The men returning home are scarce as it is. And I want to love the man I marry. You understand. I can't just conjure up a man out of thin air." She thought for a moment of Wesley and Captain Spencer. Her thoughts were interrupted when there was a knock at the door. She opened it, but almost didn't recognize the man that stood before her.

"Johnny? Jack Wade?"

"Hey, there, Charlotte!" He said, his voice was light and happy, but deeper than she had remembered. Two years away at war had changed him. He had grown up and matured. He looked slightly underfed with no excess fat on his body. His hair had darkened to almost black and fell in a shaggy disarray. He had even managed to grow himself a beard, scraggly and unkempt.

"Oh, John!" Charlotte threw her arms around him, and held him tightly. "When did you get home?" She pulled back and held his forearms in her hands. "Let me look at you!"

"I got home around suppertime yesterday. Mama only just let me out of her sight now."

"Well, I don't blame her for wanting that. She finally has all of her…boys home."

John noticed the slight hesitation in her words. He took her in his arms again and held her tight.

"Yes, I know." He had tears in his eyes and didn't try to hide them. "Mama told me about everything." Charlotte started crying as well, holding John tightly.

"How are you handling it?" She pulled away and led him to the table. John brushed tears from his eyes with the heel of his hand.

"I've seen a lot of death these past two years, friends and such, but finding out about Ginny…" he shook his head. "It just hit me so hard, Charlie. So much harder. She was my sister, my friend. I cannot imagine her not being around. And for you, being there, seeing it happen…I just don't know how you could deal with that."

"It wasn't easy. I still have nightmares about that day." Charlotte spoke softly. "But I have had nearly two years to adjust and accept it. It is brand new for you, Jack. It could have happened yesterday for all you knew." John nodded.

"Yes." It was almost a whisper. "And then Jack too..." Charlotte covered his hands with hers. It was a well-known fact that John Wade had looked up to Jack Skelley.

"It was not a good time for us, that's true." Charlotte said. "I still feel the void sometimes. There are times when I think I am fine, but then something will remind me of Ginny or Jack, and I'll have this feeling of emptiness."

"Babababababa..." a small voice came from the corner that Mary was in. The babble made John smile.

"I suppose that is the little present that your dad left you." He said in a light, teasing voice.

"A present, huh?" Charlotte smiled. "I suppose your mother really did tell you everything." She stood and headed to get her sister. "Don't go anywhere."

John smiled and watched her. The child grinned at John, who stood and held out his hand.

"Hey there, Mary." The girl reached out and grabbed John's finger. "She's very beautiful, Charlotte."

"Thank you, Johnny." Charlotte laid Mary on a blanket on the floor. The toddler immediately began playing with some wood blocks. "She's pretty much the best thing in my life. I can't imagine loving one of my own children as much as I love her."

"So. Mother also mentioned you got a chance to see Wesley Culp before he died. She overheard you talking to Ginny. Mother said you were in love with Wesley."

Charlotte went to the oven to check on the chicken, then poured John some fresh coffee. She sat back down at the table and, keeping her eyes on her sister, answered.

"I fell in love with Wesley a long time ago. I loved him with all my heart. But looking back, I see now that I loved him as anyone would feel about their first love. It was an immature love. I'm sure if given the chance, that love could have matured and we could have had a wonderful life together. But there are times when I think that I put Wesley on a pedestal of sorts. I made him perfect in my mind when he really wasn't. I was enamored with the idea of being in love, because

Ginny and Augusta and Alex, all had their loves and I had strong affections for Wesley that, in my mind, I turned that into the type of romantic love that my friends had. I will never really know now." She paused. "I hope that made sense."

"It did. Your babbling always makes sense to me." John smiled. "But you would have married him."

"Yes. Especially with Mary to raise and the farm to run. And I feel as though he really loved me."

"You did say that." John paused, a bit unsure if it was the right time to say what he really wanted to say. "But Charlotte, Mary does need a father. This farm needs a man."

"I suppose so. In time, when I find someone willing to marry me, with all this baggage."

"Charlotte, will you marry me?"

Charlotte looked at him, the shock apparent in her face. "John, I don't know if that would be a good idea..."

"Charlotte, you know I have always loved you. Admired you. I have wanted to marry you since I was a little boy. I know you turned me down before, but..."

"John..."

"You need a husband. Mary needs a father. I can be both. I know you think that I'm too young for you, but the war..."

"John, I love you, you know I do." Charlotte reached across the table to hold his forearm. "And I really, really appreciate how you would marry me, just like that, just to be my protector and be a father to Mary. But Johnny..." she paused, unsure about how to go on. "John, your family needs you right now. Your mother needs you. And you need to be free to marry someone who you really truly care for, that you feel a passionate love for. Like Ginny and Jack. Augusta and Michael. Alex and Will. I love you and I always will love you, but it is just as a good friend and little brother."

"And there is nothing I can do that will make you change your mind?" John flashed a grin, both dimples showing, his eyes shining. Charlotte was again reminded of how much he had grown and matured.

"I am sorry. I want what's best for you and for you to not be tied down and I don't think that I am the best thing for you. I'm not going to change my mind."

"Well, then, I suppose we will have to simply remain good friends."
He stood and came to stand in front of her. "Friend?" He held out a
hand to her and she took it. He pulled her up quickly and kissed her.
She quickly backed away.

"Johnny..."

"Sorry. I had to try, just once." He muttered, smiling.

"Johnny, I wish I could feel for you the way you feel for me. But
you will find a nice girl who will love you with everything she has.
What about Tillie Pierce? You could try courting her."

July 1
Lewis Home

In the parlor, Augusta turned a page in her book and stretched. Michael Joseph was in the bedroom, napping. She had received no word from Michael, had not heard anything about him since hearing he would be released from the hospital weeks ago. Augusta rubbed her eyes and turned back to the book she was reading. As Charlotte had suggested, Augusta was reading a Jane Austen novel, *Emma*. It was light-hearted and more comical than some of her other stories. Just as Emma was about to discover Mr. Elton's feelings towards her, Augusta heard the door open and close. She frowned. Mr. and Mrs. Lewis were not due back for another few hours. She stood and walked to the open doorway.

"Hello?" A familiar male voice called out.

"Michael?" She whispered, unable to move. Her husband stood there, full beard, tattered uniform, looking unbelievably thin and tired, but clean and happy. All she could do was stare. Two arms, two legs, two hands and fingers where they should be. He met her eyes and quickly crossed the kitchen. He pulled her into his arms, lifted her off her feet and twirled her around.

"Oh, Michael." She clung to him tightly. His hat fell to the floor.

"Augusta, I have missed your voice." He murmured into her hair.

"Is that all you missed?" She teased, running her hands over his face, then to his shoulders.

"Not at all." He smiled. "I missed your smile, your laugh, the way you look at me. I have missed holding you, talking with you, just being with you. I missed you and I love you and now that we are back together, I am never going to let you go."

"Sounds good to me." She smiled and pulled his head down for a kiss.

July 2
Clark Home

"I can't help but be worried, Charlotte." Alex confided. "The 87th Pennsylvania was mustered out in Alexandria on Thursday. Many of the men have been coming home but none seem to know where Will is. They said there was a lot of confusion between the siege of Petersburg and the Appomattox campaign and then the end of the war. Where can he be?"

"I'm sure he'll be here as soon as possible, Alex." Charlotte replied. She had brought Mary over to the Lewis home and then went over to visit with Alex while Augusta watched the children. "He may have been stationed farther south."

"Maybe." Alex hugged herself, her worry apparent.

Charlotte looked towards the stairs. "How is your brother?"

"He's doing okay. As well as he can be."

Alex's brother, Aaron had been wounded at the siege of Petersburg. He had taken shrapnel to the calf and had to have his left leg amputated below the knee. Alex continued. "He's lucky he didn't die. Mother and Father are both broken up about it, but he is at least here..."

A knock on the door interrupted her. Alex crossed the room and opened the door. On the other side was a Union soldier. He had shaggy, dark-blonde hair, and a full beard and mustache covered his face.

"Are you Mrs. Will Sadler?" The man asked.

"I am." Alex replied nervously.

"Ma'am, I'm Sgt. Daniel Reigle, from up in Mount Joy. I served with your husband the past few years and we became quite close. May I speak with you?" His voice made him seem younger than his appearance did.

"I apologize, I have forgotten my manners. Come right in." She led him to the parlor. "It's so good to meet you. Will did mention your name in a couple of the letters he wrote me. And your reputation in town precedes you as well. Everyone was talking about you back in October. Congratulations on your reception of the Medal of Honor." She quickly introduced Charlotte, then offered him a seat. He took it, looking nervous.

"I am so sorry to tell you that Will hasn't returned home yet."

"I'm afraid to hear that he isn't back yet, but I might have an explanation for that."

Alex's head began to spin, and her vision blurred. Charlotte quickly stood and hurried to Alex's side, putting an arm around her.

"What?" Alex could barely choke the word out as she braced her arms on her knees.

"A month or so before the surrender at Appomattox, we were in Petersburg, part of the regiment lying siege to the town. He was sent on a scouting mission, just something routine, he'd done it many times before. He and two others, Jonnie Webster and Billy Jordan went out, but, only Jordan came back. They'd been ambushed by some Rebs. Webster and Will were apparently shot down, and Jordan barely made it back himself."

"But...no...scouting? Why? How? Will didn't even have a horse. How could he have been out scouting?" Alex's mind reeled, she tried to make sense of it all. Will could not be dead. She would have known, she would have felt it deep in her heart. She didn't feel this at all. Just empty. She focused on the man in front of her and read the sincerity of his words on his face. But she still could not believe it.

"Well, ma'am, he borrowed the horse of another man. We all took turns with the scouting. He didn't volunteer for the job or anything. But Will, he wasn't the type who would pretend sickness or hurt to get out of his duty. He was a good man, saved my life more than once. The horse he borrowed did come back. Without Will. I'm not saying he's for sure dead, but..."

Alex stood abruptly and turned, staring into the flames of the fire. "But he's missing and probably is." She took a deep breath. "No!" Alex sank slowly to the ground, her legs completely giving out on her, her mind going completely blank. She curled into a ball and began whimpering, then choking out sobs. "Will..." Charlotte was at her side in an instant, arms around her in an attempt to console her.

"Ma'am, I am sorry to have to be the bearer of this news. Pease let me know if I can be of further service." Daniel Reigle said to Charlotte "I may be a few hours away, but Will was a good man, and I would like to do something if I can. I can let myself out." The former sergeant quickly left.

Alex continued pouring out tears. Charlotte cried too, hugging her friend tightly, knowing all too well what she was feeling.

"Will!" Alex choked out through her tears. "No." She couldn't believe it. Couldn't believe that she would never again see his smile or feel his arms around her. She couldn't believe they wouldn't grow old together or raise a family. They would never cuddle after a long day and talk about everything and nothing at all. She couldn't believe that she would never again see his face; that he was lost to some unmarked grave, in a place she would never find. She trembled, her body shaking with sobs. Her mind was blank, except for a vision of Will, on their wedding day. He had been so handsome, and they had been so happy.

Alex's mother returned. With one look at her sobbing daughter, and Charlotte's tear-stained face, she knew what had happened. She had been dreading this news for the past few weeks. She quickly crossed the room, pulled Alex up in her arms and held her tightly. Charlotte stood, and then explained. "It's Will. He went missing and is believed to be dead."

Alex's mother nodded, stroking her daughter's hair. "Thank you, Charlotte."

Charlotte knew she had been dismissed, and so left quietly, giving Alex a quick pat on the back before heading out the door.

September 19
Clark Home

"Alexandria, dear, are you sure you wouldn't like to come?" Alex's father asked, concern on his face. The concern had been there often since the day the family had found out that Will was missing.

"I'm sure, father." Alex said softly. "And please, don't stay home on my account. I know how much you have been looking forward to this. This is one of the first town gatherings we have had since the men came home. You should go and enjoy yourselves." In reality, Alex just wanted to be alone. Her parents had been hovering, watching her very carefully as if they expected her to do something careless. Charlotte was by far the easiest person to be around. She was the one person in Alex's life that understood what she was going through. She understood that there were those times when you just wanted to be alone, or times when she wanted to talk. Alex could now better understand why Charlotte had acted the way she had when Ginny died. If it hadn't been for her strong faith, she would have completely fallen apart.

"Well, Alexandria, we just wanted to make sure that you're okay." Her mother said.

"I'll be fine." Alex tried to smile, but it didn't fool her parents. Mrs. Clark opened her mouth to speak again when Aaron spoke up.

"Mother, just leave her alone." Aaron shifted his weight on his crutches. It was going to be his first outing since he had returned home.

Alex sighed with relief once they shut the door. She knew they were just concerned, but they could be very overbearing. She had thought that with Aaron making it home from war and with his wound that they would pay more attention to him. That wasn't the case.

Her stomach rumbled. Most days, food tasted bland in her mouth, and she didn't want to eat. Bread had been all she could eat for most days, occasionally she was able to eat a more substantial meal. Now though, all she wanted was some milk. While in the kitchen, she heard the front door open and close. She sighed and wondered who was checking up on her now.

"I'm fine, really, there is no reason…" she trailed off staring at the person who had entered. He was thin, with a haunted, injured look in his eyes, but she would know those forest green eyes anywhere.

"Will?" She whispered, not quite believing. He took a shaky step toward her and she noticed a limp in his walk before she launched herself at him. He was real, not a dream and he was holding her more tightly than he ever had before.

"Oh, Allie." He murmured into her hair. She pulled slightly away and began running her hands all over him, along his arms and down his chest then she held him tightly again.

"Will, you were missing, no one knew what had happened to you...we all believed that you were dead." She whispered into his shoulder. He smelled like a cow pasture and his face had several healing scars, but he was alive. She reached up and pulled his face down to kiss his chapped lips, then hugged him again. "What happened?" She pulled back and looked deep into his eyes. They were sad and had dark bruising underneath, as if he had not slept in months. She gently ran her fingers along them.

"Oh, Allie." He pulled her hands to his lips and kissed her fingers, then leaned down and kissed her. "Allie, I've missed you so much..."

"I cannot believe it, my prayers have been answered." Alex murmured. "I can't believe you're here, alive with me." She gave him a long kiss. "Where have you been?"

"I wish I could tell you everything, Allie, but there are parts of the story that I don't even know." He pulled her to a chair, sat, and pulled her onto his lap. She ran her hand through his unkempt hair. "I was in a battle. We were part of the unit that was laying siege to Petersburg. It was some tough fighting at times and boredom at others. My colonel sent me and two other men to scout around and see if we could find any weaknesses in the Confederate line. We ran into some Confederates who immediately fired upon us. We were riding away and got separated and were just about to get away when I was hit. I was able to stay on my horse until I lost the Confederates, but I couldn't hold on and fell off the horse I had borrowed. "When I fell, I hit my head and must have wandered off or something." Will rubbed his head and continued.

"The next thing I knew, I woke up in the home of some Northern sympathizers who took me in and nursed me back to health. They were a wonderful family, but had been torn apart by war. The father, Samuel, was an officer in the Union army. Suzannah, the mother, was from Petersburg, and so the family lived down there with her family.

However, she also had two grown sons who were fighting for the Confederacy, against their very father."

"How horrible to have to go through the war with those worries." Alex said.

"Yes." Will agreed. "They were very kind to me, though. When I was well enough, I wrote a letter to let you know what had happened to me, but I see you never received it. We heard the war was over, but I still wasn't quite healthy enough to travel north. As soon as I could, I started making my way back home. I had to stop at the capital to make sure I got my discharge papers in order. I wanted to make sure nothing could keep me from you once I got to you." He smiled and kissed her again.

"And now that you're home, I am never going to let you go." She said, smiling back.

October 3
Turner Farm

Charlotte wiped a strand of her hair out of her face. She was preparing dinner and thinking how happy she was for her friends and how things had turned out. It was so good to see Will back. Charlotte hadn't had a chance to talk to him about his time in Petersburg, but the story she had heard made her wonder how her family in Petersburg was doing.

The meager crop Charlotte had managed to plant in the spring was harvested and things were looking better. Mary continued to grow and was learning new things almost every day. God was good. There was a knock on the door. She looked up, puzzled. She hadn't been expecting anyone.

She opened the door to a face she had never expected to see again. He was not in uniform, instead he wore a basic white button-up shirt and tan jacket with tan pants. Charlotte knew him without a doubt.

"Captain Spencer!" She exclaimed. In her excitement, she threw her arms around his neck, before remembering how improper it was. She quickly pulled away from him. He smiled.

"Miss Turner." He reached forward and brushed her cheek, and his hand came away with white powder. Her heart fluttered a bit at his touch. It was so slight that she barely noticed it.

"You had some flour there." He smiled. "Please call me James. I'm not a Captain anymore." He paused, taking in her pale face and wide, surprised eyes. "Forgive me for asking, but are you all right? You look like you have seen a ghost."

"Am I not? I heard you...I heard you were dead."

"You did?"

"Yes." Charlotte said, then quickly explained about the letter. "And you never wrote again...I figured even if you weren't dead, you just didn't ever want to see me again."

"Toby did send a letter." James said, understanding crossing his face. "I can explain. If you read the letter, you know that I wrote it and gave it to a friend to make sure it was mailed if anything happened to me. Well, I was wounded a second time, I fell behind and was being cared for by an old widow. When I returned to my unit, I learned that Toby had died. I didn't know he sent you that letter. And since I never heard from you, I assumed you didn't want to hear from me."

"I wasn't about to write to someone who I believed to be dead." Charlotte said.

"I believed you were going to give up on me and marry that farm hand of your father's."

Mary chose that moment to wake up from her nap. Charlotte could hear her whimpering.

"Excuse me, Captain, I will be right back." She hurried upstairs to grab her sister. When she returned, James Spencer looked hurt and crushed.

"I see you changed your mind about your father's farm hand. You two didn't waste any time, either. Congratulations. I should go." He turned, heart shattered, and started to walk out the door.

"James, wait." Charlotte set Mary Elizabeth down and grabbed his arm. "If you were so sure that I was married to someone else, then why did you come back here?"

He looked down at her, his eyes full of longing. "I had to make sure that you were okay. I had to see you this one last time." He smiled a sad smile. "I'm glad to see you have moved on. You seem happy. Content."

"I am content, but it has nothing to do with me being married. It has everything to do with my finally accepting my life and what God has planned for me."

"So you just 'accepted' your lot as a wife and mother." James said. He had to leave, and soon. Looking at this woman, talking to her only made him hurt more.

"If that is what God has planned for me, yes. But I will have you know that I am neither a wife, nor a mother."

James looked at her, puzzled. "What do you mean?"

"I mean, little Mary Elizabeth in there is my half-sister. Our father died after being wounded in the battle of Cedar Creek. Her mother died in childbirth."

"And your fiancé?"

"Gone to Maryland. Apparently, he was wounded and fell madly in love with a volunteer nurse whose family lives there. Her farm might have more acreage than we do."

Hope surged in James's heart. "So you're unattached? Unmarried?"

"For now." She smiled. "You know, I don't know your plans, Mr. Spencer, but I could use some help around here. The barn has a room that could be converted into a bedroom of sorts. I could really use your knowledge. Unless you have somewhere else to be. I don't want to presume…"

"Miss Turner." James placed a finger over her lips to quiet her. "I have no pressing engagements. I would be happy to stay on and work as your farm hand."

October 18
Evergreen Cemetery

Charlotte, Augusta and Alex stood at Ginny's new headstone. Her remains had been reburied in Evergreen cemetery earlier in the month. Charlotte felt it was a good thing. She had trouble returning to the McClellan house, the place where she had lost her best friend.

"This is a nice spot." Alex commented. She had been the one to suggest the three women go and visit the gravesite together.

"It is." Charlotte agreed, pulling her maroon wool cloak tighter around her shoulders.

"Ginny's not there, though." Augusta gestured to the grave. "I have no doubt that she's in heaven, watching over us."

"The newly confirmed Catholic makes a good point." Alex said, referring to Augusta's recent confirmation to the Catholic Church.

"That's very true." Charlotte said "It's so comforting to know that Ginny is in heaven, looking out for us."

"Our own guardian angel." Augusta added.

The three stood for a few moments saying silent prayers. Finally, Augusta spoke up.

"This might be the last time the four of us are all together." They began walking back toward the center of town.

"What do you mean?" Alex asked.

"Michael and I have decided to move west. He's been thinking on it for a while. I agree. We both need to get away from the constant reminders of war. Even though he fought for the Union, some people still make comments about my background. Out west, we shouldn't have to worry about that."

"That's true, but you shouldn't have to worry about that anywhere." Charlotte agreed. "We will miss you. So much."

"I will miss you both as well. But the west is opening up, becoming more populated. Michael has a cousin near Denver in the Colorado Territory. Michael is fairly certain that he can get a job out there. It will be nice for him to have a job that won't give him nightmares."

"Nightmares?" Charlotte asked.

"Will has had a few as well." Alex added. "He'll wake up and not really remember where he is for a moment."

"That's too bad." Charlotte said, remembering the night during the battle when Wesley had woken up after having a nightmare. "Hopefully, they will stop having them as time goes on."

"I hope so too." Augusta said. "It's so nice to have him home. Now that we're together, I feel like we can get through anything."

November 8

Mary Elizabeth quickly formed an attachment to the former Captain, and Charlotte was becoming more and more fond of him as well. He was easy to talk to, but it was just as easy for the two to sit in comfortable silence. He had moved into the barn, and while some people hinted at impropriety, most accepted the fact that he was just working on her farm.

Charlotte soon discovered that James was extremely knowledgeable about agriculture. He had many ideas for her land, and always talked to her as if she were his equal partner in the farm. She recalled that Thomas had never done that, nor her father. They had reminisced about Fredericksburg and discussed their worries about not hearing from their friends and family. Charlotte had yet to hear anything about her cousins. It worried her, but mail was still tough to get through. James had suggested going back down to Fredericksburg to visit.

The two were out walking one day. Charlotte wanted to go to Devil's Den to think, and James accompanied her, as he was in the habit of doing. Mary had been left with Augusta and Michael in town. Augusta had welcomed the girl and with a smile, said that taking care of both Mary and Michael Joseph would be good practice, hinting at the fact that she was going to have another child. Charlotte couldn't be happier for her friend

The sky above threatened rain, but Charlotte felt as though they could make it to the Devil's Den and back in no time. James broke the silence.

"It's hard to believe that the Lewis's will be leaving."

"I know. I will miss Augusta so much. She has become such a dear friend. At least Alex and Will are staying, for now."

"Michael is excited to move. I'm not sure I would be able to go west like they are."

"I know. Augusta is excited as well, but nervous. It will be an adjustment for both of them, I believe, to go west and farm, but they are quick learners."

"Does she ever talk about going back to the family plantation?"

"She wants to, but if they do, they won't stay long. She received a letter from her brother. Both he and her other brother survived, but their plantation is destroyed."

"That's too bad." James said. They reached the rock formation. He helped her climb, and she sat on one of the large stones. He sat next to her, hands bracing him from behind. His hand was inches from hers. "Michael said he needed something else to do. Said he is sick of the army. Staying here would remind him too much of the war. He wants to go where he is not constantly reminded of fighting."

"I will miss them." Charlotte said, looking out in the distance. Some of the buildings were still damaged from the battle. Charlotte doubted that the town would ever be back to the way it was. People from all over the country were still coming to visit the "famous battlefield".

"I heard the McClellans are also leaving. Heading west toward Iowa."

"They are." Charlotte nodded. "They say it's mostly for opportunity, like with Michael and Augusta, but I know the rumors and stories about Ginny and her death hurt. Judgmental people like John Burns. People who are just jealous. You know I think Mr. Burns is jealous that Ginny got more attention than he and was called a hero of the battle. He's not the only one who speaks badly about them. Maime Williams occasionally makes comments, but luckily, the battle changed her daughter. Abigail is not as horrid as she used to be."

"Mrs. Williams approached me the other day. She said if I wanted to court an accomplished woman of high stature and beauty, she would be more than willing to have her daughter court me. Said I was ruining my own reputation, staying out here."

A flash of jealousy rose in Charlotte. "Well, you would make a good husband." She blushed, then paused. "But you could court her, if you really wanted to. I don't have a say in who you befriend."

"Miss Williams is not the one I want." James assured her. The two fell into silence. A light rain began to fall. Charlotte stood, needing to move. She climbed to the very top of the rock structure, looking across the fields, hugging herself. She could see the mountains in the distance. What did James mean: *Abigail is not the one I want*? Since he had come back and found out she was available, he hadn't said anything about courting or a future. In spite of their parting words during the war, he had not mentioned anything about the attraction they had felt at the time. Maybe he just wanted to pay her back from when she nursed him back to health. Maybe the danger of the war had made the attraction stronger than it really was.

"Have you thought any more about going down to Fredericksburg to visit your cousins? I would really like to see if Nathaniel made it through the war."

"I have thought about it. I would like to. There was so much fighting down there, I really don't know if the family plantation made it through unharmed. I can only hope and pray."

"So you would like to go down there?" James asked.

"I would. But there are some…complications. Could we take Mary? Would she be able to travel with us? And…the two of us traveling together…well…it could be looked at as improper. People might think…well…" She looked down, slightly embarrassed at the impropriety of traveling with a man who was not her husband.

As she started to walk away, James stood and took hold of her elbow. She turned.

"You know, I lost a child, a little boy, along with my wife." His hair was beginning to get damp, but he didn't seem to realize it.

"You mentioned that you lost your wife. I didn't know you lost a son." Charlotte's eyes were locked on James's. She didn't even notice the drizzle.

"I think…I think that I could love little Mary Elizabeth, just like she was my own, like you have."

"What are you saying?" Charlotte's heart sped up, just a little bit.

"I'm asking you to marry me, Charlotte." He took her hands, one in each of his.

She backed a few steps away, breaking his grasp. Marriage to this man would make her life a lot easier. She would be able to provide better for Mary and give her a father. He was a farmer with a college education and could probably do wonders with her land. The load would be lighter for her. She was already in love with him, she knew that now. But she wasn't sure what he wanted. Would he see her as simply a replacement wife? Someone to feed him and give him children, and a ready-made family? Paying off that debt to her when she nursed him back to health? She felt he was attracted to her on a physical level, but she wanted him to want her for her heart, and she was scared that she might be making a mistake by saying yes. What would a kind, handsome, smart man like him want with a plain woman like her with all of her burdens?

"I don't know, James." Charlotte turned away, but he came up behind her and placed his hands on her wet shoulders.

"I know how you are feeling, trust me, I do. You feel as though you will never feel the same way about anyone else, the way you felt about Wesley Culp." She turned and looked at him, surprised that he knew her feelings for Wesley. He shrugged.

"Alex told me." He took another step closer, she could almost feel his body heat. "I felt that way too, when my first wife died. That's why I can tell you that you can love again."

"And you know that for a fact?" His warm hands moved up and down her wet sleeves. The water had soaked through her shirt and chemise.

"Yes, I do."

"How do you know that?" Water dripped down her face. She was sure she looked frightful.

"Because, Charlotte I have fallen in love again. You must know that. I was in love with you the first day I saw you stand up to those Union soldiers. I was probably in the process of falling in love with you, even in Fredericksburg."

James's blue eyes searched hers as water ran down his face. The rain had clumped strands of his hair together. He put one hand to her cheek, the other took her hand. "I love you, Charlotte Turner. I love the way you care about people, I love your strength. I love the way you are raising your sister, and the way you have survived when everyone around you seems to be leaving. I want to marry you and build a home with you and give Mary brothers and sisters." He paused. "Well, I guess technically nieces and nephews." He pulled her close, then pushed some hair away from her face and tucked it behind her ear. "I know you might not love me now, but I know I love you, and I will wait for you to fall in love with me too."

Charlotte threaded her fingers between his on the hand he held, and reached up to touch his wet hair.

"I don't think you'll have to wait very long, James." She said softly, almost a whisper. He lowered his head and she closed her eyes as he kissed her forehead, then her temple, then her eyes. Her heart fluttered.

"Are you sure?" He whispered. "I can wait if you're not."

"I don't think I have ever been surer about anything." She said, and then she pulled his head towards her and kissed him. "I do too."

"You do what?" He smiled.

"I love you too. I have for a while."

341

The smile James gave her was the biggest she had ever seen on him.

"So does this mean you'll marry me?"

Charlotte smiled back. "Anytime that you're ready, James."

"Well, then, we should head back. We have lots of planning to do."

As they headed back to the farm, Charlotte's thoughts turned to Ginny and how her friend had made her so much stronger in her faith. She was no longer afraid to love. She remembered Ginny's favorite Scripture verse, the words she read just before she had died. "Though war shall rise against me, I shall not fear."

And Charlotte was no longer afraid.

Author's Note

I have always had a love of history. To me, history isn't just the famous people and events and dates, but it is about the stories of those who lived through these times. When I was in college, I visited Gettysburg and first heard the story of Ginny Wade, Jack Skelley and Wesley Culp, true historic people. The story intrigued me, so I began forming thoughts of a book I could write.

While this novel is considered fiction, it is based on real events. It is historically accurate to the best of my knowledge. The characters of Ginny, Jack, and Wesley, along with John Burns, the Wade family, Tillie Pierce and Sallie Meyers are actual people who lived at the time. Most of the one-time mentioned characters were citizens of Gettysburg as well. The Turner, Clark, Sadler, Byron and Lewis families were created by me.

There are so many people who I would like to thank. First and foremost, my mother, who instilled in me a love of history and accompanied me when I visited the historic sites and helped me gather research material and information. She was also invaluable in the editing process and as moral support. This would not have happened without her. There are so many other people: family, friends and students, who gave me support and encouragement.

Also, I would like to acknowledge the many authors who gave me information. Some of the books that helped me in my research include: Michael Shaara's *Killer Angels*, Albert Nofi's *A Civil War Treasury*, Cindy L. Small's *Jenny Wade Story*, Margaret S. Creighton's *The Colors of Courage*, Philip Katcher's *The Civil War: Day By Day*, and Jim Slade and John Alexander's *Firestorm at Gettysburg: Civilian Voices*, as well as primary documents, including "Tillie" Pierce's *At Gettysburg*, and letters in Enrica D'Alessandro's *My Country Needs Me: The Story of Johnston Hastings Skelly Jr.*

Be sure to look for Book 2 of the Turner Daughters series. In *Be Strong and Steadfast*, we follow Isabelle Turner, her family and friends, in the city of Fredericksburg.

Images

Mary Virginia "Ginny" Wade

Johnston Hastings "Jack" Skelly

John Wesley Culp

Georgia Wade McClellan

Elizabeth Salome "Sallie" Myers

Tillie Pierce

John Burns

Peter and Elizabeth Thorn

Wedding Photographer
Charles Tyson

Daniel Skelly

Dr. Charles Horner

Dr. Robert Horner

McClellan House

Pennsylvania College

Camp Letterman

346

About the Author

Erica "Marie LaPres" Emelander is a middle school social studies/religion teacher and lives in West Michigan. Erica has always enjoyed reading and writing. With her love of history and God, she has incorporated all four loves into this book. Erica has begun writing the second novel in this series of the Turner cousins.

When not working on or researching her books, Erica can be found coaching middle and high school sports, being a youth minister, traveling, and spending time with her friends and family especially her beloved nieces and nephew.

Erica loves hearing from her readers. You can keep in touch with her at the following locations:
e-mail~ericamarie84@gmaill.com

Facebook~"Marie LaPres"

Pinterest~https://www.pinterest.com/ericamarie21/book-1/

GoodReads~Though War Shall Rise Against Me: Marie LaPres

Twitter~@marielapres

Instagram~marielapres